Rosa trapped the phone between her ear and shoulder, then pushed the final bin into place. "What's going on, Daddy? Why are you so worried about the drug world?"

"Because now they'll think I'm actually David's partner. The only way to get at me is through you. And you won't even let me hire security for you."

"Then, let's work with the DEA. Set up a sting. Samson will help us."

"No, Rosa!" Ernesto snapped. "Why do you think the DEA never made the connection between David and me? David has agents in every agency to ensure the connection was never made. David isn't the only one with agents on his payroll. If one of the crooked agents found out I was cooperating with the DEA..." he trailed off. "I won't jeopardize you."

She turned off the light in the storage room, then went into the basement and lay on the carpeted floor. She hadn't furnished the basement, so it was empty. "You're killing me, Daddy."

"I know this is hard for you, but I can't involve the DEA."

She couldn't dispute his point that David had agents in his pocket, but Samson wasn't one of them. "Please talk to Samson. He can help."

"No, Rosa. This is my decision to make. Are you with me or not?"

She blew out an exasperated breath. "Yes. I'm with you."

CAUGHT UP

DEATRI KING-BEY

Genesis Press, Inc.

Indigo Vibe

An imprint of Genesis Press, Inc.
Publishing Company

Genesis Press, Inc.
P.O. Box 101
Columbus, MS 39703

ISBN: 1-58571-178-0
Manufactured in the United States of America

First Edition

Visit us at www.genesis-press.com
or call at 1-888-Indigo-1

DEDICATION

For my hubby, Collier King-Bey, or as the family and I call him,
"The King."
Without your support, this book would have never come into
being. This one's for you.
Love ya,

Dee

In Loving Memory of Catherine Shaw
February 10, 1916 – November 03, 2005
You'll always be my heart, Grandma

ACKNOWLEDGMENTS

I thank...

God for the gifts he has given me and for surrounding me with supportive family and friends.

My hubby, Collier, for always being in my corner and saying, "Dee, if you want to write, write." Then, he removed obstacles so that I could do so.

My babies: Daetriel, Shanna, and Daiaunne, for allowing me to miss a few matches of Mario Tennis and Mario Cart.

My nephew Joshua Lang for brightening my day with his dimpled smile.

My mother, Mary Hodges, and my sister Tanja Hodges, for reading everything I've written (Trust me, folks, some of it really STUNK) and giving loving advice on how to improve.

My spiritual twin, Angelique Justin, for believing in me.

My critique group: Turgenia Knight, Pam Olumoya, Javan Shepard, and Mitchell Thomas... Whose turn is it to submit? SMILE.

My critique partner, Freddy Traynor, author of *Bless the Thugs and the Lil' Chil'rens*, for teaching me the importance of research.

My newfound friend Evelyn Palfrey, author of *Three Perfect Men*, for her willingness to reach back.

My editor, Lois Spangler, for forcing me to overcome my fear of the flashback.

Last, but not least, I thank my writing coach, Cheryl Ferguson. She took me under her wing and nurtured my growth as a writer in ways I cannot begin to articulate.

THE CATALYST

Miami, June 15

"This is not up for discussion, Rosa. You're not moving to Chicago." Ernesto stalked across her bedroom to the window. They'd moved to Miami when she was twelve to protect her from Harriet's drunken fits and distance himself from David.

"But, Daddy."

"The Senior Vice President of Marketing position was vacated a few months ago. I've held it for you to fill after your graduation." He checked his Rolex. "In two hours, you graduate and take your rightful place as one of my Senior Vice Presidents. Someday Bolívar International will be yours."

Rosa twirled the tresses beside her ear between her fingers.

He crossed his arms over his chest. "Whatever you're calculating, forget it."

She released the hair. "Let's talk about this like the two rational adults we are." She motioned toward her beanbag chairs. "Please take a seat."

"I thought I told you to get rid of those things."

"That would be my fuzzy, pink dice chairs."

"This room is in need of serious redecorating," he grumbled as he situated his large frame onto the chair across from Rosa. "Order new furniture before you leave for Italy, so it will be here when you return."

"When I return, it will be to Chicago, not Miami," she stated calmly. "And thank you, but I won't be accepting the Vice President position at this time."

His expression matched hers, stoic. "Are you saying you need a longer vacation, maybe a year off? You've worked hard, you deserve it. I'll keep the temporary replacement until you're ready."

"No. I'm saying I'm moving to Chicago when I return from Italy and starting a computer networking firm with the hundred thousand dollar trust Mom gave me."

"I'll expand Bolívar International to include a computer networking unit. You'll be its Vice President."

"That won't work, Daddy. I'd still be working for you. Just as I have since I was nine. I want to be on my own. I want to build and run my own company. That's also why I'm not using the trust you've set up for me. I want to build my company from the ground up."

Ernesto had never been as proud of Rosa as he was at this moment. He could remember, many years ago, when he'd purchased the technology firm that grew into Bolívar International. At the time, he'd wanted to be free of David to prove to himself that he could be a success on his own. "I admire that you wish to do this on your own, but run your company here. Not Chicago. You can't save Harriet." *Just as I can't save David.* He couldn't pinpoint the exact time it happened, but he no longer envied David's fire. He didn't want David's type of power, which was rooted in the fear of others. Ernesto craved the power that was rooted in respect: the respect he received for being an industry leader, the respect he received for improving the community, and most importantly, the respect he received from his daughter for being her hero.

Rosa looked away. He leaned forward and weaved his hands through her long, bushy, black hair. "Your mother has to save herself."

She rested her caramel cheek on his shoulder. "I know I can't make her stop drinking. But I miss her. Perhaps I can encourage her to seek help. I have to try. Please don't stop me."

Weighed down by family burdens, he knew he couldn't cut ties with David—just as Rosa couldn't cut ties with Harriet. "All right, I didn't get this far without knowing how to negotiate. You may go to Chicago and babysit your mother, but I expect you to stay up on Bolívar International business. And you will continue attending the strategy and status meetings. I want you ready when it's time for me to turn over the reins."

"Yes, sir." She backed away with a salute.

He chuckled with his own salute to her. "Go get ready for your graduation, soldier."

Later that night, David staggered across the hotel room, slurring, "I'm so proud of Rosa. *Mi* Rosa." He stumbled over nothing and fell onto the bed. "Damn, Ernesto, we did it. We're gonna pull this shit off."

Ernesto continued watching David from the chaise lounge in the corner. Though Rosa was going against his wishes, he was proud of her. "You need to sleep it off if you want to have a real discussion about Rosa, Paige, and the DEA."

"My ass ain't drunk. What the hell's goin' on? You been actin' funny all night." He rolled onto his back. "Rosa's gonna be the head of the largest fuckin' drug syndicate ever! They won't know what hit 'em."

Ernesto hopped up from the chaise lounge. "What are you talking about? When did we ever agree to something like that?"

"What the fuck?" David stood with his arms out to his sides. "So you sayin' you don't remember the original deal?" Accent thickening, he harrumphed. "And I'm the one who's drunk? Don't let your white ass get this shit twisted, amigo. Not now. Not after we've come this far. Now when does Rosa return?"

Ernesto reined in his anger. Rosa was his to protect, and he had no intention of relinquishing control. "Four, maybe five months."

"Shit! My girl will finally be at her rightful place, by my side. You hear me, Ernesto? Rosa is my baby! When she returns, she'll be all mine!"

"She's mine!" Ernesto glared down on David. "No blurring of power! I decide what we do with Rosa!"

The two stood toe-to-toe staring at each other. Ernesto had never noticed just how short David really was. Ernesto was as tall for a man as David was short. Looking back, Ernesto realized David's presence had made him seem bigger than life. Ernesto internally chuckled at himself for all of the years he'd chosen to stand in this little man's shadow.

David drew in several deep breaths, calming himself. In Spanish, he said, "This is a time to celebrate our daughter. We have time to discuss Rosa's future when she returns from Europe. Grab a seat." He motioned to the chaise lounge, then sat on the bed.

Guard up at an all-time high, Ernesto took his seat. This was one fight David wouldn't win. He'd protect Rosa at all costs.

"We need to talk about the DEA," David continued in Spanish. "I've made sure those bastards won't bother you again. I know you want out, but I need your ass to continue laundering for me. I don't trust anyone else with my money. And that fucking Barry Paige." David nodded his head "I'm thinking about having his ass whacked."

Unsure how to handle this new change-of-subject tactic of David's, Ernesto half-listened while figuring out what to do to protect Rosa.

"Damn, damn, damn!" Ernesto stormed into his study with Harriet close behind. He regretted allowing her to stay with them for the few days she'd be in Miami for Rosa's graduation. He wouldn't have agreed, but having Harriet close meant so much to Rosa.

"You're just angry because Rosa's decided to move to Chicago to be with me," Harriet taunted. "There was no way you could keep her away from me. You're losing control over her, and you can't stand it."

"I never kept Rosa from you. Your drinking did. Now leave me alone, so I can think."

She pursed her lips. "I saw David at the graduation ceremony. He's getting closer and closer to telling Rosa the truth every day. Wait until she finds out her precious daddy is nothing but a lackey for a drug dealer."

"Shut the hell up! David isn't telling Rosa shit." He thumped his chest. "I'm her father, that's the only truth she'll ever know."

Harriet's drunken laugh filled the room. "Not if David has anything to say about it, lackey."

CHAPTER ONE

Six years later
Florida, June 1

A corrections officer escorted David from his prison cell along the hallway into a small office just outside of the death-row unit. "You've only got five minutes," the guard said as he unshackled David's hands from behind his back.

David massaged his wrists. He didn't know who Ernesta Wells was, how she organized this call, or why, and he didn't care. He'd do anything for a temporary reprieve from his twenty-three-hour, seven-day-a-week cage. Legs bound in chains, he shuffled across the office straight to the phone sitting on the messy desk. He unfolded the little slip of paper the guard had given him earlier and placed his call.

"Hello."

"What do you want?" he barked into the line.

"Is that you, David?" came a hushed female voice he couldn't quite place. Whoever she was, she must have had plenty of money to be able to set up this call. He'd always taken good care of his women. Since his time was drawing near, maybe one of them had called for old time's sake.

"Yeah. I'm busy. What the hell do you want?" He watched the corrections officer pace about the room, acting as if he weren't listening to the conversation.

"I have something important to tell you that I won't say over the phone. I'm being put on someone else's guest list, but I have made arrangements to see you."

The more she spoke, the more certain he was that he knew the voice. "Damn, after they hear this call, you actually believe they gonna let me see you?"

"I'm not stupid! I paid a hell of a lot of money to ensure we aren't recorded. The only reason I'm calling is to make sure I have the ins I've been promised. Now that we've spoken, I see this was money well spent. I'll see you in a few days." She disconnected the line.

Chicago, June 1

Rosa stepped off the elevator and walked down the corridor to her mother's condo. She checked her watch—8:47. Harriet didn't usually wake until noon, but Rosa had a lot to do before Ernesto arrived in town. She'd told her mother she'd be by before nine. Harriet was so forgetful; Rosa hoped that she remembered.

She ran her hands over her short-cropped hair, straightened her gold crinkle skirt and rang the doorbell. To her surprise, Harriet opened the door immediately, with a big smile on her face and her arms opened wide.

"Happy birthday, Rosa!" Harriet hugged Rosa, then ushered her in and shut the door.

"Good morning, Mom." Rosa was glad Harriet had remembered she'd be arriving early, but looking into her mother's hazel, bloodshot eyes, hurt Rosa's heart. Another reason she'd wanted to visit Harriet early was so she'd see her before Harriet got drunk.

"This waking up at the crack of dawn business is highly overrated. I've made coffee." She held out her mug. "You want a cup?"

Over the years, the dash of Kahlúa and brandy Harriet put in her coffee had changed to a dash of coffee in her Kahlúa and brandy. Disappointed Harriet couldn't stay sober for this special day, Rosa declined.

"Well, you have me up. Let's make the best of it and go shopping. My treat. It's your birthday!"

"Thanks, Mom, but I have a lot of work to do. Maybe another time. Why do you have it so dark in here?" Rosa went from window to window, opening the curtains. "You have a prime unit on the corner, lots of windows, yet you choose to live in a cave." She stood with her hands on her hips. "Now, that's much better."

The light poured in through the bay windows, bringing the place to life. Rosa had decorated her mother's home in soft shades of baby blue and pastel green. The three-bedroom condo had more than enough room for Harriet.

"Are Ernesto and his whore in town yet?"

Rosa approached her mother, then sank onto the plush suede sectional, readying herself for her mother's tirade about how no good men were, especially her father. True to form, fifteen minutes later Harriet had connected every problem she had in her life to Ernesto.

"...How can you stand by him after all he's done to me?" Harriet stared into her Kahlúa brandy concoction. "He's turned you against me."

"No one's turned me against you. I love you. I just wish we could talk about anything besides how much you hate Daddy."

Harriet pointed an accusing finger at Rosa. "There you go taking his side again. He took everything from me and humiliates me at every turn, yet you continue singing his praises..."

Rosa glanced around at the works of art, the handcrafted furniture, the oriental rugs, and the designer fixtures. Unsure of how to keep things from becoming worse but knowing things couldn't remain the same, she massaged her temples.

"...When you were a child, you couldn't understand what was going on between Ernesto and me. You're grown now. There's no excuse for you taking his side. He cheated on me with that whore, threw me out of my home in the middle of the night, and stole my child from me."

Harriet's words worked like an air pump. Each word filled Rosa with anguish, resentment, and pain. Maximum capacity reached, Rosa felt as if she'd explode.

"I don't have to defend his actions," she said with a calmness she didn't feel as she unbuttoned the second to top button on her blouse.

"They can't be defended. That bastard—"

"Don't say another word!"

Shock replaced the anger on Harriet's face.

Rosa tilted her head to the side and scrunched up her face. "Who paid for this condo and everything in it? *That bastard.* You say you're sick. Let me tell you what I'm sick of. I'm sick of the lies. You've repeated them so much you actually believe them. You were the one cheating on Daddy, not the other way around. You are the one who left us, not the other way around. You are the one who continually pushes me away, not Daddy."

"He's filled your head with lies about me. He's twisted the story and has you believing I'm the monster when it's him. He wouldn't even let you visit me after you moved to Miami."

"Daddy has never spoken a negative word about you to me. He thinks you need help. It's you who's always putting him in the negative light. You always have."

"He told you I was cheating, and I left you! Lies, lies, lies!" She slammed her coffee mug onto the end table next to the overstuffed chair she was sitting in. "I found out about his affair with Anna, and he forced me out of your life."

Back straight, hands folded neatly across her lap, Rosa's silent rage worked as a shield. "The first time I saw you cheating on Daddy, I was around four. It was you and that guy who used to do the lawn."

Harriet drew her shaky hands to her face. "Oh my God," she gasped as she rocked back and forth, sobbing.

"I didn't understand what I was seeing." Rosa shook her head. "I remember the day you left us. You told me that Daddy didn't love me." She narrowed her gaze on her mother's tear-soaked face. "How can you tell a six-year old something like that? You'd been divorced at least a year before Daddy started dating Anna."

Still rocking, Harriet stammered, "H-he forced me to l-leave. I wouldn't leave you." She choked on her tears. "I didn't leave you. He made me."

"Do you take any responsibility for the things that happen in your life? This is partially my fault. I've held in my feelings because I've always wanted to protect you. But, I'm doing more harm than good. I don't want to resent you or avoid your calls. I want to love you. But, you won't get better until you start facing reality and dealing with your past."

"The only thing wrong with me is Ernesto! He ruined my life. He divorced me, threw me out, then turned you against me."

"Daddy told me that he initiated the divorce, but he would never tell me why. Looking back with my thirty-year-old eyes, I finally understand why he did. Have you ever considered he was tired of putting up with your mess?"

Harriet took on a distant look, as if she were experiencing déjà vu. Focusing over Rosa's shoulder, she said, "He forced me out and turned you against me."

"I don't need Daddy to tell me anything. I remember the final straw. I remember breaking my arm. I remember you left me at the hospital."

"Ernesto made me leave you."

"He was scared and angry and probably told you to leave. I don't have any children, but I feel pretty confident saying that nothing and no one could have made me leave my baby at that hospital." She wiped her stinging eyes. "Do you know or even care how much that hurt me, Mom?" She inhaled deeply, fighting to regain her cool veneer.

Harriet continued rocking back and forth. "I was upset. He was so angry. I couldn't stay. I was scared."

"Scared of what? Daddy never hurt you. Now that I think about it, that was the first and last time I'd ever seen him raise his voice at you. But, let's say you were so afraid of this man who had never laid a hand on you. When we got home, where were you? Were you worried about me?"

"I was worried sick about you."

"So worried that when we came into your room, you were sound asleep. Did Daddy make you go to bed also? Again, I don't have any children, but there's no way I would have gone to sleep until I saw my baby was home safe and sound."

"He's twisted everything."

"Give it up, Mom. The next day you picked me up from school trying to turn me against Daddy. I was only six!" Tears moistening her face, she pointed at Harriet. "Then that night, you left me." She pointed at herself.

"No, he forced me out!" Harriet shouted, picking at the pastel upholstery with her nails.

"Reality check. When we came to visit you, you said you weren't ready to see me. I heard you through the door."

"I was hurt. I didn't want you seeing me like that."

"I needed you. I thought you'd left because I wanted Daddy to stay. I blamed myself. How could you turn your crying child away?"

"It... It wasn't your fault. It was Ernesto."

"Stop this!" Harriet snapped to attention. "While you were busy feeling sorry for yourself, Daddy had a child to raise. He sent me to counseling to help me understand that I shouldn't blame myself for your choices in life. And while we're at it, he didn't keep me from visiting you when we moved to Miami. I chose to stop because I had better things to do with my teen-age years than play nursemaid to my drunken mother."

Realizing she was now speaking from pain, Rosa stopped herself. "I'm sorry," she said as she hugged her mother. Harriet's tears soaked through Rosa's blouse. "I don't want to fight. I know you aren't perfect. I never expected you to be. Please, Mom, try the Alcoholics Anonymous group I told you about. I'll go with you."

Harriet snatched a tissue out of the box that sat on the end table, then dabbed under her eyes. "I can't."

Rosa could see her mother physically withdraw into her shell of denial.

"Let's stop all of this foolishness," Harriet said. "It's your birthday. Having you was the happiest day of my life." She fingered the short curls that framed Rosa's face. "You look so much like your father and act like your aunt Angela."

Rosa knew Harriet was drunk now. "I love you, Mom."

DEA agent Samson Quartermaine dragged his large, dark hands over his face, smoothing down his goatee. "We only have ten days before the execution. There has to be a way to make him talk. Everyone has a price." He slammed his notebook closed, then tossed it toward the coffee table. The notebook skidded across the table and fell to the floor.

"Martín plans on taking his secrets with him to the grave," agent Alton Miles said as he swung his golf club at the imaginary tee. A

Miami thunderstorm had made them miss tee-time, and, as usual, they ended up talking shop. "That's one price we can't beat. If we could only convince the FBI to put him into witness protection."

"He's always been able to hide his money trail. How? Who? He'll never roll over on his silent partner. If he went into witness protection, he'd take up where he left off. The Feds can't allow that. We need his sentence commuted to life without the possibility of parole." Samson watched his partner pace around the living room of the small apartment, swinging his golf club.

"I know he'll never give up his partner," Alton said. "What I don't understand is why he'd rather die than turn over the Sierra syndicate. They were his competition."

David Martín had been sentenced to death for murdering a DEA informant and his gang. The informant had infiltrated the Sierra organization and copied account records, pipeline routes, business connections, and other information the DEA needed to bring the syndicate down.

Alton carried a straight-backed chair from the dinette area into the living room. "Who is Martín protecting and why? And what's the purpose in giving us free rein if they won't let us truly have free rein? Do they want us to break these syndicates or not? Hell! This is my career riding on this case. We have to bring Sierra down."

Samson understood Alton's frustration. Their team was given the "freedom" to bypass much of the strict structure and red tape of government agencies, but what good had it done them? "You know there's no such thing as total freedom. I agree with the chief on this call. Offering witness protection to the head of the largest drug syndicate is out of the question. Sorry to sound politically correct, but we need to think outside the box."

He trained his warm brown eyes on Alton's cold blue ones. They'd been best friends since preschool, yet were as different as a monsoon and a drought. "What if he doesn't have a silent partner? What if he didn't obtain the information?"

Alton waved him off. "Martín never said he didn't have the information."

"Would we have believed him if he had? Would we believe him if he said he was the only leader? What if he doesn't have a bargaining chip?"

"So you think he's been dickin' us around this whole time?"

"I don't know. I'm throwing every possibility out there. After he was taken out of commission, his organization hiccupped, then continued with business as usual. His silent partner must have run things for a while. Otherwise, there would have been a struggle for power. Yeah, he definitely has a silent partner." He ran his hands over his cleanly shaven head, and then leaned forward, resting his elbows on his knees. "Lately something else has been needling me. Why didn't the witness to the murders have a fatal accident before the trial? No one had ever lived to testify against David Martín. The man testified, then died in a car accident an hour later."

"I've been wondering the same thing, man. I think his silent partner double-crossed him, but that brings us back to square one. I sure as hell wouldn't die for someone who double-crossed me."

"We need more time."

"They won't commute his sentence unless he gives up his partner or Sierra. Hell, you're the lawyer. How can we have his sentence commuted?"

"Good question."

"Well, something's got to change. I'm too close to let this slip by."

Drifting into his own world, Samson looked around the one bedroom flat. *Boy, has my life changed.* He went from having a promising career and beautiful home to an all-consuming job and somewhere to sleep. The worn-out, tacky tan furniture was even part of the rental agreement. Three years had passed since the divorce. Tired of punishing himself, he wanted to live again, practice law again, and take control of his life again. But, he couldn't bail out on Alton.

After Samson left his law firm, Alton kept him from shutting himself off from the world and convinced him to join the DEA. Alton had been there to kick sense into him when he needed kicking. The change of pace had worked wonders initially. Being a DEA agent was exciting and kept his mind off his troubles, but now he was ready to move on and do his own thing. After David's execution, he planned on turning in his resignation.

"Anybody home?" Alton knocked the coffee table with the head of his golf club. "Hell, forget this. It's Sunday. We're off. Let's go to the pool hall and worry about this in the morning."

"I'm with you." He stood to leave. Only thirty-four years old, Samson still had a lot of life to live. Thoughts of his large family comforted his aching heart. He hadn't seen them since his sister's funeral a year ago. She'd been on his mind a lot lately. "I forgot to ask your status on the Ernesta Wells' call David received."

"I've already run her. Of course, her name is totally bogus. We'll allow the guards to believe they're getting away with smuggling her in until after we've interviewed Ernesta. The warden's gonna call us as soon as she arrives." Alton stood and reached in his pocket for the keys to his Mustang.

"She's our only lead," Samson said. "That and flowers. He's been obsessed with them lately. His cell walls look like he has floral print wall paper."

"Maybe he's dreaming about his funeral. Martín dies in ten days. We need to find out who he's actually protecting and why, or get his sentence commuted. I don't give a damn how we do it."

Chicago

"Happy birthday, CNN," said the news correspondent. "The nation's first all-news station debuted on this day in 1980…"

Opening the door, Rosa heard CNN, and her spirits lifted. The news playing could only mean one thing. She dropped her keys into her purse, setting it on the entry table.

"Daddy!" She rounded the corner into the living room where he stood with his arms held out. She hugged her grizzly bear of a father. "You're early." Though he lived in Miami, they had keys and the combinations to each other's residences.

His hearty chuckle filled the room. "You want me to leave and come back?"

After the dose of disappointment her mother injected, Ernesto's loving embrace was just the antidote she needed. "You'd better not."

She fought the urge to cry. She couldn't save her mother if she refused to recognize that she needed saving.

"What's wrong?" he asked.

"I visited Mom today. That's always draining."

He lifted her chin with his fingertip. "She's the one losing out, not you." He wiped the tears from her face. "I have something for you." He turned her around.

A glimpse of brown beside her large, white sofa caught her eye. "You didn't." She walked around to investigate. "You did! An African stool." She knelt beside the Asante chief's stool, running her hand over the fine dark wood of the concave surface. Excited to see Ernesto, she'd missed the stool when she came in. The craftsmen carved each stool out of a single piece of wood. The base of this particular stool was an elephant, a sign of chiefly authority. "Thank you, Daddy."

"You have two ends to this couch."

"Two! You got me two?" She went to the other side of the couch, and sure enough, there was a second stool. This one's base was a lion, reserved for royalty. Both stools were only two feet tall, making them perfect end tables. She knew the antiques' original purpose, but she didn't want people sitting on them.

"You need to get dressed. We've only begun to celebrate your thirtieth."

"Why didn't I turn thirty years ago? How should I dress?"

Arms crossed over his chest, he raised a brow. She laughed. He always wore designer suits, handcrafted Italian leather shoes, and Egyptian cotton or some other fine-fabric dress shirt. He did everything in first class style.

"I guess bowling and Burger King are out."

He moved several large throw pillows out of the way, so he could sit comfortably. "Who's Burger King?" He winked.

Rosa and Ernesto boarded the Odyssey cruise ship, which was docked at Navy Pier on Lake Michigan. Known for its elegance, the Odyssey had three levels, each ensuring its guests a great time.

"Let's have our picture taken," Rosa suggested.

The photographer positioned Rosa and Ernesto along the railing and snapped shots. "You're a very lucky man," the young man said.

Pride filled Ernesto's light eyes. "My daughter is something, isn't she? It's her birthday."

Ernesto missed the man's double take, but Rosa didn't. She didn't resemble either of her parents, so she figured she must look like some of her family that she didn't know, which was all of it. With Ernesto growing up in foster care and Harriet's only sister disowning her, Rosa considered herself family-poor.

As the man clicked more pictures, she observed Ernesto. In his early sixties, he was still a handsome man. She reached up and ran her finger through an area of his hair that had more gray than black.

He smiled down at her. "I'm getting old."

"Mature." She hugged him.

They had spent the majority of their day at the Art Institute enjoying the exhibits, with her talking about the children she tutored during the school year, and him giving her pointers on how to expand her computer-networking firm.

Ernesto had raised the bar, using Bolívar International as the example. Proud of her father, Rosa listened to most of his advice because she knew it was sound.

The pictures printed out instantly. Liking what they saw, Ernesto paid for the photos, and then escorted Rosa around to the Topaz deck. The ship left dock and cruised Lake Michigan, providing a breathtaking view of Chicago's night skyline.

"Where's everyone?" Rosa asked. The outside portion of the deck was deserted. "The main point in these cruises is to see the skyline from the lake."

Ernesto frowned. "This is strange. I'll go inside and see what's going on. Stay here." He walked around the deck chairs toward the entrance.

Rosa followed. "I'm coming, too. You're not leaving me in the *Twilight Zone*."

The perfect gentleman, he opened and held the door open for her.

"Thank you, kind sir." She stepped into the Topaz dining area.

"Surprise!" cheered the crowd.

Rosa clutched her heart in fear, and then realized what was happening. The dining hall was filled to the deck's two-hundred-person capacity with her tiny family, friends, and co-workers.

Juan, one of the children she babysat, ran to her with his hands held up. "Wosa!" She lifted the three year old, swinging him around. "Wheee!" he squealed.

She stopped spinning and placed him on her hip. "*¿Como estas, Juan?*"

"English, Rosa," Ernesto chastised. "He must learn."

"Yes, Daddy." Not in the mood for an English lesson, she held the child close. Often, she wondered if Ernesto was ashamed of his Colombian blood. He'd claim to be a proud Afro-Colombian, and they were both fluent in Spanish, but she knew there was so much more to the culture. It was Anna who had taught her about El Choco, Colombia, also known as the African Heart of Colombia, where Ernesto's family came from; Anna who had taught her the many similarities between African-American and Afro-Colombian history, Anna who had convinced Ernesto to take Rosa on a trip to Colombia for her high school graduation gift.

Then again, it was Ernesto who sparked her love for African art, and Ernesto who had raised her a proud black woman.

Juan, tugging on her arm, broke her musings. Ready to enjoy her special day, she gazed into his smiling face. Someday, she'd have a child of her own. The crowd continued gathering around to wish her happy birthday.

Someone pulled on her waist. She looked over her shoulder. "Mom!" Juan remained planted firmly on her hip as she hugged Harriet. "I can't believe you didn't tell me about this."

"And ruin the surprise? Never! Stand back and let me see you."

Rosa handed Juan to Ernesto, then spun to show off her new designer dress. The sheer black rayon shell and Georgette lining were close-fitting without being tight; the sleeves were capped and the sides slit up to the knees. A rose border print swept diagonally across the front and along the hemline.

"You're simply breathtaking."

Rosa bowed gracefully. "Why, thank you. You're looking pretty good yourself." She had to give Harriet her props. She always dressed nicely, and tonight was no different. Harriet sported a burgundy silk pantsuit and had her hair in a French knot with a few curls falling freely.

She waved Rosa on. "Go ahead with your friends. Have a good time."

Grateful Harriet wasn't drunk, she kissed her mother's chocolate cheek. "I love you."

"I love you, too."

Rosa turned to greet everyone else and bumped into Anna. "Someone's been keeping secrets."

"One…two tops." Anna winked. "Harriet's right. You're breathtaking."

Harriet grumbled under her breath as she pushed her way past Anna and stalked off toward the bar.

Rosa narrowed her eyes on her mother. *She'd better not cause the usual scene. Not tonight.*

She returned her attention to the dark statuesque beauty her father had married. Anna would never replace her mother, yet Rosa had carved a special spot in her heart for Anna. Many a night, she spent talking to Anna about her troubles, wants, and desires. Many a night, she spent wishing Harriet were more like Anna.

"I'm sorry about—"

"Stop apologizing for your mother." Anna fingered the curls about Rosa's face. "I love this new look." She hugged Rosa. "Everyone's waiting on you to get out there and shake your groove thang."

Anna's attempt at slang had Rosa laughing. "Groove thang? Okay, I'm out." She took Juan from Ernesto and headed for the dance floor.

"I'm worried about Rosa," Ernesto said. Dinner finished, most of the party guests were on the dance floor or on the boat's deck enjoying the view. Ernesto remained at the head table with Anna, watching Rosa.

Anna patted her husband's hand under the table. "She has such a kind heart. Look at her out there with Juan." Rosa was on the dance floor teaching Juan how to step to a R. Kelly jam. "I don't think his mom will ever get him back. Our baby is ready to settle down and have children of her own."

Ernesto's brows furrowed. "I'm not talking about that. I was only thirty-two when I married the first time, and look what a disaster that turned out to be. She has plenty of time to start a family. I'm worried about her trying to save Harriet. That woman's the pilot on a one-way trip to self-destruction. I don't want Rosa caught up."

Harriet stumbled over to Ernesto's table. "How could you bring your whore to my daughter's party?" she slurred.

"Please, Harriet," Anna said before Ernesto could speak. "Not tonight. I'm willing to leave. This is too special for Rosa."

"My point exactly. Your ass shouldn't be here!" She stomped on the floor, spilling a portion of her Long Island iced tea on her silk suit.

Ernesto glared at Harriet. The party was Anna's idea, but she was willing to stay away because she didn't want Harriet to cause a scene. He'd told Harriet, and she'd insisted that she knew how to behave. He'd prayed that for once Harriet would put her child first. Having the three of them in the same room without a fight would have been a long-awaited, much-needed first for Rosa.

"What the hell you looking at?" she asked Ernesto.

Ernesto stood to drag Harriet out of the party if necessary. He should have followed his own mind instead of Anna's, and not invited Harriet.

"Mother!" Rosa spun Harriet around to her. "Grab your wraps," she said through tight lips. "We're leaving!"

After the boat docked, Rosa dropped her mother off at her condo, then called Ernesto and told him that she wasn't returning to the party. He tried to change Rosa's mind, but the moment had been ruined for her. Instead, she went home, showered, and readied for bed. Mind weary, she reached into her nightstand for her two best friends: journal and pen.

Ernesto had started her writing journals when she was eight. He said women had all of these extra emotions and journaling helped get the emotions out before they drove the men in their lives crazy. A smile warmed her heart as she readied her pen, thanking God again for her father.

I love Mom, but things have to change. She doesn't respect my feelings or care about the awkward positions she continually puts me in, and I'm tired of it.

She wrote everything that had happened throughout the day regarding Harriet. *Maybe the books are right, and I'm an enabler.* She tapped her chin with the end of the pen. *I've remained quiet out of respect; but if I remain quiet, things will never get better. I hate to admit this, but it felt good telling Mom off this afternoon. Freeing.* She doodled a few scribbles. *Things have to change.*

CHAPTER TWO

Upset that Rosa refused to return to her party, Ernesto claimed one of the deck chairs and watched the skyline as the Odyssey cruised Lake Michigan.

The city has changed so much.

The boat passed the high rise where he had lived some thirty-odd years ago.

I've changed so much.

He could remember the Thanksgiving when he'd learned of Harriet's pregnancy as if it just happened. Looking back, he had a lot more to be grateful for than he'd realized...

Chicago, thirty-one years ago

A quiet David equaled a dangerous David. Ernesto knew David's somber mood had something to do with his girl. The previous day, David had hung up on her and closed himself off in the spare bedroom. He stormed out a few hours later and didn't return until late.

"I bought a few more buildings." Ernesto pushed the specifications for the properties across the kitchen table to David. The real estate, car dealerships, and other businesses they owned weren't enough for Ernesto to launder their drug money, and Barry Paige was trying to muscle in on their trafficking territory. They didn't have time for distractions. "You're bringing in the money too fast," he joked, hoping to lift David's spirits and get him talking. "We need to make our move." He pulled the plate of bacon over to his side of the table and took a few slices.

"Well, ain't this some shit!" David skimmed through the papers while continuing to eat. "I knew we were moving up, but damn. Who'd a thunk two *niños* nobody wanted would rule the world someday?" He tipped his forkful of eggs onto a slice of toast. "We've come a long way."

"Yeah, we've come a long way." Thoughts of their years in foster care, bouncing from one abusive home to the next, always brought Ernesto down. If it weren't for his friendship with David, he would have never made it.

At the age of fifteen, they had their first corner. Seventeen years later, they controlled the drug trade in the majority of the Midwest of the country. David handled the seedier side of the business, while Ernesto handled the rest.

Ernesto's thoughts returned to the present. He needed to break David out of his funk before it affected their expansion. "I'm quitting my job and buying a technology firm." He used his position as a corporate lawyer to network both the legal and illegal sides of business and start several legitimate businesses of his own. David saw the legitimate side as a necessary evil, but Ernesto wanted to fit into it, be accepted by it.

"It's an up and coming firm," he continued between bites of bacon and eggs. "Software and hardware. They have several large contracts pending. I'm sinking all of my assets into this."

"How many times have you told me not to put all of my eggs in one basket?" David said, his Spanish accent coloring his words deeper than Ernesto's.

"I've already developed a vision for the company that will propel me by leaps and bounds. I don't know. I just have a feeling about this. I'm going for it."

David nodded. "That's cool." He forked through his food. "I always knew your white ass was corporate."

"I'm not white, I'm Colombian," Ernesto retorted to rile David.

"Humph, Colombian, my ass." David tossed his fork onto his plate. "Your ass ain't neva been to no Colombia. We, Chicago boys, born and raised. You need to change your name to some shit like Ernest Bowman!" Their laughs ricocheted off the kitchen walls. "A wholesome white-sounding name that'll keep a few doors open for your corporate ass. Jews do it all the time. You wanna be corporate. I say go all out. Hell, you even sound like a white boy."

"When I'm at the top of the Fortune 500 list, I want my mother to see what she gave away." His joke had an undercurrent of truth. His earliest memory was when he was three and his mother's lover said he wasn't raisin' no white man's kid. A few days later Ernesto's mother dropped him at David's house to spend the night. She never returned. David's mother, Maria, kept Ernesto so David would have someone to play with while she worked. A year later, she was murdered by one of her johns, and the boys were placed in foster care.

"Oh yeah, I'm sure she follows the list religiously, Ernest."

Relieved David was climbing out of his stupor, Ernesto smiled.

"Seriously though, I'm glad you bought this company. I'm sure you'll take it far. If there's anything I can do, you know I got your back."

Ernesto knew. He couldn't count the number of times David had saved his butt over the years. Throughout their whole lives, the only people they could rely on were each other. David would get into a bind—Ernesto's charm and cunning would get David out of it. When Ernesto needed unabashed, brute force—David was willing and able to oblige. But, Ernesto wanted to do this entirely on his own. This was his company, and he would be the reason it succeeded or failed.

He watched David toy with his food. Prying conversation out of him was awkward. It was time to stop fooling around and go in for the kill. "What's going on with your girl? You might as well say it before your black ass explodes," he said with a smile, eliciting the same from David.

David became somber, stared at Ernesto a while, then pushed away from the table. "*Esa puta* got pregnant! No, make that, she got pregnant, then had the audacity to tell me I'm gonna pay for her abortion. Now ain't that some fucked up *mierda*? I ended up kickin' *Jorge's* ass."

Now this sounded more like his David! The more upset he was, the thicker the accent, until he'd finally switch to Spanish completely.

"You're out of your damned mind," Ernesto said as he lifted his mug and inhaled the rich aroma of the Colombian coffee. This turn of events didn't bode well for Ernesto. A baby in the mix would complicate their already difficult life exponentially; there had to be a way to turn this around. "You'd better chill out with these married women before a jealous husband comes after you." He set his coffee down and continued eating.

"Aw, hell naw! I know you ain't tellin' me to watch who I'm screwin'. I'm not the one who almost got his brains blown out. How the hell you gonna sleep with Mac's girl? Damn, man. You're lucky I was followin' his ass."

"I was only seventeen, and Vanessa was too fine to pass up. You're thirty-two. What's your excuse?" Hunger gone, he dropped his fork onto his plate.

"That was one of my best kills." David positioned his arms and hands as if he were shooting a rifle. He closed one eye and looked through the sight, following along the diamond print wallpaper, past the refrigerator, to the patio door. "Taking over his territory was a good idea. Sleeping with his woman was stupid." He readjusted his imaginary rifle. "S.W.A.T don't have shit on me." Pulling the trigger, he jerked back. "Bang!"

Ernesto flinched, haunted by nightmares of Mac's head exploding: the blood, the brains, the body. He loved the control the money and power associated with the drug trade afforded him, but he couldn't stomach the violence. He envied David's fight. David would do whatever needed doing. Ernesto knew he'd be unstoppable if he could somehow harness David's power.

David lowered his arms. "I'm sorry, man. My ass got carried away."

"I'm fine." Ernesto forced himself to stop trembling.

"Hell, naw! Your ass really is white now. I was out of line. That bastard had a gun to your head. I know that shit fucks with you." He returned to his seat. "I need to learn how to shut my damn mouth."

"I'll be fine." He lifted his cup of coffee with shaky hands, then replaced it on the table.

David's brows furrowed. "You sure?"

"Yeah." He pushed his plate, the cup, and the memories away. "Do you think they'll go to the police? Maybe I should smooth things over with George and give him a payoff. We can't afford for you to be arrested over this stupid stuff right now. Paige is standing at our back door with a battering ram, and the DEA is at the front."

"*Jorge* ain't goin' no fuckin' where; Paige ain't shit; and the DEA hasn't even learned to tie their damn shoes yet."

"What did you do to George?"

"I pushed him around a little." He strummed his fingers on the wooden tabletop. "I can't take him out. My stupid ass was drunk. I drove over there like I owned the damn place. I know someone had to see my car."

They both fiddled with their cups of coffee, calculating their next move. Contrary to David's assessment of Paige, the man was very important. Paige controlled the second largest trafficking territory in the United States and was primed to squeeze in on David's. The Drug Enforcement Agency might be only a few years old, but they were hungry to make a name for themselves. Ernesto groaned. He needed to get this baby situation under control fast so that David would concentrate on business.

"Why don't you just marry Harriet?" Ernesto suggested, knowing what David's reaction would be. "That way you'd have your son. It's not like you have to be faithful."

"My ass would be *el pinche* Pope before it was married, especially to a *puta* like Harriet. And if that *pinche* Paige found out about my boy…" he trailed off.

It was never proven, but they suspected Paige ordered the drive-by that killed David's son. "You're right," Ernesto said, voice laced with concern. He chewed on his inner jaw as he ran his hand over his short, dark, wavy hair. "I'm about to be the CEO of a company. We've always kept my image squeaky clean. Even the drug world doesn't know I'm your clean-up man. Corporate moguls have wives and children."

"No!" David choked on his coffee. "Don't even start."

"I don't like this either. I'm a free man. I have no ties, and I don't want any, but hear me out. I need a wife that looks pretty on the arm, is the perfect hostess and, most importantly, will stay out of my business. From everything you've told me about Harriet, all I have to do is toss a little money at her and tell her I love her every once in a while. She's already pregnant."

David ran his hands through his short, curly hair. "So you'd raise *mi hijo*."

"This is the perfect way for you to have your son and keep him hidden from the cartels." The more David was pressured, the more he would resist, so Ernesto continued eating, allowing his words to sink in.

A second helping of scrambled eggs and bacon later, David grudgingly admitted, "This could work. Yeah, let's do this shit. "

"I just need time to figure out what to do with George."

"He gonna kick her greedy ass out for this shit. I'll go over and apologize. I'll tell him I was all emotional and shit after she said she was gonna kill *mi hijo*. Hell," he chuckled, "when I'm finished, he'll want to *dot* Harriet's *eye*. I'll pay off his bills, and all will be forgiven. Hell yeah!" He clapped his hands. "It'll work. She'll make the perfect show piece."

"If the baby turns out to be George's, I'll pay him off to get him to sign over custody. Either way, Harriet will make the perfect trophy wife for my picture-perfect family."

"That punk ass bastard can't make no babies." He grabbed his crotch. "Hell, my troops cancel everybody's shit out."

Ernesto chuckled as he brought his coffee cup to his lips and took a sip. The only time Ernesto saw David break down was when his son was murdered. Somehow, that child had done the impossible— touched David's heart. "What if the baby is yours?"

"What about it?"

"Do you want to be a part of his life or not?"

"Hell no! I'm keeping her ass from killing him. Ain't that enough? Shit, that ought to be worth a point or two when my ass is whacked."

David's words didn't ring true to Ernesto. Even as children, David believed he'd be dead by the time he was fifty. Ernesto thought this was the reason why he lived life so dangerously. From what Ernesto could tell, this child was his best friend's way of keeping death from destroying him.

David sighed heavily as he dragged his hands over his face. "I'm not going through that shit again. Hell yeah, I want *mi hijo*, but damn…"

Ernesto saw the pain in David's black eyes, heard it in his voice. He would never fully recover from the death of his son. Pondering his next move, Ernesto finished his cup of coffee. If he took this child, he could have a part of David's fire as his own. Ever since David saved Ernesto from Mac, Ernesto felt indebted to him. Raising this child would finally put David in his debt. "We're doing this, but this child is mine."

"Hell yeah, it's yours. What the hell would I do with *un bebé*?" He paused. "I want you to be a hands-on father. Minimal contact with Harriet."

CAUGHT UP

"Hold up a second. I'm a businessman, not a babysitter. I'll raise *my* child as I see fit." David ground his teeth. Ernesto continued, "You know I won't let Harriet ruin the kid. I'm insisting on full control. This is business. I don't tell you how to run your part, and you don't tell me how to run mine."

"Then maybe I should just kill the *puta* after she has the baby. Her ass is more trouble than it's worth."

"No," Ernesto said calmly though his heart raced. He'd had two mothers taken from him and wouldn't deny this child a mother. "That would call too much attention to me." Manipulating Harriet wouldn't be a problem. Greedy people were so easy to control. "We do this my way."

David chewed on his thumbnail. "You're right." He relaxed. "No blurring of power." He smacked the table. "This shit'll work. You'll see."

"DEA paid me another visit."

"They'll never give up on you. Guilt by association and all. Fuck 'em. They can't prove shit. I got it covered." He strummed what was left of his fingernails on the table. "I can't stand those crooked-assed bastards."

"Okay. Just thought I'd mention it." He paused. "About Harriet, how will I contact her?"

"I'll bet your ass she calls me. I'm tellin' you, *Jorge* is gonna kick her ass out. She has nowhere to go. All she cares about is *es dinero*, and her pride will keep her from returnin' to *Jorge* until she's desperate. She'll call or end up at Tony's to try and seduce me into taking her back."

"Tony's?"

"Yeah, that new spot I've been hangin' at over in Wrigleyville." He looked around the average sized kitchen. "These luxury apartments are great and all for a bachelor, but if you gonna be with Harriet, she's gonna want a big-ass mansion." He stretched his arms out. "Really big."

"I have someone who's into me for about a mil. His family doesn't know about his gambling habit. I'm sure he'd give me a great price on his estate."

"What the?" David leaned forward, head tilted and brows fur-

26

rowed. "Why didn't you tell me? I would have made sure that *chimba* paid you. A million? Hell naw! You can't let that shit slide."

Unaffected, Ernesto continued, "I'll be able to use him someday. He's a senior vice president over at Diligent Telecommunications."

"That Caldwell guy you told me about?"

"Yep, that's him."

"Oh." David relaxed his small frame in his seat. "As usual, you have the shit under control."

CHAPTER THREE

Florida, Present Day

David turned his back to the corrections officer and allowed him to unshackle his hands. "This is fuckin' unbelievable. You're actually gonna leave me alone in a room with a woman. I should have paid for this shit years ago." A death row inmate, David wasn't allowed contact with his visitors except Alton and Samson. Not that anyone visited him besides his lawyer and the agents.

The officer chuckled. "Hell, I'm being paid a grip, but not enough to be caught on tape. The leg irons stay on. Hurry up." He opened the door.

❧

"You look like shit!" David couldn't believe Harriet had let herself go so badly. He could get past the filthy, baggy clothes and burgundy wig she wore as a disguise, but her eyes had washed-out-drunk swimming in them. And she smelled like a distillery. He'd bet she sweated two hundred proof.

Harriet's tight smile looked as if it would crack. "We don't have time for pleasantries, dead man. Our child's in trouble, and you're going to help me save her." She tugged the ragged sleeve of her denim shirt up and checked her watch.

Panic sent his heart racing, and the small room felt like it was caving in on him, but he forced himself to maintain control. "Why the hell would I help you?"

"Because we're both fuck-ups, and she's in danger we placed her in." She strummed her nails on the metal tabletop. "She's more than earned her inheritance. If I go to the authorities, she'll lose everything. No. You have to do one good deed before you die."

Harriet may have changed physically, but he noticed she was still about the money. "Your ass always needs money. Tell me something new. What danger?"

"I'm not saying shit until you ensure my financial security."

"What the fuck?" He hopped up from the table, the chains about his legs rattling. "You said our child is in danger! Your ass is still fucked the hell up!"

She tapped her watch with the tip of her nail. "I don't have time for this, David," she said through clenched teeth. "I risk everything coming here because I love her. But, I'm realistic. I need money to survive. I should have spoken up years ago when you first approached me."

"Fine." He smacked the back of his chair. He'd suspected Ernesto set things in motion for him to end up on death row, but he couldn't have his lifelong friend murdered on a hunch. He'd spent years searching for the truth. The truth pointed to David making a mistake of arrogance and Ernesto continuing with business as usual. Ernesto even saw to the change of power in the cartel when David received the death sentence. He followed David's orders to a "T", except that Ernesto kept none of the power for himself. At the time, David was disappointed, but not surprised. Ernesto never wanted the cartel. He got off on the juice he received from being associated with David, and only continued laundering because they were so close and David didn't trust anyone else with his money.

"I'll make arrangements for your financial security. My ass is dead anyway. Now tell me what you know." He grabbed his metal folding chair and set it next to hers. "Speak quietly. You never know who's listening."

She quickly looked around the small room, resituated her wig and huddled close to him. "He came from your room after the graduation ceremony, enraged," she whispered. "He said after all of these years you wanted her back, and he wasn't giving her up. He wouldn't let the drug life have her. A month before she returned from Europe, you were arrested for murder."

David remembered him and Ernesto celebrating Rosa's graduation from college perfectly. He'd gotten drunk and said lots of things he didn't mean to follow through on. He pushed away from the table. *"Hijo de puta!"*

He'd clung to the reports of Ernesto's innocence because he could-n't bring himself to admit his lifelong friend, the man whose life he'd saved time and time again, the man he'd trusted to raise his child and handle his money, would betray him like this. Why hadn't Ernesto come to him for clarification when David was sober? Didn't Ernesto owe him at least that? *This shit must end!*

He drew in several breaths and released them slowly. Harriet hated Ernesto so much that she would lie, and she hadn't said what "danger" Rosa was in. In his heart he knew Ernesto loved Rosa and would never hurt her, and if Ernesto did set him up, it was because he was protect-ing Rosa. He smiled internally. They'd changed a lot over the years. All and all, none of this mattered. Rosa deserved to know the truth. "I'll take care of everything."

Harriet's lifeless hazel eyes sparked to life. "Very good." She peeked at her watch. "My time's almost up." She stood to leave.

"Clean yourself up."

She rolled her eyes as she quickly exited the room.

David, hands re-shackled behind his back, shuffled along the dark-ened corridor with his guard escort. "How would you like to make a quick hundred grand?"

"It depends on what I have to do," the guard replied.

"If you can get me a disposable phone within twenty-four hours, the money is yours." David always used throwaway phones when he didn't want his calls traced or bugged.

"Two hundred grand."

"A million if you hand me a disposable phone within five min-utes."

The guard stopped in his tracks and looked around for eavesdrop-pers. Harriet's money had ensured they were alone. "Are you serious?"

"Dead serious."

He was just as serious as when he'd decided to allow Ernesto to raise Rosa. Ernesto had tried to convince him that the baby might not be his. He'd reminded David that Harriet wasn't the most faithful of women. But David knew in his heart the baby was his. It had to be. He could see himself lying across his bed after he'd broken the news to Ernesto…

Chicago, thirty-one years ago

First his whorish mother tried to destroy him, then the foster care system tried to destroy him, then society tried to destroy him. He dragged his hands over his face. His rivals thought by killing his son that they'd destroy him, and now this. David closed his eyes. The baby Harriet carried was a part of him. He wouldn't allow her to destroy him or his son.

He reached into his back jeans pocket and pulled out his wallet. Lying on his stomach, he sorted through the scraps of paper he found in the slits. He unfolded a picture of him holding his three-year-old son and hugging the love of his life, Rosa.

He brushed his thumb over Rosa's image. She'd survived the drive-by physically, but died emotionally. He couldn't let the world know Harriet was carrying his child. He smiled, knowing he'd be having another son. This time, he'd do it right.

Using Ernesto would be perfect. This way David would have access to his son without the drug world ever discovering his secret. Then when his son was older, he could run the cartel at his real father's side. And if Ernesto ever got out of line—David folded the photo—he'd be handled. He replaced the picture, then stuffed his wallet into his back pocket.

◦∽✕∾◦

Samson and Alton circled the desk officer like sharks around prey. He'd already said the mistake was his fault, but the agents weren't satisfied. The heavyset warden leaned on his desk with one hock on the edge of his desk and one foot on the floor as he watched the agents debrief the officer.

"Let me get this straight," Samson said. "You *forgot* to call Warden Jackson when Ernesta Wells signed in?"

"This mindless ass thinks we're as stupid as him." Alton poked the officer in the center of his forehead. "How much were you paid?"

The officer wiped the sweat from his brow, then gripped the arms of the chair. "I wasn't paid. I swear."

"You should have been, because when I finish with your ass, you won't find employment anywhere," Alton snapped.

The officer avoided eye contact with Samson and Alton, but looked with pleading into the warden's eyes. "We go way back. My record is clean. I only have a year until retirement. You know me. I made an honest mistake. Please, don't let them do this to me."

"I'll vouch for him," the warden relented as he heaved his leg off the desk and approached the officer. "But, I'm suspending you without pay for three months. Now get."

The agents watched the officer scurry out. "He wouldn't have told us shit anyway," Alton said. "I'm still having his ass watched though. I want every guard associated with David changed. Their asses are on the take."

"May we have some privacy, Warden?" Samson asked.

"Sure. I'll have the guards changed immediately." He left the agents alone.

Samson popped in the video of the mystery woman into the VCR. "I don't recognize her from our files. What about you?"

"Nope. And what's this shit about their child? He had a son, right? He was killed in a drive-by. They must be talking in code."

Samson smoothed down his goatee. "Can we crack the code before we run out of time? What about the taxi service she took?"

"I'm checking into it. With our luck, we'll hit another dead end. Same for her fingerprints."

"I need to speak with David."

"I know you're his buddy-buddy and all," Alton said with an over-dose of sarcasm, "but he's about to go on the warpath. You need to step back and watch his every move. He'll slip up."

Samson sat at the warden's desk, thumbing through a file on David, writing all of the names associated with David on a notepad. "What are we missing? Who would know about a child, his child, his daughter?"

"There ain't no daughter. Daughter's a codename. I'm having extra cameras placed every damned place and wiring them to our office in Miami."

Ignoring Alton, Samson began crossing names out. "Who would he trust?" He continued eliminating names when one name yelled at him. The same name that David had plastered all over his cell.

"I've figured it out."

"What?"

"The code."

"Well, hot damn. Lay it on me." Alton rolled an office chair from the conference table to the desk.

"Ernesta was talking about Rosa, the mother of David's child. She disappeared soon after the baby was killed. I'll bet David put her in hiding."

"Sorry, man, but there's no way in hell he's still protecting Rosa. Her ass cracked up after the kid was killed. He isn't the type to stand by his woman through thick and thin." Alton stood to leave. "I'm checking in with the taxi service. Maybe they have something for us."

"I'm visiting David."

"Suit yourself, but it's a waste of time we don't have."

David set the stack of typing paper to the side, then leaned against the wall and pulled his feet up on the bunk.

By the time Rosa earned her masters degree, he'd grown tired of hiding in the audience while she showered Ernesto with the affection that should be for him. Her strong personality rivaled his. He could see her being not only the first big-time female drug lord, but also the drug lord of the largest syndicate. He lowered his head to his knees. Those were only drunken dreams that he had never really considered. He looked at the bars. He'd given her to Ernesto to save her from the life and, at the time, save her from himself.

If there were only a way to see her one last time before I die.

An anxious chuckle escaped him. The knowledge of impending death was a mind-altering event. His priorities had changed since he was assigned his death date. Now all that mattered was Rosa. If the drug world discovered her identity, they'd never believe that she wasn't involved. He'd die before he allowed another of his children to be destroyed by the drug world. He regretted giving her to Ernesto, but he couldn't go back. The call he'd made a few minutes ago would ensure her safety once he was gone. Only the truth would protect her.

He heard someone with a long, even stride approaching. It had to be Samson. He heard a second set of footsteps, but he didn't recognize the stutter-step rhythm.

The new guard let Samson into David's cell, then left.

"Where's that lanky-assed bastard you call your partner?" he asked in Spanish.

Samson grinned. "He said to tell you he misses you." He sat on the opposite end of the bunk, which creaked from his weight. Leaning forward, he rested his elbows on his knees and his face in his hands.

David considered Samson. He was young, single, honest, and actually a good person, so how the hell did he allow Alton to convince him to join the DEA? Samson had been visiting him twice a week for the past year. David knew the game. Samson's assignment was to befriend David. He'd never admit it to Samson, but over the months David began looking forward to the visits. It helped relieve some of the boredom and loneliness.

"You just gonna sit there or you got somethin' to say?"

"I thought I'd just sit here."

"Suit yourself, smart-ass. You got somethin' to write with?" His pen had run out of ink, and he wanted to sign the pictures he'd drawn. Even as a child, drawing had calmed David.

Samson handed him an ink pen and resumed his resting position. David didn't know if Samson was brave or stupid. He could kill Samson with the pen, and what could they do to him? Send him to death row? There was no way Alton would have lowered his guard. He smiled internally. Samson knew that he didn't have anything to worry about. Somehow, the jerk had become a friend of sorts.

He took the stack of typing paper and signed the top picture, which was a rose. He'd missed his little girl's thirtieth birthday. He closed his eyes, this time praying to see her again.

"Where's Rosa?" Samson asked.

David coughed violently. His sketches dropped to the floor, the pages scattering. He hopped off the bunk and bent to retrieve them.

"If you give us Sierra, I'll ensure no one harms your lover. Just tell me where she is."

"My lover?" David quickly gathered the pages, laughing. "My lover!"

Samson picked up the last stray page and displayed the rose design to David. "It's too late. I've already seen your reaction. Who's threatening her?"

David snatched the page. "You don't know shit." He returned to the bed and leaned against the wall as if it would fall if he moved. Ernesto had been correct; naming Rosa after his lover was a stupid move.

"Help me and I'll help you."

"I take care of my own. Always have. Always will."

"We can put her into witness protection."

Placing Rosa in protective custody would be the same as taking her freedom. He held the drawings close and closed his eyes. He'd kept Rosa's identity secret this long, he wouldn't ruin it now. In a few days he'd be gone, and his baby would be safe.

"Do you believe in fate?" Samson asked.

David heard Samson but didn't answer. His fate was sealed; he was a dead man and would never have the chance to tell his daughter that he loved her. If he could replay his life, he'd be thirty-two again and raise his child on his own as a legitimate businessman. He'd have the guts to be Ernesto.

Samson touched the drawings. "Rosa needs you."

He handed over Samson's ink pen, certain Samson didn't know about the visit from Harriet yet and that Harriet had covered her tracks. She'd never risk losing the money he promised. "I'm tired and ready to die."

"Okay, I'll drop it. Think about what I've said. Officer," he called.

David watched Samson as he waited by the cell door. He and Rosa would make a good couple. Maybe he should make another call and set up meetings between the two for after he died. He dismissed the idea as insane.

The officer escorted Samson out. At times, David didn't know what to think. All he knew was he couldn't stand being caged much longer. The sound of Samson's long stride faded. He did look forward to their visits. They helped maintain his sanity.

Samson stared out the window of their cramped office onto the parking lot a few floors below. It was raining outside and people darted to and from their cars.

What is David running from?

The terror in David's black eyes when he mentioned Rosa threw Samson. He'd caught him off-guard on purpose, but David's reaction was past shocked. Core-shaking fear had gripped him.

Alton drew his hands through his brown hair. "Are you out your damned mind? You want me to waste the little time we have finding Rosa Shields? You've gotten too buddy-buddy with him. I'm trying to bring down a cartel, and you want to play matchmaker."

"You didn't see him. When I mentioned her name, he turned from a black man to a white ghost. He's protecting her. Finding Rosa is our only chance."

Alton knocked a stack of folders off his laptop onto his messy desk. "Fine. I'll do it." He pushed piles of papers about. "Have you seen the adapter to my laptop?"

"Clean your desk." He unplugged the power adapter from his laptop and handed it to Alton. "How long do you think it'll take you to find her?"

"Too long. But we don't have anything else. Ernesta Wells covered her tracks too well."

"I can't believe I didn't think of Rosa before. David's been acting strange for the past few weeks. He's been obsessed with flowers."

"If she's alive, I'll find her. Hell, you're probably right. I'll lay odds she knows who his partner is."

CHAPTER FOUR

Rosa jumped at the chance to leave Chicago for Miami. Ever since Harriet acted up at the party, Rosa had needed a break from her mother. She unzipped her garment bag and hung its contents in the hotel closet. She would have stayed at Ernesto's, but the hotel was only a few blocks away from the work site. Opening a second office in Miami looked better every day. In the past three months, she'd picked up nine new clients in the area, and traveling expenses were climbing. She usually sent a technician to conduct estimates, but she would take this opportunity to visit Anna.

She might need to crawl on the floor to see portions of the current computer network configuration, so she kept a pair of dark brown twill slacks and a gold cotton blouse to wear.

Hackers had attacked this client's network three times. Word of her firewall protection had spread like wildfire, and this customer contacted her firm.

On the flight, she'd read through the list of software the company presently used and discovered an incompatibility that made the company's network vulnerable. As she organized the closet, she organized her day's schedule.

Thoughts of cramming a two-day job into one tired her out. The day being Friday made matters worse. No one wanted to work on Friday, including Rosa. But if she finished early, she could spend the weekend with Anna until Ernesto finished working, then they could all enjoy a family outing. After the way Harriet had shown her butt, she thought her and Anna could use some special time. Recollections of Ernesto telling her that women needed their alone time came to mind. At the time she felt like he was trying to get rid of her, but now she realized he was correct. She'd enjoyed her times with Anna and prayed someday she could enjoy her time with her mother.

CAUGHT UP

Thoughts of Ernesto's impending doom had Harriet giddy. She'd been waiting years for this moment and could barely contain her excitement. Showered, perfumed, and dressed in her normal designer attire, she strutted into his Miami office as if she owned the place.

Ernesto pointed the remote control at the wall across from him. It was tiled with flat screen televisions, each playing a different news channel. "What do you want?" He lowered the volume on the one he'd been listening to.

Afraid of heights, she stood in the center of his office. His back wall was floor to ceiling windows. Even though she was at least ten paces away, she felt as if she'd fall. Lightheaded, she lowered herself into one of the leather armchairs in front of his desk. The only reason she selected her high-rise condo was because it was the most expensive; thus in her opinion, the best.

As a child, she'd had nothing but the abuse of perverted men because her no good father only stuck around long enough to get Harriet's mother pregnant twice. Her mother had to beg men for money to keep food on the table, clothes on their backs and a roof over their heads. Harriet had fought her entire life to be on top. And now, thanks to her visit with David, she'd be rich and Ernesto would fall. He'd fall for all of the men who had used her mother. He'd fall for every man who had tipped into her room while her mother was passed out drunk in the living room. He'd fall for taking her daughter from her. He'd fall.

He shoved his suit sleeve up slightly and checked his Rolex. "Already 2:30. Of course, you're drunk."

"I haven't had a drink all day," she snapped. "I'm here to apologize for my behavior the other night." She drew in several deep breaths, then went over to the wet bar, sure to avoid the lovely fifteen-story view.

"You should be apologizing to Rosa and Anna, not me. Now what do you really want? If it's money, forget it. I give you more than enough."

She poured herself a cola, wishing it were brandy. With Ernesto out of the way, Rosa would need a sober mother. "Why must we always fight?" Memories of some of their better times brought a lazy smile to her face. "We were so good together in the bedroom. Why couldn't we take it elsewhere?"

"I'm not sleeping with a drunk."

❧✕❧

"Hello, Mrs. Walker." Rosa liked Ernesto's assistant. The middle-aged woman always had a genuine smile and funny stories about her family to share.

"Well hello there, stranger. You're early. It's only 2:53." She waved Rosa fully into the front office.

"Want me to leave and come back?"

Mrs. Walker giggled. "You sound like your father. I hear you had a birthday."

"I'm thirty years old. All grown up," she said with pride.

The assistant's clear blue eyes opened wide in feigned surprise. "The big three-O? Congratulations!"

Rosa tilted her head graciously. "Thank you." She headed for the large wood doors across from Mrs. Walker's desk.

"Two things before you go back. First, Ernesto wants you to apply the new patch to the network."

Rosa plopped her hands on her hips. "I hired a perfectly good system administrator to do these things. It's just an upgrade, not a big deal."

"Talk to your father. You know how he is."

"You're right. I'm sorry. I'll install it from his office."

Ernesto barely allowed anyone to touch his networks besides Rosa. She blamed herself. Her time in college as a hacker had him paranoid. She laughed at herself, thinking she'd shown him things no "normal human" should see. At the time, he hadn't found her hacking funny and made her find legal outlets for her abilities.

A few years ago, she'd linked the Bolívar International network to the computer at her home, so she could apply patches and updates and fix problems when possible. Working as Ernesto's lead system administrator and running her own business was like having three full-time jobs. She shook her head.

No wonder I don't have a love life.

"What's the second thing?"

"You're mother's in there with him now."

Shoulders slumped, Rosa asked, "Has she been drinking?"

"I don't think so, honey." Mrs. Walker pressed the button to unlock Ernesto's door. "Why don't you peek in and see if it's safe?"

"Good thinking." Rosa gently cracked open one of the large oak doors.

"You were a good lay," Harriet said. "But nowhere near as good as David Martín." She giggled and shook her body as if a shiver had gone up her spine. "I still tingle from his love-making."

Rosa had heard the name somewhere before. Trying to figure out why the name was so familiar, she closed her eyes. He was obviously one of the men her mother cheated with, but this felt more recent.

"Then have him pay to support you."

"You're just jealous because he's Rosa's father and not you."

"What?" Rosa burst fully into the office and went straight to her mother. "What are you talking about?"

Harriet released the cola as she drew her hands to her face. "Oh my God!" She looked around the office as if for help. "I...I...I didn't mean..." She stumbled on the spilled ice as she rushed past Rosa to one of the chairs in front of Ernesto's desk and grabbed her purse. "I'm sorry," she cried as she ran out.

He's Rosa's father and not you, her mother had said.

Rosa felt faint. Ernesto quickly rounded his desk and helped her to a couch in his office. He encouraged her to lie on the sofa.

She stared blankly into his light brown eyes a long while, trying to figure out what just happened. "David Martín is my father?" she uttered.

"I'm your father."

"This doesn't make sense. Why would Mom say you're jealous of this David?" The picture taken of her and Ernesto on the Odyssey was displayed on the end table, mocking her. "Oh my God," she gasped. "Why don't I look anything like you or Mom?"

"He was nothing more than a sperm donor." He wrapped his arms around her. "I'm so sorry you found out, baby. I'm so sorry for everything."

As always, she felt secure in his arms. But her life had just spun out of control, and she needed answers, not to break down. "Who is David Martín, and why did you lie to me all of these years?"

"I was protecting you. I'm about to ask the impossible. Pretend you never heard of David Martín. Times have changed. I have changed."

She focused on the wall of flat screens, and it clicked; she recognized the name. "He's that drug lord guy, isn't he?"

She shot up from the couch and crossed the room to Ernesto's desk. She grabbed the remote and surfed the channels on the wall. Sure enough, there was a report about the reputed drug lord David Martín's execution.

She'd always flipped the channel or ignored the reports about David, but now she stared at his picture and saw her eyes, her hair, her complexion.

Ernesto slowly stepped behind her and caressed her back. "Breathe, baby, breathe."

She gazed over her shoulder into his worried eyes.

He gently shook her. "Breathe, Rosa!"

She crossed the room and turned the two leather armchairs in front of Ernesto's desk to face each other, then sat in one and motioned toward the other. Emotions replaced by disassociation, she asked, "Why do you know this man? And how did you end up with his child?"

Ernesto took the second seat. "Drop this, baby. You're better off not knowing."

"No more lies. No more secrets. I can't live like that! I won't." Staying detached was impossible; this wreck was her life. She softened along with her voice.

He leaned forward, taking her hands into his. "I'm not perfect. I've made so many mistakes."

"I never expected you to be." No matter how hard she tried, the reality of what she'd just learned was too difficult to grasp, to accept.

After a long pause, he said, "As foster children, the only constant thing David and I had in our lives was each other. We were best friends." He took on a far-away look. "He even saved my life. He needed me, and I couldn't turn my back on him. A life for a life," he said proudly, then lowered his gaze into his lap.

The guilt in his eyes scared Rosa. She couldn't imagine what he'd done to honor the life for a life pledge. She prayed raising David's child was all, but knew there was more.

"I've made so many mistakes. Back then, I felt I owed him my life. In a way, I wanted to be David. He had this presence…" He sighed. "I can't explain it. I was trapped by the allure for a while, but I've changed."

"Is Bolívar International a front for his drug cartel?" Though her faith in her father cracked, her voice didn't. "I've heard of legitimate businessmen doing that sort of thing." That she could even consider Ernesto was a criminal sickened her.

Without missing a beat, he lifted his head and calmly answered, "No," then lowered his head. "I'm ashamed of my past. I want to leave it there."

Relief washed over her. Though she didn't agree with him, in a way she understood why he hadn't told her about David. The important thing was Ernesto was her father, the man she loved, respected, and adored—not some lying, conniving criminal. "We all make mistakes. Mom's a mess, but because I know the truth, I can deal with it. Not knowing will drive me crazy."

It tore her heart out seeing Ernesto so defeated. She really didn't want to hear anything that would shatter the image of her perfect father. But, the one lesson she'd learned from Harriet was that hiding from the truth did more harm. She'd sworn to stop enabling Harriet to hide from the truth, and she had to do the same with herself and Ernesto. Still not ready to consider that someone else was her father, she went on. "If you two were so close…did you do anything illegal?"

"Leave the past in the past, Rosa. The here and now is what's important."

"Daddy, please. Did you do anything illegal?"

"I used to launder money for David."

Breathing had become almost as difficult as comprehending what was happening. This was all too much, too fast, too unreal.

He walked over to the window and looked over the city. "I know I was wrong. I'm a different person now."

Mind racing a thousand places with no destinations in site, she silently prayed for the strength to pull herself together. "How did you end up with me?" Afraid of the answer, she watched the giant of a man—who now looked minuscule and beaten—she loved as her father.

Eyes closed, he leaned his head against the glass. "Harriet cheated on her husband with me."

Rosa choked on Ernesto's words. "What?" She rushed to his side. "Mom was married before you?" Her world spun out of control. She held onto Ernesto for balance, but he couldn't balance her. Not as before. She no longer knew who her parents were. "How could you sleep with a married woman?" was the best question she could muster.

"I didn't know she was married at the time. I also didn't know she was screwing my best friend. Your mother divorced her husband and married me. I loved her, but a few months into the marriage, I found out she married me for my money."

Rosa hated to admit it, but this sounded like something Harriet would do.

"I didn't find out Harriet was sleeping with David until you were born looking like him. To make a long story short, David and I had a huge argument and decided to go our separate ways. He couldn't raise a child, and throughout the pregnancy, I'd thought you were mine. Our last act of friendship was to do what was best for you. I loved you as mine." He caressed her face. "I love you as mine. You are mine."

There was no doubt in her heart that Ernesto loved her. And no matter what the DNA said, he'd always be her father. Yet, she couldn't reconcile him being a money launderer—a criminal. He didn't fit the image. He'd instilled in her how important the rules of society were and had a no tolerance policy on crime. He'd even threatened to call the authorities on her for hacking into networks.

"You were actually friends with a drug lord."

"I was young, dumb, and had a skewed sense of honor and friendship. When David slept with my woman, I knew we had to end our friendship. He'd crossed the line."

"Why did you stay with Mom?"

"Knight in shining armor complex, I guess. I loved her and thought I could save her. That's why it hurts me so much to see you doing the same. We can't save Harriet. Only Harriet can save Harriet." He paused. "I thought if I gave her everything her heart desired, she wouldn't stray;

but she was unappreciative and became disrespectful. The last straw was when she had an affair with a lawyer friend of mine. He told her to divorce me, and they could live off the alimony and child support."

Rosa rested her weary body against Ernesto. The woman's best friends were MasterCard and Visa.

How many times has Mom told me that men are here to serve women?

Rosa knew how she used men over the years. She'd slept with several married men and told Rosa this proved men were no good. Harriet loved to show off the gifts married men had bought her, saying, "They should be home with their wives instead of buying me things."

Ernesto lifted her chin up with his finger. "I'm sorry about all of this. You should have never found out. I'll never live down the disappointment in your eyes."

Torn, she didn't know how she would manage, but she knew she would. "I love you."

"I love you more." He tapped her nose with his knuckle. "Knowing these dark secrets has only hurt you. There was no need. You're my daughter. You're my heart."

The need to see how this David fit into her family's life puzzle was too great to ignore. She wasn't ready to deal with the reality of her parentage, but she knew he would die in a few days. "I want to visit Martín before he's executed."

He stiffened. "Stay away from David. If the drug world finds out you're his child, you'll be in danger. I'm your father. I know what's best."

She detected more jealousy in his voice than fear. This had to be hard for him, especially after Harriet had just emasculated him. "You'll always be my only father, but I need to meet him before it's too late."

"No. I forbid it."

"Forbid?" First he'd hid her parentage from her, then his illegal activity, now he was forbidding her, a grown woman, from seeing her biological father days before he was slated to die. She'd never disobeyed Ernesto before, but this was an order he had no right to make.

"I'm not a child anymore. I love you, but this is something I need to do."

He tilted his head to the side. She saw a flash of panic before he snapped his business face into place. He stalked over to the desk and made a call to his chauffer. "Rosa needs a ride to the airport. Be down-stairs in five minutes."

He hung up. "I love you too much to take any chances. You're going to Italy, and that's final. I have to stay and take care of this distribution company we're acquiring. I'll meet you in a few days." He made a call to his pilot.

She massaged her temples. How had everything gotten so out of control so fast? And going to Italy? That was insane!

"I don't want to run away. There's no need."

"Let's go, Rosa." He held his hand out for her.

"I don't want to."

"Now!"

Bottom lip poking out, she stuffed her fists under her armpits and stomped toward him.

He raised a brow. "Pout all you want. I'm doing this for your own good."

Hand-in-hand, she did her best Frankenstein walk as he dragged her to the limo. She hadn't been ordered to her room in years, and this was worse. He'd actually ordered her out of the country. His protective-ness had gone too far this time. Full-grown and with a multi-million dollar business to run, she had no intentions of leaving.

She plopped onto the back seat and watched him through the win-dow as he spoke to the driver.

He opened the back door and knelt, using the seat to steady him-self. The harsh lines of his face had softened. He reached out, gently pinching her chin. "I love you."

"Then don't make me leave."

"I don't have a choice." He kissed her cheek. "I'll call you tonight." He stepped fully onto the curb and closed the door.

She watched him out of the tiny back window as the stretch limo drove away. He didn't move until the limo rounded the corner. She turned in her seat and closed her eyes. The soft sounds of Anita Baker's soulful voice filled the car, calming her. She respected Ernesto's author-ity and knew he wanted what was best for her, but he'd crossed the line this time.

She pressed the button for the intercom. "Marcus, I'm not going to the airport. Drop me at my hotel."

"Your father gave me specific orders."

"If you drop me at the airport, I'll just take a taxi to the hotel. Why not skip a step? I'll take full responsibility."

Thoughts of her pouting tickled her. She hated how she'd regressed, but it had to be a funny sight. Only Ernesto had this power over her. She shook her head.

No more pouting.

It was way past time to be an adult in more than the business world.

Ernesto stood at his office window and watched over the city. Rosa was becoming feistier with him every day, but he could still control her. Six years ago when she went against his wishes and opened her own company in Chicago, he knew the next few years would be rough. If he could maintain control until after David's execution, she'd never find out the whole truth.

He assured himself that he would recover from this small setback. By giving her a piece of the truth, he'd shown her that he was human. All humans make mistakes. All the years he had invested into Rosa's emotional well-being would pay off. He tapped his knuckle on the window. There had to be a way to stall Rosa until he had time to cover his tracks. *Fear.* He sighed as he leaned his head against the window. *Fear for my life? No, her life.*

"You know I wouldn't call if it weren't important. Please, Angela," Harriet begged. "Please call me! Rosa found out Ernesto isn't her father. I need your help."

"To delete this message, please press seven—"

Angela pressed seven, then wiped the tears from her eyes. She loved her sister, but refused to get caught up in Harriet's games. Memories of the last time she was pulled into one of Harriet's messes still haunted her...

Chicago, thirty-one years ago

"You can't stay in this hotel forever." Angela rolled the armchair from the small table to the bed, then sat knee to knee with her sister. "Humble yourself. Beg George for his forgiveness. Do whatever you need to save your marriage and give this child a father."

"She's got a father—David."

"First off, he's a no good drug dealer. Secondly, it could be George's."

Harriet *tsked* her teeth. "George and I haven't had sex in at least six months."

"What?" Angela gasped, and her eyes flew wide open.

Harriet continued, "I'm not sure what I want anymore. How could he kick a pregnant woman out on the street in the middle of the night, knowing I had nowhere to go and no money?"

"Get real! Not only did he find out you were cheating on him and got pregnant by the guy, but David kicked his tail."

Fanning herself, Angela drew in several calming breaths that in no way soothed her. "Okay, we can make it through this. I'm not saying George was right or this'll be easy, but you have to try. Your marriage is a union made before God—"

"Don't start with that God mess again. Did God keep those nasty ass perverts out of our beds when we were kids?"

Angela flinched at the memories.

"The one thing I do know is I don't want George."

"I know you're not leaving George for that monster!"

Harriet stared at her sister as though she'd gone from having an Afro to straight hair in sixty seconds flat. "Have I ever allowed a man to beat me? I'm not a child anymore. Men will not use me. I told you, I've learned from Mama's mistakes. I'm through with George *and* David." She looked at the clock setting on the end table. "It's almost noon. You need to leave before you miss your bus, and I need a nap. I'm trying to make a baby here."

"You mean you're *having* the baby?"

Harriet slowly nodded her head. "Men come and go. But blood," she rested her hand on Angela's, "is forever. This baby is a wakeup call.

I need to change my life. I want to change my life."

"I'm so proud of you." Angela closed her eyes momentarily and silently thanked God. "I'll help you with the baby. I'll get a job and transfer to Chicago State."

Withdrawing her hands, Harriet jerked back. "Oh no you won't! You have a full scholarship at Vanderbilt. You're almost done. I expect you to graduate from Vanderbilt."

"But what will you do for money? I only have enough for one more night. Come to Tennessee with me for now."

Harriet tapped her earrings—Chanel set, 14 karat gold, with full-cut, round, brilliant diamonds. "Do you realize how much jewelry I have?"

Angela looked at Harriet as if she'd become a nun. "I know you're not pawning your jewelry." Harriet's light giggle warped Angela back in time, back to when they were four and five years old and all they cared about was playing in the park, picking dandelions, and making clover necklaces. Back to before their mother's visitors stole their innocence. How she prayed her sister could regain some of that childhood innocence.

"I sound crazy, don't I?" Harriet fanned herself, finally calming. "Seriously though, I need time alone. I don't know. I guess to figure out what I want out of life. Now get going before you miss the bus."

"Are you sure?" Angela wanted to have faith in Harriet, but it was hard. She'd been let down so many times before. Harriet was so much like their mother that it scared Angela.

"I have to stick around here until the divorce is final. Then, who knows? I may check Tennessee out."

Angela hugged her sister. This time things would be different. She could feel it.

The truth is in Florida, so Florida is where I'm staying. Repositioning herself and her journal on the hotel bed, Rosa propped a fluffy pillow under her arms.

I'm finding it hard to digest the fact that David Martín is my biolog-

ical father. An eerie chill filled Rosa. *The father of my heart is the head of the business world, and my biological father is the head of the drug world.*

How can I be from a man like that? It's true, so I have to deal with it. I don't know if Daddy is more afraid of the drug world or afraid I'll start considering David Martín as my father. Either way, in the long run, he'll see he's worried needlessly. He's being his usual overprotective self. She drew a mustached happy face. *And I love him for it.*

While gathering her thoughts, she bit on the end of her ink pen. *No matter how out of whack my life was, I knew I'd make it because I had Daddy. He's always been my anchor.* She paused. *Had been my anchor. I'll always love him, but I don't know who he is anymore. I don't know who I am anymore. We're both adrift.* She sighed. *Daddy was the one person I totally trusted and knew I could depend on. Now I feel betrayed. I don't know what to believe. I'm scared. Scared of what else he's hiding, scared that I can actually believe there may be more that I don't know. Scared.*

Reluctant to delve deeper, she closed the journal, then set it and her pen on the nightstand. She surrounded herself with fluffy pillows and fell into a fretful sleep. Eventually she relaxed, and a version of her favorite dream visited her. Instead of images, she heard children laughing and felt the warm, loving embrace of a man. These weren't just any children and any man, but her children and her husband.

Banging at the door startled Rosa to full alertness. She hopped out of bed, grabbed her robe and wrapped herself with it. "I'm coming." She slipped on her house shoes and rushed across the room. "I'm coming." She peeked through the suite's peephole. "Daddy?" She flipped on the light and opened the door. "What are you doing here this time of night?" She closed the door as he blew by her into the living area.

"What am I doing here?" he roared. "You're supposed to be on a flight to Italy."

Readying for the storm, she battened down her emotional hatches, stood tall, squared off her shoulders, held her chin high and kept her face stern. Appearing grown in rainbow print pajamas and fuzzy, blue bunny slippers wasn't easy to pull off, but she thought she could swing it. "After I finish my business in Miami, I'm returning to Chicago."

Ernesto trained his light stare on her. She thought she would buckle under his scrutiny, but she maintained her stance. This was a battle of wills. He would have to recognize her as an adult who made her own decisions. She didn't expect him to agree with all of them, but she did expect him to accept that she would be making them. This was also a battle to save her family. The secrets were killing them. He and Harriet were unable to deal with the past, so she'd have to step up and do what needed to be done.

"You're disobeying me?" he raged.

"I'm being the strong, independent woman you raised me to be. I have a thriving business that I can't and don't want to walk away from. I'm building a life in Chicago." She paused to reorganize her thoughts. "My own life." She softened. "I love you, but try to understand that I need time to live somewhere besides in your shadow. In Chicago, I'm Rosa Bolívar; anywhere else, I'm Ernesto Bolívar's daughter."

The fight slowly dissipated from his face. She remembered the last time that they had an argument. Then, too, she'd wanted to have a life outside of his shadow. She sighed. Six years and not much had changed—he was still her commander-in-chief.

He sat on the couch, leaning back as he ran his hands through his hair. "Then return to Chicago tonight. Do not return to Florida until I'm sure you're safe. I can't lose you, Rosa."

She knelt before him, knowing he wanted her to leave Florida before she met David. He was afraid of losing her love. Her gaze tenderly caressed his worried face. He appeared to be aging, right before her eyes. "Love is thicker than blood, Daddy." Telling him her plans to see David would only upset him more. Though she hated to admit it, he was acting so irrationally she thought he'd try to physically stop her from seeing David. "I have more business here. I'm not leaving for Chicago until I'm done."

"Business, my foot. You're here to see David. You're not even doing estimates. I spoke to your new client earlier today. He said you finished the estimate before you came to my office."

"First off, I didn't even know David was my biological father until you told me this afternoon. I came here to spend time with my real father, Ernesto Bolívar. Secondly, we received another request for an estimate. I thought I'd check it out while I'm down here." Glad she'd been able to tell the truth, she crossed her arms over her chest. "And let's be honest. I can't hide anywhere. I'm Ernesto Bolívar's little girl," she added for sympathy points.

He smoothed his mustache down a few times. "You win. But, you're not to visit David Martín. I'll tell you everything you want to know about him. I even have a few pictures at the house."

"Thank you." She changed the subject before he made her promise to obey him. "Do you want to sleep here tonight? I'll take the couch."

"Anna's waiting up for me." He kissed her on the cheek. "Do not disobey me on this, Rosa. He's a dangerous man from a dangerous world. I don't want you drawn in. Now that I think about it, I'm getting you security."

Her eyes shot wide open. "No way! You know I don't do the security thing. I don't want bodyguards following me all over the place like puppy dogs."

"These aren't bullies from the school yard, Rosa. You need around-the-clock protection. I'll make arrangements first thing in the morning."

She folded her arms over her chest. "No disrespect, Daddy, but I refuse to be spied on."

"They aren't there to spy, but to protect you. I don't care what you say; you're getting protection."

"If I even *think* someone is following me, I'll call the cops on them. That includes your security service."

He heaved a long, drawn-out sigh. "I can't leave you unprotected."

"Let's be realistic here. Their protection couldn't stop a sniper or a bomb. I don't need to draw more attention to myself. I haven't had security since I went to college, and I never want it again. I'm not giving up my freedom. I'm sorry, but end of discussion."

After Ernesto's visit, she hadn't slept well, and her nerves were shot. Guilt for going behind Ernesto's back nipped at her heels, but she had to do this. Grumbling, Rosa sorted through the few outfits she'd brought to Miami with her. She tapped her rabbit-slippered foot on the floor as she stared at the bright and bold contents of the closet. She made due with a black pantsuit and a firebrick red shell.

Her day would be full. She had to visit the work site she'd told Ernesto about, then catch the helicopter that she'd chartered to the prison's city. She padded across the carpeted floor of the suite to her journal and ink pen. Lately, her journal had become her sole confidante.

Be careful what you pray for. I wanted Daddy to recognize me as a grown-up. I longed to prove myself. She steadied her trembling hand. *Now, here I stand, wanting Daddy to hold my hand while I meet my biological father. I want him to protect me as he always has. I want him to be my anchor.*

I feel like I'm working through some sort of rite of passage. She prayed silently. *I can make it through this test. We'll all make it.*

CHAPTER FIVE

The ride from the helipad to the prison wasn't long enough. Rosa wanted more time to prepare emotionally. She paid the taxi driver, and then walked toward the crowd. Supporters and anti-death penalty factions yelled across an ocean of police at each other. She saw a few reporters swimming about like sharks, and others who she couldn't identify.

Her pace slowed. She wasn't as sure of herself as she had been when she'd stood up to Ernesto. The closest to a prison that she'd come was seeing reruns of the HBO jailhouse series *Oz*.

She bumped into a woman holding a toddler. "I'm sorry." She smiled at the little, curly haired girl. "You have a beautiful daughter."

"Thank you," said the young woman. "We're here to see Daddy. Aren't we, Julie?" The little girl nodded, but she didn't look happy.

Rosa could identify with the child. She was also there to see her "Daddy," and she wasn't too happy about it either. A chill went down her spine as her gaze traveled from the double fence, to the barbed wire, to the guard towers. Her blood had earned his place on the wrong side of the double fence. Her blood had given her away. Her blood. She worked her way through the crowd, reminding herself that love is thicker than blood. She was nothing like Harriet or David. She was Rosa Bolívar.

She looked into the green eyes of the burly guard who stood on the inside of the entrance gate. During her approach, she'd watched him. He seemed patient and respectful of everyone. "Excuse me, sir," she said through the fence, keeping her voice steady and calm. "I'd like to see David Martín."

He cocked his head to the side. "David Martín?"

"Yes."

"Sorry, ma'am, but that won't be possible. He doesn't have anyone on his guest list."

"This is very important. How do I go about being put on his list?" If she didn't see David today, she knew she'd lose her courage.

"Excuse my French, but the warden would need a hell of a reason to approve a visitor."

"May I speak to the warden then?"

"Don't waste your time."

Other spectators listened while pretending they weren't. Rosa ignored everyone, except the guard. She was on a mission and wouldn't be turned away.

"Would you please call the warden for me? I'd at least like to try."

"Fine. But, don't say I didn't tell you."

He walked further back onto the lush green grounds toward a tall brick wall that surrounded the prison and made a call.

"They won't give you permission," said a fifty-something-year-old, white male over her shoulder. "I've been trying for two weeks."

"They have to," she whispered to herself. "They just have to."

The officer shook his head as he returned. "Sorry, ma'am."

Panic gripped her almost as tight as she gripped the fence. "But, I have to see him. It's extremely important." Afraid of losing her chance forever, her mind scrambled for bait to throw out they couldn't resist.

He leaned against the fence. "I'm not trying to be smart, but everyone thinks their reason is important. The warden's an extremely busy man."

"Tell the warden I'm David Martín's daughter," she whispered to the guard.

His boisterous laugh turned many heads in their direction. "You won't give up, will you? David Martín doesn't have any children."

She rolled her eyes. Couldn't he tell she was trying to keep this on the down low? "But he does," she continued, softly. "Please call the warden and tell him."

He walked away mumbling, "I don't know why I'm doing this." He called the warden and told him about her claim.

"Hey, Rolland," yelled the man standing behind her. "Tell the warden, I'm his long lost son." The gathering crowd joined in the laughter.

Rosa glared over her shoulder at the man, and everyone went

silent. Slapping the snot out of him wasn't an option. "I suggest you step off now," she warned.

Taken aback, the man stared into her eyes, as if seeing her for the first time. His own eyes opened wide with recognition, then widened with fear. "Oh, my God. You *are* his daughter." He stepped around her, shaking the fence. "Rolland, Rolland, she's telling the truth. She's telling the truth!" He pointed at her. "Look at those eyes." Fear clearly etched on his face, he turned to her. "I'm sorry, Ms. Martín. I meant no disrespect."

Many people had said that she'd be put behind bars for killing someone with her evil eye someday. She hadn't meant to whip it out, but the eavesdropping jerk had worked her last nerve. She bowed her head slightly. "No problem. And my name is Bolívar, not Martín," she said proudly. The man behind the bars helped to conceive her, but he wasn't her father, and she wouldn't accept his name.

"What are you drawing?" Samson asked in Spanish. David only had three days until his execution, but Samson wasn't ready to give up on him. He'd given David a sketchpad, colored pencils and an art eraser, encouraging David to feel again, to see that he had someone to live for. He peeked at the picture. David had drawn the flower of a fully opened rose in deep reds and shaded the background in black. "You miss her a lot, don't you?" The more Samson thought about it, the more he was convinced that Rosa was the key to David. The fear in David's eyes when Samson had dropped her name had haunted Samson ever since.

"How's your family?" David asked.

"I miss them."

"Join the club." He'd written "Rosa" in large gold script letters at the bottom of the image. "You tell the bastard you're leaving the agency yet?"

Samson doubted David knew Alton's real name. The two hated each other at first sight. "He was shocked I stayed this long. I need to write my letter of resignation." He paused. "You and Rosa were high school sweethearts?"

"Don't ask shit you already know. You can leave if you're here to play that psycho-babble shit. I'm in no mood for it today."

Samson could tell David was on the edge, ready to bare his soul, so he waited patiently. Over the year, David had become more than a case, he'd also become a friend. And soon, this friend would confide in him.

"I have so many regrets," David mumbled. "Now that I know what's important…" he trailed off. "Family's more important than anything, Samson. Go see your people while you can. Enjoy them while you can."

"You can still see your family."

"Not the one person who matters most to me." He looked down the corridor. "Here comes Giles. I wish he'd pick up his damn feet. All that shufflin' and scrapin' is working my damn nerve."

"Everything is working your damn nerves," Samson mocked. He kept his voice jovial, but he could kill Giles for ruining the moment. "I'll be right back."

"Tell that mutha' to pick up his damn feet or don't bring his ass down here."

Giles led Samson a few feet away from the cell. "A woman claiming she's David's daughter is here," he whispered, barely audible.

"*¿Qué?*" Samson momentarily looked over his shoulder at David who was drawing, seemingly in his own world. "There must be a mistake," he said in English. "His only child was killed years ago, and that was a son." Ernesta's claims of a daughter rang loudly in Samson's ears. All of the pieces were finally falling into place.

"The warden says she looks an awful lot like David. Her name is Rosa." He closed his eyes. "Umm, Rosa, Rosa Bolmiva, Boltivar, Bolivar…"

Samson recognized the name. *Bolívar*. He swiped his powerful hands over his shaved head. "He has a daughter," he mumbled to himself as he glanced over his shoulder at the small man sitting in the cell. The fear in David's eyes upon hearing Rosa's name confirmed Samson's suspicions. *He has a daughter. That's why he's been acting so irrational lately.* A revelation hit him, releasing a nervous chuckle. *Ernesto-Ernesta. I'll be damned.* He returned his attention to Officer Giles. "Has

Agent Miles been contacted?"

"Yes, sir. He'll be here shortly. The warden wanted to know what to do with the Rosa woman."

"Set her up in an interview room."

Samson returned to the cell and sat on the end of the bed. Everyone knew the name Bolívar. If he remembered correctly, Ernesto Bolívar did have a daughter.

"What did the hack want?" David asked in Spanish.

"You have a visitor."

"Is the bastard here? Can't I die in peace?"

"It's not Alton." He rested his elbows on his knees and lowered his face into his palms. Samson wasn't stalling for dramatic pause or mind games. He literally didn't know how to proceed.

"I ain't in no mood to play twenty-fuckin' questions."

He took the sketchpad from David, then flipped through page after page of roses. At a total loss, he closed the pad. David obviously loved his daughter and was trying to protect her, but from whom?

"She's here, isn't she?" David asked quietly.

"I need for you to trust me, David. To be honest with me."

David looked straight into Samson's eyes. "Have I ever lied to your ass? I don't tell what I don't want to."

"Who is Rosa Bolívar to you?"

David shot up from the bed and paced from one end of the cell to the other. Though a small man, it only took him a few steps to reach each end. "She's here, isn't she?" He continued pacing. "Rosa's my daughter. That punk ass Ernesto must have told her I'm her real father."

"So, she didn't know?"

"She was never to know. Ernesto shouldn't have told her until after I was long dead. I don't know what that dumb-ass was thinking. She has my fire. There was no way he could keep her away."

"Give us Sierra, and I'll ensure she goes into witness protection." His team was linked to all of the government agencies, providing additional options.

"Do you understand who her adoptive father is? Ernesto Bolívar. Everyone who's anyone in business, thus the drug world, knows about Ernesto and his daughter Rosa. She's too popular to hide. I'll protect her as I always have. I just need time to think." He tangled his fingers into his short, curly hair.

"She's here to see you for the first time?"

"You could say that. If you can get the DEA to stay away from her, the drug world will never know about her. We can have this little meeting, and no one will be the wiser."

"There's no way to keep your daughter a secret now. The only thing we can do is place her into protective custody. But, the agency won't allow that unless you give us something."

"No! I won't take her freedom away."

"What the hell do you want me to do, David?" Praying for patience, he smoothed down his goatee. "Explain how your telling me about the Sierra cartel will endanger Rosa."

"Simple version. Drug lords have to love the drug world more than anything. But, I love Rosa more. If I tell you and my sentence is commuted, then Rosa will be murdered to punish me. If I tell you and you don't commute my sentence, I go to my grave knowing that she'll be murdered to punish me. I caused my son's death. I won't be the cause of my daughter's death."

"But they didn't know she existed. You could have told us years ago."

"Well hell, Samson, I'm an asshole. Why the hell would I cooperate?"

"Humph, you got me there."

"You gonna let me see her or not?"

Samson peeked into the interview room through a bent slat on the mini-blinds. The small room was nothing special: cream walls, metal table, a few folding chairs, and a speckled linoleum floor. On the other hand, the woman sitting at the table thumbing through a magazine was very special.

He'd seen pictures of David's mother and thought her a beautiful woman. This Rosa was an improvement of her grandmother's perfection. David's father was African-American and his mother Afro-

Colombian. Rosa posed an exotic blend of cultures.

She toyed with one of the curls by her ear as she read a magazine. Amazed such an innocent move could arouse him, he shook his head. If he were to draw his hands through her hair and pull her close enough to kiss her full lips, her curls were just long enough to wrap themselves around his fingers. He smoothed down his goatee, needing to stop his train of thought: she was off limits, she could be involved in the drug trade, she lived in another city, she probably already had a man.

He'd grown to know David and thought he told the truth about Rosa, yet he still wanted to verify things for himself. He brushed the sleeves of his black tailor-made suit, straightened his tie, and entered the interview room.

Soft and innocent, yet deadly, came to his mind as Rosa stood. She was definitely the type of woman to make a man do stupid things.

"Hello, Miss Bolívar. I'm DEA Agent Samson Quartermaine," he said in his most official voice.

She nodded slightly as she took his outstretched hand. "The pleasure's all mine, DEA Agent Samson Quartermaine."

Their gazes held, seemingly freezing them in time. He wouldn't mind remaining lost in her eyes forever. He forced himself to snap out of it and do his job. "Would you like some coffee or tea, Miss Bolívar?"

She returned to her seat. "No, thank you. Could you do me a favor and call me Rosa? Miss Bolívar sounds like an old maid."

"You're no old maid, for sure." They both rolled their eyes. "Sorry about that, Rosa." He sat across from her, switching his mind back to business.

"Will I be able to see David Martín?"

"Yes. I needed to speak with you first."

"Go for it."

"Are you any relation to Ernesto Bolivar?"

"He's my father."

He appeared calm, though he was anything but. Ernesto Bolívar, CEO of one of the largest corporations in the world, was now the No. 1 candidate as David's partner. "What's your biological mother's name?"

"Harriet Bolívar."

"Her maiden name."

She *tsked* and crossed her arms over her chest. "I was told Wells. You may wish to double check that fact out for yourself." She cut her eyes away.

Giving her time to compose herself, he wrote a few notes. The pain behind her words was loud and clear. She'd obviously been kept in the dark about her family's dynamics. He could only imagine the surprises that she was in store for as the investigation continued. It reminded him of his own family troubles.

He remembered how shocked he was when his brother-in-law was arrested for embezzlement. Lenny stealing a piece of candy seemed impossible, let alone a million dollars. Lenny skipped town with the money and his secretary, leaving Samson's sister to deal with the fallout.

Missing his sister, he lowered his gaze. There was nothing he could do to save her now. On the other hand, Rosa had no idea what she was in store for; perhaps he could help soften the blows.

He brought his mind back to the case at hand. At least the Ernesta Wells mystery had been solved. Ernesta was most likely Harriet Wells. "What do you think should be done with David?"

"He's a drug lord, DEA Agent Samson Quartermaine. He can never be allowed on the streets again. His sentence should be commuted to life without the possibility of parole."

Except for teasing his name, she sounded emotionless. "Why are you here?" he asked.

"To meet my biological father. You called him David. Do you know him personally?"

"In a way."

"What's he like?" She hunched her shoulders. "I mean, I know his criminal record, but what else is there to him?"

"I'll let you form your own opinion. How long have you known he's your father?"

Her voice and face took a harsh edge. "Ernesto Bolívar is my father." She softened. "I apologize for my tone. I didn't get any sleep last night. I know what kind of man David is and that I'm of his blood." She drew in and slowly released a long breath. "It's just a bit much. I'm exhausted, and I'm worried about this meeting. None of this excuses my rudeness. I found out about David Martín yesterday."

"No apology is necessary." He made a mental note of her defensiveness where Ernesto was concerned. "It had to be a shock to you."

"That's putting it lightly. Daddy's gonna have an aneurysm when he finds out what I've been up to. Maybe I'll get lucky and can keep this out of the media. If so, I'll tell him in a few weeks."

"Why doesn't he want you to visit David?" Debating on whether he should tell her the media would find out shortly, if they already hadn't, he remained silent.

"I think he's jealous, but according to him, the drug world will come after me if they find out our family secret. When can I see David?"

Someone from the drug world would seek out Rosa to see what she knew, but Samson didn't think they would harm her: she didn't know anything, David had never shown any concern for her, and her father was Ernesto Bolívar. The heat they'd bring down on themselves wouldn't be worth the risk. Samson saw Ernesto as the most likely danger. Ernesto probably turned on David and now Harriet was afraid he'd do the same to Rosa.

"Thank you for your cooperation. You've been very forthcoming, and I appreciate it. A few more questions, then I'll bring him to you." He wondered if she'd continue being forthcoming after he asked his next question.

"I understand you have a job to do."

"Do you know how Ernesto ended up with you?"

She studied him a long while, then repeated the story Ernesto had told her, minus the money-laundering portion.

He frowned. "They grew up together?" Nothing in the old case files indicated Ernesto and David knowing each other. Ernesto and David's acquaintance was a major red flag and should have been thoroughly investigated.

"He made a lot of mistakes when he started out in business. Mistakes he regrets. He is a changed man now." She twisted the baby hairs beside her ear between her fingers.

He didn't blame her for protecting her father. She thought he was innocent now, and that's what was important to her. From Samson's brief conversation with her, Rosa appeared to be your everyday, run of the mill, drop-dead gorgeous, sexy, African-American, Latina, law abiding citizen who loved her family.

"I have a favor to ask, Rosa."

"Yes, DEA Agent Samson Quartermaine."

He hated his name, but could listen to "Samson" roll off her tongue all night long. "Okay, you win. Please call me Samson."

"If you insist," she said with a coy smile that sent his heart racing and temperature rising. "What can I do for you, Samson?"

"David has information the DEA needs to bring down one, maybe two, drug syndicates. He plans on taking this information with him to his grave. I was hoping you could speak with him."

"Me?" She cocked her head to the side and drew her hand to her chest. "How? Don't get me wrong. I want the drug trafficking to stop, but I don't know the man." An anxiety-laced laugh escaped her. "You're on a first name basis with him. You speak to him." She calmed herself. "I'm sorry. I wish I could help you, but I wouldn't know the first thing to say. I don't mean anything to him. To tell you the truth, I'm shocked he agreed to see me."

The sorrow in her voice touched him, reminding him of his sister. "You're correct. Forget I asked. Are you ready to meet him?"

"Not really, but I won't have peace until I do."

He stood to leave.

"Thank you," she said.

"For what?"

"When the warden told me the DEA wanted to speak with me, I had visions of being interrogated. I guess I watch too much television. You're easy to talk to. Thanks for disproving the stereotype."

He bowed his head slightly. "And thank you for your cooperation. When are you returning to Chicago?"

"Tomorrow. But once I fall asleep, I may never wake up."

"We'll speak again later."

Rosa nervously thumbed through the magazine with the amazing man who just left on her mind. "Samson," she said softly to herself. *A powerful name for a powerful man.* She wished she could have told him everything. According to her lawyer friend, there was a statute of limitations for money laundering, and Ernesto had it beaten by years, but she couldn't reveal Ernesto's secret past without his knowledge. Though disappointed, she respected her father and wouldn't blindside him. She also still had faith in him and knew he would tell the authorities the truth once he realized that she wasn't in danger.

She was grateful and attracted to Samson's patience and understanding. He could have made the interview a bad experience. The authorities always had more information than they let on, yet he went easy on her.

She closed the magazine the warden had given her to pass the time. Soon, she'd meet her "father." She inhaled a few calming breaths. She was afraid of what she'd learn about her parents, but she still longed to know.

David stepped into the room with Samson behind him. An automatic smile tipped her lips. She finally looked like someone, and he looked pleased to see her.

"I'll be across the hall if you need me," Samson said in Spanish. He gave Rosa a supportive nod and left the two alone.

All her prepared questions escaped her. She held her hand out and followed Samson's lead of speaking Spanish. "Thank you for agreeing to meet—"

"Damn, Rosa," David interrupted as he walked around her. "You didn't get shit from your mama." He chuckled. "I couldn't deny you if I wanted, and Lord knows, I don't want to."

Rosa blinked at his admission. If he didn't want to deny her, why hadn't he ever contacted her?

"Aw hell, hold the press." He shook his head, slowly pinching his chin between his thumb and index finger. "That ass has Harriet written all over it." He winked at her, and she couldn't help but laugh. His joking broke the ice and put her at ease.

"Come and sit with me." He held the chair out for her like the perfect gentleman. "Damn you're tall."

"I'm only 5'6". It's the heels." She pointed at her short cut, black leather boots as she sat.

"Well I'm 5'4", so I say you're tall." He took a place at the metal table. "How's your mother? Still money hungry?"

"I'm afraid so."

"How did you find out about me?"

"Daddy told me everything."

"Why that stupid son-of-a-bitch! What the hell was he thinking?"

"Who you callin' stupid? You're the one behind bars, not him."

He cocked his head to the side. A slow smile appeared, identical to hers. "Well hell, at least he didn't turn you into a punk-ass pussy. Don't pay me no never mind. I'm a asshole from way back."

Tickled, she said, "I can agree with that." He was the biggest jerk she'd ever met, but he pulled it off with a twist of charm. The laughter dancing in his big black eyes made it hard to stay angry with him.

"Seriously though, I knew giving you to Ernesto was the way to go."

"That's what he said, but why did you give me away if you wanted me, and what in the hell possessed you to have a baby with a married woman?" To keep from seeming like she was attacking him, she didn't ask why he'd slept with his best friend's woman. This was their first and maybe last meeting.

"I thought a married woman would be more careful about birth control. Then Harriet got pregnant, and I thought I'd have a son."

Slightly hurt, she said, "So, you gave me away because I was a girl."

"Don't get your ego bruised. How the hell can a girl be a drug lord? That don't mean I didn't love you. I gave you to Ernesto, knowing he would raise you right."

She had unsuccessfully tried to convince herself that she didn't care what he thought about her, so hearing he loved her lifted her spirits. "How did you meet Mom?"

"One day I saw Harriet walking out of the Sears Tower and was like, 'Damn, look at that ass!'"

They both laughed.

"You're a mess." She dabbed at the tears gathering in her eyes.

"Hell, I'll admit it. I'm a one hundred percent ass man. At first when she told me she was pregnant, I wanted to kick her ass. But then,

I thought about my son." He paused. "Your brother."

Mouth dropped wide open, she asked, "I have a brother?"

"Had," he said reverently. "He was killed in a drive-by when he was three."

"Oh my goodness." Heart mourning, she reached across the table and held his hands. "I'm so sorry."

"I was being given a second chance. They killed your brother because of me. Giving you to Ernesto was the right choice. Would you do something for me?"

"If it's legal," she teased to lighten the mood.

He brought his chair around to her side of the table, then whispered into her ear, "Harriet had two sides to her. I killed the fun-loving part. Would you apologize to her for me?"

"What did you do to her, and why are we whispering?"

He pointed over his shoulder to the upper corner of the room. "Big Brother's watching. Wave hi to Samson."

With a wide smile dominating her face, she waved. "Samson is one handsome man." Mortified, she covered her face. "Oh my goodness. He heard that."

David belted out a laugh heard around the world as he smacked the table. "Damn, I haven't had this much fun in years. I'll bet that bastard's having a heart attack about now."

"Samson's not a bastard."

Joking stopped, he stared at her. "I'm talking about his partner." He slowly turned to the camera, showing all thirty-two pearly whites.

"No, David," Samson said to the monitor.

"What the hell is this shit?" Alton asked.

Samson lowered the volume. "He's trying to fix me up with Rosa."

Alton stalked about the small room, hitting at the folding chairs as he passed. "I can't believe this shit. I saw that travesty of an interview you did with Rosa. I love a big butt and a smile as much as the next guy; but damn, you can't sleep with her. We have work to do."

"Heather Wilkins, Olivia St. John, Margaret Stapleton…" Samson continued naming women Alton had slept with who were directly involved in cases Alton had worked over the years. Unlike Samson, Alton always kissed and told. Samson had never crossed that line and didn't intend on crossing it with Rosa, no matter how much he wanted to.

Alton glared at Samson. "How you gonna throw that shit back in my face?"

"Don't start with me." He folded his arms over his chest, looking down at Alton. "I do my job, and I'm damned good at it. I won't jeopardize our case. I also won't crucify the innocent for a bust."

"Innocent? Stop projecting. This is totally different. Ernesto Bolívar is the moneyman for the Martín syndicate, and Rosa is up to her pretty Colombian neck in it. Hell," he motioned toward the monitor, "he isn't even wearing shackles. Why don't you just free his ass now?"

"I felt if we took off his shackles while he met with Rosa, he might be more willing to cooperate with us. Rosa didn't even know about David until yesterday."

"So she told you," he spat sarcastically.

"You need to step back and regroup. Not all Colombians are drug lords."

"Hell, the Sierra syndicate has moved up over the years. I'll bet Ernesto sent her in here to get the information from David. You see how he whispered in her ear. Look at them." He pointed to the monitor. Rosa and David were laughing and having a good time. "She has known him her whole life. She's here to say a final farewell and get the information on the Sierra syndicate."

"You've gotten desperate. It's obvious that Rosa doesn't have anything to do with any drug cartel and didn't know about David."

"Obvious! What the hell? We made no connection between Ernesto and David. Damn, man, they share a child. What else have they been able to hide?"

"I know you're ready to pounce, but don't rush into something we can't get out of. We knew David was protecting someone. It's Rosa. He's always blamed himself for his son's death. He would die before he allowed another of his children to suffer because of his sins. Ernesto must be using Rosa against him."

"More of that psychological bull. It's simple: David's a drug lord, Ernesto's his No. 2 guy, and Rosa's their secret weapon."

"We've got to have our ducks in order before we approach Ernesto. If you alienate Rosa, she'll warn Ernesto before we have a chance to reach him." The thought of Rosa in danger kicked Samson's protective streak into overdrive. She would never protect herself from Ernesto. She was a sitting duck. "We've got to clamp down on the media. Keep this story from hitting the news circuit."

"We'll get to Ernesto, and you might as well forget about the media. Right now, I have more questions for Rosa. Her Little Miss Innocent act doesn't work with me."

"You're not going to badger her. She's innocent until proven guilty. Ernesto is innocent until proven guilty. Do I think he's involved? Yes. But what I think doesn't mean squat."

"Why you always got to be the damned cavalry? Listen, I'm sorry about your sister. But Rosa *is not* your sister. Rosa *is not* an innocent bystander. Ernesto and David are in on this together, and Rosa is their child. They've trained her to take over some day. No one would suspect a female drug lord. Damn, I'm impressed. The shit is brilliant."

A year had passed, but the pain of losing his sister drowned Samson in a flash flood of emotion. She'd had such a promising life ahead of her. If he'd only been there for her, she might still be alive. An image of Rosa twirling the tiny curls beside her ear came to his mind. She didn't deserve what was headed her way. With her family in such disarray, he worried she wouldn't have the support she needed, just as his sister hadn't.

Alton stopped mid-tirade. "Oh hell. I'm sorry, man. I was out of line. This case has me by the balls."

"It's all right. I'm fine." Samson had found her lifeless body hanging from a beam in the basement.

A long, awkward pause passed between the lifelong friends. "You know," Alton said, "your sleeping with Rosa may be a good idea. We can work you into the Martín syndicate through her. Crooked agents are a dime a dozen."

"I'm not sleeping with her." Samson chuckled. All Alton thought about was sex and running the DEA someday.

"Sure you won't," he said with a hint of sarcasm. "I'll have them prepare the chopper for our trip back to Miami. I'll find out what hotel she's staying at, so you can pay her a visit."

"Forget it."

Alton left the room. Samson turned the volume up on the monitor. He wanted Rosa, but for more than her body. He had never felt this strong of an attraction before. Not even for his ex-wife. He longed to explore things with Rosa; but, unfortunately, she was off limits.

"Can you do me a favor?" Rosa asked.

"As long as it's legal." David winked.

"Tell Samson about those Sierra people, so they'll commute your sentence."

Folding chairs placed so that they were sitting knee to knee, he took her hands into his. "I wish I could, but I can't."

"Why?"

"For one thing, I don't want my sentence commuted. I always knew I'd be dead by the time I was fifty. Here I am in my sixties, healthy as a horse, and still kickin'. I'd rather they kill me now than die slowly in that cell."

She didn't know how to comment, so she remained silent.

"And why should I help these assholes?"

"Because people are dying," she said quietly.

"Look, baby girl. If they bring down Sierra tomorrow, there's already someone there today to take their place."

"Did you really kill that DEA informant and his crew?"

"Samson tell you to ask these questions?"

"He asked me to talk to you. I read everything I could about you on the Internet and couldn't figure out why you killed them."

"The DEA should pay you." He sat up in his chair. "I'm not a nice person, Rosa. He wasn't the first person I've killed."

The little man sitting and joking with her all afternoon didn't fit the mold of a cold-blooded murderer. It just couldn't compute in her mind. "Why'd you do it?"

"After I got his ungrateful ass into the Sierra organization, the bastard tried to blackmail me."

"Did you know he was working for the DEA?"

"Hell, yeah. But I made him and his crew pay. Look. They're gonna come for me soon, and I haven't had the chance to say 'happy birthday' to my little girl." He wrapped his arms around her, holding her tight. "I'm sorry I'm not the man you wanted me to be. I'm ninety-nine percent monster." He gazed into her eyes. "That last percent is all heart and belongs to you."

Unsure of her feelings, she leaned her head on his shoulder. How could she love a murderer? She smiled internally. She didn't love a murderer; she loved that one percent heart. "Thank you for giving me to Ernesto. You did the right thing." Now she fully understood why Ernesto kept David a secret. He didn't want his baby to know the ninety-nine percent monster who had fathered her.

"I'll always do what's best for my little girl." He released her and reached into his breast pocket, pulling out the picture of the rose on a black background he'd drawn. "I know it isn't much." He handed it to her. "But I want you to have this."

She unfolded the paper. "It's beautiful. Did you actually draw this?" He nodded. "Amazing. Thank you. I'll buy a frame for it when I return to Chicago." He flushed with embarrassment, and she laughed. "Uh-oh, the big bad tough drug lord has a soft spot. Do you think they'll let me visit you again?"

"I'd love to see you every day, but I won't allow it. I have a lot of enemies. If they find out I care about you, your life won't be worth shit. They killed my son. I won't sacrifice my daughter. Promise me, you'll never return."

"I'm not afraid of—"

"Rosa, please."

She held the picture of the rose close to her heart. This convict had shown more love and concern for her in two hours than her mother had in thirty years. "I'll do as you say."

A corrections officer stepped into the room. "It's time to go."

David embraced her tightly, whispering, "Don't trust anyone but

Samson. He'll take care of you. I love you, Rosa."

"I love you, too."

He kissed her on the cheek, then walked out.

CHAPTER SIX

Samson stood in the doorway of the interview room and cleared his throat. Rosa didn't lift her head or acknowledge his presence in any way. She continued twirling the curls by her ear and staring through the speckled linoleum floor. He stepped fully into the room, then tilted her chin up with his finger. Her sorrowful eyes gripped him, drawing him into her pain.

"Come with me." He held out his hand.

She took his hand and followed him out. He led her through the maze of corridors into the warden's office. He'd arranged for the debriefing interview to be there to help her feel more comfortable.

As she looked out the window, he watched her. "Penny for your thoughts."

Her slow smile warmed him. "He thinks a lot of you," she finally said. "I think you're the only one he didn't call a bastard."

Samson chuckled. "He's a bit much, isn't he?"

She returned to watching the prison yard. The sun was setting and soon the protesters would be going home. "I didn't expect to feel anything for him," she said softly. "I wanted to know who he was. How we're alike. I don't want to feel for him. I have a father. I love my father."

"Your feelings for David don't diminish your feelings for your father."

"But he's a murderer."

"He's not the same person anymore. He's still an asshole." They shared a smile. "But his heart has changed. Over the past year, I saw him change from that ninety-nine percent monster to ninety-nine percent heart."

"He wouldn't tell me who Sierra is. He doesn't care about the people they're hurting."

Samson was impressed that she'd asked. Because of her, they no longer had to suspect why David had killed those men. "You're more important to him than those people. He's trying to protect you. He thinks if he tells about Sierra, they'll kill you to punish him." He paused. "And he's right. He won't risk your safety, especially when he knows another drug syndicate is ready to take the place of Sierra."

"So he dies?"

"I'm afraid so."

She closed her eyes and leaned her head against the window.

"What is it?" he asked.

After a long while she answered, "I'm afraid of what else I don't know." She opened her eyes and a tear fell.

He drew her into his arms, rocking her gently. "I can't begin to imagine how hard this is for you. If you need anything, I'm here for you." She fit as if she'd been made for his embrace, for him to protect, for him.

Alton walked into the warden's office. "What have we here, Frick and Frack?" He motioned toward the two. They were both wearing black suits: Rosa had on a firebrick red shell to add a little color, and Samson wore a black tie with a thin swirl of red.

"Don't start," Samson warned before he made introductions.

"Pleased to meet you, Agent Miles." Rosa held out her hand.

He brushed by her. "Umm-hmm. Grab a seat." He tossed his legal pad on the table, set his briefcase under the table and took a seat.

Samson rolled one of the office chairs out for her, then pushed it in gently as she sat. He would check Alton about his rude behavior in private.

"Thank you, Samson," she said.

"Why are you here?" Alton snapped.

Her eyes turned as cold, hard, and deadly as black ice, but her voice remained calm. "If you wish for this interview to continue, I suggest you step to me correctly."

Samson had seen Alton stare many a soul down, but Rosa didn't flinch. Alton had finally met his match.

"My apologies," Alton grumbled as he straightened his tie.

"I'm here to visit my biological father, David Martín."

"And you didn't know he was your father until yesterday?"

"My father is Ernesto Bolívar," she stated matter-of-factly. "I didn't know David Martín was my biological father until yesterday."

Waiting to see where Alton's line of questioning would lead, Samson stood off to the side. He knew Alton would try to connect Ernesto and David, but *how* was the question.

"Your fathers grew up together in Chicago?"

"Yes."

"Then David gave you to Ernesto."

"Yes."

"Wow, that's some friendship." He waited for her comment, which she didn't volunteer. "Your biological father is the head of the drug world and your 'father' is the head of the business world. Interesting."

"Very."

"Ernesto just acquired a major European distribution company," Alton said as he stared into her eyes.

"I'm sorry, Agent Miles. I missed the question. Bolívar International acquires companies all the time."

Samson knew Alton was insinuating that the distribution company would be used to traffic drugs. He also had a feeling Rosa knew.

"No question. I'm just thinking aloud. Too many coincidences is no coincidence." He drew a small tic-tac-toe board on his legal pad. "Ernesto is a Colombian of the lighter variety, correct?"

"Yes. Just as those of African descent are in this country, Afro-Colombians come in all shades."

He put an X in the middle of the board. "He found out about David's affair with his wife, correct?"

"Yes."

He marked X in the upper right corner. "He was moving up in the business world when you were born, correct?"

"Yes."

He placed an X in the lower left corner. "What are the chances of an upwardly mobile, Colombian male raising the black female baby of the man who cheated with his wife?" He crossed the three X's.

She raised a brow. "You are aware that is a two person game, aren't you?"

He smirked. "You are aware that upwardly mobile, Colombian males do not raise black female babies of men who fuck their wives, aren't you?"

"So who raised me?" Rosa didn't flinch at Alton's vulgarity, but Samson was ready to strangle him. Witnessing how the investigators had probably treated his sister increased his protectiveness for Rosa. For some reason Alton had decided she was the enemy, but Samson would ensure objectivity.

"It's not who," Alton continued, "but why. Men aren't that great friends, yet he took the responsibility of raising a known drug lord's child. Do you know how much scandal it would have caused had word leaked out? This is back in the seventies." He flipped open the file and sorted through documentation. "Hell, he actually raised you on his own when he had the capital to hire a nanny."

"So because he's a good father and friend, he must be dirty? Yeah, that makes perfect sense."

"It doesn't add up."

"They'd been friends their whole lives. David even saved his life before."

"Yes, Ernesto's best friend was working his way up the drug syndicate ladder while he worked his way up the corporate ladder, yet they never decided to join forces." He held his hand up. "Wait a second." He drew another tic-tac-toe board. "I feel another round coming on."

Samson had to give it to Rosa. She seemed unfazed by Alton's antics and accusations. She sat patiently, expressionless. He'd never seen a better poker face.

"Have you ever seen your birth certificate?" He placed an X in the upper right corner.

"Yes."

"Ernesto has always been listed as your father." He marked X in the lower left corner. "Can you explain why Ernesto went against the laws of nature and raised the child of the man who his wife cheated with?" He put an X in the center, then drew a line through the three X's. "They'd always intended on raising you to take over the syndicate and Bolívar International. They hid Ernesto from the DEA's radar to raise you."

Rosa laughed. Not a light feminine laugh, but a deep belly laugh that sent tears streaming down her face. "I'm sorry. We just went through this whole production for..." she paused, "for nothing, I guess. Maybe your friendships are as shallow as you, but others have something of substance. I'm tired, hungry, and have a flight to catch. This is a waste of my time and the taxpayers' money." She stood, nodding at Samson. "It was a pleasure meeting you. How do I get out?"

"There's an officer waiting outside the door."

"Thank you." She walked out.

Samson waited a few seconds after Rosa left. "That had to be the most counterproductive interview in the history of the DEA—make that any government agency. Alienating someone who we need to work with wasn't good enough for you. No. You had to go all out. If she or Ernesto is involved in this, you just showed how weak our hand is. We have to go back sixty years and start from scratch. It'll be days before we're ready for Ernesto. Do you know how much damage control he can do in that time? Yes, I'm attracted to Rosa, but I'm not allowing it to interfere with what we need to do. Instead of worrying about my love life, you'd better check yourself."

"This is all too neat, too pretty. How could she not know about Ernesto?"

"Maybe you're right, but you're going about this wrong. Take a step back and think about what you've just done."

"I know. I know. I just..." Alton pushed away from the table. "I can't stand that little bastard. He's winning."

"What does David have to do with your blowing this interview?"

"I saw him in the hallway. He was his usual ass of a self, gloating and shit. I wanted to slap him tall. Then when I saw you two together in here, I just snapped." He ran his hands through his hair. "Damn, I fucked up man. Do you think we can recover?"

"I don't think Rosa's involved. She doesn't want Ernesto to know she visited David until after the execution. If we can keep this out of the media, we may have enough time to do the research before Ernesto can cover his tracks."

"I'll see what I can do. In the meantime, why don't we pay visits to George and Harriet Wells?" Alton ripped the tic-tac-toe covered sheet from the legal pad and crumpled the page. "Do you honestly believe

Rosa isn't involved?"

"She isn't."

"What about Ernesto?"

"I don't know yet. I'd need to speak with him in person." Samson had become an expert at reading people. He saw more than what they said. He could sense what they weren't saying. "And David loves her. I can't believe he'd just walk away, not even in his early days."

"Then you do think she's involved?"

"No, I know she isn't involved."

"You need to run over to her hotel and get a little somethin'-somethin' so you can think straight again. You just said it didn't make sense for David to walk away." He tossed the crumpled paper at the garbage can. The shot banked off the corner of the desk and went in. "That's what I'm talkin' 'bout."

Samson watched out the window as Rosa hailed a taxi. "I don't know what happened, but she didn't know about David. No one is that good of an actor. We need to check out Ernesto."

"I made a file on Rosa." He reached under the table for his briefcase, then set it on the table and opened it. "She's a trust fund baby worth over a hundred million. I have the guys working on Ernesto, Harriet, and George." He fished Rosa's file out of a sea of a documents, fast food wrappers, and napkins.

"I want to know why the connection between him and David wasn't made sooner." In Samson's opinion, the fact that the information was missing placed more guilt at Ernesto's door. Why else would the connections be erased?

"That makes two of us," Alton added. "I'm on it. You need to get going." He grinned from ear to ear. "Don't keep Rosa waiting."

"I'm not sleeping with her, Alton."

I'm not sure how I feel about David. I love who he is, but I can't accept who he was. I guess I shouldn't dwell on his past, but thank God he's changed. I'll pray that he'll give the DEA the information they need. Rosa curled her legs underneath herself, resituating the journal on the arm of the hotel sofa.

I'm shocked Daddy hasn't come banging on my door yet. I'm sure he's checked with my new client. I need to tell him about my visit. I don't trust that Agent Miles. I see why David calls him the bastard. She drew a smiley face. *I wouldn't put it past him to fabricate evidence to make a bust. Daddy needs to protect himself.*

Samson. Her body warmed. She took off her robe and tossed it to the side. *How can so much umm umm good be stuffed into one person? Whew, what a man! And that voice. Lawd, have mercy! It's as deep and rich as his skin. Boy howdy! Let me stop before this becomes an erotica entry.*

Laughing at herself, she set the journal and pen on the coffee table and picked up her book. Though exhausted, she knew Ernesto would be pulling a "surprise" check on her. She'd rather stay up than be woken.

She fought against it, but fell asleep. Samson visited her in her dreams. They were just about to kiss when a knocking sound woke her. "Aw, Daddy, what timing," she said as she dragged herself to the door.

Samson tapped the door lightly with his knuckle to avoid waking Rosa. He'd gone home, showered and changed to jeans and a gray T-shirt. Restless, he drove around Miami. The next thing he knew, he'd pulled into the parking lot of her hotel. He stepped away to leave.

The door flew open. "Daddy!" Rosa froze, big black eyes wide open and hands to her mouth. She swung the door closed. "I'm so sorry. I'll be right back."

She was the cutest little thing in her rainbow print pajamas and bunny slippers. He'd expected to see her wearing a satin negligee. He grinned, admitting he'd fantasized about seeing her in a satin negligee.

She opened the door, this time wearing a robe over her night-clothes. "I'm sorry. I don't usually answer the door like that."

He followed her into the living area. Her suite was the same size as his apartment. There was no way he could afford a woman like Rosa. She'd want to be wined and dined in the manner she was accustomed to.

Her strides were determined, yet feminine. He quickly found himself hypnotized by the sway of her hips. The dark suit she'd worn earlier did nothing to accentuate her shapely figure. The robe's material was light and fell about her figure nicely, leaving just enough for the imagination.

"Would you like some juice?" she said over her shoulder.

His eyes moved from her backside to her face a tad bit too late. Face heated almost as hot as his loins, he commented, "Nice robe." Her light laughter helped ease his embarrassment.

"Men," she said as they settled on the couch. "What can I do for you, Samson?"

Oh the things you could do for me. "I wanted to apologize for Alton. He's usually more professional."

She reached over and turned his wrist around. Her soft touch had him wanting to touch her soft places. She tapped his watch. "It's after midnight. Why are you here, Samson?"

Her voice and demeanor were innocent; her loaded question was anything but. The last time he mixed work and pleasure ended in a nasty divorce. Tempted as he was to cross the line, he wouldn't make the same mistake twice. "To prove to myself that I can stay away from you."

"Honesty. I like that."

He could feel her gaze glide over him from head to toe, breaking down his defenses. She looked into his eyes, and he knew he'd lost.

"Is it working?" she purred.

He leaned forward, whispering into her ear, "No. Not really?" His hands weaved through her hair. He'd been correct; her curls wrapped perfectly around his fingers as if custom made for his hands. And she smelled so sweet. This off-limits woman was someone he could fall in love with.

"What would you do if I kissed you?" he asked huskily.

"Enjoy myself thoroughly."

Not ready for the challenge, he dropped his head back to the couch. "You're not going to make this easy on me, are you?"

Her jovial laugh matched the mischief in her eyes. "You came to my room. Not the other way around."

"You got me there. I'm sorry. I've started something I can't finish."

Until he made certain she wasn't a player in the Martín syndicate, he'd stay away. He was angry with himself. He wouldn't use her as Alton wanted and should have never gone to her room. "I truly apologize." He resisted the urge to carry her into the bedroom of the suite and make love. "I have a job to do and shouldn't even be here. This is a major conflict of interest."

Brows furrowed, she asked, "Do you think I'm involved with David's syndicate?"

He took her hands into his. "I know in my heart that you aren't. But that isn't good enough for the DEA."

"What about innocent until proven guilty?"

"That's all well and fine for a court of law, but this isn't a court of law."

"You'll also have to investigate Daddy, won't you? I don't trust your partner. You can prove Daddy's innocent."

Knowing she wouldn't like what he was about to say, he prepared himself for a tongue-lashing. "My job isn't to prove Ernesto's innocence or guilt, but to find the truth. I have to look at every possibility."

She sighed. "I wish I could be mad at you for being so thorough, but I can't. I understand." She kicked off her bunny slippers, then snuggled into his side. "I'll be glad when this is all over with."

He stared at the top of her head. His ex-wife would be throwing a fit about him not using his position to help a friend. He wrapped his arm around her, thankful for her analytical mind.

"I'm afraid your partner might try to frame Daddy."

"He isn't like that, Rosa. He was out of line today, but he was in rare form."

"All I know is your partner thinks I'm a *femme fatale*. Daddy raised me right. Anyway we can help, we will. Within reason," she added slowly. "We don't have to take his insults, insinuations, or disrespect."

"I agree." Comfortable silence joined them in the room as she relaxed against his side.

"Even though you're a tease, I'm glad you came by. I wanted to thank you for supporting me today. My life hasn't been a bed of roses, but I've always known what I'm dealing with, so it had order. Since I turned thirty, my life has lost all order. Daddy doesn't understand I need to know about David. For the first time in my life, I'm alone, and it's scary." She laced her fingers through his. "Well, I was alone, until you came along."

Her sincerity touched him as much as her faith in him gave him strength. Both qualities his ex-wife didn't possess. "Your mother never told you anything about David?"

"The only thing Mom talks about is how much she hates men. I'd bet she doesn't even know what my degrees are in." She closed her eyes. "I know this will sound horrible, but as a child I felt the only reason she had me was for child support."

She'd tensed up when speaking about her mother. He gently stroked the rim of her ear with his finger, and she relaxed. "It's not horrible," he said. "Who wants to be thought of as a paycheck?"

"David actually showed more love and concern for me than she ever has. He isn't what I expected." She placed her hand palm-to-palm with his. He'd bet his were at least twice the size of hers. As she played with his fingers, he could tell she had more on her mind than finger games.

"When you interview her, don't let your partner antagonize her."

"His name is Alton."

"I can't stand him. Jerk."

"Like father, like daughter. Neither of you like Alton."

"I can't believe I had a brother. Now I understand why Daddy didn't want me to see David. I thought it was jealousy. I still think jealousy plays a role, but he's afraid someone will come after me like they did David's son. They're all monsters. That's why he's being so irrational. Do you think anyone will come after me?"

"They may snoop around, but you don't know anything, so you should be safe. Try not to worry about that. I won't let anyone harm you."

She pulled back and their gazes locked. "Are you applying for job as my bodyguard?"

"Something like that." Though she looked mind-weary, he admired the way she'd handled the upheaval. To be bombarded with so much information that was contradictory to what you'd been raised to believe was too overwhelming for him to imagine. He silently prayed

Ernesto had given up all ties with the drug world shortly after Rosa's birth.

"You know everything about me," she said. "Tell me about yourself."

"I'm number three of five children. My mother was a teacher. My father was a police officer, who died in the line of duty when I was fourteen. My older brother was already in college, so I became the man of the house."

"I'm sorry to hear about your father."

"It was hard at first, but we made it. I love having a large family." Thoughts of his sister darkened his mood.

As if sensing his pain, Rosa hugged him. He rested his head on hers, thinking this was just what he needed.

"You don't have to tell me what happened if you don't want to," she said silently.

He'd never spoken about his sister's suicide because he couldn't; but now he wanted to, needed to. He knew it was crazy, but he felt comfortable telling Rosa things that he couldn't even admit to himself. He told her everything about the embezzlement, his brother-in-law running off with the secretary, how the investigators totally demoralized his sister, and her subsequent suicide. A DEA agent at the time, he'd told her to tough it out. The investigators were only doing their job. It would all blow over once they saw that she didn't know anything. Now he wished he'd recognized her pain, the shock she was in, her call for help.

Comfortable silence returned as they held each other.

"Thank you, Rosa."

"I'm here if you ever need to talk." She rested her head on his shoulder. "How did you become a DEA agent? You don't seem to fit the mold."

"Oh, really." Thinking David would agree with her, he smiled.

"Nope. Alton does though."

"Actually, I'd just gotten a divorce. My ex-wife was a paralegal at the law firm I worked for."

"What was your job?"

"A lawyer."

"You gave up being a lawyer to become a DEA agent? Whew."

"My law degree helps me as an agent, but I joined to run away." He was tired of running and was ready to take control of his life again.

"My parents are running away from their pasts. You can't run forever. Eventually your past will catch up with you and run you over."

"I agree."

"If you don't mind me asking, what caused your divorce?"

"I wanted children. She had an abortion, and I found out about it. Then later, I found out she'd been having an affair with one of my partners."

"So that's why you're having a hard time believing Daddy wanted me after he found out about Mom and David?"

"Yes," he said slowly. "After the divorce, I quit the firm and joined the DEA."

"It's understandable that you'd need a break." She squirmed a little, then nervously said, "Have you ever just met someone and felt you've known them your whole life? I know this will sound crazy, but …" she trailed off. "I'm sorry. I've been under a lot of stress. I'm talking crazy." An uneasy smile tipped her lips.

"Before today, I would have thought you were talking crazy. After today, I know that anything is possible."

Searching for a reason to stay longer, he spotted two books and a pen on the coffee table. "What are you reading?" He picked up the purple book. "*Indigo* by Beverly Jenkins."

"She wrote it back in the eighties, but it's my favorite book. No, make that my second favorite book. *Their Eyes Were Watching God* by Zora Neale Hurston is my favorite. This is a close second though."

He went into the bedroom and returned with a pillow and a comforter. He handed her the pillow, covering her with the comforter. "I want to see what this Beverly woman has." He brushed his lips over hers.

She nibbled on his bottom lip. "Don't start none, won't be none," she murmured.

He'd only wanted a taste to hold him over until he could feast. He backed away. Some temptations were too great. "You're killing me." He rolled the leather office chair from the desk in the back of the room around to the coffee table. He flipped open to the marked page and read aloud. Peeking up occasionally, he watched her reaction to his voice. She closed her eyes and laid her head on the pillow. She looked so peaceful, content.

He stopped reading and her eyes opened. He'd thought she'd fallen asleep.

"Done already?" She yawned, stretching. "Thank you. I'll have to get a recorder next time, so I can listen to you whenever I want."

"Would you like for me to read more?"

"I'd never put you out like that."

A few chapters later, he heard a light snore. Her choice of books said a lot about her. *Indigo* was a romance novel about a former slave who finds love as she runs a station on the Underground Railroad. He also found it interesting that the heroine was named Harriet, yet was the total opposite of Rosa's mother. He set the novel on the coffee table and picked up the second book. It had a canvas cover with an embroidered rose on it. The bottom was cross-stitched Rosa Bolívar. *An artist like her father*, he thought and opened the book to the marked page. *I'm not sure how I feel about David. I love who he is, but I can't accept who he was.* He quickly closed the journal. He wouldn't betray her trust.

He set the journal on the table, kneeling before her, watching the swell and fall of her chest as she slept. Hot blooded, she'd knocked the comforter onto the floor.

An uneasy feeling had settled in him. He wanted to give Ernesto the benefit of the doubt, but who else had the perfect ammunition to use against David? He fingered through the curls about her ear. This time, he prayed for their sake that Ernesto was clean.

CHAPTER SEVEN

"Hello, Mrs. Walker," Rosa said as she entered Ernesto's front office. She'd come to tell him about her visit with David and the DEA. Instead of the usual cheerful reply, she was greeted with a grim nod.

She rushed to the secretary's desk. "Is everything all right? Is there anything I can do?"

Mrs. Walker took Rosa's outstretched hand and squeezed gently. "You've always been such a sweet child. I'm truly sorry." She picked up the phone and dialed Ernesto's line. "She's here." She hung up.

Rosa stared at Mrs. Walker. Eyes all puffy, shoulders slouched, face drawn: the woman looked like she'd just lost her best friend. "Do you want to talk about it? I'm a great listener."

"You have a good head on your shoulders, Rosa. You've grown into a fine young woman. Don't worry about me. I'm fine. Go ahead and see your father."

Rosa crossed her arms over her chest. "I don't like leaving you like this, but I'll go." She hugged the secretary. "If you need me, you know where to find me."

The moment Rosa stepped into Ernesto's office, she knew something was desperately wrong. He was standing at the floor to ceiling windows, looking over the city, which she'd seen him do a million times. The odd part was the tiled wall of flat screens weren't on. The man couldn't be in a room with a television and not have on the news. He even listened to news radio.

First Mrs. Walker, now this.

Fear gripped her as she thought of the two things that could cause these events. "Daddy, has Mom been in an accident?" She'd worried Harriet had gotten drunk after she rushed out of the office and caused a car accident. She'd tried calling several times, but Harriet didn't answer the phone.

He continued staring out the window.

Heart pounding loudly in her ears and eyes welled up with tears, she crossed the room to him. "Daddy, please. What's wrong with Mom?" She tugged his suit sleeve.

He looked down on her. "She is well. No one is hurt," he said, then returned to staring out the window at the busy, morning-rushed city streets.

"What's wrong?" Her heart continued on its quick descent as the second event that could cause Ernesto's mood readied to reveal itself. She'd been so emotionally drained after leaving the prison yard, she hadn't even thought of damage control. She silently prayed it wasn't as bad as she knew it could be.

"What happened to the obedient little girl I raised?" he quietly asked. "When did she grow into the hard-headed woman standing beside me?"

The slap of disappointment in his voice knocked the wind out of her. "I'm sorry. I had to do what I felt was right."

"Have I ever led you astray before?"

"No, sir. But this was different."

"Yes, it was. I've never known you to make a decision without having all of the facts first."

"You wouldn't give me the facts, so I had to work with what I had."

"Instead of trusting me, you shot off on your own like a child because I wasn't telling you what you wanted to hear." He stalked over to his desk.

How could she tell him her trust in him had been shattered? "You should have given me all of the facts and allowed me to make my own decision. I'm not a little girl anymore."

"I know what's best, Rosa." He thumped the newspaper on his desk. "Come see your handiwork."

The headline read *Mystery Daughter Pleads to See Father*. Under the headline was a giant split photo: one side of her shaking the prison fence, the other of David. A full feature article about Rosa Bolívar's plight followed.

She weaved her hands through her hair. "I'm so sorry. I was in shock, desperate, and not thinking straight."

"There are more repercussions from your lack of judgment." He aimed the remote control at the screened wall and flicked. All of the televisions came on. To her horror, channel after channel reported some version of the "Bolívar connection" to the largest drug syndicate in the world. "Our stock has already plunged fifteen percent. Do you know how many millions that is?"

She lowered herself into his executive chair. "I feel so horrible. I'm so sorry."

"And do you know what the worst part is?" he calmly continued. "I'm not sure how I can protect you from David's enemies." He knelt in front of her. "Can't you see you're more important to me than the air that I breathe?" He gently swiped his thumb under her eyes, wiping her tears away. "You're my only child."

"I'm sorry."

He held her hands. "You don't understand the drug world. I have to protect you, Rosa. You're going into hiding."

"Please, Daddy, no."

"I don't have a choice."

"But I'll always be David's biological child. I can't hide forever." His facial expressions went from compassionate to all business. "Let's face them down now," she added.

"If I must hide you forever, then I will. I'd rather have you alive and mad."

"This is ridiculous. I'm sorry news of my parentage leaked out, but I'm not about to hide for the rest of my life. How do I know they won't come after you because I've gone into hiding? I messed up. Just as you've taught me, I must suffer the consequences."

"The consequence for this is too high. I won't risk your life." He flicked off the flat screen televisions. "I don't mean anything to David, but you do. You're the one in danger." He tapped on the picture of her at the prison gates. "They'll never believe you aren't a part of his organization. They'll think we raised you to control Bolívar International and the Martín cartel."

The fear in his eyes told her there was more. And, quite frankly, she was too disappointed to completely trust him. "What aren't you telling me?"

"I'm protecting you."

"I know about David's son. I'm not a three-year-old, defenseless child. You should have told me about David years ago."

"Look what happened when I told you."

"That happened because you didn't tell me. I thought I was losing my only chance, and I panicked. Omissions aren't protections, but lies. I'm not a child. This involves me." She thumped her chest. "I have a right to know everything!"

"You don't understand, Rosa. I know the life. I lived the life. I saw his son die. I saw how it tore David apart. I can't live with that pain."

"The only thing I don't understand is why you don't have faith in me. You raised me, and I think you did a damn good job. You're not on your own. I'm grown. We can get through this together, but I need to know what's going on."

He stared at her a long while. Acknowledgement sparked in his eyes. She could tell he saw her for the woman she'd become instead of his little girl. He had finally relinquished control as her commanding officer.

He turned away and walked to the wet bar. "What are we going to do, Rosa?" He took out two glasses and began fixing their drinks.

She wanted to run down the hallway calling out, "He said we! He said we!" Instead, she calmly said, "I have a friend in the DEA. I say we work with him. He can tell us who to look out for and maybe set up some sort of sting thing."

He poured her soda. "You're joking, right?" He handed over the cola. "We may be black, but our surname is Colombian. They think we're all drug lords. We're on our own."

"Samson isn't like that," she said more harshly than she intended. "We can trust him."

He lowered his cola from his lips. "Who is Samson?"

"A DEA agent I met yesterday. We don't know anything about these drug people." She followed Ernesto to his desk. "He can help."

"Do you realize who David is? He's dying in a few days, and they haven't brought down his syndicate. Think about it. Our friendship was so tight that I've secretly raised his child all of these years. What else have we done in secrecy? To run a syndicate the size of David's requires *legitimate* businessmen." He hunched his shoulders. "Who would make a better choice than me? The DEA's job is to catch drug lords, not protect you."

"Why did you agree to raise me after you knew David cheated with Mom? I mean, they both betrayed you."

"You know how we grew up. David and I vowed our children would never want for anything, and we'd raise them right. He loved his son and Rosa."

"Who's Rosa?"

"The love of David's life. He insisted I name you after her."

"Where is she now?"

He stared at her a long while. "After her baby died, she had a nervous breakdown. David moved her to Mexico and hired people to care for her."

"Is she still there?"

"Yes. I make sure she's well cared for."

"Let me get this straight. You raised his child and are caring for his lover, even though he betrayed you? This doesn't add up."

"David and I aren't blood, but we're family. Yes, I was angry about the affair, but he's still my family. It's like your aunt Angela and your mother. She loves Harriet, but doesn't agree with her lifestyle. That's me and David. He wanted to raise you himself. I couldn't allow you to be raised in the drug lifestyle.

"To make a long story short, he finally agreed that he couldn't raise a child and live as he was. He loved you and didn't want the same fate that befell his son to happen to you." He took her hands into his. "Next thing I knew, I had a beautiful baby girl."

She relaxed considerably. "What role did David play in raising me?"

"We traveled in different circles. He was my friend, but I couldn't afford to have friends like him. He understood my dilemma. We agreed it would be best for everyone if he stayed away. Over the years, he would ensure our names were never connected in government agency files. We didn't want anyone finding out about you." He ran the tip of his finger along her jawbone to her chin, which he gently pinched. "You've lived a protected life. I can't stress how dangerous the drug world is. You have to keep a low profile."

Ernesto's explanations made perfect sense to her. If they'd remained in contact, the authorities and business community would have thought Ernesto was guilty by association. She still felt his stress on the danger surrounding her situation wasn't warranted, and dismissed it as him being his usual overprotective self.

"We should go to Samson before the DEA comes to you," she said. "It's been thirty years. The statute of limitations is over, and they'll find out about your past eventually. It's better to go to them with it first."

"I don't care about the DEA investigating Bolívar International. We made sure they'd never find anything to hurt me, and Bolívar International was never involved in anything illegal. I'm worried about keeping you safe."

She released an exasperated sigh, thinking her father had a one-track mind today, and it was set on her safety. "But a drawn out investigation and any indication that we aren't cooperating will kill our stock price. You've worked so hard—"

He held up his hand. "Stop worrying about me. You're more important to me than Bolívar International's stock price."

"But you can have both if we go to the DEA."

"And what if David's enemies think we're telling the DEA David's secrets? They'll come after you to silence us. We need to try and continue with life as usual and avoid the DEA as much as possible."

"We don't know any secrets."

"I know that and you know that. But the DEA and David's enemies don't know that. The worse the DEA can do is hurt Bolívar International's stock price. The company is strong and will survive this. Drug syndicates could kill you."

Rosa watched him skim through the article about her and David. She couldn't allow him to sacrifice his business for an irrational fear, but she couldn't think of a way out. He'd never cooperate with the DEA if he thought she were in danger. He wouldn't save his business, so she'd have to do it herself.

Knowing the article was just the tip of the iceberg, she asked, "Daddy, can you keep the media from hounding me?"

"I've already taken care of it." He looked up from the article. "I need to know everything David told you, and what happened with the DEA." He set the paper to the side. "But first, you're going to explain why you flush when you speak about this Samson."

Her eyes flew wide open. "I don't."

"You practically bit my head off to defend him. You need to be careful. He's using you to find out information on me. He can't be trusted. We can't trust anyone but each other."

She squelched the urge to proclaim Samson's innocence. "You should meet with him before you judge him."

"We'll see."

"Have you seen the news? Martín has a daughter."

He switched his cell phone to his other ear, then brushed his hand through his short, mousy brown hair. "Of course, I have. I'm on it. I'll have to tread lightly." Sitting in a local café, he set down the *Daily Herald* in exchange for *The Wall Street Journal*. There was an article about Paige Industries that he wanted to read before he headed for Chicago.

"Agreed. Keep me informed of your progress."

"As always."

CHAPTER EIGHT

Chicago

Harriet snapped her flip phone shut. *She has always thought she's better than me!* Harriet had been calling Angela for days and was ready to give up. Talking about giving up, she hoped Rosa would stop calling her. Harriet knew Rosa would confront her eventually, but Harriet intended on putting off "eventually" for as long as she could.

On television, a woman rushed from the hotel entrance to the waiting taxi, reminding Harriet of when her sister had abandoned her for the first time…

Chicago, thirty-one years ago

Harriet stood at the hotel window and watched Angela's taxi merge into the holiday traffic. Angela was so gullible, it made Harriet sick. *Typical goody two-shoes.* She smirked. *Tell her what she wants to hear, and she'll lap it up.*

Missing her fluffy down pillows and bright, cheerful comforter, she returned to the hotel bed and pulled back the ugly brown and orange splotched spread. She would call David after her nap, sure that he'd be plenty worried by then.

Rolling onto her stomach, she stuffed the pillows under her arms. She couldn't get over the way he'd pulled his punch instead of hitting her. Her heart smiled. He really did love her and wanted to have a baby with her. Yes, even the mighty David had fallen to her will.

She slipped her hand between her stomach and the bed. If not for the baby, she would be stuck in a loveless marriage and missing out on all the things David would buy her.

Maybe I'll name her Miracle, she thought.

If she played her cards right, she'd be married to David and living the life she deserved by Christmas. But first, she needed to get rid of George. After he showed his butt by throwing her out, she knew he never really cared for her. He'd obviously wasted their money on a woman and blamed Harriet for their financial troubles.

Finished napping, Harriet told herself this was the last time she'd try David's number. She'd left him a message over an hour ago, apologizing. Though in love, she didn't want to sound desperate and lose the upper hand. Her mother had learned that lesson the hard way.

She laughed in delight. David was actually hers, and soon she'd have more money than she could dream of. She prayed George wouldn't try to weasel in later. When she'd called him, George apologized for kicking her out of the house. He said he would move into an apartment and leave her the house, but Harriet wasn't hearing it. She told him to sell that cheap-assed house and give her the money. She'd found a man that knew how to treat a woman. A tinge of guilt pricked at her for being so hateful to George. After all, he had been a good provider, initially. But David had so much more to offer that she had to love him.

She dialed David's number, then placed the phone to her ear.

"Yeah."

"David, honey, I've been worried about you," she said in a voice so sweet it made sugar taste sour.

"What the hell do you want? I aint payin' for no fuckin' abortion."

The hostility pouring through the line brought a frown to her face. "Didn't you receive my message, love? I'm sorry about yesterday. I don't want an abortion. I was so worried this was George's baby that I hadn't considered this could be our child," she lied as easily as she had when she told Angela that she hadn't had sex with George for six months. "Please forgive me for being so emotional." A nervous giggle escaped her. "The hormones of pregnancy have me acting out of sorts."

"Yeah, right. Back to my original question: What the hell do you want from me?"

She didn't appreciate his tone of voice, but would remain silent on the subject. Before yesterday, he'd only spoken to others in such harsh tones. She rationalized his pain was speaking, not David. The idea of her aborting their love child obviously cut him deeply.

"I thought we could go to dinner and discuss the baby, my divorce, the wedding." She smoothed down her mauve wrap around skirt as she waited for his reply. His silence worried her. Perhaps she should have waited until tomorrow to call. The hotel room was paid for one more night.

"You don't honestly believe I'm marrying you, do you?" His sinister laugh crept through the line, then rappelled down her spine. She shook it off. She couldn't have miscalculated this badly. She knew what men wanted: how they thought and how to manipulate them. More importantly, she knew David loved her as much as she loved him. Why else would he be so distraught over her aborting their child? Why else would he spend so freely on her? "I know you're angry about yesterday, but I was distressed."

"Do I have to spell the shit out? Is my accent too thick? I…don't…want…your…ass."

"B-but, David, you said you'd marry me if I left George." Panic sent her heart racing. This hateful man couldn't be the love of her life. Someone must have answered his line. She twisted the phone cord between her fingers. "I'm divorcing George," she stammered. "We-we've already started the paperwork."

"You mean he's divorcing your ass. I just got back. I went to him like a man and apologized for showing my ass."

"Why are you doing this? You said you loved me." In a daze, Harriet sat on the edge of the bed, crinkling the comforter with her free hand. She'd actually believed David and George's professions of love. She cursed herself for being so arrogant, so stupid, so… She felt like she'd throw up, and not because of the baby.

"I said whatever the hell I had to get your ass in bed. You're nothing more than a high-priced whore. You're no better than your mama."

"I'm nothing like my mother!" The sound of her mother crying after yet another man walked out on them resounded painfully within Harriet. "How can you speak to me like this? I don't understand." She drew her hands through her lye-straightened hair as if to find the answers between the black, shoulder length strands. "George threw me out. I have nothing. Don't do this."

"I ain't doin' shit. You knew you were married. What the hell did you think he'd do when you get pregnant by a *real man*? Hell, I'm not stupid. You punked *Jorge*. I ain't goin' out like that."

"But what about the baby? It's yours. I can feel it." She blinked away her tears. She'd given him something that she'd never given another man—her heart. Biting the tips of her French manicure, she rocked on the bed. This couldn't be happening. Not to her. She was too smart, too cunning, too beautiful to be taken for a fool. What would she do for money until she found another man? After the way she'd cut up on the phone, there was no way George would take her back.

"I'm a man. I take care of my responsibilities, but that don't mean I have to marry your ass."

"But, I love you."

"Love my money."

She gripped the phone with both hands as if that would double her sincerity. "You've got to believe me. I've never felt like this before."

"You were supposed to be on birth control," he bit out, accent thickening along with his anger. "I told you what happened to *m'ijo*."

"David, please. This is your chance to have another son."

"I told you I can no risk havin' *no mas...*" he trailed off.

"David, please listen to me. I love you. I love our son. He needs you to be his father."

"You think I'm gonna let you manipulate my ass? That shit's the oldest trick *en el libro*. You bled *Jorge* dry, now you're after me. Fuck that. I ain't havin' it."

"No!" She wiped the tears away. She couldn't give up. His money was her future. "I love you. I never thought I'd love—"

"Don't waste your breath," he cut in.

She heard him draw in a few deep breaths. Praying she hadn't pushed too hard, she remained silent. But his heavy accent told her she'd shoved him over the edge.

"A hundred grand is more than enough to raise a kid." He inhaled deeply. "To keep your trick ass from abortin' my son, I'll give you cash *after* he's born."

Her ears perked up to the sweet melody of a hundred grand. Assessing her situation quickly, she fingered her belly like the buttons of a calculator. "I'll need at least half a million, David. Please. How will I survive until the baby comes? I know you want a healthy son."

His laugh was so loud that she had to pull the phone away from her ear temporarily. "I thought your ass was in love with me. You seem to have recovered quickly. Two hundred big ones—after my son is born. Don't even think about asking for more."

Noticing his accent had dissipated, she felt more secure. "But, I need money now." He didn't reply. "David?"

"Meet me at Tony's. I'll give you a lil' somethin' to hold you over for a few days. But you need to get back in your house and get your things. Pawn some of that shit I bought your ass. You have money."

She heard the phone slam on his end. The line went dead. The phone fell from Harriet's trembling hand. She'd given him her heart, and he'd crushed it. Sounds of her mother crying returned. She would never allow a man to use her as they had her mother. No, she was better than her mother. Harriet would never be the used again. She slumped to the bed.

Never again, she swore.

CHAPTER NINE

Samson couldn't believe how close he'd come to crossing the line with Rosa last night. She was perfect for him, but the timing was anything but.

David entered the interview room minus his shackles. "What's the special occasion?" he asked in Spanish. "Why are we in here?" He sat across from Samson.

"This is the only place I could speak with you privately."

"What about them cameras?" He nodded toward the corner of the room, but the cameras were missing.

"We need to talk about Ernesto."

"I can't stand his stupid ass. Is that Rosa?" One of her pictures was sticking out of the folder. Samson slid Rosa's folder across the table to him. "I still can't believe I made someone so beautiful." David flipped through the folder. "I've missed the last six years of her life."

"But, I thought she didn't know anything about you until the other day?"

"Don't get your shorts in a bunch. I kept an eye on her from afar. She's my little girl."

"I want to protect Rosa, but I can't unless I know the whole truth." The truth behind his own words scared Samson. She was someone he could fall in love with. He corrected his thoughts: *was* falling in love with. Setting the timing issue aside, they came from two totally different worlds. He'd never fit into hers, and she'd never fit into his.

A slow grin eased across David's face and mischief sparkled in his eyes, putting Samson in mind of Rosa. "So now, you're her champion?" David straightened his posture and spoke through his nose. "My, aren't we the gallant one?"

"I'm being serious."

"So am I. She'll need someone to watch over her after I'm gone."

"Well, that someone isn't me. Is Ernesto your silent partner in the syndicate?"

David's larger-than-life laugh filled the small room. "Subject change time. Okay, I'll play along. Will you arrest his ass if I say yes? If so, hell yeah! I saw the newspaper. That stupid bastard's big mouth is gonna get her killed. Lock his ass up. There's an open cell across from mine." He began reading through articles written about Rosa, the business prodigy. "She was only thirteen when she orchestrated her first company takeover. Yeah, you'd better lock Ernesto up fast."

"Stop being facetious and answer me."

"I like you, Samson—but I love Rosa. Even if Ernesto were part of my organization, I would never tell. Bolívar International will be hers someday. I won't ruin her inheritance or her name."

Samson expected as much, but he thought he'd give it a try. "Do you have the information on the Sierra syndicate?"

David patted himself down. "Not on me. I already told you, I ain't turnin' over shit."

"I'm not asking you to turn anything over. I'm asking if it exists."

David took a recent picture of Rosa out of the folder. "Can I have this?"

"Sure." Samson had grown accustomed to David taking time to choose his words carefully in deciding what he'd reveal. He smiled internally. Rosa did the same thing.

"I have it in a safe place. No more questions about it."

Samson could tell that David had a love-hate-admiration-jealousy relationship with Ernesto, but David had trusted him as he had trusted no other. Samson worked through different scenarios in his mind as he thumbed through the folder on Ernesto. Two rang out clearly.

In the scenario Samson preferred, Rosa was on the right track. Ernesto was no longer a part of any drug syndicate, and David gave the information to Ernesto to use as security against the Sierra syndicate. The two men were doing what they thought was necessary to protect Rosa.

In the second scenario, Ernesto was neck deep in the Martín syndicate, and he was using Rosa to gain more advantage over the Sierra syndicate.

David pulled the file on Ernesto to his side of the table. "Ernesto is a self-centered bastard. Always has been. Don't get me wrong. He has his moments, like when he agreed to take Rosa for me. I thought he'd pawn her off on a nanny, but instead, he raised her himself. I'm impressed."

"Why did he agree to take her?"

"I fucked up gettin' Harriet pregnant. He was the only person I could trust with my baby."

"But why did he agree to take her?"

"Let the truth be told, I'm just as self-centered as Ernesto. For once in our lives, we were thinking of someone else. We agreed he'd raise my child, and I'd stay away."

"What if Rosa had been born a male?"

"Sex didn't matter. In raising Rosa, we are selfless. She is our center."

"After Rosa was born, did you remain in contact with Ernesto?"

"Before my ass was locked up, he'd send me pictures and updates every few months. Rosa doesn't know this, and I expect her to continue not knowing."

"I understand." Samson opened his notebook and began writing notes.

"Have you contacted your family yet?" David asked. "What's your brother's name, Derrick?"

Samson continued writing. "Don't start. I've been too busy."

"You couldn't keep your sister from killing herself anymore than you can stop my execution. Her death wasn't your fault. My death isn't your fault. You can't save the world."

"Mind your own business," Samson warned. He'd failed his sister, and it cost her life. When his family needed him in control, he was busy wallowing in self-pity about his divorce. He missed his family, but he had to ensure Rosa was safe before he contacted them. It had been over a year, so a quick phone call wouldn't do.

"I'm dying in a few days and can't look after you. Call your brother."

"You're looking after me?" Samson said, voice filled with amusement.

"Hell yeah! I know some of that psycho-babble shit. Your sister had just died when you started 'befriending' me. In saving me, you save your sister. I can't be saved, Samson."

"You're talking crazy."

"Am I? I don't know how or when it happened, but we've become friends, and I'm dying. You feel helpless, just as you did with your sister."

"Be quiet." The folding chair screeched against the speckled linoleum floor as Samson pushed away from the table. "Are you ready to return to your cell?"

"What's this, you sending me to time out? Stop fighting battles you can't win. Rosa needs you in your right mind. Re-connect with your family."

A chill went down Samson's spine. The blood drained from his face. "Ernesto's part of your syndicate, isn't he." He rounded the table, smoothing down his goatee. "Rosa will be crushed."

"You won't find anything on Ernesto, but Rosa needs you."

It wasn't what David said, but what he didn't say that terrified Samson. "Say it, David. Why does Rosa need me?"

"Don't pay any attention to me. I've been locked up too long. Stop feeling sorry for yourself and contact your family. You finish that letter of resignation yet? I thought you were quitting after my execution."

"I'm not letting you off the hook so easily. Give me the Ernesto connection. What danger is Rosa in?"

David stared into Samson's eyes a long while. "I'm an asshole. I know how you always ride in like the fuckin' cavalry to save the day, so I told you Rosa was in danger."

"Why?"

"It's my way of matchmaking."

"You're lying."

"It won't be the first time."

Samson clinched his fists and let out a frustrated sigh. "How can you play these stupid games and say you love Rosa? You're the one who'll get her killed."

"Then hop on your white horse and protect her."

"Why are you trying to push me and Rosa together?"

David looked at Samson as if he'd lost his mind. "Because I'm about to die, and I need someone I trust to take care of my little girl!" He pushed away from the table. "Damn." He brushed his hands over his hair as he shook his head. "I'm dying," he said softly. "I can't leave her alone."

Taken aback by David's show of emotion, Samson asked, "What

CAUGHT UP

about Ernesto? Why don't you trust him to take care of Rosa?"

"You mean the dumb-ass who told her who I am? I stayed away from my child all of these years to protect her, then that stupid mutha' blows everything. Don't you think I wanted to tell her? That I wanted to be the one she adores? Ernesto's usefulness has ended. She doesn't need a father—she needs a husband."

"Wait a second." He held his hands up slightly. "Hold up. I'm interested but... Well hell, we come from different worlds."

"You can come up with a better excuse than that. I know what the hell I'm doing. I picked her father, and I'll pick her husband. I know where you spent last night."

"How the hell did you find out?" Samson snapped.

"I didn't. I guessed and you just confirmed."

"You're a piece of work."

"How the hell you think I became the head of the largest drug cartel in the world?" David marked time about the interview room, using his hands as he spoke. "I know I'm the big bad drug lord, but I love my child. I even care about your ass. Between Rosa's visit, Father Mike talking about I need to atone for my sins, you talking about fate and my impending death, I know what needs to be done."

"You don't have to die."

"I can't live in a fuckin' cage for God knows how long! I don't want to." He drew in a deep breath in an attempt to calm himself. "But, I can't leave Rosa by herself. I got to thinking about fate and atoning for my sins. Hell, there ain't that much atonin' in the world, but you. You work for the DEA, but you're not DEA. We should have never met. Rosa should have never found out about me. You two should have never met. You spent the night with her because it was meant to be. Fate."

"This is crazy. I hate to break it to you, but last night I went to Rosa's hotel room to apologize for Alton showing his ass. We didn't do anything. I don't mix business and pleasure. I've learned my lesson." Talk of fate brought Rosa's comment about feeling as if you'd known someone you just met your entire life to his mind. In a way, Samson felt the same way for her. They'd just clicked, and he couldn't find a logical explanation for why.

"You didn't do anything because you're falling in love with her. Hell,

100

you two were made for each other. Stop blaming yourself for your sister's death. Stop punishing yourself for the divorce. Stop playing martyr and live. I wish I could be thirty-four again. I would leave the drug life behind and raise my daughter. Yeah, I've been lookin' after you." A sheepish grin overtook his face. "What the hell else have I had to do? I pray you don't get to be my age, looking back at a life full of regrets." He paused. "I need for you to grant a dying man's last request."

Samson watched as David fiddled with Rosa's picture.

"I want you in Chicago when I die."

"I told you I'd be here for you, and I meant it. You're not dying alone. I'm not doing this because of the job. I want to be there for you."

"Rosa needs you." He shrugged his shoulders. "How did two ass-holes like me and Harriet have such a loving child? She cares too hard. I want you there with her. She'll need you." He reached in his pocket and pulled out a letter. "Give this to her for me—after I'm gone." He hand-ed the letter over.

Conflicted, Samson accepted the letter. He wanted to open it and see if David finally told Rosa the truth about Ernesto so she'd protect herself.

"Don't get your hopes up," David said, breaking into Samson's thoughts. "It just tells her I love her and am sorry we didn't have more time together. If you want, I'll write another letter so you can read it before I seal it."

Samson placed the letter between the pages of his notebook. "That won't be necessary."

"Then, I think it's time for me to leave." He rounded the table and gave Samson a brutha embrace. "Take care of my baby girl. No more regrets."

"No more regrets."

Samson stared out the window of their cramped temporary office onto the parking lot a few floors below. The rain didn't keep the protest-ers away. David's words continued to ramble in his mind. Samson's life was already full of regrets, and he didn't want to make Rosa another.

"We need to get up out of here for our flight to Chicago," Alton said from his desk. "George Wells is out of town, but we have other interviews we can conduct before he returns."

"What about Gains, the original agent on the Martín case?"

"David must have paid him off. He kept a low profile after he retired. He moved to France about five years after his retirement and lived well above the means of a former agent. He died six years ago of a heart attack. Every ex-agent that has worked on this case retired a little too nicely." He slammed his fist on the desk. "Hell, Ernesto and David were doing their dirt before there was even a DEA. They slipped Ernesto in under the radar, kept all of his connections hidden." He thumbed through the list of people they needed to interview. "The people old enough to help are either dead or senile. The bookkeeping back then was horrible at best, but I have our guys digging through old boxes and reading though every scrap of paper they can find."

"Are any of their high school teachers still around?"

Alton opened his notebook. "I was calling them while you were wasting time on David." He tapped on the list. "There are actually three I'd like to check out before we interview Harriet tomorrow. I've already made the arrangements. Let's go before we miss our flight."

❧❧❧

Ernesto stood at his floor-to-ceiling windows overlooking the city. "I should kill you for this, Harriet," he said loud enough for the speaker-phone to pick up his voice.

"I said I'm sorry. I didn't mean…"

He stalked over to the phone and snatched it from its cradle. "You never mean to! Did you see the news? She's on every channel, pleading to see David. Do you know what you've done?"

"I… I'm leaving town for a while."

"The hell you are! Rosa's worried sick about you. Why haven't you returned her calls?"

"I can't face her. I'm so ashamed. And, the DEA called me. They want to interview me in the morning."

"Shit! The cat's out of the bag now. You'll have to talk to them. I'll tell you what to say." He repeated his new and improved version of how he came about raising Rosa.

"No! I won't do it. You make me sound like a slut."

"If the shoe fits… and you will do this! Your worthless butt will finally do something for your child. If the DEA finds out about my business, Rosa will lose everything." He paused. "Maybe even her life."

"Please," she cried, "there has to be another way. Rosa needs to be told the truth about you and David. No! I won't do it. I'll call Rosa and tell her the truth, and then leave town before the agents arrive."

"Who do you think Rosa will believe? The bitter, drunken mother who never told her she got pregnant by a man other than her husband, and then married another man who wasn't the baby's biological father— or the man who has showered her with love her whole life? I've already admitted to Rosa that I knew David and laundered money for him. She'll never believe you because you never take responsibility for your actions."

"All of the evidence points to my story being true." He continued to pound in his point. "No one will believe a drunk over a successful businessman. The DEA won't believe you and neither will Rosa. All that will happen is Rosa will disown you just like Angela did."

"I hate you!"

"Hate me all you want. You'd just better do as I say."

Chicago

A long day had passed, and they still had one interview to go. Samson noted that the previous interviews had two common threads. Both retired teachers recalled how tight Ernesto and David were. Each recalled being interviewed by at least three agents, at different times, over the past forty years about David, which led to them telling the agents about Ernesto.

"I don't remember the agent's name," Mr. Terry said as he settled his rickety old bones in his well broken-in lazy-boy. "But one came by years ago asking about David and Ernesto."

"We're just re-tracking," Alton said as he situated himself on the couch.

"I can't believe you all haven't caught Ernesto yet." He nudged his cola bottle glasses up on his nose with his index knuckle. "Then again, you really didn't catch David on drug charges."

Alton cleared his throat. "You were telling us about Ernesto and David."

"They were both extremely bright young men and closer than an ionic bond." The retired chemistry teacher laughed at his joke, but the agents didn't. "They were both too smart for their own good. Ernesto was the charismatic one, and David was the muscle. They combined their strengths to succeed. As teens they moved out of their foster homes and into an apartment together. I would have called the authorities, but I knew they'd just run away. You know they opened their first money laundering business when they were only sixteen, don't you? A barbershop. By the time they were eighteen, they had restaurants and a few other businesses."

This was new information, but Samson had finished being shocked after the second interview. They finished questioning the teacher, thanked him for his time, and then went to Samson's hotel room to regroup and search through the government's computer files.

Samson and Alton sat at the room's desk, reading through all of the information they could find on Ernesto, and the teacher was correct. They did have their first business when they were sixteen, but it wasn't in their name. They'd had an adult sign as the owner. Over the years, their joint business empire grew.

"Damn, I have to give it to them. They were some smart bastards." Alton propped his feet on the coffee table. "For every restaurant opened in Ernesto's name, there's one in David's name. For every building Ernesto purchased, David purchased one. They have mirroring business acquisitions until Ernesto bought the computer company. Then, it looks like Ernesto went his own way business-wise."

"Too much of a coincidence, but not proof." Samson couldn't get Rosa off his mind. She was in danger and wouldn't believe him if he told her. He'd have to stay close to her.

"We'll find it. David's time isn't the only one's running out."

"Let's work the case from our Chicago office for a while."

"I thought you were quitting after the execution?"

"I've decided to stick around a while longer."

"She's in on it, man. Ernesto is in Miami. Unless you're planning on buttering up Rosa for the case, that shit's out."

CHAPTER TEN

The Next Morning
"All I want is the truth, Mom."

"Would you please close the curtains?" Harriet asked. "The light is killing me. I need to move."

Rosa did her mother's bidding, then returned to the couch and watched Harriet fumble with a cup of black coffee. "Tell me what happened."

"I don't want to talk about this. Giving up drinking is hard enough." Harriet focused on the steam rising from the cup. "I'm sorry I didn't call. Yes, it's true. I was married when I met Ernesto. Can we please drop this? You've been out of town a few days. I'm sure you have business you need to catch up on."

Rosa was proud of Harriet. She hadn't had a drink in two days. She didn't want to make sobriety harder on Harriet, so she dropped the subject for the mean time. She also allowed her to get away with rushing her out. "I love you, Mom." She leaned forward and hugged Harriet. "We'll speak when you're ready. I'll leave the pictures from my party." She set the packet on the coffee table.

❧✕❧

The only thing Harriet wanted more than to tell Rosa the truth was to hide it from her. Ernesto was correct—Rosa would side with him. He had always been a smooth operator.

"He got me good," she whispered, remembering when she'd met Ernesto...

Chicago, thirty-one years ago
"Place your bets."

Harriet tipped the glass to her mouth as if the wine hadn't run out two tips ago, then slammed the glass onto the wooden edge of the blackjack table. Several of the other patrons in the illegal gambling house glared at her, yet continued with their games. After all she'd given David, he'd tossed money at her and dismissed her. What the hell was she supposed to do with a measly grand? How was that supposed to hold her until the baby came? She'd broken her own rule and fallen in love. She couldn't believe she'd been so stupid.

"Are you in?" the dealer asked.

She narrowed her eyes on the potbellied, balding man. David paid her debt, then had the gall to tell Tony he wouldn't cover her credit any longer. She crumpled her last ten spot between her fingers. Even Lady Luck had abandoned her. She snatched her wine glass up, weaving her way through the crowd of people to a corner table. Sitting slightly beneath the thick layer of bluish-gray cigarette and cigar smoke that filled the room, she inhaled deeply and coughed. The air had a stench to it. She tipped the glass to her lips. Nothing came out.

"May I help you, ma'am?"

Harriet clutched her money and wine glass to her heart.

"My apologies," the waitress said. "I didn't mean to scare you."

"I must have been daydreaming." She tapped the rim of her wine glass with the ten spot. "Another white wine, please. Keep the change." She handed over the last of her money. Ten paltry dollars couldn't supply her needs anyway. She needed a man, fast.

"Coming right up," the waitress said with a smile as she turned to leave.

What quality of man could she get with a baby in tow? But, she couldn't pass up the two hundred grand. She lowered her head into her palms. She could put the child up for adoption after she collected the money. That would satisfy her needs and keep Angela off her back. *I can give Angela fifty thousand to adopt the kid. That way I can get more out of David later.* She chewed on her inner jaw. *Twenty-five thousand is more than enough for Angela.*

She chastised herself for treating George so poorly before she had what she needed from David. She'd have to give George a few days to cool off before she could even attempt to ease her way back in. Not that she actually wanted him, but he'd do until she found someone better. She strummed her nails along the tabletop.

"Is this seat taken?" said a low, sexy voice.

Harriet's gaze quickly traveled from the man's handcrafted leather shoes, along his silver designer suit—the same suit she'd wanted cheap-butt George to buy, but he'd said five hundred dollars was too much to spend to look like the Tin Man from *The Wizard of Oz*. The man was so tall that she had to crane her neck back to see his face. And what a face it was: chiseled features, light-skinned, and short, wavy, black hair.

Realizing she was staring, she flushed. "I'm sorry." She motioned toward the second chair at the table, which was no more than a padded stool with a short backing. "Please sit."

"Thank you." He nodded politely.

His massive hands looked like they'd never seen a day of manual labor, and his watch was a Rolex—the gold one with the diamond accents. She heard a lovely "ka-ching" as she tallied his worth. The man oozed money and power. She'd been attracted to David's dark persona until he dismissed her without a second thought. She now realized that she'd been in love with the money, not David, and there was nothing wrong with that. Money was safe, predictable. David's type was exciting, but too unpredictable. She longed for excitement, but she couldn't risk being burned by David's type again. If she found the right man, she could get her excitement elsewhere.

The mystery man reached into his inner suit pocket, then took out a gold Cross pen and a small note pad. He pushed them to her side of the tiny round table. "Write down his name and address."

She tilted her head to the side. "I'm sorry, but I don't know who you're talking about."

"I want the name and address of the person who hurt such a lovely lady. I'll ensure he never hurts you again."

She didn't know if it was her hormones raging out of control, the buzz from the booze or her longing to be protected, but she felt like crying.

The waitress set Harriet's wine on the table. "May I take your order, sir?"

Harriet swooned in his whisky-colored eyes as they caressed every inch of Harriet's face.

"I have everything I need," he said, his faint Spanish accent drawing her in. The waitress nodded and moved on to the next table.

Impressed that he hadn't so much as glanced at the shapely brunette waitress, Harriet suddenly felt hot and shy. She couldn't recall ever feeling shy in front of a man. "I'm Harriet, and you are?"

"Your knight in shining armor."

Stifling a giggle, she drew her hand to her mouth. He was too sweet to be true.

He reached forward, took her hand into his, then touched her wedding ring. "Oh, I see," he said, voice laced with disappointment. "I meant no disrespect. Forgive me, milady."

She quickly withdrew her hands and placed them in her lap. "You've done nothing wrong," she said softly. "I'm pleased to meet you, knight in shining armor."

"The pleasure is all mine." He pushed away from the table. "I'm new around here and…" He shrugged. "I'm sorry. I guess I should leave before a jealous husband comes after me."

Her ears clung to his words "I'm new around here." This piece of fresh meat would be an easy mark. She couldn't allow all of that money to land in the hands of one of the whores spying on their table. If he wanted to be a knight, then she'd let him be a knight. He'd be hers in no time. Trying to call up a few tears, she sniffed, but they didn't come. She covered her face with her quivering hands.

"Oh, no, no." He scooted his chair around close to hers. "Don't cry." He embraced her.

Giddy as a child at a candy factory, Harriet smiled inside. She'd hit the softie jackpot. Men like him were few and far between; and men like him *with money* were virtually impossible to find. She buried her face in his shoulder. It felt good to be held.

"I'm told I'm an excellent listener," he said. "No strings attached. If you need to talk, just talk. Or we can sit here until your husband comes to beat me for touching the most beautiful woman in the world."

"He won't come." She paused for dramatic effect and to calm her adrenaline-charged heart. He was buying her act hook, line and sinker. Her luck had finally changed. She sighed heavily. "He kicked me out of our home."

"What?" he snapped as he pulled back slightly.

She dabbed at the imaginary tears building in her eyes with her knuckle. "I'm pregnant." She choked up and lightly patted her chest with her shaky hand. "He said if I don't get an abortion, I had to get out of his house."

Seemingly oblivious to the other customers who were watching, he pressed her head to his shoulder. "Men like your husband give real men like me a bad name." He shook his head. "I'd kill to have a wife and children, and this idiot throws away a family like last week's newspaper."

Harriet straightened her posture and brushed off the wrinkles that were nowhere to be found on her v-necked, orange jumpsuit. "I'm sorry. I didn't mean to burden you with my problems. You've been so kind." She batted her eyes to remove her crocodile tears. "I'm sobbing all over you. You must think me a mess."

"Not a mess," he said gently. "A damsel in distress."

Her breath actually caught. "And does my knight have a name?"

He held his hand to his chest and bowed his head slightly. "Ernesto Bolívar, at your service. And you are?"

"Harriet. Harriet Wells."

She took a sip of wine. "I don't know what I'm going to do." She averted her gaze to her lap, where she nervously twiddled her fingers. "He took everything from me," she said barely above a whisper. She really didn't know what to do. She was married so couldn't overtly chase after this jackpot. She had to think long-term with this mark.

"What about your family?"

She fed off the concern in his voice. Oh yes, Lady Luck had definitely returned to her side. She would tread lightly with this one. Too much was at stake. "My sister is a student out of state. She gave me her last hundred bucks to put me in a hotel for a few nights, but the money is gone. He always forbade me from working. I thought we were trying to have a family, so I didn't object." Her shoulders slumped. "He's left me with nothing." She sipped at her wine.

Ernesto frowned. "He made you dependent on him, then threw you out on the street." He rubbed his chin as if calculating. "Do you know how to type?"

She stopped mid-sip and cocked her head to the side. "Excuse me?"

"Can you type?"

Harriet fought to keep her brows from furrowing. She didn't want a job, but maybe this could work in her favor. "I'm out of practice, but yes."

"I could use an assistant."

She grumbled internally, but smiled externally. The position would do until she could work her way into his wallet. "You're being too kind. Thank you."

Samson saw Rosa as Alton maneuvered their sedan around the parking garage of the condo complex. "Let me out," he said to Alton.

Alton stopped the car. "Unless you're getting close to her for the case, you need to cease and desist this behavior."

"I heard you the first ten times. Like you said, I need to get close to her."

He exited the car, trotting toward Rosa. "Hey, pretty lady." He took her hand and held it out so that she would spin for him. She was wearing a black wrap-around skirt with giant yellow sunflowers printed on it and a bright yellow blouse. "I don't have to worry about spotting you in a crowd for sure."

Her smile didn't light up her eyes. He gently pinched her chin with his fingers. "Is something wrong?"

"I'm searching for the same thing you are: the truth. Mom is in no shape to help me. I feel like I've hit a brick wall."

"Maybe we should join forces."

"Thanks, but I don't trust your partner." She intertwined her arm with his and continued to her car. "Go easy on Mom. She's an alcoholic and hasn't had a drink in days. I don't want her falling off the wagon."

"I'll be as gentle as I can, but I don't control Alton. You know how he can act."

"I'm sure you'll do your best." She stopped in front of her Nissan and flicked the alarm off.

"Is this a company car?" he asked, looking at the mid-sized, mid-priced sedan that appeared to be at least three years old.

"It's mine, all mine." She scrunched up her nose. "I know. It needs washing. I think I'll head over to the car wash on my way to work."

"Can I call you tonight? Pleasure, not business."

"I've been thinking about this, and I'm not sure. Maybe we shouldn't contact each other out of the business realm. I'll always put my father first, and you must put the agency first."

"Those two things don't have to conflict. We're both seeking the truth. What time should I call?"

She chewed on her cheek a while. "I won't be home until late. Seven, maybe even eight."

"I'll call after eight. Have a great day." He helped her into her car, then watched her drive off. He convinced himself that to protect her, he must stay close to her. He wouldn't cross the line and begin a sexual relationship. That wasn't what she needed, wasn't what either of them needed right now.

Samson couldn't believe his eyes. Rosa had just said Harriet was a drunk, but the haggard, jaundiced lush who sat across from him looked nothing like the gorgeous, dark-skinned woman in the photos of thirty years ago. He was amazed her liver hadn't totally dissolved yet. He took a sip of coffee, then set his cup on the kitchen table. She was definitely Ernesta Wells though and had repeated the same story about how Ernesto ended up raising Rosa, but it didn't ring true.

"How active a role did you play in Rosa's life?" he asked.

"I was very active until Ernesto moved her to Miami when she was twelve. Then, I barely saw her."

Samson and Alton couldn't figure out why Ernesto had moved to Miami. All they knew was that he'd sold a large number of holdings after the move. Further investigation revealed that the majority of those holdings turned out to have drug connections.

"When is the last time you saw David?" Alton asked.

She played with the handle of her cup. "The day he found out I was pregnant."

"Are you sure?"

She stared into her coffee. "Positive."

"Do you recognize this woman?" He took a security camera picture of Ernesta Wells out of his folder and pushed it across the table. Harriet glanced at the picture, then began choking.

"What's going on?" Alton demanded as he hopped up, causing his seat to thump back to the floor.

She stared at the picture for what seemed an eternity, then she pushed away from the table. "This interview is over. The next time you want to speak to me, speak to my lawyer." She headed for the door.

Alton blocked her exit. "If you turn evidence over on Ernesto, we can work a deal out for you. Put you into protective custody."

She stepped around him and continued to the front door. "I don't need your protective custody."

"If you can't explain these photos, then maybe I should ask Rosa about them."

Now in the center of the living room, she turned on Alton, poking him in the chest with her finger. "Stay away from Rosa or I swear to God—"

Samson slid between them. "We're searching for the truth, Harriet. You told David that Rosa was in danger by the man who set him up to go to prison." She looked away. "We know it's Ernesto. Help us protect Rosa." He turned her to face him. "Help me protect Rosa."

She studied his face a long while. He was sure she could hear the genuine concern in his voice, but would she act on it? Rosa had said David had shown her more love and caring in the short time she'd known him than Harriet had Rosa's whole life.

"I can't," she cried. "Please leave." She rushed to the front door and opened it. The agents gathered their brief cases and notebooks.

Harriet grabbed onto Samson's sleeve as he walked out of the door. "David will protect Rosa. He always has." She released him and closed the door.

Alton cursed all the way back to their rental car, tossed his brief-case in the back seat, and settled behind the steering wheel. "What the hell's goin' on?" He started the engine and slammed the door closed. "I knew we had her. What power does Rosa have over these people that they'd rather go to jail or die than tell the truth? You'd better be careful messin' with her."

"I don't understand the Ernesto-Harriet dynamic. He still pays for everything of hers, yet she hates him. This doesn't make sense."

Alton checked the rearview mirror as he backed out of the parking space. "That's simple. He's a control freak, and she's money hungry. Do you think she'll tell him about the interview?"

"She'll tell him she was interviewed, but she won't mention her visit to the prison. She was trying to set him up, after all."

❧❧❧

"Angela, please call me," Harriet cried into the cordless phone. "I said I'm sorry. I need your help. Agents…DEA agents were here asking questions. What if they go to Rosa?" The line indicated Angela's answering machine had filled. She replaced the phone in its cradle on the end table.

Her cravings for alcohol were worsening, but she wouldn't give in. Rosa would need her when Ernesto was eliminated from the picture. Thoughts of Ernesto finally falling gave her strength. Seeking a distraction, she sorted through the pictures Rosa had left on the coffee table. Everyone seemed to enjoy the party, except for Harriet. Picture after picture showed her by herself. *They never accepted me into their world. I don't need them or Angela.* Her mind returned to when she first tried to enter Ernesto's world…

Chicago, thirty years ago

Harriet stood at her bedroom window and watched Ernesto work the crowd below. Everyone seemed to be enjoying the Fourth of July pool party. Hundreds of society's who's-who had shown up, eager to welcome the Bolívar baby, but Harriet felt like an outsider and sneaked to her room for a short reprieve.

"So, how's Paris?" Harriet switched the phone to her other ear.

"It's great," Angela replied. "I can't believe I'm actually in Europe. Thank Ernesto again for me."

"You graduated with high honors. We're proud of you."

"How's my niece?"

"She still doesn't sleep through the night, but she's the most beautiful child I've ever seen. Did you get the pictures? She has David's caramel complexion and good hair. Unfortunately, she also has his coal black eyes. Think of how beautiful she would have been with my hazel eyes."

"I'm tired of you degrading our hair texture. It's just as good. Plus, she's a baby. You have no idea what her hair will be like later."

Ernesto looked up at the window with the baby in his arms. He waved at Harriet. She waved back with glee painted on her face as if she were a clown. Her life was perfect: she had a mansion, rooms of designer clothes, cars and, most importantly, lots of money. But, she still wasn't happy. She even missed the arguments she used to have with George. The closest she'd come to having an argument with Ernesto was when he had told her she couldn't even socially drink until after the baby was born. Those months without her booze security blanket were tough. Nightmares of men violating her young flesh had filled her dreams. Glad the dreams had subsided, she swirled her brandy in her glass, then took a sip.

"Ernesto's great with Rosa. You should see him parading her around." Bothered that Ernesto seemed more interested in the baby than her, she finished off the brandy, setting the glass on the window ledge.

"Is something wrong, Harriet? You don't sound like a happy newlywed and mommy."

She fiddled with the heavy green drapes. "I'm just down."

"It's only been a month. I've heard that sometimes new moms go through a depression for a few months. Give it time."

"It's not the baby." Hating that the only person she had to confide in was Angela, she paused. Her sister felt she was the prosecutor, judge, and jury.

"What's wrong?"

"To be honest, it's Ernesto." She picked up the base of the phone and propped it under her arm, then padded across the Persian rug to the sitting area and slouched onto the chaise lounge. She might as well tell Angela the truth and get it over with. "He's boring me to death with this white bread life. Don't get me wrong. He gave me my own bank account. I'm a millionaire," she boasted. "He even puts an additional ten grand a month in to ensure I have enough. He says I shouldn't have to beg him for money." She propped the phone between her ear and shoulder, then ran her hands along her inner thighs. "And he makes love like no other man, but," she sucked air through her teeth, "I don't know. All he cares about is being 'Super Dad.' I need some excitement."

"Don't start this again," Angela warned. "He's perfect for you. I don't know many that could afford you."

"Don't worry. I never make the same mistakes twice. I had my tubes tied."

"Harriet!"

She laughed at the squeak in her sister's voice. "Don't Harriet me. He has his secrets, and I have mine." She thought about his home office. He always kept the door locked. She was his wife and should be allowed in every part of her home.

"Stop making excuses to sin."

Harriet released a belabored sigh. Angela always forced her into the bad guy role. "Don't start that holy mess again. You're my sister. You're supposed to be on my side."

"Because I won't give you your way that means I'm not on your side? I'll tell you what I'm not. I'm not doing this again. God has placed an excellent man in your life. Ernesto took your child as his own and worships the ground you walk on. How can you disrespect him and yourself like this? Think about your child."

"I am. I took the money from David and put fifty thousand of it in a trust fund for the baby. I also convinced Ernesto to set up a fund for her. He thought it was an excellent idea. She'll never have to worry about money or depend on anyone."

Angela's voice rose an octave. "Are you fooling around with David again?"

"Of course not!" She'd approached him, but he wouldn't touch her. He said when he was through with someone that he was through. When he saw she'd had a daughter instead of a son, he had tossed the bag of money at her and walked out. "I can't risk him approaching Ernesto like he did George. I have my eye on someone else."

"You have everything, yet it's still not enough. You'll never be satisfied. I'm not covering for you."

Harriet gritted her teeth. "I'm so sick of your butting in."

"Butting in? You keep drawing me into your mess, expecting me to bail you out when you get in over your head. I can't sleep at night from the guilt I have for covering for you."

"Why are you always so melodramatic? Cool it, Angela. I'm not hurting anyone."

Angela heaved a long, exasperated sigh. "I love you, but I can't live like this."

"What are you talking about now? Okay. Alright, I'll stop talking about my men." She placed her hand on her chest. "I didn't mean to offend your sensibilities. I'm just tired of these prejudiced snobs. I can tell they only tolerate me because of Ernesto. I'll bet they haven't even noticed I've left the party."

"God's given you a blessing in Ernesto and Rosa. Don't—"

"I'm sick of this same ol' sermon, Reverend Angela," Harriet cut in. "I thought you called to tell me about your trip. Stop preaching and tell me about your trip."

"This is more important. I won't stand by and watch you ruin your life."

"I don't need your judgment. I need your love."

"I do love you."

"Then support me! I'm stuck in this lily-white world, not you. I need an escape so that I can be a good wife and mother."

"You are unbelievable," she sniffed.

"Are you crying?" Harriet asked as she crossed the room to the window. Ernesto motioned for her to join the party. She nodded an acknowledgement, then turned her back to him.

"I can't stand by and watch you destroy yourself," Angela said. "You keep asking me to compromise my morals. I can't live like this any longer. It's killing me."

"Here we go again," she drawled out. "You'll beat a point through ten reincarnations. Well, I'm not hearing it. I need to get back to my guests."

"I can't help you if you won't help yourself."

"Help? I don't need help. You're in Paris on my money, aren't you? My way of life is fine when it benefits you."

An extended pause settled on the line.

"You're right. I shouldn't have accepted this gift from you. Why I keep putting my faith in you is the real mystery," she stated. "I'll send you money every pay period until you've gotten every dime back, with interest."

Harriet didn't know how to react to Angela crying. Surely, she wasn't serious. Angela wouldn't abandon her. "Stop this nonsense. It was a gift. I'm sorry. I shouldn't have—"

"I'm partly responsible because I always cover for you. I have to take my responsibility in your situation. I refuse to compromise my principles. I quit."

"But you can't."

"I'll always love you."

Angela's voice contained too much finality for Harriet. "If you loved me, you wouldn't be doing this," Harriet explained.

"I'm doing this because I love you. I can't save you. Only the Lord can. Goodbye." She hung up.

Harriet slammed the phone onto its base. "I don't need you. I don't need anyone!"

CHAPTER ELEVEN

Rosa rushed home from work, took a shower, readied for bed, and then pretended like she wasn't waiting on Samson's call. The clock on the nightstand read 8:13. She opened her journal and began to write.

When I spoke to Mom on the phone, she was sober but she sounded shaken up. She liked Samson, but said Alton was a complete ass. I have to agree with her on this one.

She drew a stick figure with horns and a pointy tail, then labeled it Alton.

I'm glad she likes Samson. He's a good man.

She peeked at the clock—8:16.

I'm afraid Daddy's hiding more from me. He's stressing that I'm in danger too much, like he's trying to make me believe it. I'm not sure if I doubt him because of his past or because of my own insecurities. I'm so off balance right now. I need to steady myself. I need the complete truth.

She picked up the phone, heard the dial tone, and then replaced it on its cradle.

Talking about complete truth. I don't know how this happened, but I'm falling in love with Samson. She felt her face flush with embarrassment. *This doesn't make sense. I'm a logical, rational person. How can I fall so deep, so fast? And don't get me started on the timing.* She paused. *I don't know. All I do know is that when surrounded by darkness, he has become my light, and I'm afraid. I can hear Mom in my head saying how men like Samson are the worst ones, the most deceptive. My logical, rational mind tells me not to listen to her, but that emotional part is afraid he's using me to find out more information about Daddy.*

I can't stand how insecure I've become since finding out about my father. She lifted the pen, ready to scratch out "my father" and replace it with David, but stopped herself. Samson had been correct. Her love for David didn't diminish her love for Ernesto. *David, my father.*

I don't like being afraid of loving someone. I don't like being afraid of what I'll learn next. I guess I'm not insecure, I'm tired. I want peace.

David wants peace. His execution is slated for tomorrow. I've called the warden a few times, asking him to allow me to spend the day with David, but David refuses to see me. I wanted to convince him that he could find peace without dying. A warm comforting feeling enveloped her. *I love him. I'm not ready to give him up. I need more time. We need more time.* She set her pen and journal on the nightstand, then rested her head on the pillow and drifted into sleep.

The phone rang, startling her to full alertness. She inhaled deeply, trying to catch her breath. "Hello."

"Hello, Rosa. It's Samson. Is something wrong?"

Her heart raced, but not because of the start. "I'd dozed off. I'm fine. How was your day?"

"Better now that I'm speaking with you."

"We've got to get you some new lines," she teased.

"That was pretty lame, wasn't it? You'll have to forgive me. I'm out of practice."

"Good."

They talked into the wee hours of the morning about her feelings for David. Samson told her how he'd grown to know him over the past year and how David was no longer the same person as the murderer who was convicted. Rosa felt connected to David through Samson and was grateful they both had come into her life, though she wished it had been under different circumstances.

"The sun will be up shortly," Samson said. "One of these days, we'll have to watch the sunrise together."

"Let me know the time, place, and date, and I'll be there."

"Would you like to go out for lunch tomorrow? Or should I say today?"

The thought of sharing the day with someone who understand how she felt about David lifted her spirits. "I'd love to. Since this is my town, how about I pick the place?"

"Sounds great. Just let me know the time and place, and I'll be there."

"I'll call you in the morning." She looked at the clock, and then laughed. "Or should I say in a few minutes?"

Samson parked their rental car in the hospital parking lot. "Does he know we're coming?" He was exhausted, but they had work to do.

Alton glanced up from his notepad. "Yeah. I just wish we'd waited to talk to Harriet until after we interviewed him. We need to stop rushing and do this right. Connecting all the dots decades later is almost impossible, and they've been together for sixty," Alton said as he drew connections on the paper. "Forty-some-odd years ago, David was the suspect in the murder of a small time drug dealer." He circled the name MacKenzie.

"He's been suspect in several murders." Samson took off his sunglasses and put them in the cubby. Unlike Miami when they'd left, Chicago was bright and sunny. He smiled. *Kind of like Rosa.* He rolled his eyes at himself for being so dopey.

After this interview was their date, and he could hardly wait. When she spoke on the phone about David's execution, she'd sounded withdrawn and lost. David was correct; she did need him.

"Yeah, but this one actually involves Ernesto," Alton said. "When the police interviewed MacKenzie's girlfriend, she said that Ernesto had been harassing her. Mac, that's what they called him, confronted Ernesto. She thought David killed Mac for threatening Ernesto."

"Her story sounds flaky to me." He got out of the car and headed for the hospital entrance.

"To me, too," Alton said as he stepped out of the car and closed the door. "But it's all we have to work with. I'll bet she was banging Ernesto, and Mac found out. David ended up taking over Mac's territory. He killed two birds with one stone, so to speak. David's always protected Ernesto."

"Isn't that kind of odd how he's always protected Ernesto? I don't get it. Rosa said David saved Ernesto's life before. Why are they so tight?"

"I'm not sure, but in the old foster care files it looks like David and Ernesto were raised as brothers. Somehow, David's mother had custody of both boys when she was murdered. The authorities didn't even know they weren't related until they'd been in the system for two years and Ernesto's mother decided to show up. Ernesto was even in the system as Ernesto Martín."

Samson raised a brow.

"That's not it. His mother was a hype when she returned and couldn't regain custody. None of that shit matters anyway. The guys found a box of old files and stuff they think belonged to Gains. Maybe they'll uncover something. How are you making out with Rosa?"

"We have a lunch date."

Alton raised a brow. "Oooh, a little lunch action. I'll bet someone returns with more pep in his step."

"I'm not sleeping with her. I wouldn't use her, or anyone for that matter, like that."

"Listen to me, man. You might as well sleep with her, because once we take down Ernesto, she'll blame you and want nothing else to do with you."

They walked through the revolving doors, weaved through people and down the hallway. "I say get yours while you can. She's too sweet a piece to let slip by. Hell, if she were interested in me, I'd sho' tap that ass."

"I will put my foot up your ass," Samson warned as he punched the button for the elevator. The few people waiting nearby decided to take a different elevator.

"Sorry, man, I got carried away. She's not my type. Fine as hell, but too rich. I can't stand rich people. They think the world owes them everything." They stepped onto the elevator. Alton stared at his large friend.

"What?" Samson asked as he pressed the button for the second floor.

"I'm just thinking that we're closer than that ionic bond crap the nutty professor told us about, but if I show any interest in Rosa, you'd kick my ass...and you two aren't even an item. It's a territory thing."

"You're right. I'd kick your ass, so don't even think about it." The door slid open and they exited. Samson looked at the plaque on the wall to see which direction to go. He motioned to the left.

"Why is Ernesto lying about how he ended up with Rosa, and what's the truth?" Alton commented. "This makes absolutely no sense."

"I'm wondering about why he's lying about the part that isn't illegal but told her the truth about his illegal activity."

Alton stopped in his tracks. "She told you he was laundering money? Why didn't you tell me?"

"She didn't come out and say it, so we have nothing; but yes, she told me." They continued down the hallway.

"I can't believe she told you. Damn, man, think of what she'll tell you after you tap—"

Samson smacked him in the head, then opened the office door.

"May I help you?" asked the receptionist sitting at the front desk.

"We're here to see Dr. Wells," Alton said. "He's expecting us. Mr. Miles and Mr. Quartermaine."

"Go on back." She motioned to the door. "It's the third door on your left."

George welcomed the agents into his office and offered them a seat. "I'd just returned from vacation when you called this morning, Agent Miles. I came into the office just for this meeting. What is this about, gentlemen? Is there something going on in the clinic?"

"We have a few questions about your ex-wife, Harriet Bolívar."

George almost tripped. "Harriet?" He settled behind his desk. "What would you like to know?"

"Let's begin with the circumstances of your divorce."

"It had nothing to do with drugs."

"Why would you think it had something to do with drugs?" Alton asked.

"Why else would the DEA be knocking at my door?"

Alton laughed at himself. "I'm sorry. I'm also sorry our questions make you uncomfortable, but we must ask. We know she was cheating on you."

George stiffened. "Yes, she was," he said through tight lips. "Is she in trouble? I know David's execution is tonight."

Alton and Samson moved to the edge of their seats. "You know about David?" they asked in unison.

George tilted his head to the side. "Of course, I know about David. She was cheating on me with him."

"What!" Alton hopped out of his chair.

George's eyes grew large. "What's going on?"

"You mean you saw in the newspaper or on the news that David is actually Rosa's biological father?"

"No," he answered slowly. "I thought you knew about the affair."

"Why don't you tell us in your own words what you know about David, Harriet, and Ernesto?" Alton asked.

George glanced at the picture of his present wife and grown children that sat on his desk. "She cheated with David on me. I kicked her out of the house, and David ended their relationship because she'd threatened to have an abortion. Then she met Ernesto. I tried to warn him about Harriet, but he was so in love. I know how he felt. Harriet had a way of making a man feel like he was the master of the universe. He divorced her within a few years. I'm glad he kept the baby though."

"What is the time period between the time you kicked her out and David broke up with her?" Alton asked.

"In less than twenty-four hours I kicked her out, David broke up with her, and she met Ernesto." He shook his head. "She's a fast worker."

Alton stomped and slapped his leg. "This is un-fucking-believable."

"What's going on?" George asked.

"We're investigating Ernesto," Samson said.

They'd assumed George and Harriet were separated when Harriet met David, then the divorce followed later.

"You two divorced for irreconcilable differences, correct? Didn't you think the child may be yours?"

Shame marred George's dark features. "I know what you're thinking," he replied softly. "How could I walk away from what could have been my child without a fight?" He paused. "Everything happened so quickly. I was hurt, angry, embarrassed, demoralized…the list goes on and on. Then Harriet found another man the next day," he bit out. "I'll admit it. I hated her. I wanted nothing to do with her, including her child. I tried to warn Ernesto, not out of concern, but out of revenge. She was winning again. She always got over…always.

"I was so consumed with hating Harriet that I never considered the child she carried could be mine. It took me years to admit that I may have a child out there who I'd turned my back on, and the guilt was overwhelming. Then when Harriet divorced Ernesto, I had to know what I'd put my child into. I went to Ernesto. He showed me pictures of Rosa and explained about Harriet's drinking problem." His eyes returned to the family portrait. "She'd started drinking heavily during our marriage. I'm just grateful Ernesto kept Rosa."

Both agents remained silent while George composed himself.

Samson wrote a few notes on his legal pad. They were running out of time, and he needed to speak with David before the execution and convince him to open up. He checked his watch, forty minutes until his lunch with Rosa. He would call David after the date.

"Ernesto left a few messages on my answering service," George said. "He said it was important. I thought it was about Harriet, so I didn't answer."

"The government is about to send you on an extended vacation," Alton said.

George frowned.

"Protective custody until we're sure you're safe." Samson didn't believe the information George divulged warranted protective custody, but they'd rather be safe than sorry. There was no telling what Ernesto would do once he saw the lies he'd spun unravel.

Samson laid the comforter out under the shade of the tree, then helped Rosa spread out their lunch. He wished his mind were half as peaceful as the view of the lake. He'd barely said a word to Rosa; all he could think about was what George had said. "It's beautiful out here, and the weather is perfect."

"I love June. And not only because it's my birth month." She placed a fried chicken breast, a heaping helping of potato salad, collard greens, and cornbread on a sectioned plate, then scooped out some garden salad into a plastic bowl. "What type of dressing do you want?" He didn't answer. "Samson, what type of salad dressing do you want?" She set his plate of food and bowl in front of him.

"Italian."

She handed him the dressing and a bottle of hot sauce.

"Thank you. Did you make this?" He took two sodas out of the cooler, handing Rosa one.

"Of course," she said as she fixed her plate. "I also made dessert."

His brows rose. "When did you have time to do all of this?"

"I skipped work today." She hunched her shoulders. "I just didn't have it in me to go." After saying grace, they began eating.

"Whew, you can cook!" He took another bite of chicken and returned to replaying the interview with George.

"Why, thank you," she said softly without feeling.

A cool breeze kicked up off the lake. Rosa was wearing jeans and a Cubs T-shirt. She rubbed her hands on her arms. He took off his suit coat and draped it around her shoulders. "It's a little large, but I think it'll do." He returned to his plate of food, knowing David may not answer his questions, so he needed to ask her about Ernesto and Harriet.

"It's perfect. Thank you." Her smile was sad, yet gracious.

"Before your parents divorced, what was their relationship like?"

"Daddy loved Mom to death. He gave her everything she ever wanted." She picked the skin off her fried chicken leg and tore it into tiny pieces. "Grant Park is fabulous. It's big, but still intimate. If that makes any sense…" She forked the leaves of her collards.

According to his research, after Ernesto purchased the technology firm, he sold many of his original business ventures. Upon further investigation, he found the majority of those businesses turned out to be fronts for money laundering. Directly after Ernesto's divorce, he sold more businesses that could have easily been used for laundering. Ernesto went on two more dumping frenzies: one right after he moved from Chicago to Miami, and the last directly after David was convicted of murder. He wondered what happened to instigate these sales and if Ernesto owned any more money laundering businesses. He'd make sure to keep an eye out for Ernesto's future deals. "Do you remember the last time Ernesto started unloading his holdings in companies outside of Bolívar International? It was after you finished grad school. He sold off his auto dealerships and restaurant chains."

"I thought this was a date."

"I'm sorry." He scooted closer to her but couldn't take his mind off the sales or the interview with George. He tried paying attention to Rosa, but all he kept thinking about was Ernesto didn't meet Harriet until after George had kicked her out. Thus Ernesto had known she was pregnant, possibly with David's baby. What he couldn't figure out was why she married Ernesto instead of David or why Ernesto decided to marry Harriet.

"…Are you listening to me, Samson?"

"Oh yes. It's a beautiful park."

She pushed him away. "I said that I haven't been to the Field Museum in years. I was asking if you'd like to go sometime."

"Of course, I'm sorry. My mind was on other things." He ate some more of the perfectly seasoned greens. "This is excellent. Really."

She continued talking about the sights they could see and events they could attend while he was in Chicago. Deep in thought, he wondered if Harriet knew Ernesto and David were friends when she met him. None of this made sense. "How did Ernesto and Harriet meet?"

Her eyes turned to black ice and face became hard. "Goodbye, Samson." She pulled off his suit coat and tossed it at him.

"I'm sorry. I'll stop."

"Too late. You aren't using me against my father." She grabbed the bowl of potato salad, snapped on its lid, then threw it into her basket. "I'm such an idiot." She snatched the platter of chicken, dropping a few pieces off.

"I was out of line. I should have left work at work. Please stop."

"You can't leave work at work. I'm part of the work. Daddy's changed. Yes he did a few things he shouldn't have, but the statute of limitations is up."

"Why don't we start this date over?"

"Let's not and say we did." Hands shaking in frustration, she threw them up. "You can have the food." She walked off.

"Damn," he said under his breath. He couldn't believe he'd been so stupid and rude. "I'm sorry, Rosa." She didn't even glance over her shoulder. Instead of following, he cleaned up, thinking she needed time to cool off, and he needed time to get his act together.

"Please don't say I told you so," Rosa drawled as she plopped onto her plush white sofa. Using one of the smaller throw pillows to prop up her head, she resituated the phone.

"He grilled you today because he's trying to tie me to David," came Ernesto's agitated voice. "I know you have feelings for Samson, but you're nothing more than a case to him. He'd do and say anything he needed to use you against me. It doesn't matter that I've changed."

"I know, I know. I just..." she trailed off. He'd acted so kind, caring and loving. In a way, he reminded her of Ernesto. She had a thing for knights in shining armor. She didn't want to believe it had all been an act, but she couldn't take any chances. They'd punish Ernesto for the person he was, not is, and she couldn't allow it.

"What did he ask?"

"Questions about how you and Mom met." The sound of Ernesto cursing under his breath perked her ears up. He rarely cursed, and she didn't see why his meeting her mother would upset him or Samson for that matter. Samson's aloofness bothered her, but what worried her was his obvious distress. "How did you meet Mom?"

"I met her in a bar. It doesn't matter. We have more important things to cover. Has David tried to contact you?"

"No, he hasn't, and what bar?" Ernesto drank liquor even less than he cursed and went to bars even less than that. But, this was thirty years ago. She rationalized that maybe he'd changed after he married.

"I already have the DEA after me. I don't need you hounding me, too!"

She couldn't believe that he'd spoken to her like that. Dumbfounded, she sat up.

"I'm sorry," he said gently. "I'm just under so much stress."

She couldn't speak. The possibilities of what he wasn't telling her had robbed her of her voice.

"Please, Rosa, I'm worried about your safety; I'm worried about your mother; I'm worried that Anna won't forgive my past; I'm worried they're trying to send me to prison. I'm innocent. It's all getting to me. I apologize."

"I understand," she said, but she didn't.

What isn't he telling me? What did Samson find out—what?

"Let's tell the DEA everything. They're going to find out anyway. You're making yourself look guilty."

"No. This is my decision to make. I'm not telling. I won't risk you. You need to be worried about your safety, not how I met Harriet. Has David tried to contact you?"

This couldn't be her father on the phone. It wasn't like Ernesto to repeat himself. He was acting so strange. Then again, she'd gone through a lot of changes in the past few days also. This whole situation was wearing on everyone involved. "No, he hasn't." And she didn't know the drug world. Maybe she was in danger and should listen to him. He'd never led her wrong before. The answers weren't clear. She'd just follow her own heart.

"Be careful. David was always up to something. If he tries to contact you in any way, call me immediately."

"I will. I need to get going. Love you."

"Love you more." They disconnected.

I hope I didn't come on too strong, thought Ernesto as he exchanged the phone for Rosa's first grade picture. She'd had to start school with a cast on her arm. He tapped the glass. *I'll always protect you...*

Chicago, twenty-four years ago

Ernesto looked over the top of his newspaper at Rosa, who was sitting at a miniature oak desk, similar to his, and a multi-colored balloon tapestry office chair custom made for her. She glanced from her work, smiled sweetly, then continued writing.

His heart swelled with pride. She was definitely a daddy's girl. Ernesto found himself doing double time to undo any damage he thought Harriet might be causing. At first, he resented being stuck with Rosa, but somehow she had worked her way through his protective shields and commandeered his heart.

Unsure what to do about Harriet, he felt trapped. He'd given her everything and treated her like she was his all and all, yet she never had enough. He looked around his office. Inside these four oak paneled walls was his sanctuary; the only place in the house where Harriet wasn't allowed.

He chuckled to himself. When Rosa was around a year old, she'd toddled in saying, "Dadda." He'd instinctively known she was trying to escape from Harriet.

He set his *Wall Street Journal* on his neatly kept desk. "What are you working on over there?" He'd enrolled her in summer school, so she wouldn't be stuck with Harriet while he was at work. The school was more of an all-day playgroup, so she shouldn't have had any homework.

"I'm writing a report," she said with all seriousness and a hint of a Spanish accent as she brushed her naturally curly, black hair behind her shoulders with her hands.

He raised a brow. "A report?"

"*Sí.*" She skimmed over what she'd written, pushed away from her desk, straightened her pink and white pinstriped dress, grabbed her report, and marched over to Ernesto's desk.

To match her seriousness, he snapped his business face firmly into place and slowly spun his chair around to her. She stood tall in front of him with her head held high and shoulders back, yet was the tiniest little thing.

"Can I go to your next board meeting?"

He'd taken her to the office a few times, and she'd loved it. "Not my next one, but I'll see what I can arrange."

She twirled a few of the baby hairs beside her ear between her fingers. "Then would you peezent this to them for me?" She handed the report to him.

"Present," he corrected.

"Present," she repeated with a charismatic smile and business face similar to his.

He read the report to himself. *Objetib. To git Daddy time auf to do what he want to do and spend time with his frindz...*

He hugged his baby girl, the only person who always put him first and cared about his well-being. He kissed her forehead, then picked her up and set her on his lap.

"When I grow up, I'm going to buy you this whole wide world." She took the report from him and stretched forward, placing the report in his outbox.

His eyes opened wide, and he pulled back slightly. "The whole world?"

"Umm hmm and the moon," she tossed over her shoulder.

"Whoa, the moon, too. What about you? Don't you want anything?"

"I want," she flashed a billion watt smile and tapped her lip with her index finger, "for you to take me to your next board meeting, so I can make them stop working you too hard."

"So hard," he corrected.

"So hard," she repeated. A much better reader than speller, she turned to the newspaper and began pointing out the words she recognized.

She had the same fire that he always envied in David. Now, he had his own piece to do with as he pleased.

If David had been tamed and trained properly, the DEA wouldn't be hounding him. He controlled the drug industry in the Midwest, most of the eastern half of the country and parts of Canada, but Ernesto worried David's wild streak would lead to their ruin. Ernesto had made it too far in the legitimate world to be taken down by David's actions. David wanted Ernesto to take the second-man role in the drug side of the business, claiming Ernesto's hands had been clean long enough; it was time for him to come out of hiding. Ernesto reminded David that the reason they'd done so well was because they'd never mixed territories and Ernesto's laundering role remained secret. No blurring of power.

Unsure of what he wanted, he dragged his hands over his face. His legitimate business had grown to be comparable to David's drug syndicate, but he wasn't ready to let go of his piece of the drug world. The drug world brought a rush to him that he couldn't explain or let go of—not yet.

"What's this word, Daddy?"

"Erickson." He watched over Rosa's shoulder, helping her with the words she didn't know. She would grow up to be his soldier. With the realization of what he wanted came a grin; he wanted it all, and Rosa would be his way of obtaining it. His crowning glory would be when she was head of both the business and drug worlds.

He never had anything of his own: not as a foster child or as David's partner. Even thirty percent of Bolívar International belonged to other stockholders. He stroked her bushy hair with his fingers and straightened her pink headband. He finally had something of his own.

"Hey!" She pointed to an article about Bolívar International winning a riverboat casino contract. "That's our name. What does it say?"

Every day he'd read at least one article to her and explain its content. His computer technology firm had grown quickly and taken over a large share of the market. He could envision every household having a home computer in it someday. With inspiration from raising Rosa, he had also capitalized on the children's educational software and computer markets.

A knock at the door interrupted him. "Come in," he said.

Harriet stood in the doorway of the office. "The car's outside, sweetie. Time to go. I know you don't want to miss the fireworks. Have you changed your mind, Ernesto?"

"I think I'll pass this year."

"Can I stay here with you?" Rosa asked.

He placed her on the floor. "Women need special time to themselves. This time is for you and your mother." He tapped her nose with his knuckle. She hugged him, and then skipped out of the room a happy six year old. Harriet followed close behind.

Ernesto crossed the room and slid the portrait of him and Rosa that hung on the wall opposite Rosa's desk to the right, revealing a safe. Turning the knob left, then right, then left again, he opened the safe. His head of security had suggested updating the surveillance in the house so every inch would be watched at all times, but Ernesto balked. He didn't like the idea of anyone having recordings of who entered and left his residence or what went on inside of his home. He conducted minimal cartel work from home and didn't believe in leaving paper trails, so his safe provided more than enough interior security.

He took out a long velvet box and examined the emerald bracelet inside. Anna would love the bracelet he'd bought for her. Unlike Harriet, she was truly appreciative.

"Daddy!"

Rosa's terrified scream sent Ernesto into virtual cardiac arrest. Harriet's cries for help followed almost simultaneously. The bracelet and jewelry box fell to the floor as he ran for his baby.

"Daddy!" She continued calling for him between loud crying fits.

The hallway seemed to lengthen with his every stride, turning his home into the house of horrors. What if one of the cartel's rivals put a hit out on his baby like they'd done David's son? How had they found out who he was? Speaking of security, where was his? How had anyone gotten close enough to hurt his Rosa? He'd never imagined he could experience more fear than when Mac held a gun to the base of his head. Now he was living it. He chastised himself for considering allowing Rosa into the drug world.

"*Papi!*"

"I'm coming, baby!" He couldn't move fast enough. Rounding the corner, he looked over the balcony. Harriet was crouched over Rosa who was lying on the marble floor crying. He missed more steps than he hit on his way to his baby. "What happened?"

Rosa swiped the tears out of her eyes, then reached her hand out to him.

Harriet's whole body quaked. "Sh-she fell. She fell!"

Thinking she'd sprained an ankle, he put his arms under Rosa's legs and back. As he lifted her, her forearm turned an unnatural way. Rosa screamed out in pain and buried her head in his chest.

"Oh my God!" Quickly, gently, he grabbed the arm before causing more damage and ran her outside to the limo that was to take them to the fireworks show. "Hospital!" he snapped at the driver.

Harriet barely had time to hop in before the car sped off.

Rosa's dazed, blank stare traveled over Ernesto's face. He knew her arm had to be killing her, but she'd stopped the loud crying. She was a tough cookie, just like David. Tears still flowing, she buried her face in the crook of his arm.

Harriet stroked Rosa's hair. "It'll be okay, sweetie."

Ernesto ripped his focus from Rosa to Harriet. "How did this happen?" he bit out.

She continued stroking Rosa's hair. "She fell off the banister."

"How the hell…" he trailed off, drew in several deep breaths and released them slowly. "Why was she on the banister?"

"She'd wanted to slide down. I didn't think she'd fall." She wiped the tears from her eyes.

Rage quickly consumed him. "How could you be so stupid? She could have been killed." He turned his massive body, so Harriet couldn't touch his daughter. "We'll discuss this later."

❧

"Is it safe to speak?" Samson asked into the phone in Spanish. He knew the trouble he would be in for arranging this call outside of the agency's radar, but he needed privacy.

"Yeah," David said. "I guess shuffling-ass Giles ain't all bad."

"I need your help."

"I'm busy preparing to die. What the hell do you want?"

"I messed up with Rosa today." Now he could clearly see how distraught she'd been. Just as he'd done with his sister, he'd allowed his job to interfere. *Shit.* "She won't even speak to me." Deciding if he should tell David everything, he smoothed down his goatee. There was no sense in denying his feelings. He knew what he wanted. "I've fallen in love with her."

"Why the hell you tellin' me? Go tell her."

"I can't. Everything's so convoluted. Please, David, give me some clarity. Give Rosa and me a chance."

After a long pause, David said, "I can give you a little clarity, but I won't cop to anything illegal."

"How did Ernesto end up marrying Harriet? Why did they divorce? Why does Ernesto go through selling spurts every few years? And what happened in the MacKenzie murder?"

"Damn! You want to know all my business. I'm not telling you shit about Mac unless you promise not to stall my execution with another prosecution. I'd deny everything anyway, so you'd be ass-out."

Knowing David wouldn't give him enough information about the murder of Mac, he agreed to the terms. David spent the next two hours telling Samson everything from his affair with Harriet, to how he'd watched Rosa grow up from afar. He also told Samson that every few years Ernesto tried to make a break from the drug world and how he'd saved Ernesto's life from Mac.

"You set Harriet up." Alton would get a kick out of this. He mulled over if he should ask the next question. The old saying, "nothing beats a failure but a try," came to mind. "When did Ernesto stop laundering for you?"

"All I can say on that subject is that Ernesto isn't the same person today as he was when we set Harriet up. He was never really in the game."

Samson grabbed onto the tiny ray of hope and ran with it. "So he's changed. His money laundering days are over."

"He's changed. Don't worry about Ernesto. I'll take care of him. You just protect Rosa from my enemies."

Samson noted David didn't include Ernesto as his enemy. Maybe he'd been wrong about Ernesto, and David was actually angry with him about letting out their secret.

"Thank you." David spoke in double meanings quite often to throw people off, so he needed to meet Ernesto and judge for himself.

After a long pause, David said, "No one can replace the son I lost, but I consider you my son. I take care of my family."

Samson was left momentarily speechless by David's admission. "You mean a lot to me, too."

"Now, don't go all soft on me. You're a good man. You'll be good for Rosa."

CHAPTER TWELVE

It was done. Rosa used the remote control to turn off the television, then she balled up in a fetal position on the living room couch in a heap of tears. Her father was actually dead. It was all so senseless. He was young and full of life. He shouldn't have died.

She reached across to the coffee table for the cordless phone, dialed the first six digits of Ernesto's number and hung up, thinking it wasn't fair to seek comfort from him. The phone fell from her hand and quietly thumped onto the plush carpet.

Piled on her sorrow was worry about Samson. She knew he'd grown close to David and would need comforting. In a way, they were both isolated from their families, thus needed each other.

The phone rang. "Hello," she answered.

"I know it's late, but I knew you'd be awake," Samson said. "I'm sorry about earlier. I'm sorry about David. I'm sorry."

Relief swept over her. She knew he was in a difficult position, and she should have been more understanding. She wiped the tears from her eyes. "How are you holding up?"

"Come to the door and see."

Emotionally drained, she thought she'd heard wrong. "Excuse me?"

"I said come to the door and see."

Cordless phone in hand, she padded out of the living room and peeked into the entry hallway at the frosted windows framing the front door. She would recognize Samson's giant of a silhouette anywhere. She slid across the marble floor and opened the door.

Samson stood in the doorway with his arms outstretched. "We have to stop meeting like this."

She hopped her bunny-slipper, rainbow pajama-wearing self into his arms. She'd never been so happy to see anyone in her life.

He carried her into the house and gently kicked the door closed. The moonlight streaming through the kitchen window provided the only light. "Which way?" he asked.

"Just go straight and turn left." She rested her head on his shoulder and felt anchored for the first time in days.

Samson stepped into the living room. "I'm putting you to bed." He turned and went down the other hallway. "Which door is it?"

"Last one on the left." She gazed into his face, wondering if they had a chance. Ernesto wouldn't protect himself, so she had to protect him. What would Samson do when he found out she'd been withholding vital information? She relaxed in his arms. She wasn't ready to deal with the future. She needed to accept David's death. "I'm glad you came."

He set her on the bed. "I'm glad you allowed me in." He knelt in front of her, took the slippers off her feet and set them under the edge of the bed, then rolled down the covers. "You've been through a lot these past few days. I know you're exhausted." He tucked her in.

"What are you planning on doing?" she asked. "Leaning on the bed all night?"

"If I have to." He fingered the curls by her ear.

She scooted back and patted on the bed for him to lie beside her. He hesitated, then kicked off his shoes, set his cell phone on the nightstand and lay on the bed, fully clothed. They eventually fell asleep in each other's arms, and both had their first peaceful sleep in a long time.

Harriet drank sparkling grape juice to celebrate David's demise. "One down, one to go."

She wanted to call Rosa and console her, but she still hadn't figured out how to explain why she hadn't stayed at the hospital when Rosa was a child and had broken her arm. After she could come up with a good enough answer for those questions, she'd work on an explanation for her marriage.

Thinking back, she could see Rosa's point. *I should have stayed at the hospital, but everything happened so fast. I was distracted...*

Chicago, twenty-four years ago

Harriet had never seen Ernesto so angry, but she understood and agreed with him. They were both terrified. In a way, his anger turned her on. It showed he had life.

She went home from the hospital and poured herself a rum and Coke. If anything ever happened to Rosa, she'd never forgive herself. She guzzled down the drink, and then poured another, this time straight rum.

A chill went down her spine. She'd actually considered aborting the one person who loved her unconditionally. She thought about the bouquet of dandelions and clover that Rosa had picked for her. She'd spent all afternoon in the park selecting only the best flowers for her mommy. Harriet held the glass of rum close to her chest, wishing it were Rosa.

She walked out of the study and headed up the winding stairwell to her bedroom. She was lucky to have caught a man like Ernesto. He was generous and genuinely loved Rosa. She looked over the banister and thanked God for saving her baby. Her neglect could have killed her little girl. She rushed down the hallway, away from the scene of Rosa's fall.

The house line rang as Harriet passed Ernesto's office. She stopped at his door. He'd never allowed her into his home office. The shrill ring of the phone continued. She hesitated, then marched into the office and answered the phone. This was her home, too.

"Hello, Bolívar residence."

"Hello, honey," Ernesto said, sounding as warm and loving as usual. "I wanted to let you know the baby is fine, but more importantly, I wanted to apologize for yelling at you. I overreacted. This was an accident."

She settled in the leather executive chair behind his desk. A sensitive man, he had never raised his voice to her before. "I don't know what I was thinking. How is she?"

"She's my little trooper." He chuckled. "She'll be taking over the hospital any second now. We'll be home in a few hours. I love you."

Ernesto's sweetness brought a smile to her face. He was so unlike the men of her childhood, or any man for that matter. "I love you, too." She hung up, then leaned back in his chair, inner thighs tingling with thoughts of how he'd make up for his behavior. Ernesto was always so controlled. The only place he showed her true fire and passion was in the bedroom. None of her men had come close to Ernesto's lovemaking skill, not even David. If she could get Ernesto to be the same tiger out of the bedroom, she wouldn't have to look elsewhere for excitement.

She saw a picture of Ernesto tossing Rosa, who was a toddler, into the air sitting on his desk. They were so cute together. He seemed to come to life whenever Rosa was around. Sometimes she thought he pushed Rosa too hard. Her baby girl was bilingual, had a larger vocabulary than most of the adults Harriet knew, and acted more mature.

Harriet didn't interfere with Ernesto's teaching. Somehow he'd found a way to control the fire she'd inherited from David, adding in his own charisma and business sense. With Ernesto's training, Rosa would be CEO of the largest corporation in the world someday and never have to depend on anyone.

She scanned the office from his desk. There were several pictures of Rosa throughout, but none of Harriet. A familiar feeling stirred in her gut. Ernesto said and did everything like a man who loved his wife, but she didn't feel any emotion behind his words. Often, Harriet felt as if he married her for the baby. She pushed her jealousy of Rosa away as silliness. Ernesto spent freely on them both. It was she who couldn't love a man.

Anxious to see what type of "work" her baby was into, she crossed over to Rosa's desk and searched. Just about every time Harriet asked Rosa to go shopping with her, Rosa would say, "Sorry, Mommy. I have work to do."

Seeing a picture of herself, Harriet smiled. Rosa was the one person Harriet knew would never turn on her. She sighed, missing her sister, twisting the ends of her shoulder length hair between her fingers. Someday Angela's dirt poor, preacher husband would show his true colors, and Angela would come running back to Harriet. Of course, she'd take her in. Angela may have disowned her, but Harriet would never turn her back on her sister.

The open safe grabbed her attention. She returned Rosa's desk to the way she'd found it. Like Ernesto, Rosa was orderly and would notice if anything were out of place. She padded over to the safe and tried to peek in. The safe was too high for her to see into. She dragged a straight-backed chair from his four-seat conference table and placed it under the safe.

The glitter of a bracelet on the floor caught her eye. She picked up the string of emeralds; Ernesto obviously wanted to surprise her. She dismissed all misgivings about his feelings toward her. He was just giving them both what he thought they needed. She set the bracelet back on the floor beside the box to keep from ruining Ernesto's surprise.

She climbed on the chair and fingered through the safe. A pile of papers presented nothing exciting. She reached further to the back and pulled out a stack of cash, fifty-dollar bills. So far, his office was as boring as Ernesto. She didn't know why he wasted energy keeping her out.

A whiff of Tea Rose enticed her to sort through the papers to see if Ernesto had hidden a bottle of perfume for her, but she found none. She wasn't crazy. She knew the faint scent of her favorite perfume. She looked through the papers and saw a few colored envelopes. Realizing some of the envelopes were scented, she frowned and opened one.

…The diamond earrings are beautiful, but I'm not comfortable accepting them. I love you for you, not the things you buy me.

Furious he'd spend her money on some other woman, Harriet cursed. Ernesto was just gullible enough to fall for such a lame line. She'd kill him. Ernesto's money belonged to her, and she had no intentions on sharing. *Humph, all this time he's been pretending, just like David.*

…I'll always love you. Anna

She only knew one Anna—Rosa's kindergarten teacher. Seething, she slammed the box on the desk. She, Harriet, was way more attractive than Anna. Not only was Anna as big as an ox, she looked like one, too. She reread the love letters. There was no way she'd be played for a fool by Ernesto or any man. She'd tolerated him long enough. Men weren't worth fighting over. It was time for her to move on with her baby and collect a fat alimony and child support check. Staying a part of Rosa's life would cost Ernesto dearly.

Quickly, she put everything back into the safe, replaced the chair, and straightened the office. She had a lot of calculating to do and calls to make before Ernesto returned home.

Rosa woke in Samson's loving embrace, but she didn't want to open her eyes. Hurt that Ernesto never called to comfort her, she wanted to stay in this place forever.

Samson's cell phone rang. She felt him roll away. From the first moment they'd met, she had known he was special. She searched her soul for why he'd become so special so fast, but she couldn't find a logical explanation. It was as if their being together was fate. Whatever the reason, she thanked God for his goodness and prayed Samson would continue standing by her. She wanted everything with this strong, loving man, but couldn't give her all until after the DEA finished investigating Ernesto.

"What do you want, Alton?" he said quietly as he spooned Rosa into his body. "I didn't realize it was so late. I overslept... I know I'm not in my hotel room, but thanks for telling me..." She felt him toying with the curls by her ear. "None of your business. I'll be in when I get in." He disconnected, gently kissed Rosa on the ear, then got out of the bed.

A few seconds later, she heard running water. She opened her eyes and saw he'd left his cell phone on the nightstand, so he wasn't in the bathroom having a secret conversation with Alton.

He returned to the bedroom. "Go back to sleep." He grabbed his cell phone. "I need to go to the hotel and wash my funky butt."

"You really know how to turn a girl on."

"I wish I could stay with you today, but we have a lot of work to do. I'm already an hour late. I heard about a free concert in Grant Park the Chicago Symphony Orchestra is giving. Do you want to go tonight?"

"Sounds terrific."

He rested his forehead on hers. "I know your mind and heart are being tugged in a thousand directions right now. I know there are things you want to tell me but can't. Just know that I'm here for you. I'm not going anywhere."

Grateful for the reprieve, she hugged him tightly, praying he could feel the love she felt for him through her touch. He kissed her lightly, then reached in his back jeans pocket and pulled out a letter. "I meant to give you this last night, but I forgot. It's from David." He handed it over.

She fumbled with the letter, then slowly opened it.

"I guess I should give you some privacy," he said nervously.

She reached for him. "I'd like for you to stay." Two photos fell out of the envelope. Joy from David's love and sadness from his death battled for control. The first photo was of David holding his son and embracing his lover, Rosa. The second photo was of David beaming with pride as he held his baby daughter, Rosa.

"He always loved you," Samson said as he embraced her.

"I wish we'd had more time," she murmured. "Would you please read the letter?"

Holding her with one arm, he unfolded the notebook paper with his free hand. "I wish I had eloquent words to take away your pain. I wish I had chosen the path in life that would have allowed me to show my love for you. I pray you understand that no one can take me from you. I pray you understand I am always with you, loving you, protecting you. My love for you will never die. Your father, David."

Missing her father, she sunk fully into Samson's embrace.

After a second and third call from Alton, Rosa insisted Samson leave. She tried to take her mind off her fathers by throwing herself into work, but it took her three hours to apply a small update to Bolívar International's network system when it should have been an hour job. She knew it was irrational, but she was angry with Ernesto for not calling her. David was his best friend and her biological father. How could he just let his death pass without a word? How could Ernesto not realize that she needed him to be there for her as he always had?

The phone rang, startling her. She peeked at the caller ID, inhaled and exhaled deeply, then answered the phone in the calmest voice she could muster. "Hello, Samson."

"Hello, baby."

She warmed at his term of endearment. "Aren't you supposed to be working? Alton's going to get you," she teased.

"I think he can hold down the fort alone for a few minutes. How are you coming along?"

"Honestly, I've been better. But I'll make it." She looked out the window of her small home office. Her old journals were packed away in the basement. Maybe it was time to read through them, see if she'd mentioned David and forgotten.

"You will. We will. What did you eat for lunch?"

She tilted her head to the side. "Lunch?"

"Yeah, lunch. You skipped breakfast, so I'm asking about lunch."

She bit on her bottom lip. "Actually," she paused, "I haven't eaten today."

"Go eat something."

"I'm not hungry. I think I'll clean out the basement."

"Rosa, it's three. Make a sandwich, heat up some soup, eat a piece of fruit, cheese and crackers, anything. I don't want you fainting on me tonight at the symphony," he said jokingly, but she heard the concern behind his words.

"Since you put it that way, I guess I'll eat a little something." She heard Alton in the background fussing. "Say hi to Alton for me."

"Stop instigating and go eat. I have to get going. The weatherman says it'll be in the lower seventies tonight by the lake, and we'll have a full moon. Sounds like the perfect night for an outdoor concert."

"I can hardly wait," she answered honestly.

They ended their conversation. Then she went into the kitchen to fix a grilled ham and cheese sandwich. She opened the refrigerator door and found ham, but no cheese. Since it was such a beautiful day outside, she decided to take a walk to the corner store to clear her mind.

She slipped on her sneakers and headed out the door. "Hello, Mr. Stapleton," she said to the mailman.

"Good afternoon, Rosa." He handed her mail over instead of placing it in the box. "How are you holding up today?"

Thanks to the news, everyone knew about David being her father. Mr. Stapleton had always been such a nice man. She knew he was being sincere.

"I'll be fine. Thanks for asking."

She stepped into the house as she sorted through the mail: invoices, junk mail, electric bill, and a package—nothing out of the ordinary. She dropped the junk mail into the kitchen trashcan, filed the electric bill in the appropriate slot in the bill holder, went to her office and set the invoices on her desk, then took a closer look at the thin cardboard package.

It appeared to be another free firewall sample from an upstart company. She didn't feel like opening it. She was tired and needed to eat before Samson called again. She placed the package on the stack of other samples that she needed to go through on her office bookshelf. Her bookshelf was getting cluttered. She sighed, thinking this was kind of like her life. She'd have to clean both up soon.

Samson watched Rosa as she watched the Chicago Symphony Orchestra perform. A cool breeze off the lake chilled the night air. He wrapped his arm around her in the guise of keeping her warm, but he actually wanted to be near her. Holding her last night was the most wonderful, yet one of the hardest experiences, he'd ever had. Making love with her was his desire, but not an option. He took her hand into his and held it to his heart. She'd accepted him, had faith in him and trusted him.

With each passing moment, Ernesto's guilt became more certain An old notebook of Gains had been discovered. Gains had noted connections between David and Ernesto from the time David's mother took Ernesto in when he was three until David and Ernesto were well into the drug industry. Unfortunately, at the time, all of the connections only led to guilt by association where Ernesto's laundering for David was concerned.

Samson didn't know what to do about Rosa. He knew she wouldn't support Ernesto's illegal activity, but how would she feel about Samson after he brought the truth to the light? How could he soften the blow?

After the concert, they took a nice, long stroll through Grant Park and ended up sitting under the same tree where they'd picnicked the previous day.

She settled between his legs with her back leaning against his chest. He wished she could remain within his protective embrace forever. He broke the silence, saying, "Tomorrow morning, we're returning to Miami to prepare for our interview with Ernesto."

She looked over her shoulder into his eyes. He didn't see anger but saw concern. "I know how difficult this is for you," she said. "We're both stuck between that proverbial rock and hard place. I trust you'll find the truth." She returned to watching the moon's reflection shimmer on the lake.

"What if the truth is something you won't like?"

She fully faced him, then took his hand and held it to her heart. Their gazes locked, and he knew that she loved him. He could see it in her eyes, feel it in his heart, and he had no intention on losing it.

"What's your greatest fear?" he asked.

"Daddy's done some things I'm not proud of." She paused. "I'm afraid he's about to make himself look guilty by not cooperating. I'm afraid Alton will use his lack of cooperation as evidence of his guilt. I'm afraid Alton will make up his own truth. I need for you to find the real truth."

"What is the truth?"

"I know my father. The man he is now. He isn't guilty."

Her words said one thing, but her tone said another. He held her close. "Are you convincing me or yourself?"

A long pause was the only thing that stood between them.

"He isn't guilty," she said silently.

She'd been through too much over the past few days. She wasn't emotionally ready to consider Ernesto's possible guilt. After he returned to Chicago, he'd broach the subject again.

"How long will you be in Miami?"

"It depends on what we find."

"Friday the thirteenth is coming up. Maybe you should stay here where I can protect you."

"You're going to protect me?" He rocked her gently. "We'll make it through this, Rosa."

CHAPTER THIRTEEN

Rosa smiled politely across the desk at Jeff Paige, thinking with the way he'd been flirting all morning, there was no way he recognized her. She wasn't shocked or disappointed. They'd never traveled in the same circles. He'd been a senior in high school when she was a freshman. He was a jock, and she was a computer geek. Everyone knew his name, and she was known as "you mean that black girl?" Being one of the few black children in the school was difficult. She swore that her children would only attend racially diverse schools.

He rolled his chair around his desk, closer to hers. "I'll send a limo for you at six for our date."

"I'm flattered, Mr. Paige. But I make it a policy not to date my clients." She continued studying the layout of his current network configuration.

He raised a brow. "I'm not a client yet. Let's say we discuss the possibilities over dinner. And please, call me Jeff."

"How's your father? I haven't seen Mr. Paige in at least three years." She checked her watch. It was almost noon. Samson would be interviewing Ernesto by now.

"If I'd known you would have grown to be so beautiful, I'd have paid more attention to you in high school."

A genuine laugh erupted from her. "You never give up, do you?"

"No." His slow, sneaky grin did nothing for her. "Resistance is futile."

"Why are you setting up a totally different network for this annex?"

"You have a one-track mind." He brushed his hand through his short, mousy brown hair, then leaned back in his executive chair. "I'm experimenting by separating marketing from the rest of Paige Industries. Marketing has become lax because they feel they have a definite client. My intention is to make them work to earn our business. Our business units will now have the option of using outside firms if our marketing team doesn't suit their needs. Cheaper isn't always better, you know. We may even cut the marketing department eventually."

Satisfied with his answer, she asked, "And you want me to test the main corporation's firewalls, correct? Have you been having trouble with hackers?"

"Besides the usual viruses from the Internet, not really. But, I want to make sure. You're the best." He rolled his chair behind his desk, rifled through his bottom drawer, then pulled out a file. "I've checked your record." He set the file on the desk in front of her. "You've hacked into the Pentagon's and NASA's mainframes. Amazing. And it doesn't stop there."

"With permission, of course," she said with a smile she didn't feel. She legally infiltrated systems; therefore, she wasn't a hacker, like in her college days.

"If we have holes in our system, you'll find them. And I want your company to plug them."

"I have all the information I'll need for now. I'll call tomorrow with an estimate on setting up your network for the annex. Who's my contact for testing the main system's firewall?"

"That would be me. We don't trust just anyone with our network system."

"I don't blame you."

"Let's discuss it over lunch."

She laughed as she gathered her paperwork. If nothing else, he was persistent.

He stood, holding out his hand. "I'm wearing you down." He helped her stand.

"I'm afraid I'll have to pass on lunch. I need to get back to the office and write up these plans."

Samson and Alton read over their notes while waiting in the front office for Ernesto. So far, all of their evidence was circumstantial at best. They didn't expect to gain any incriminating evidence from the interview with Ernesto. Instead, Samson would observe him carefully and read between the lines. Samson peeked from his notes at Mrs. Walker. She was warm, kind and full of smiles for him, while she was coldly polite to Alton.

"Are you sure I can't interest you gentlemen in a cup of coffee, tea, soda?" Mrs. Walker asked as she approached them. "I made a special trip on my way in for apple juice, Agent Quartermaine."

"You shouldn't have gone to any trouble for us," Samson said. "Thank you. I'll have apple juice, please."

"It was no trouble at all," she said with wide-eyed enthusiasm. "Anything for Rosa."

Alton grumbled and resituated himself in his seat. "You've been working for Mr. Bolívar for forty years now, right? Since the beginning?"

"Your records are correct." The cheer in Mrs. Walker's voice was nowhere to be found, and the laugh wrinkles about her eyes seemed to frown at Alton. "If you wish to interview me, Agent Miles, you'll need to make an appointment," she stated flatly, then crossed the office to a paneled wall. To the agents' surprise, one of the panels slid to the side, revealing a convenience center.

Samson hopped up. "How did you do that?"

"Magic," she answered, cheer returned. Once Samson stood beside her, she pointed her toe toward two small buttons on the floor.

"You had me going for a second there," he said.

She took a bottle of apple juice out of the small refrigerator and a glass out of the cabinet, then gently stepped on the close button. "My grandchildren get a real kick out of the wall." She handed him the apple juice and glass.

"Thank you."

"And thank you for being there for Rosa."

"You care a lot about her, don't you?" He set the glass on her desk and opened the bottle.

"She has a way of commandeering your heart."

Samson could relate. He poured the juice into the glass, then tossed the bottle into the trash.

"Ernesto's a good man," she directed toward Alton as she took her seat. "But he isn't rational where Rosa's concerned. He's overprotective. Always has been."

"What are you trying to say?" Samson asked.

"I want you to understand that his family was taken from him when he was a child, and I don't think he ever recovered. That's why he's so protective of Rosa. He isn't a money launderer. He isn't a drug lord. But he'll fight against anyone he perceives as threatening his family. I guess I'm asking you to consider his frame of mind when you question him."

"Why are you telling me this?"

A sad smile tipped her lips and moistened her eyes. "Because I love the Bolívars. Over the years I've seen their struggles, failures, and successes. They're like family to me. Ernesto hasn't been himself since Rosa found out the truth. I'm afraid he'll point guilt at himself to keep these drug people away from Rosa. He has changed so much over the years. He isn't the same person anymore."

"Did you know David was Rosa's father?"

"Yes."

"What do you know about David?" he calmly asked.

"I used to send pictures of Rosa to David." She scooted to the edge of her chair. "Now this doesn't mean Ernesto is a money launderer or a drug lord."

"I agree."

The worry lines in her face softened. "I knew you'd understand."

"When you say Ernesto has changed over the years, what do you mean?"

"After Rosa was born, he slowly cut off his relationships with people like David. By the time he was divorced, all ties had been cut. He is a good man now. Please don't prosecute him for mistakes he made so many years ago."

Absorbing this new information, Samson drank his apple juice. Without coming out and saying it, she'd confirmed that Ernesto laundered for at least six additional years. Ernesto had told Rosa he'd quit laundering when she was born. Yet there were still businesses that Ernesto dumped later, which turned out to be fronts for money laundering. He wondered if he would ever discover the entire truth.

"Thank you for your assistance and the apple juice, Mrs. Walker. The Bolívars have a good friend in you."

She flushed, waving him off. "If you need to know anything else, call me." She wrote her home and cell phone numbers on a piece of paper. "I don't care if he fires me. I won't allow him to sacrifice himself needlessly."

⟟⟟⟟

Samson groaned, thinking he should have heeded Rosa's warning about Friday the thirteenth. As expected, Ernesto wouldn't admit to laundering money for David. Instead of following the game plan of observation, Alton went into attack mode. Samson had to give it to Ernesto, he remained calm through out Alton's verbal attack. Too calm.

Samson observed Ernesto's lawyer who was sitting off to the side. He'd forgotten the man was there.

The tiled monitors were on, but the sound was off. Ernesto used the remote to turn off the screens, then set the remote on his desk. "What are your intentions with my daughter, Agent Quartermaine?"

The burgundy leather of the armchair Samson was seated in suddenly became hot. "I only have honorable intentions." Samson loosened his tie.

"Define honorable."

"I wasn't finished," Alton interrupted.

Ernesto nodded slightly. "My apologies. Please continue," he answered, while maintaining eye contact with Samson.

"We know you laundered money for David. We just need a timeline to clear this up. If the statute of limitations is over, you don't have a problem."

"I'm a lawyer, Agent Miles. Even if I'd laundered money for David, I'd never admit it."

Alton smirked. "You insist on doing this the hard way."

Samson could see where Rosa learned her poker face. Ernesto appeared totally unmoved by Alton. He remained seated and calm, as if to seem smaller. Even at sixty-two years old, Ernesto was a physically imposing figure.

"Rosa said you laundered money for David. Are you saying she's lying?" Alton asked.

"Unlike you, Rosa doesn't lie."

The meaning behind Ernesto's statement swung like a pendulum between Alton and Ernesto. There was no misunderstanding. Rosa couldn't be used this way against Ernesto.

"Since we're on the subject of honesty, how did you come about raising Rosa as your own?"

"Does it matter?"

"Do you know who Randolph Caldwell is?"

"Years ago, he sold me his home," he answered smoothly.

"A three million dollar home for one million. Why such a bargain price?"

"Luck. I was in the right place at the right time."

"Caldwell could have used some of your luck. He was murdered."

"Oh really? I wasn't aware."

Samson noted Ernesto's human nature didn't kick in to ask how, when, or why he was murdered. According to the trial transcript and other sources, Caldwell had a serious gambling problem and owed one of David's crew more than a million bucks. In exchange for forgiving the debt, Caldwell was supposed to embezzle money from Diligent Telecommunications. The authorities didn't catch Caldwell until he'd already sapped over five million from the company.

Caldwell had claimed to be a Martín insider. In exchange for protective custody, he'd promised to tell the authorities everything he knew about the cartel. Unfortunately for Caldwell, someone cut out his tongue and slit his throat before he had a chance to testify. This information had been missing from the case files. A few months later, Ernesto moved from Chicago to Miami.

"Do you know who Judge Winston Truman is?" Alton asked.

"I'm not sure, the name sounds familiar. I meet so many people."

"He's the judge who granted your divorce." He sorted through his notes. "From the time you filed for divorce to the decree only took two days. Wow, that's fast service."

Ernesto remained silent.

"This may interest you. In 1986, Judge Truman was on the opposite side of the bench. Turns out he was on the take for David Martín. He was also murdered before he could turn evidence against the Martín cartel."

"Yes, that's very interesting. It would make for a good book."

"Your name seems to keep popping up with direct ties to people who worked for David. How can you explain that?"

"Six degrees of separation. David and I grew up together, and we were best friends. No crime in that."

"More like a half degree in your case. I'm shocked Mac didn't shoot you for screwing his girl."

Ernesto stiffened and lost the little color he had. Samson saw the fear in his eyes. Not of them, but of something he'd seen, maybe lived through. Ernesto quickly regrouped.

Alton smirked. "Yeah, we heard about how Mac took you out to the swamp to cap you, yet somehow he ended up capped. Looks like you have at least two bestsellers on your hands."

Ernesto's lawyer spoke up, startling everyone. "That will be enough for today, gentlemen." He walked around the desk toward the agents. "My client has been very cooperative and giving of his time. If you have further questions, please contact me."

David was actually gone. Ernesto stood at his floor to ceiling windows, watching the rush hour traffic. The cartel, Rosa, Harriet, all were Ernesto's for the taking, but he couldn't bask in the glory of victory. *Victory.* He leaned his head against the window. The prize for this victory was a cartel he never wanted and the loss of everything: his best friend, his business, his child.

"It wasn't supposed to be like this," he whispered. "What have I done?" He massaged his temples. His guilt had already kept him from comforting his child in her time of need. He didn't have time to wallow in self-pity. He had to do damage control before Rosa found out the truth. As long as he saved his relationship with Rosa, everything else could be damned.

He tapped on the window with his knuckle. He'd known the agents would ask about Mac. He had prepared himself. Yet Alton's timing caught him off guard. He ran his hands over his salt-and-pepper hair. They couldn't touch him. Just as the agents of the past, these didn't have any real evidence.

Mrs. Walker walked into his office. "They're gone."

He glanced over his shoulder at her. "You did a good job. Thanks." He returned to watching the city below. Before the agents arrived, Mrs. Walker had turned on the intercom so Ernesto could hear everything said in the front office.

"I only told the truth." She sat in one of the leather armchairs in front of his desk. "Well, mostly the truth. Samson's coming to my place tonight to continue questioning me."

"I'm not surprised. I'll tell you what to give him."

"What are you going to do about Samson and Rosa?"

"Good question." He turned away from the window, walked over to his desk, then settled into his executive chair. "We'll be working out of the Chicago office until this blows over. I need to see her journal. Find out what's going on in her mind."

"She's not a child anymore. Getting to her journal won't be easy."

"I have a key to her place." An awkward pause filled the air. "I should have never allowed her to move to Chicago."

"You 'allowed' her to move to Chicago? Allowed!" Mrs. Walker laughed, and eventually Ernesto found himself chuckling. "Now that's rich."

"Maybe 'allow' was the wrong word."

"Maybe? Rosa's always been obedient, but she has her own mind. She's independent. We both know why she started her own business in Chicago. You can't control her. She'll find the truth eventually. You can't have Rosa and the cartel."

"I'm too old for this. I'll admit, when I was young I wanted it all, but now that I can have it…" He sighed shaking his head. "I've made too many mistakes."

"You can't have it all. Focus on what's most important to you. You have my support. You won't lose Rosa."

He raised a brow. "And who says Rosa is most important to me?"

A sly grin heaved the corners of her lips upward. "The pride in your voice every time you speak her name." She walked around and positioned herself behind him, then massaged his shoulders. "We entered the drug trade for the money. I know you and David went through that male power struggle thing for a while, but now we're older and wiser. You haven't laundered money in years. Now that David's gone, your last tie to the drug world is gone."

He bit on his inner jaw.

She looked around his shoulder and narrowed her blue gaze on him. "Ernesto! What have you done?"

"I still…" He drew in a deep breath. "I still have five small businesses that launder for the cartel."

"What!" She smacked his shoulder. "How could you? I thought that you finished selling off your laundering businesses after David was sentenced."

"I know this'll sound crazy, but…" He shook his head. "I don't know. They were a souvenir of sorts. They were small-time. Not even a million a year combined," he rambled. "I can't sell them off right now or I'll draw more attention from the DEA. All laundering has stopped, but…" He pushed away from his desk; she moved out of the way of the chair. "I'm not worried about the DEA. They'll never find anything on me or learn of the extra-curricular activities of these businesses, but if Rosa starts searching…" he trailed off. "I've made so many mistakes. She can't find out, Jill."

She took his hands into hers. "Listen to me, Ernesto. You have to tell Rosa the whole truth."

"I can't. She'll never forgive me. That's the one thing I can't take."

"She knows you laundered money for David. Yes she's disappointed, but you've raised a fine young lady. She'll be angry when she hears the truth, but she will forgive you. But she has to hear it from you."

"She's so much like David," he lamented, recalling how David had totally dismissed Harriet.

"What are you saying?" she asked softly.

"When David is through with someone, he is through. Rosa is the same way. It just takes her longer to reach that point. I think I've almost reached that point with her. I can't risk it."

"You should tell her. You have changed."

An anxiety-soaked chuckle weighed him down. "How can I say I've changed when I still have businesses that laundered money until she found out about David? She'll never understand." He tapped the picture of Rosa when she'd broken her arm. He used it as a constant reminder of how he'd failed her. "I've lost two families." He wouldn't give his or David's mother any prizes, but they had cared for him, and he loved them as well. "I can't go through that again. I can't lose Rosa. She's all I have. I don't care what I have to do. She'll never find out about the businesses."

The night he took her home from the hospital, he swore to never fail her again...

Chicago, twenty-four years ago

Ernesto didn't remember leaving his office unlocked until well after he'd sent Harriet home from the hospital.

Rosa woke as he shifted her to his other shoulder. She saw the safe was open. "Ooo, we never leave the safe open, Daddy," she said weakly, the painkillers and long day slurring her speech.

He kissed her forehead. "You're right." He looked through the safe and office, then released a sigh of relief. He should have known everything would be as he'd left it. He had Harriet well trained. He'd have to give her a special treat for being so obedient. He picked the bracelet off the floor and put it into his pocket, closed the safe and allowed Rosa to secure it properly.

He locked his office on the way out. "Time for someone to go to bed."

"Where's Mommy?"

He stopped off at his bedroom, and they both peeked in. Harriet was sound asleep. Disappointed she hadn't waited up until Rosa was safe and sound in her own bed, he carried his baby to her bedroom. He needed time to cool off before playing the adoring husband. He wasn't sure how much longer he could—or should—keep up the act.

He helped Rosa change into her nightclothes and grabbed a brush and spray bottle of water out of her bathroom.

Rosa's light giggle tickled him. "You can't fix hair."

He chuckled as he set her between his legs on the bed. "We can do

154

anything we set our minds to." He moistened her hair enough to loosen the curls, then brushed her hair to the back. "When you grow up, you'll be CEO of Bolívar International. There are no limits." He sang her favorite Colombian lullaby as he worked on her hair.

His large hands were agile, but he needed more practice. He styled her hair into one long, scraggly braid, tying it with a band at the end. "It's not the most beautiful, but at least you won't suffocate yourself with all that hair."

Eyes barely open, Rosa leaned on Ernesto. "It's the most beautiful braid in this wide world," she dragged out with a yawn.

He pulled the covers back and laid on the bed. "I love you, Rosa." "I love you more."

He stroked the tiny curls that framed her face, then softly sang a lullaby about healing. "*Sana, sana, colita de rana. Si no sanas hoy, sanarás mañana...*" As she slept, he gently tapped her cast. He could still hear her terrified scream and her calling for him. He was her only protection from the drug world and Harriet, and he wouldn't fail her again.

The next morning, Ernesto covered his face with the pillow to block out the sunshine streaming through the large picture windows of his bedroom. Too tired to move, he called for Harriet to close the curtain. After giving Harriet the emerald bracelet, he'd spent the remainder of the night having sex. The one place Harriet was giving was in the bedroom. Her sexual appetite almost matched his, and there was nothing off limits. If she'd be more selfless in other aspects of their life, maybe she'd be happier somewhere besides the bed and stores.

He peeked from under the pillow at the clock—7:43. He kicked off the sheet and headed for the shower. If he hurried, he'd be able to drop Rosa off at school. He could imagine her telling everyone how she'd jumped off the balcony and broken her arm. She'd be the talk of the playground.

By the time he finished, Rosa had already left and Harriet was nowhere to be found, so Ernesto went to his home office and called Anna. If he worked things properly, he could meet Anna for a little afternoon action before Rosa came home from summer school.

"Rosa is doing great," he said as he repositioned the phone. "She was up and out before I woke." He heard Harriet pass by his door and continue down the hallway. "I'm sure by the end of the week, she'll have broken her arm from jumping off the roof of the house." He thumbed through a jewelry catalog. He'd need to order another bracelet for Anna.

Harriet walked fully into his office and stood in front of his desk with her arms crossed over her chest and a few papers in her hand. She wore a bright red, warpath business suit and had determination firmly entrenched on her face.

To appear calm, he nodded a polite hello. *Who the hell does she think she is, invading my sanctuary? She must have banged her head against the headboard one too many times.*

Reminding himself to play the loving, docile husband, he maintained his cool façade. He'd lost his control yesterday, but wouldn't slip again. At least not until he found out what she was up to. After the way she'd endangered Rosa, he was seriously considering cutting Harriet loose. "The love of my life needs me. Have the report ready for our one o'clock."

Tapping her foot, Harriet *tsked* and rolled her eyes. "Don't rush on my account."

Harriet was only twenty-seven, too young to be suffering from menopause. He didn't care what the problem was. All he knew was she'd better fix it before he lost his patience. He hung up the phone.

"Won't Anna be upset with you for rushing to speak with your wife?" She tossed the papers in her hand onto his desk. They scattered, littering his otherwise neat and orderly desk.

Cold-busted and shocked, Ernesto had a coughing fit as he sorted through the photocopied love letters Anna had written him.

Smug satisfaction twisted Harriet's delicate, dark features. Her emotionless hazel eyes locked on him. "It would hurt the company's stock price if the world learned of your indiscretion, so I'll remain silent for now. A quick divorce and a settlement will be best for all concerned." She relaxed her arms, allowing her hands to rest on her hips. "I've been to a lawyer. He said you don't have a leg to stand on, and our prenuptial agreement isn't worth the paper it's written on. You will cooperate. I'm no man's fool."

Fully regrouped, Ernesto watched in amazement as she told him what he was going to give her, ticking off the items with her fingers as she spoke. "Two hundred and fifty million to start, then twenty thousand a month in spousal support, and we haven't come to an agreement on the child support." Lips pursed, she rotated her neck. "I know Rosa's worth more than a measly ten thousand a month to you, especially if you wish to see her on a regular basis."

A deep rumble worked its way from his stomach out of his mouth as a laugh. He'd never heard anything so ridiculous in his life. And she stood there so sexy, believing he'd follow her demands.

"This is no laughing matter. We had a good thing, and you blew it."

He continued playing the docile role; her arrogance and greed had led to her ruin. He knew her lawyer told her to remain quiet, but of course, Harriet would do things her way. He remained seated at his desk. With his size towering over her, he wouldn't seem as helpless to her. "I'm sorry, baby. She meant nothing to me."

"Have your shit out of my house by the end of the week." She turned to leave.

He approached her from behind, drawing her into his body. "Honey, please. How can you throw me out after last night? Let me make it up to you." He suckled along her neck, kissing while grinding his arousal into her. Angry sex was some of the best sex. She was so angry with him, she may not be able to walk after they finished. "Don't I mean anything to you?"

She returned his kisses, whispering, "Yes, a paycheck and half-way decent sex." She backed away. "I can get laid any day of the week, and with the two hundred and fifty million…" She hunched her shoulders. "Let's just say, you're dismissed. School's out. Go be with your teacher." She walked out.

He had to give it to her. When it came to money, Harriet didn't take prisoners. He closed his door to start placing phone calls. The only type of check Harriet would be receiving from him was from the bank of reality.

Samson followed Mrs. Walker into her den. The evening sunrays poured through the sliding door, providing plenty of light. Each wall in the sparsely furnished room was covered by built-in bookshelves.

"Please have a seat." Hands full with a snack tray, she nodded her head toward the only seats in the room, overstuffed chairs close to the fireplace.

"Are you sure you don't want me to take that?"

"If you could just clear the stool for me."

He set the magazines on the Oriental rug, then ran his hand along the fine wood of the stool. The base of the stool was carved into a man lying on his back, supporting the seat with his arms and legs. "Rosa has end tables similar to this."

Mrs. Walker set the tray on the stool. "Ernesto gave them to her for her birthday. I do all of the ordering, so I ordered myself one." She turned on the lamps that stood behind each chair. "It'll be dark before we know it."

"You have a lovely home." He found the chair opposite Mrs. Walker very comfortable.

"Thank you. I'm glad you didn't bring your partner."

"Alton takes a little getting used to. I really appreciate your taking the time for me."

"I'll do whatever I can to help." She poured them both a cup of hot chamomile tea. "Would you like sugar, lemon?"

"No, thank you."

She handed him a cup, with a raised brow. "Rosa drinks her tea plain also." She smiled warmly. "You two make a handsome couple."

"I'm worried about Rosa. She's been through so much these past few days."

"She's a strong, young woman. Give her time to adjust."

He took a sip of tea as he sorted through the questions in his mind. If Ernesto was still involved in the drug trade, Mrs. Walker would know, but she wouldn't betray Ernesto to protect Rosa. "Do you know how Ernesto ended up with Rosa? We've heard several versions."

She told him the complete truth, including Ernesto was laundering money for David at the time. "I'm only telling you this to protect Ernesto," she insisted. "He's a changed man. Those days are behind him."

Her admission shocked him, but he remained calm. "What about the divorce?"

She told him Harriet and Ernesto were both cheating, but when Rosa broke her arm because of Harriet's neglect, that was the final straw for Ernesto. Harriet's drinking could have killed Rosa. "Ernesto called David and asked for a favor," she continued. "He said he needed a divorce fast."

"So David set Ernesto up with Judge Truman. But why did Harriet agree to the divorce?"

"All Harriet cares about is money. Ernesto threatened to cut her off if she didn't sign the papers. He had the money and power behind him to do it."

"He still pays her bills, doesn't he?"

"He isn't a monster. Yes, they manipulated Harriet into marriage, but he treated her well and cared for her. He divorced her to protect Rosa."

"Do you know about Rosa Shields?"

Her gaze lowered to her lap. "David's lover. That was so sad."

"Where is she now?"

"In Mexico. She was so full of life. I visit her once, sometimes twice a year."

He tilted his head to the side. "How long have you known Ernesto and David?"

"We all grew up in the same area of town."

"So you really have been there since the beginning." *Another bit of information missing from the files.* He took a sip of tea. "I have to ask something very personal."

"Go ahead."

"Where you and Ernesto ever lovers?"

She choked on her tea. "Oh my. I'm sorry. No, darling, we were never lovers. It would be like dating my brother."

Samson stepped into his apartment.

"What did you think about her?" Alton asked. "What did she say?"

Samson set his briefcase on the coffee table. "You know how the

President sends the Vice President out to say things he can't say himself? Well, that's the relationship Ernesto has with Mrs. Jill Walker." He sat on the small tan couch, kicked off his loafers, then propped his feet on the coffee table.

"So, she knows everything."

"Yep. And she'll only tell us what Ernesto wants us to know. He can't tell us himself or he opens himself up to all types of questions he doesn't want to answer. They're slick. I don't know how we'll catch them. He'll use her to give us information we would have eventually found anyway."

"I know you don't want to, but you have to work the Rosa angle or he'll get away. We have to bring these cartels down."

Samson leaned his head back onto the couch and stared at the ceiling. "I know," he reluctantly admitted. *The best hiding place is in plain sight.* He knew where to look, but he'd need Rosa's cooperation.

"I can't rush Rosa," Samson said.

"With David dead, we're in no hurry. We know Ernesto's our man. I'll make arrangements for our transfer to Chicago."

CHAPTER FOURTEEN

When Harriet first picked up the phone, she thought she was ready to comfort Rosa and answer the questions she knew would come her way. As the ringing filled the line, the excuses she'd made up suddenly sounded flimsy. She quickly hung up.

How will I explain?...

Chicago, twenty-four years ago

Harriet pressed the intercom button to speak with the limo chauffer. "Would you please drive around the neighborhood for a bit? It's such a beautiful day, perfect for a drive."

"Yes, ma'am."

Rosa glanced out the window, then continued admiring the designs and signatures her friends had put on her cast.

Harriet stroked her little girl's hair. *I didn't think this would be so difficult.* "I need to speak to you about something important."

Rosa pointed to the only clear area on her cast. "Don't worry, Mommy. I saved the best spot for you."

What if she thinks the divorce is my fault? I can't lose my baby. I have to make her understand this is all Ernesto's doing.

"You are too sweet. I'll be sure to put a special design for my special little girl. We need to speak about your father." Searching for the right words, she paused. Though advanced for a six-year-old, Rosa was still a young child. "Your daddy has decided he doesn't want to be married anymore and wants a divorce."

Rosa tilted her head to the side and scrunched her face. "You mean like on *The Parent Trap*? I don't have a twin sister. How can I trap you into getting married by myself?"

Harriet stifled a smile. The old Disney movie was one of Rosa's favorites. They'd watched it hundreds of times. "You're correct, darling. You don't have a twin, and you can't trap us into remarrying."

Refusing to be outdone, Rosa quirked her mouth to the side as if it would help her think and twirled the baby curls by her ear with her free hand. "Well, then we can't move to California, and you can't move to Boston."

Harriet was hurt that Rosa had associated herself with living with Ernesto. All this time Ernesto had been slowly turning her child against her. Pure and simple, men were evil. The kinder and gentler they appeared, the more dangerous and manipulative they were.

"That was a movie, darling. It works differently in real life. Since we'll no longer be married, your father is moving out. You and I will have the whole house to ourselves," she said with enthusiasm, trying to lift Rosa's spirits. "Think of the fun we'll have."

Rosa's brows knitted together. "Where will Daddy live? He can't leave. Who will take care of us?"

"I'll take care of you." The amused look on Rosa's face cut deeper than any knife ever could.

What has Ernesto done to you?

Rosa's facial features seemed to take on the wisdom of an eighty-year-old. She trained her black stare on Harriet. "You can't take care of anyone. We need Daddy. When I get home, I'll write a report to show him why he can't leave."

"It's about time you learned that men can't be trusted. No man! All men do is use and abuse, including your precious Ernesto!"

"He's not a man, he's a daddy," Rosa replied matter-of-factly. "And daddies take care of their babies." She scooted as far away from Harriet as she could.

Harriet's hands wouldn't stop trembling. She pressed the intercom and told the driver to take them home. "I'm sorry I raised my voice. I know you're young, but someday you'll understand what Mommy's telling you." Harriet turned away from the intensity of Rosa's black ice eyes. "Men can't and don't love. All we have is each other. I love you."

"My daddy loves me," Rosa said through clinched teeth.

Chicago, Present day

I can't stand that Mr. Caldwell. His beady eyes are always staring at me. I think he's one of those pervert people Anna told me about. Daddy must think he's a pervert, too, because he told me to make myself scarce when Mr. Caldwell is around. I'll be glad when Daddy's business with him is finished, so he won't come here anymore.

Rosa's butt had fallen asleep. She resituated herself on the cement floor of the basement storage room and continued reading. A few pages later, she had to stop and re-read.

See, I told you Caldwell was up to no good. I saw on the news today that he was arrested. She fingered the curls beside her ear. What had Anna told her about Caldwell? It was so long ago. She continued reading.

Two journals later, she found the answer. *You're not gonna believe this. That Caldwell guy was murdered. They cut out his tongue! Ewwwwww. Something about him working for some drug lord. I'm sorry they murdered him, but I'm glad he won't be coming around here anymore.*

Daddy said we're moving to Miami. Mom's not happy about it, but I am. All Mom does is drink, sleep around, and put Daddy down. I hate visiting her. I hope Daddy doesn't make me come back to visit her. She closed the journal and set it on the floor with the others.

She was twelve when they moved to Miami. She needed to find out whom Caldwell worked for. She closed her eyes, silently praying it was any cartel besides the Martín cartel.

The sound of her garage door opening broke her out of prayer. She glanced at her watch. It was barely noon. Ernesto wasn't due until eight. She quickly gathered the journals and placed them in her keepsake box. She couldn't believe she was sneaking around in her own house through her own things because she didn't want Ernesto to know what she was up to.

She held her latest journal in her hand. She'd seen Samson open, then close it quickly when he realized what he was reading. He'd called several times since his interview with Ernesto, but she wasn't ready to speak with him. Ernesto had called and told her how they grilled him, and then tried to manipulate Mrs. Walker into saying Ernesto was a money launderer.

Torn between her loyalty to Ernesto and her love for Samson, she placed the last journal in the keepsake box. She had to put her family first. She closed the box and set it inside of a large plastic container.

She pushed the bin into the corner with the others. She'd have to wait until Ernesto left before she could do more research into Caldwell. She went upstairs to greet her father.

The news wasn't on, which worried her. Ernesto always turned the television on before he'd set down his keys. So who was in her house?

Her heart thudded against her chest. She pulled an eight-inch knife out of the rack, then stood against the kitchen wall, close to the doorway that led into the rest of the house, and listened. She could hear someone in her bedroom.

Don't panic. Ernesto had been correct. She cursed herself for her arrogance and not listening. He'd never steered her wrong before, and even Samson had said someone would be around to check. Now she had a drug-world goon in her home.

She couldn't go out the front door or the intruder might hear her. Her cell phone was in her purse, which sat on the entryway table. The nearest house phone was in plain sight. She focused on the door that led to the garage. *What if he has buddies with him?* She bit her bottom lip. Ernesto was right, goons had come for her. She chastised herself, again. *How did they crack the security code?*

Footsteps approached. There was nowhere to hide in the kitchen, so she remained silent, pressed against the wall, clinging onto the knife for dear life. The footsteps passed the kitchen. She relaxed slightly, but she had to get out. She looked across the room at the sliding door. It would only take her a second or two to unlock the door and get out. The thug wouldn't have time to catch her.

The television came on and anger mounted on top of her fear. This hoodlum had the nerve to watch her television. The channel switched to CNN. She heard keys slide across the coffee table.

Knife still in hand, she marched out of the kitchen into the living room. "Daddy!"

He jumped around, facing her. "Dammit, Rosa!" He clung to his heart. "You scared me half to death. What are you doing here?"

"I live here. I thought you were drug people coming to get me."

He folded his arms over his chest and raised a brow. "What on earth would possess you to go after criminals with a kitchen knife? You know better. Call the cops."

"Dad," she drawled. "It didn't take me long to figure out it was you. Sheesh."

"Your car isn't in the garage."

"The motor in the window burned out, so I'm having it fixed before it rains. Why are you here so early?" she asked, but wanted to ask, "Why were you in my bedroom snooping around?"

"I figured we could start our Father's Day celebration early." He stepped forward and kissed her forehead. "I'm sorry I scared you. You should allow me to hire security for you."

"No thanks. I'll be fine. Did you need something out of my bedroom?"

"I was thinking about taking a nap while waiting for you," he answered smoothly. "I hate the bed in your spare room. Have you heard from Samson?"

His answer didn't satisfy her, but she let it go because she was afraid of what the real answer might be. She tossed the knife at the coffee table and plopped down on the couch. "He's called a few times. I left him a message telling him to leave me alone."

Ernesto sat beside her. "I know you have feelings for him. I'm sorry I've put you in this situation. I feel horrible."

His sincerity made her feel guilty for thinking he was rifling through her belongings. Just because he'd hidden his past didn't mean she should cancel out everything she knew about the man he'd become.

She wrapped her arms around him. "I love you, Daddy." The journal entries regarding Caldwell haunted her, but she couldn't wipe away all the years of love from Ernesto. She didn't want to. She had to believe in his innocence. She had to give him the benefit of the doubt. He'd earned her belief in him.

He rested his head on hers. "I love you more."

"Have you found anything?"

Jeff resituated the earpiece to his cell phone as he turned into the parking lot of Bolívar Networks. "I'm about to meet with her now. I have

to be careful not to tip our hand, Dad. If Ernesto's who we think he is..."
He shook his head. "We just need to be careful. I can't believe we didn't
make the connection sooner. With her haircut, you can really see her
resemblance to David. I'll bet Ernesto is the reason the organization did-
n't crumble. He's the real leader."

"May I speak to Ms. Rosa Bolívar?" Samson asked the receptionist at
the front desk.

"Sure," she said with plenty of bubble behind her voice. Samson did-
n't know the young lady, but people with so much cheer quickly annoyed
him.

He glanced over his shoulder as a tall, dark-skinned woman entered
Bolívar Networks. "Hello, Gail," said the beauty as she walked past.

Gail hopped out of her seat, reaching forward as if there were some
sort of emergency. "Wait a second, Ebony. Would you mind showing
Samson here back to Rosa's office?"

He narrowed his eyes on the perky secretary. "How did you know
who I am?"

Her smile widened. "Rosa can't shut up about you. By the way," she
delicately placed her hand on her chest and batted her big green eyes,
"I'm Gail Cooper, the too-nosy-for-her-own-good secretary. Pleased to
finally meet you."

Fat grin on his face, he nodded. "The pleasure is all mine."

"And I'm, Ebony Pacini, the fresh-off-maternity-leave wreck."

They stood eye to eye. He glanced down to see if she wore heels.

She laughed. "I'm six-one without heels, six-four with them."

"I'm sorry, I didn't mean..." He shook it off. "Pleased to meet you
both."

Ebony and Samson conversed as she led him though the hallways
toward Rosa's office. Ebony stopped when she heard a male voice around
the corner from them.

"Take a right at the corner. It's the first office on the right. You can't
miss it."

He noticed she'd become tense. "Is something wrong?"

"That guy rubs me the wrong way," she said in hushed tones. "I'm sure it's nothing. It was nice meeting you."

"You, too. And congratulations on the baby."

"Thanks." She left him alone.

Samson waited along the wall, listening.

"It's been so many years, Rosa. We have so much to catch up on," the man said.

"It has been a long time. Do you ever see any of our old classmates?"

"I've lost touch with just about everyone. I don't plan on losing touch with you again."

Samson strained to hear Rosa's reaction to this jerk's flirting. She was silent, so she was probably blushing. After five more minutes of the man's incessant boasting about himself, Samson thought he'd be sick.

"So we're on for tomorrow?" Rosa asked.

Samson's eardrums burned. No way had his Rosa just confirmed a date with this guy. He smoothed down his goatee.

"I wouldn't miss it for the world," the man said. "I've kept you from your work too long. Give me a call."

"I'll do that."

The man rounded the corner, making brief eye contact with Samson as he passed. Samson forced the scowl from his face and nodded a hello as he quickly assessed his competition: average height, sleek build, brown eyes, white, thirty-something, mousy brown hair, arrogant gait, and looked like money. After he saw the man had clearly left, Samson went to Rosa's office.

He stepped into the first office around the corner, but there was no one in it. He thought he was in the wrong office until he saw her nameplate sitting on the mahogany desk. Instead of the normal black leather executive chair, hers had a flowered tapestry design. He smiled, thinking Rosa sure loved her colors. On the shelf behind her desk were photos. He crossed the room for a closer look. They appeared to be Rosa at a picnic. There were kids everywhere and Rosa was in the center having a good time.

He turned and noticed her computer screen. The monitor displayed an article from the *Chicago Tribune* archive—Former Diligent Telecommunications Executive Murdered.

"Why are you snooping around my desk?"

Samson jerked his head up. "I wasn't... I mean..." He rounded the desk to her. "We need to talk."

"About what, you accusing my father of being a criminal, you trying to manipulate Mrs. Walker, or you spying on me?" She brushed by him and closed the Internet connection.

"You knew I had to question them, Rosa. You're being unreasonable."

"You've practically convicted my father, yet I'm the one being unreasonable. This is a clear case of guilt by association, guilt by being born Colombian."

"Since when did Ernesto claim anything Colombian?"

"I'm not arguing with you." She took her seat. "This won't work. I have to support my father, and you have a job to do."

He crossed his arms over his chest. "You'd so easily dismiss me?"

"I'm in no mood to pamper your ego."

"Who was that man who just left your office?"

"A client." She straightened her already neat desk.

"Well, make sure it stays that way."

Brow raised, she asked, "You're not serious, are you?"

"What's his name? I'll check him out." He reached inside his suit coat pocket and pulled out a small notepad and pen.

"I'm warning you, Samson, leave my clients alone."

"He didn't sound like a client to me."

Rosa stared at him a good long while, then picked up her phone and dialed the front desk. "Excuse me, Gail. Could you get Mr. Paige's number please?"

"Yes, his number would do nicely. I think I need to pay Mr. Paige a visit," Samson said.

Rosa hung up, then dialed the number. "Hello, Jeff, it's Rosa." She listened a few seconds, smiled at Samson and giggled. "I know you just left."

"What the hell are you doing?" Samson asked under his breath.

"I've changed my mind. I'd love to go out with you."

Samson leapt forward, almost grabbing the phone. Rosa didn't flinch. "Seven o'clock would be fine... See you tonight... Yes, I'm sure you'll show me the time of my life… Goodbye." She hung up.

"You're not going out with him!"

Rosa pushed away from her desk, then rounded her desk and stood directly in front of Samson. "Wanna bet?"

The silent seconds that passed felt like hours to Samson. No way would he allow his woman to go out with another man. But how could he stop her? She wouldn't even accept his calls. "I'll be the mature one and leave before this gets out of hand."

"You do that."

Without looking back, Samson commanded his legs to walk out, reminding himself that she was angry. She loved him. This was her way of striking back at him for doing his job. He'd give her a day or two to cool. Until then, he'd have a tail put on this Paige guy and check out his background, just in case he was one of the drug connections snooping to see what Rosa knew.

The name Paige rang a familiar bell in Samson's ear. *Damn.* He definitely recognized the name. He stopped off at the receptionist desk. "Excuse me, Gail, could you tell me where Ebony's office is?"

"No."

He didn't know if she were joking or serious. "Why not?" he asked in the most neutral tone he could muster.

"I saw the way you looked at her when she came in. First of all, she's Rosa's friend, and secondly, she's happily married. This is her third child. You need to step off." She pursed her lips. "Men are dogs."

"I need to interview her for my job, Gail. Now, would you please point me to her office?"

A few minutes later, Samson was seated across from Ebony in a coffee shop. Mid-morning, the shop traffic was at a minimum. Ebony added cream to her coffee. She reminded him of his deceased sister. They were both tall, beautiful, dark women with kind hearts. He missed his family, but pushed his sorrow away. Rosa needed him. "How long has Jeff Paige been a client?"

"He came sniffing around a week or so ago, insisting that he could only work with Rosa. He's up to something."

"That's what I was thinking." He took a sip of coffee. "What type of work is she doing for him?"

"He wants to set up a separate network for an annex office, and he wants her to test the firewall protection of their main system."

"So he hired her to infiltrate his network."

"Yes. Don't worry about Rosa. She won't fall for the likes of Jeff. She has her sights set on someone else." She tipped her coffee cup at him.

"I just ran for the 'Jerk Of The Year' award. I can't believe how jealous I was. He's not her type at all."

"Give her a day to cool off." She took a sip of coffee.

"She has a date with him tonight."

Ebony almost choked from laughing so hard. "Oh, poor Rosa."

Samson smirked. "Serves her right. Do you know if Jeff Paige is part of Paige Industries?" He asked, though he knew the answer. The DEA had several leads that pointed to Barry Paige, CEO of Paige Industries, as a major player in the drug world.

"His father is CEO."

"Is it standard to have two separate networking systems?"

"Not the way he wants it. He wants them to be two totally non-related businesses."

"Why would he do that?"

Ebony hunched her shoulders. "You've got me."

Samson knew why—Paige was keeping an eye on Rosa. Samson would sick Alton on him directly after his interview with Ebony. "Have you met her father, Ernesto Bolívar?"

"A few times. He's overprotective, but nice. He is even working from his Chicago office until you guys stop investigating him."

"Oh really?" He stirred his coffee. "So why are you being so forthcoming with information?"

"Rosa told everyone to give our full cooperation."

He thought about the article Rosa had found about Caldwell and wondered what had happened to provoke her to conduct her own investigation. He needed to apologize for the way he had acted. They were both after the same thing. There was no need to be at odds.

"I owe you an apology, Jeff." Rosa stood under the soft yellow light of her porch lantern. He'd taken her shopping, though she wouldn't allow him to buy her anything. He'd also taken her to dinner at the most expensive restaurant in town.

She forced herself to remain still as he stepped closer and placed his hands on her waist. "What's wrong?" he asked. "I had a great time."

"I had a nice time, but I don't want to lead you on. My life's a mess, and I'm not looking for a relationship right now."

He leaned back on the wrought-iron porch railing. "Oh, this has to do with David Martín, doesn't it?"

"In a way. I need to get my life back in order."

"How about this? We part as friends. If you need to talk, I'm here for you. We can do this on your terms."

When not talking about himself, which was rare, Jeff was actually a nice guy, she decided. "Thanks."

He kissed her on the forehead, said goodbye, and went to his limo. Rosa sat on the porch a few more minutes. The neighborhood was so peaceful at night. She closed her eyes and listened to the crickets, wishing for her own peace.

According to reports, Caldwell was embezzling money from his company for David Martín. She'd told Samson that he was wrong for considering Ernesto guilty by association; now here she was telling herself the same thing. She sighed and went inside.

Too tired to change into nightclothes, she chose to sleep in her full slip. She turned on the lamp and reached into her nightstand for her journal, but it wasn't there. She'd forgotten that she'd packed it away and needed to start a new one.

She frowned at the drawer. Some of the items were out of place. She always kept her extra pencils on top of the notepad. One of the pencils was off to the side. And the Post-its were in the top center instead of the bottom center.

She snatched the cordless phone up so quickly the numbers almost didn't follow. She punched in the digits, then waited.

"What's wrong, Rosa?" Ernesto asked, his voice filled with concern and sleep. "It's almost midnight."

She marched out of her room toward the kitchen. "You've been snooping in my room, haven't you?" She rounded the corner into the kitchen and headed straight for the basement door. She'd caught him reading her journal when she was a teen, but she couldn't do anything about it. She yanked the basement door open.

"Calm down."

"I'm not calming down, Daddy!" She flicked on the lights as she stomped down the steps. "You have no right to invade my privacy."

"I'm your father and worried about you, that's all the rights I need."

She slapped on the light as she entered the storage room. The cement floor was so cold it stung her bare feet, but she didn't care. "About what? That I'll find more of your dirty little secrets? I told you to tell me everything. Have you told it all?" Phone propped between her ear and shoulder, she pulled out the bin with her journals. She threw the lid, and it clattered against the wall.

"Leave the past in the past. I've changed."

She took the keepsake box that contained her journals out. "I believe you've changed. But you sneaking around my home makes you look guilty. If you're not guilty, stop acting like it." She put her most recent journal on the floor, then returned the keepsake box to the bin.

"You're right, baby. I apologize."

She began dragging all of the storage containers to the center of the room. Each had an itemized list of its contents.

"I was looking for your journal. You've always been so open with me, but since you found out about David…" he trailed off. "I'm sorry I've shaken your faith in me, but I'm worried about you. You're still my child. You won't tell me what's on your mind. I can't help if I don't know what's wrong."

She stuffed her most recent journal in with her college memorabilia items. "If you want to help me, cooperate with the DEA." She pushed the bin into a corner of the storage room, then began stacking and replacing the other containers around it.

His voice rose in defense. "Don't you think I want to cooperate? This goes against everything I am, but I have to protect you."

"Protect me? From what? The only one snooping around is you. No one's after me. I don't know anything, and your cooperating with the DEA won't change that." She continued arranging the storage units.

"You don't know the drug world. I do. I'm not worried about the DEA. I have to protect you the only way I can."

She pushed the final bin into place. "What's going on? Why are you so worried about the drug world?"

"Because now they'll think I'm actually David's partner. The only way to get at me is through you. And you won't even let me hire security for you."

"Then, let's work with the DEA. Set up a sting. Samson will help us."

"No, Rosa! Why do you think the DEA never made the connection between David and me? David has agents in every agency to ensure the connection was never made. David isn't the only one with agents on his payroll. If one of the crooked agents found out I was cooperating with the DEA..." he trailed off. "I won't jeopardize you."

She turned off the light in the storage room, then went into the basement and lay on the carpeted floor. She hadn't furnished the basement, so it was empty. "You're killing me, Daddy."

"I know this is hard for you, but I can't involve the DEA."

She couldn't dispute his point that David had agents in his pocket, but Samson wasn't one of them. "Please talk to Samson. He can help."

"No, Rosa. This is my decision to make. Are you with me or not?"

She blew out an exasperated breath. "Yes. I'm with you."

⚜

Glad that Anna hadn't woken, Ernesto disconnected and set his cell phone on the nightstand. He didn't divulge any information the DEA didn't already know, so he was still safe on that front.

Yes, Rosa will always be with me, Ernesto reaffirmed...

Chicago, twenty-four years ago

Ernesto quickly rounded the corner to see why Rosa had come into the house screaming for him. She dropped her sketchpad and ran up the stairs, skipping steps.

"I'm sorry, Daddy," she said with tears streaming down her face as he lifted her. "I promise to be a good girl. I won't break my arm *no más*." She hugged him tightly. "Please don't leave me."

Harriet didn't make it to the top step before Ernesto blasted, "What the hell have you been telling her?" He held Rosa close, rocking her. "It's all right, baby." He stroked her hair. "I'd never leave you."

"She's my daughter—"

"Don't say another word! I'll deal with you later." He stalked off to his office and slammed the door, thinking this was low, even for Harriet.

Comforting Rosa, he hummed a lullaby until she sobbed herself to sleep in his arms. The fear in her eyes of losing him was twenty times worse than her fear from the fall. David had given her to him. Harriet didn't want or appreciate him. Rosa never asked for anything and worshiped him. He gently brushed the hair out of her face. He had no intention of ever giving her up.

Painful memories flooded him: A man had taken his mother from him; a murderer had taken his surrogate mother from him; and then the abuse he suffered at the hands of foster parents stole his youth and innocence from him. A child at the time, he couldn't fight back. He kissed Rosa's forehead. No one would take what was his again.

CHAPTER FIFTEEN

Shocked that Rosa allowed him into the house without any resistance, Samson sat at the kitchen table and watched as she heated water. Dressed in jeans and an orange cotton blouse, she was as beautiful as ever, but she looked mind-weary and exhausted. The usual cheer and laughter in her eyes had disappeared.

"I apologize for my behavior yesterday. I was totally out of line." He took off his suit coat and draped it over the back of the chair. "Allow me to make it up to you. There's a strawberry festival this weekend I'm sure you'll enjoy."

She took the teakettle off the stove and poured hot water into their cups. "Thanks, but I don't think it's a good idea for us to see each other socially."

He watched as she set the teapot on the stove and opened the lower cabinet next to the oven. One of the screws fell out of its hinge.

The cabinet isn't the only thing in the room in need of repair.

She lazily set the screw on the counter, then grabbed the box of tea out of the cabinet and took out two packets. "You did want tea, didn't you?" She returned to the table, holding out a teabag. "I have apple juice."

He took the offered bag. "Tea will be fine. There's no reason we can't continue seeing each other."

"No reason? Humph. How about your job is to convict my father?"

"My job is to find the truth. We're both working toward the same goal. We're on the same side."

"I'm going in knowing he's innocent, and you're going in thinking he's guilty." She used her spoon to press the steeped teabag against the inner edge of her cup.

"Unlike you and Alton, I'm objective." A flash of acknowledgment lit her eyes before she covered her emotions. "If Ernesto's innocent, then I'll find it. What are you afraid of?" After seeing the Caldwell article on her monitor, he knew she was afraid Ernesto was still involved in the drug trade. She was near the point where she could deal with Ernesto's possible guilt, but she needed more time.

She pushed her tea away. "I have to protect my father. I don't trust Alton. Would you please give me all of the information you have on Daddy? I don't know where to look or what to look for."

"On one condition. You have to cook dinner for me tonight." He displayed a toothy grin. "Strictly business, of course."

The laughter returned to her eyes. "You are a mess, DEA Agent Samson Quartermaine."

"I'll be by around six." He went over to the counter and held up the screw. "Do you have any tools?"

"In the garage."

A few minutes later, he sat on the floor and began fixing her cabinet. She crouched down and watched.

He patted the cream tile floor with his hand. "Sit here. You should learn how to do these small jobs." She moved closer. "Your garage is a handy man's heaven. I'll bet you don't even know how to use half of the equipment."

"And you'd be correct, but I could have taken care of that screw."

"I saw a few other things that need fixing. Instead of indulging in strawberry delights this weekend, how about I make a few repairs around here?" He took her hand into his.

"I'd never impose on you." She gently tugged her hand away.

He pressed his lips to her forehead. "I'm not giving up on you, Rosa."

"The best way to find holes in Ernesto's story is through Rosa," Samson said. "In order to prove his innocence, she'll cooperate." He looked out of their second story office window onto the street below. A mid-morning rush of people hurried from here to there.

"You can't give her everything we have, man," Alton said. "You're too close. She's playing you."

He turned his body to face his partner. "I never intended on giving her everything. I'm revealing what I think she already has and a little more. I need for her to see that we're a team, working toward the same goal."

"And what's your goal, to catch Ernesto or win Rosa's heart? You've fallen for her."

"I'll admit I have feelings for Rosa; but *if* Ernesto's crooked, he's going down. I don't give drug lords free passes, and neither will Rosa."

"You actually believe she'll turn on her father? You're dreaming."

"She'll never turn on Ernesto, but she won't support his illegal activity. She's already found out about Caldwell."

"So what do you think she'll do when she finds out Ernesto's the head of the Martín syndicate?"

"*If* he's the head of the Martín syndicate, she'll deal with it just as she has everything she's learned in the past week."

"I didn't say you could open my blinds, Ernesto." Harriet stood in her living room with her arms folded over her chest, tapping her foot. David had made her a hundred million dollars richer, so she no longer needed Ernesto. She'd never have to depend on anyone else again. She wondered what David did with the rest of his drug money. She figured he had to be a multi-billionaire.

Ernesto continued opening blinds. "You did a great job with the agents. I'll have to buy you something special. Did Rosa say anything to you about Agent Quartermaine? I'm afraid she's getting involved with him." He approached her.

Harriet *tsked.* "Rosa's smarter than to become involved with some poor cop. He has nothing to offer her." Hands on her hips, she craned her neck back to look into his face. "I'm sick of you always making me look like the bad guy."

"You are the bad guy." He turned and walked out.

Harriet was so enraged, she couldn't move until after he'd already left. She grabbed a nearby vase and hurled it across the room. It smashed against the door, shattering to pieces. "I hate you, Ernesto!"

She needed vodka, but instead, rushed into her bedroom and read the information an anonymous friend of David had sent her. The correspondence said that David arranged to have everything taken care of between Rosa and Ernesto. Harriet crumpled the letter. David was taking too long, and she didn't trust this friend to come through.

She sorted through the hundreds of pictures that accompanied the letter. The friend had told her to make copies and put them away in a safe hiding place. Some of the pictures were taken from a distance, but were clear. Many of the pictures contained Ernesto and David in the shots. Another group of photos looked promising also. She grinned. Rosa would finally see Ernesto for the liar he was.

Wishing she could have just one celebratory drink, she licked her lips.

"Come in. It's unlocked," Rosa yelled over her shoulder as she stirred the homemade vegetable soup. A few seconds later, Samson entered the kitchen. He'd changed from his suit to jeans and a polo shirt. She loved bright colors, and a dark man in bright yellow—she shook her head—Lawd have mercy, he looked fine.

He tapped the salad bowl, quickly scanned the kitchen, then stepped behind her and wrapped his arms around her waist, drawing her into his chest. "The soup smells delicious, but a man needs food when he comes home from a hard day's work."

The rumble of his voice against her back comforted her. Soaking in the security, she pressed further into his embrace. "Do me a favor." She pointed to the counter corner. "Move the grill over to the island and plug it in."

She took two marinated steaks out of the refrigerator, and his eyes lit up.

"Now that's what I'm talkin' about!"

She waved off his silliness. "Oh my goodness. You'd think you never ate before."

Samson caught Rosa sneaking another peek at him. He'd known she'd like the bold yellow of his shirt. He winked at her. She blushed and averted her eyes. At his first chance, he planned to go clothing shopping.

She pulled her feet up on the white curved sectional in her living room and continued reading the information he'd given her. "Is this everything you have on him?"

"Everything I could give you. I won't allow my feelings for you to interfere with the investigation. If Ernesto's still involved in the drug trade, he'll be arrested and prosecuted."

A compassionate understanding filled her eyes. "I can respect that." She returned to the file. "You're wasting the taxpayers' money. He's innocent."

"I pray you're correct."

Her mouth opened wide, then shut. "You guys already know he was laundering money for David." She shook her head as she continued reading. "I told him to tell you."

"The statute of limitations is over." He scooted next to her and draped his arm around her shoulder. "I've never seen such a well-organized syndicate."

"You sound in awe of them or something."

"I'm impressed. It's no wonder Ernesto's at the top of the business world. What do you think about the Caldwell connection?"

She toyed with a few curls beside her ear. "I don't want to consider Daddy guilty by association. According to these," she tapped on the papers, "he bought our first house from the guy. I remember Caldwell coming to our house several times, but Daddy never liked him." She paused. "Neither did I. Daddy must have known he had ties to David's illegal activities, but that doesn't make Daddy guilty of anything."

"That's how I feel also. We have associations, but no recent proof of any illegal activity."

She tossed the file onto the coffee table and snuggled into Samson's side. "Daddy's been acting so strange lately, I was afraid you'd show me something..." she trailed off. "He's innocent."

She still sounded as if she were convincing herself of his innocence. Samson stood, pulling her along. They both needed a break. "The moon's almost full. Let's go for a walk."

"I was shocked when I saw you lived in a middle-class neighbor-hood," Samson said. "I thought for sure you'd live in an overpriced condo or mansion somewhere."

"I'm not into wasting money, and I'm only one person," Rosa said. "What would I need with a mansion?"

They continued strolling, hand in hand, along the sidewalk. "I guess I'm just trying to say that I'm glad you're down to earth. You don't seem rich."

"Rich? Describe rich."

"Uh, your father, Jeff Paige, your mother..."

"Okay, you win." They shared a laugh. "You have my mother to thank for my attitude toward money and possessions."

"Yeah right," he drawled out.

She elbowed him in the side. "Don't be mean."

"I just can't see it."

"Maybe you're looking at it wrong. She has everything money can buy, yet isn't happy. The only times I remember her being truly happy were when we weren't spending money. When I was a kid, we'd go to the park. She'd get in the swing next to me or play on the slide and have a great time. Sometimes I'd pick her a dandelion and clover bouquet. By the way her face lit up, you'd have thought they were the rarest, most expensive flowers ever. Somewhere along the line, she was taught that the things money can buy brings happiness. Her life has taught me different."

"That's sad."

They rounded the corner and continued toward her house. "So why haven't you seen your family in over a year? Too busy with David?"

"Ever since my sister died...I don't know. If I'd have been there for her, she wouldn't have killed herself."

"You got that right. How could you turn your back on your own blood?"

"What?" He heated instantly. "I didn't turn my back on her. It's not like I knew how much trouble she was in."

"Why didn't you?" she chastised, her pace increased as they entered her yard. "She was your sister, and you're a DEA agent. You should have investigated for yourself."

"I did, Rosa. The files don't contain information about her psychological well-being. Every time I spoke to her she said she was a little down. How was I supposed to know it meant more?"

They stopped at the edge of her porch. "Excuses, excuses. She said she was down." Poking him in the chest, she asked, "What did you think that meant? You should have stopped her. You should have known."

"Well hell, of course she was down. She'd found out her life was a lie. But I was there for her. She could have come to me and told me how she actually felt instead of thinking I'm a mind reader. You're going through the same thing. Are you down about it?"

"Yes."

"Do I need to call suicide prevention?"

"No."

"I loved my sister, Rosa. I did everything I could for her." Realizing she was actually projecting her situation on him, he softened. "I'm here for you."

The devilish grin that he'd seen so many times on David found its way to Rosa's face. "Are you convincing me or yourself?" She hopped up the stairs and entered the house.

He stared at the beveled glass within the front door. *What just happened?* One second they were walking, the next he was defending himself. Whatever happened, she'd made her point. He should have stopped blaming himself long ago. So many people had told him, but he never listened. Rosa was the only person that didn't tell him, she showed him. He took the steps two at a time and went into the house, worried about how he'd protect her if Ernesto were guilty.

Rosa handed Samson the cordless phone as he walked into the kitchen. "What's this for?" he asked.

"I don't know anyone in your family's phone number."

"I'll call later. We need to talk now."

"I'm not going anywhere. Call while I clean the kitchen. You can use my bedroom for privacy."

He pulled her into his embrace, loving her.

"Hello, Brianna."

"Samson? Samson! Oh my God," she screeched. "It's Samson!"

He smiled at his sister's excitement. "How have you been?"

"Wait a second. I'm putting you on three-way." He heard a click, then a short time later, "Derrick, you won't guess who I have on the line."

"You're right," Derrick answered. "I won't even try. Now what do you want?"

Samson shook his head. His older brother, Derrick, was still all business. He moved from Rosa's bed to a recliner in the corner.

"Conference in John for me, then I'll tell you."

"I'm busy, Brianna. I don't have time for this."

"Then, you'd better hurry."

A few seconds later, John's wife answered the phone. "Hello, Quartermaine residence."

"Hello, Monica. It's Brianna. Is John home?"

"Sure. I'll get him for you."

"Great, but you stay on the line also."

"We'll be right back," Monica said.

"What's going on?" Derrick asked.

"Be quiet and wait."

"This had better be good," he grumbled.

"What's going on, Brianna?" John asked. "Are you finally pregnant?"

"What?" Derrick exclaimed. "She'd better not be pregnant unless she got married and forgot to tell me about it."

Samson laughed so hard his eyes watered. He'd missed his siblings. "Y'all haven't changed a bit."

"Samson?" Derrick, John and Monica said in unison.

He sat forward, speaking as if they were in the room with him. "None other but. I've missed you all."

Everyone spoke at once, so no one was understood. Samson finally calmed his siblings.

"Well, hot damn!" John said. "Where are you at? Are you in Tampa?"

"I'm in Chicago."

They spoke for over three hours about what was going on in each of their lives and why he'd cut himself off from everyone.

"Didn't you say Rosa was waiting on you to make this call?" Brianna asked. "She sounds like a keeper. You'd best not mess this up."

He glanced at the clock. "Oh, man. Time flew so fast."

"Now I know you're my older brother and all," John said. "But since I'm the only married one, I say listen to me."

"Oh Lord," Monica interrupted. "I think it's time for us to go. Good luck, Samson, and don't ever leave us again. Hang up, John."

"But, Monica, I have really good advice."

"Goodnight, John," the remaining siblings said, laughing.

"I'm gonna let you go also," Derrick said. "Love you, bro."

"I love you," Brianna said.

"Love you, too." Samson disconnected, unable to believe he'd stayed away so long, missing out on his family. He closed his eyes and thanked God for sending Rosa into his life.

He crossed over to the bed and turned down the comforter, then went to find Rosa. He found her lying on the sectional asleep. She'd changed her clothes to a large cotton nightshirt. As he lifted her to carry her into the bedroom, she woke.

"How's your family?" she asked groggily as she wrapped her arms around his neck and leaned her head against his shoulder.

The lights were already off, so he continued their journey down the hallway. "I feel like an idiot for staying away so long. It makes absolutely no sense to me now."

"Did you speak with your mother?"

"Not tonight. I'll call her in the morning." Unlike the rest of his family, he'd been emailing his mother at least once a month. "I'm sorry it took so long. Time got away from me." He laid her in the bed and knelt beside her. "Thanks, Rosa."

She reached her hand forward, placing it on his chest. He cupped her hand into his. "My heart beats for you," he whispered. His body ached for her, but they couldn't make love, not yet. He was afraid to kiss her goodnight because of where it might lead.

"I'm worried about us." He rested his hand on her waist. "How will you feel about me if Ernesto turns out to be part of the cartel?"

"You're worrying for nothing. He isn't."

"I have to consider all possibilities, and I'm asking you to do the same. What happens to us if I have to bring down Ernesto?"

"Do you think he's guilty?"

He hunched his shoulders. "I honestly don't know." His hand slowly moved along her body to her hair, knowing this was a bad idea, but longing for the intimacy. Her curls wrapped around his fingers as he massaged her scalp.

She closed her eyes and remained silent a long while. "You're not responsible for Daddy." She opened her eyes. "If he's a part of the cartel, I'd be hurt and shocked, but that wouldn't be your fault. I might even be angry with you for a while. You know about shooting the messenger, but I'd get over it."

He brushed his lips over hers. She opened up to him, and he felt as if he'd been reborn. No one and nothing could defeat him because he'd already won.

"Lord knows I don't want to, but I think I should leave." He gently traced her kiss-swollen lips with his thumb.

"Is something wrong?"

"I have a little problem. You see, I've wanted to make love to you since the first time I saw you."

"And," she said with a coy smile.

"And to stay away from you, I've devised a scheme. I don't carry condoms." He Eskimo-kissed her. "With the way I'm feeling right now, I really don't give a damn, so I need to get out of here." He suckled along her neck to her ear. "You'll be the mother of my babies, but we'll be married."

"How do you know I don't have any protection?"

"Do you?"

She moaned as he cupped her breast. "I can run to the store."

"Not tonight, my sweet, but soon." He rested his head on her chest. "Very soon or I'll burst." Their first time together would be special, spontaneous, no stopping at the store, then attacking each other.

He covered her with a light blanket, then sat on the edge of the bed. "I can't believe I'm doing this."

"I can't believe I'm allowing you to do it."

"I want for you to be sure, Rosa. How will your parents react to us?"

"It won't be pretty."

"We don't have to rush things."

CHAPTER SIXTEEN

Rosa couldn't believe Harriet was already active at ten in the morning. She looked nervous as all get out, but she was sober. "Would you like some coffee? It's decaffeinated."

Harriet stopped biting on her nails. "No thanks."

Rosa hugged her mother. Harriet clung so tight that Rosa could hardly breathe. "I'm proud of you, Mom." She rocked her mother in her embrace until Harriet loosened her grip. "How would you like to go shopping?"

Harriet wiped the tears of joy out of her eyes as she pulled back. "You want to go shopping?"

"No. But, you like shopping, and I want to spend time with you." She returned to her seat at the kitchen table. "I'm thinking you need a new wardrobe."

Harriet looked around the room, then reached under the table and took out the large gift bag she'd placed there when she first arrived.

"I can't go shopping today, darling. Do you think you can take off this weekend? Maybe we can go to California. I want to see Angela." She handed the package to Rosa.

Rosa was so thrown off that she forgot about the gift Harriet had just handed her. First Harriet was acting like she was on the FBI's "Most Wanted" list, then she didn't want to go shopping, and now she wanted to visit the sister who had disowned her. Harriet giving up the booze had really changed her. Next thing Rosa knew, Harriet would be singing Ernesto's praises. "I'd love to go to California with you. My treat. How about we leave on Friday?" She knew Samson would understand about her ditching him for her mother. This would also give him time to work on his investigation without worrying about stepping on her toes.

"That will be perfect. Open your gift. It's my apology for my behavior at your party."

"You shouldn't have." She opened the bag and saw a leather photo album. She pulled it out for a closer look. "It's lovely. Thank you so much."

Harriet glanced from the sliding door toward the window above the sink. "I've already started placing photos in it for you."

Rosa opened to the first page. "Oh my!" The page was full of pictures of David and Ernesto when they were children. "This is great!" She pointed at the photo of Maria holding David on one of her hips and Ernesto on the other. "This woman looks like me!" Giddy, she laughed. "This has got to be my grandmother. Boy do we have some strong genes."

Harriet fidgeted in her seat.

"Come over here and look through these with me," Rosa said as she turned to the next page. "Are Daddy and David actually brothers? These are family photos."

"I…I have to leave, darling." She grabbed her purse off the edge of the table.

"What's wrong, Mom?" She closed the album and set it on the table. "Maybe you should lie down."

Harriet hugged Rosa. "Don't worry about me. I'm fine."

"I love you, Mom."

"I love you, too."

Harriet rushed out of the house. Rosa followed her to the door and watched as she sped off. Something was definitely bothering her. She thumbed through the pages of the photo album with Harriet still on her mind.

Where did she have to go?

She glanced down and froze. There was a picture of Ernesto and David sitting on a bench, watching Rosa play in the sandbox at the park. She looked like she was around four years old in the picture.

She flipped back and noticed there were lots of pictures of Ernesto and David watching over her. Trying to remember, she closed her eyes. Ernesto and Harriet took her to the park often, and they always spoke to people. She couldn't remember David, but these pictures… Her heart warmed. David did care about her. He'd always been there.

She continued going through the photos. She smiled when she saw

David had attended her graduation ceremonies.

Why didn't Daddy tell me?

The last few pages were full of pictures of Ernesto with people she didn't know.

What are you up to, Mom? Why did you give me pictures of strangers?

She stared into the strange faces and became nauseous. She wasn't ready to find out who they were. She wasn't ready to admit why her mother had the pictures. She wasn't ready. She closed the album.

⊱✦⊰

"I'm not drunk! I ordered vodka. I expect vodka, not lip." Harriet slammed her empty shot glass on the bar.

"I'm sorry, ma'am, but I'm not serving you. I'll call you a cab."

Harriet looked around the smoke-filled, packed bar. "Do you see this? She refuses to serve me! Get off the damn phone and fix my drink!" The bartender finished ordering the taxi.

"Fuck it!" Harriet snatched her purse off the neighboring stool and clumsily weaved her way through the crowd and out of the bar.

"I know my damn limit. Who the hell does she think she is?" The parking lot looked blurry. She squinted to help clear her vision. "No more driving at night, for damn sure."

When she'd arrived, her car and the employees' cars were the only ones in the lot. Now, there wasn't an empty space to be found. "Where's my damn car?" She didn't know if she was angrier with the bartender for not serving her or herself for falling off the wagon. She hadn't realized it would be so difficult to quit.

She pressed the panic alarm on her keys to find her car. The alarm blasted directly behind her. She dropped the keys, quickly squatting to pick them up, then fumbled around until she could cut off the alarm.

Sitting behind the wheel of her car, she regretted every decision she'd ever made, except having Rosa. Swearing she'd never take another drink, she started the car and exited the parking lot. This time she'd join one of those Alcoholics Anonymous groups Rosa nagged her about.

Everything looked so different at night that she was a little turned around, but she eventually merged onto the expressway traffic. Blaring horns were making her hangover come early, and why the heck was everyone using bright lights?

"These folks are driving like a bunch of damn fools."

So many lights were coming at her and horns were sounding, they were confusing her. Yet she was certain of one thing, she'd turned the tables on Ernesto. "Your day has finally come."

The last night of their married life, Harriet had stormed into Ernesto's home office...

Chicago, twenty-four years ago

"This psychological bull you're pulling on Rosa will cost you."

Without giving Harriet a second glance, Ernesto increased the volume on the news radio program and continued reading his *Wall Street Journal*.

She did a double take. First he wouldn't allow her into Rosa's room while he tucked her in, and now this. She needed to straighten him out post-haste. "Rosa is my daughter, and you have no right—"

"Why don't you take a seat?" he said calmly.

Thrown off, she pulled a straight-backed chair from the conference table to the front of his desk. She reassured herself that she knew men; their lust put them at women's mercy. She had the upper hand. His new tactic wouldn't change anything.

Financial report over, he lowered the volume on the radio and handed Harriet two short stacks of papers that were held together by paperclips. She skimmed through the paperwork.

"The top set is our prenuptial agreement, which you signed," he explained. "It states that in the event of divorce, you leave the marriage with what you came into it with. The last three pages are an itemized list of your holdings at the time. I'm feeling generous today, so I'll give you an additional million up front and ten thousand a month for ten years."

She flung the papers toward him. "Wrong answer. Do not pass go. Do not collect two hundred dollars. Go back and try again." She crossed her arms over her chest. "I don't care what the prenuptial says. And did I see in those divorce papers that you maintain full custody of Rosa? Humph, my lawyer says—"

He interrupted her, saying, "You should have paid for a real lawyer, instead of calling in a favor from a friend." He took the divorce papers off his desk, restacked them neatly, and then held them out to her. "Try being grateful for a change."

"There's no way in hell I'm taking that paltry little tease for money. You're worth over five hundred million. And if you think you're getting custody of Rosa," she paused, unable to fathom his audacity, "you're out of your mind. She's my child. You have no claim to her. You're not even her real father. I didn't allow my first husband to treat me like shit, and I'm not taking it from you either."

His sinister laugh scared her. He'd never fought back before. She'd stand her ground, and he'd relent to her will.

He dropped the papers on the desk. "Everyone will testify that I've been a doting husband and father."

"I agree. If you wish to continue being the doting father, you'll give me my fair share. I'm getting half. Wait until the courts hear about your affair. I haven't decided what news organizations to send her love letters to yet."

"When you send in that article, make sure you tell them how your first husband divorced you because of infidelity."

Her face snapped back as if she'd been slapped. She'd told him their divorce was because George didn't want children. Telling herself that he must be fishing, she regrouped. "I never cheated on my husband. The divorce decree says irreconcilable differences."

"Oh yes, you did. You cheated on him with me." He flashed a wicked smile. "Of course, I'll tell the judge I didn't know you were married at the time and that you've cheated on me numerous times throughout our marriage." He paused. "I have several men willing to testify about your escapades—including the man that will soon be your former lawyer." His voice filled with concern, and the angry, harsh lines of his face softened. "I'd begged you to seek professional help. A woman wanting sex all of the time just isn't natural."

"You liar!" she shouted from the edge of her chair, gripped the sides, prayed for grounding.

"I told you if you didn't end your latest affair, I'd seek a divorce. That's when you fabricated this affair I'm *allegedly* having and tried to extort money out of me. I knew I had to save Rosa. So I made the toughest decision I've ever made in my life." Looking truly distraught, he sighed. "I filed for divorce and am seeking full custody of Rosa."

She jumped out of her seat. "You'll never get Rosa! I...I...I read in this medical journal about this experimental testing."

"You actually read?"

She ground her teeth. "This test will prove that you aren't her father."

Eyes large in feigned horror, he drew in his hands. "So you were cheating on me *and* your husband? I'm wounded." He slapped the desk with his heavy hand. "Oh yeah, you're sunk. Bring on this test. Your lawyer should have informed you that legally, Rosa is my child: my name is on the birth certificate; I've been raising her as my own; and you have always maintained that she is my child."

He pushed the divorce papers toward her. "Sign and I'll allow you visitations with Rosa, or we can go to court and I will prove what an unfit mother you are. Even the orderly at the hospital smelled the alcohol on your breath last night."

She hadn't had a drop to drink until after she returned home from the hospital. This couldn't be happening. He had to be stopped. "George isn't Rosa's father."

"If you want to impress me, tell me something I don't know."

She straightened her back and glared at him. "Her father is a major drug dealer. He'll have you killed," she bluffed. She hadn't seen David since he'd tossed the bag of money at her. Ernesto was corporate; he'd fear confronting anyone from the drug world.

Ernesto raised a brow. "You mean my brother, David Martín? At least he was right about you. You are hell in bed."

Wind knocked out of her, she could barely stand. How had he known about David? They couldn't be brothers. This was another one of his lies. He was tricking her. Of course, he had said the name David. After all, he was the largest drug lord in the country. "I'm serious, Ernesto. I can have you killed with one phone call."

He reached for the phone. "Go for it." He held up a finger. "Wait a second. I need to make a call first." He dialed David's number, then held the phone to his ear. "Hey, David, Harriet wants to speak with you." He handed the phone over to her.

Harriet hesitated, then slowly reached for the phone and put it to her ear. David cursed her out for being so stupid and endangering his child. Then he told her to sign whatever the hell Ernesto wanted or he'd have her ass whacked.

All she could do was lower her head. "Please, don't take Rosa from me." She felt her eyes fill with tears. Year's ago, she'd sworn no man would ever see her cry. Right about now, she didn't care who saw her. The taking of her child from her hurt more than the taking of her innocence by her mother's men. "She's all I have." She wiped the tears from her eyes.

He took the phone from her trembling hands. "We'll talk later," he said into the line, then hung up. "I gave you everything, but it wasn't enough. If I choose to go by the prenuptial agreement, you get nothing. Take the money."

"What about Rosa? She needs me."

"She can see you whenever she wants. Unlike you, I'd never hurt her."

"You can have the money. I'll follow the prenuptial agreement. Just please don't take Rosa from me." She choked on the lump of emotions in her throat. "Please don't take her."

"Sign the divorce papers or we go by the prenuptial agreement, and I take you to court for full custody. Presently, I'm in a generous mood. If I have to go to court, my generosity ends. After I win—and I will win—you'll never be allowed to see Rosa again."

Her tears left stains on the paperwork. She could barely see through her watery eyes to sign.

"I've called for a service to pack your things tonight." He opened the top drawer in his desk, pulled out a set of keys and tossed them at her. "This is your new apartment. It's downtown. Class is dismissed."

Angela's warning from years ago replayed in her mind. She hadn't heard her sister's words of wisdom at the time, but now they were loud and clear: *One of these days, you're gonna get caught up in all the mess you throw out there.* She felt numb. He'd taken her one true happiness from her.

"Your day will come," she swore.

CHAPTER SEVENTEEN

"Hey, Daddy, are you all set up in your office yet?" Rosa had spent the morning supervising the network setup at the Paige annex and needed a break. She pressed the speaker button on the phone, then took the stack of software samples off her bookshelf and placed them on her home office desk. She hated that she'd gotten so far behind.

"Just about. What are you up to?"

"Catching up on some work before I head over to another site visit." She'd spent yesterday looking over the photos in the album, moping around the house and missing Samson. He'd had to work late, so he had called instead of visiting. "You'll never guess who I have for a client. Jeff Paige." She began sorting the packages by postmark, oldest to newest.

"Did you say Jeff Paige?"

Her gaze slowly traveled from the packages to the speaker on the phone. *Why did his voice sound so panicky?* "Yes," she drawled out.

"What did the Paiges want?"

"We're setting up a network in their annex, and I'm testing their firewall. What's wrong, Daddy?"

"I'm just worried about you. I wish you'd go into hiding. You can run your business from anywhere in the world."

"Well, I'm worried about you. If you're correct, these drug people think you're the head of the Martín cartel. What's to keep them from murdering you to take over David's territory? You always harp on me about security, yet you don't always have yours. You're the one they'll think is part of the cartel. Not me."

"The only time I don't have security is when I come to visit you. Otherwise, the president can't even get to me. You're unprotected.

If you don't go into hiding, I'm hiring security for you."

"I don't want to live like that. I won't."

"Why are you being so hard-headed? This is your life."

"This is ridiculous. Why won't you talk to the DEA? They already have proof that you laundered money for David years ago."

"I don't trust them."

"I don't either, but I trust Samson. We can work with him."

An awkward silence filled her small office. She'd never heard him sound so unsure, so out of control. It scared her. Why was he still forcing the danger issue? If these people hadn't come for her yet, she doubted they'd come. "Please talk to Samson."

She heard his belabored sigh. "I'll think about it," he said. "I'm not rushing you off the phone, but I have a meeting. I love you."

"I love you more."

"Damn, damn, damn!" Ernesto knocked a small box off his desk onto the floor. Pens, pencils, and paperclips tumbled out of the box. In his arrogance, he'd never really believed someone from the drug world would come after Rosa. Jeff Paige was the No. 2 man in the Sierra cartel. His father, Barry Paige, was the leader. Panic gripped him; his baby was actually in danger.

He'd send Rosa away, but there was no way to do it without drawing attention to himself, and she'd fight against him. He bent, picking up the small mess he'd made. They needed to be taken out before they could hurt Rosa.

There were too many unknowns factoring into the equation. Something had to give. He dug into the bottom of the box on the floor, pulled out a disposable phone, and called his head of security. He had arrangements to make. The Paiges' days were numbered.

"What did you find?" Samson asked.

Alton tossed a file on Samson's desk. "We already suspected that Barry Paige played a large role in the Sierra cartel. Him turning his son on Rosa puts him on the top of the list as the real leader. These cartels are getting smart. I found a few more drug connections on the Paiges. I gave a copy of everything to the Sierra team."

"So, they're after Rosa." He skimmed through the file.

"Nah, they're snooping. What do you think about Ernesto's visit with Harriet the other day?"

"If he found out about the hundred million David left her..." The phone interrupted them.

Alton answered. "Hello, DEA Agent Alton Miles speaking... No, shit! Any signs of foul play?" He shook his head. "Now that's a damn shame. Has the family been notified?"

"What?" Samson asked under his breath.

"Thanks." He hung up.

"What's going on?"

Alton didn't answer. He just stared at Samson.

"Snap out of it, Alton!"

A few more moments of silence passed. "Harriet's dead. She was in a car accident last night."

Samson gasped. "Oh, my God. Rosa will be devastated. Has she been notified?"

"Yeah. I'm just shocked. Maybe Ernesto found out about Harriet's trip to the prison and had her killed. Everyone knows she's a drunk. Making it look like an accident would be a breeze."

"Why hasn't Rosa called me?" He yanked his cell phone off the desk and speed dialed her home number. No answer. He dialed her work number. No answer. He dialed her cell phone number.

"Hello."

"Where are you? How are you doing?"

"Umm, Samson, you know I love you, but I'm conducting a site visit. We can talk later."

The cheer in her voice told him she didn't know about the accident. He cursed under his breath at the incompetence. "Can you get away? This is extremely important."

"You're worrying me, Samson. Can't you just tell me now?"

"Not over the phone. Meet me at your place."

"I'm on my way."

"No!" Rosa cried.

Samson embraced her. She fought against him, fought against what he'd told her. This wasn't happening.

"I'm here, baby. You're not alone."

"Are you sure? Did you identify the…?" She shook her head. "No!"

"I'm sorry, but she's gone."

She rested her head on his chest. "I knew something was wrong. I shouldn't have allowed her to leave," she said between sobs. "I should have made her tell me what was wrong. I should have…"

He placed his finger over her lips. "I wasted a year blaming myself for my sister's death. You helped me see it wasn't my fault. This wasn't your fault, Rosa. I know you're hurting, but don't run away from the pain. You have to live through it and continue on with life."

She gazed into his warm brown eyes and felt his love. She didn't know what she'd do without him. "She's dead."

"I'm sorry." She relaxed in his arms. He kicked a few throw pillows off the sectional and pulled her onto the couch with him. "I'm not going anywhere. We'll stay here forever if need be." They lay on the couch together.

"I know I'm being selfish," she mumbled, "but I'm scared. I've lost so much. I'm not sure I can take much more."

"What do you fear most?"

She concentrated on Samson's strong, steady heartbeat. David was gone. Her mother was gone. "If Daddy's guilty…" she trailed off.

"You won't lose him, even if he's guilty." He caressed her back. "I can't imagine how difficult this is for you."

She couldn't believe that she honestly doubted Ernesto's innocence. She couldn't believe Harriet was dead. She couldn't believe Ernesto hadn't come by to console her; but then again, he'd acted like David's death was nothing. She couldn't let go of Samson or she'd be lost forever. "Don't ever leave me."

"I'll never leave you."

She closed her eyes, praying that when she woke the bad dream would be over and all that would remain was Samson's loving embrace.

⟡

Samson thumbed through the pages of Rosa's new photo album. He'd laid her in bed and read to her until she finally fell asleep, then he returned to the living room where he'd noticed the album sitting on the coffee table. He recognized several of the individuals in the shots as soldiers from the Martín cartel, but the photos weren't proof that Ernesto was an active member of any illegal organization.

He closed the album. She hadn't asked for Ernesto, but Samson was sure she wanted him there. He took her cell phone off the lion Asante stool and scrolled through the names until he reached "Daddy," then he pressed the call button.

"What a wonderful surprise! Two calls from my favorite girl in one day. You're spoiling me," Ernesto said.

Before Samson could speak, Ernesto continued, "You know I love you, but it's awfully late. Is something wrong?"

"Mr. Bolívar—"

"Why do you have my daughter's phone, Agent Quartermaine?"

"It's Harriet." He paused. "She was in a car accident."

"Wha… what hospital are you guys at? I'm on my way!"

"I'm at Rosa's. I'm sorry but… Harriet died in the accident."

"Oh my God. How's Rosa? Put her on the phone."

"She's not doing too well, Mr. Bolívar. She has been through so much. I called because I knew she'd want you here."

"Yes, yes, of course. I'll be there in twenty minutes. Thank you, Agent Quartermaine. Anna, wake…" He disconnected.

Samson set the phone on the coffee table next to the album. He knew surveillance photos when he saw them. This was most likely David's way of showing Rosa the truth. Knowing her inquisitive personality, she wouldn't stop until she figured out who the other people in the photos were. David had planned to let her find out about Ernesto on her own instead of telling her. That made sense to Samson.

After all, she probably didn't know David when he arranged for her to receive the album. Why would she trust a stranger over the father she loved?

Wanting more time to check out the connections between Ernesto and the people he'd seen in the album before Ernesto discovered the pictures, he slid the album under the couch. He called Alton from his own cell phone and told him about the album. Then, he went into Rosa's bedroom to rest.

"Samson," she whispered as she lifted the covers.

He hesitated; he'd intended on waiting in her reading chair. She flapped the cover. He gave into his misgivings and lay beside her. She rolled over, and he cupped her into his body. "I'm in serious need of night clothes."

"Why don't you take off your slacks? You'd be more comfortable."

He smiled at the thought of Ernesto catching him in bed with Rosa with his pants off. "I'll be fine." He placed his cell phone on the nightstand, then returned to cuddling Rosa. "I love you," he whispered. More tired than he realized, both were asleep within minutes.

The sound of the garage door lifting woke Samson, but not Rosa. He'd thought Ernesto would have his own key and know the security codes. He heard a car pull in and doors opening and closing, then the garage door lower.

He tried to pull the arm that embraced Rosa away so they wouldn't be caught in bed together, but she held on for dear life. A few seconds later, he heard the door to the mudroom open and Anna say, "The house is so dark, but her car is in the garage. Do you think he took her to his place?"

"They're here," Ernesto replied.

Keys plopped onto a table, then footsteps headed down the hallway. Samson closed his eyes and pretended to be asleep.

"What the?" Ernesto said in hushed tones.

"Aww, aren't they cute? I'm glad she has someone," Anna whispered.

"She does have someone. She has me."

"Be quiet before you wake them. Come on, we can stay in the guest room."

"He can't be asleep. It's only been what—a half hour?"

Rosa's grip loosened, so Samson uncoiled his arm and brought a finger to his lips as he looked over his shoulder at the two. "She's asleep."

Ernesto rounded the bed. "Rosa," he said softly as he sat on the edge and took her hand.

She cracked her eyes open, then bolted out of Samson's embrace into Ernesto's arms, leaving Samson feeling empty. "Daddy!"

Samson was glad the room's only light was from the small bit of moonlight that escaped between the drawn curtains. He was sure his jealousy was evident on his face.

Ernesto rocked Rosa gently. "Don't worry, baby. Daddy's here."

Samson exited the bed to give them privacy. Rosa turned, holding out her hand. "You're not leaving me are you?"

He ran his hand through her soft curls. "I'm here to stay." The panic in her voice showed she needed them both. He wouldn't allow his jealousy to interfere. This was her family.

"Anna." Rosa reached out for her.

"My little rose." Anna sat on the bed and wrapped her arms around Rosa.

"I don't know…I can't…bury her."

"Your father and I will take care of everything. You need your rest." She kissed Rosa on the forehead. "We just wanted to let you know we're here for you and we love you."

Ernesto held the covers up so his baby could lie down. He tucked her in and kissed her goodnight. "I love you."

"I love you more," she mumbled.

"I have nightclothes in the spare bedroom," Ernesto said to Samson. "I'm sure you'll fit into them."

Samson acknowledged their truce with a nod. After seeing this family scene, he fully understood why Rosa couldn't see Ernesto as the head of a drug cartel. He obviously loved his daughter more than anything in the world. David had once told him that a drug lord must love the drug world more than anything.

"I'll be right back." Samson went across the hall to the spare bedroom and searched through the drawers for a set of nightclothes. The irony of the situation gave him pause. The government spent billions trying to bring down drug lords, when love was free and actually worked. First David fell, and next Ernesto would fall.

Anna dropped a platter of scrambled eggs onto the kitchen table between Samson and Ernesto. "Rosa is going through more than enough. You two will come together and act civilized for her sake," she bit out through clinched teeth. "I swear you're worse than my students ever were."

Both men piled eggs upon their plates without taking an eye off each other.

"Anna's correct." Ernesto grabbed a piece of toast. "Thank you for being here for Rosa. I appreciate it. When she wakes, I'll tell her you had to leave for work. She'll understand."

Samson placed four slices of bacon on his plate beside his eggs. "This smells delicious, Anna." She smiled her thanks. He tipped his glass of apple juice toward Ernesto. "When Rosa wakes, I'll be sure to tell her you two had to make the funeral arrangements, but will call later. She'll understand."

Anna grumbled as she pushed away from the table and stormed out. Ernesto chuckled lightly. "I love a woman with fire."

"Anna is very nice. Rosa thinks a lot of her."

"She stepped in as Rosa's mother figure and did a great job." He stretched his arm out to see the time. "It's almost nine. I can't believe Rosa's still asleep."

"We stayed up all night."

Ernesto's brows furrowed.

"We were talking. She finally dozed off around seven. I don't think either of us will be seeing her today. I'm not leaving. She needs me." He took a bite of eggs.

"How can you pursue Rosa and investigate me at the same time?"

"I love her."

Ernesto's mouth opened, then closed. "If I find out you're using Rosa, you will pay," he warned. "I don't care what kind of agent you are or who you work for."

"We have a lot to do today, Ernesto," Anna interrupted as she stepped into the room. "I'm sure Samson can take care of things while we're out." She took Ernesto's unfinished plate and dumped his food into the trash.

Ernesto laughed as he stood. "See what I mean? Fire." He pulled Anna close and kissed her neck. "Okay, Anna. You win. I'll leave them alone for now."

❧⋈❧

Samson peeked through the living room curtain, watching Ernesto and Anna drive off for the funeral parlor. He darted to the couch, grabbed the photo album from underneath, then rushed to the front door and waved outside.

Alton hopped out of a blue sedan that was parked down the street. Digital camera in hand, he ran for the house.

Samson set the album on the porch swing. "Hurry up, Rosa's asleep."

"I've got this." Alton quickly snapped pictures of the pages of the album. "Damn, Ernesto's sunk. Look at these. David was having his ass followed." He continued turning, and clicking. "Some of these are only a few years old. Look at the cars."

"Yeah, I know. This must be David's way of telling Rosa the truth about Ernesto. He knew she'd find out who the men in the photos are."

"Finished." Alton handed the album to Samson. "Now, all we need to do is prove that he's head of the cartel."

"Easier said than done. Did you bring my clothes?"

"I forgot them in the car. What was Ernesto's reaction to you being here?"

"He was ready to explode, but played it off for Rosa."

"She's his weakness."

"His weakness and his strength. This has all gotten out of hand. It's like Rosa is trapped in the center of a love triangle. David, Ernesto, and Harriet make up the points. They all wanted to claim her as their own."

"I guess Ernesto won." Alton kicked about an imaginary rock.

"Would you tell Rosa I'm sorry about Harriet? I mean… Well, hell, I know what it's like to have a drunk for a mother. Shit, just tell her I'm sorry."

"Time to get up, Rosa," Samson whispered as he spooned her into his body. She didn't move or acknowledge him in any way. "I allowed you to lie in bed all yesterday, but not today." Rosa groaned as he pulled her out of bed. "I've already run your bath."

"Where's Daddy?"

He ushered her into the restroom. "Probably at the airport picking up your aunt Angela and her husband. He said he'd call. We're on our own until the funeral tomorrow."

She grabbed the toothpaste and her electric toothbrush off the light blue marble sink. "I haven't seen Angela since I was small. She cut Mom off years ago."

"Do you know why?" He took the toothpaste from her and applied a small amount to his toothbrush.

"According to Mom, Angela was jealous. I think it has more to do with Angela not agreeing with Mom's life choices. She emails every few months to check on me. She's a good woman."

Samson knew Angela was in college during the time Ernesto, David, and Harriet got together, but he still wanted to interview her; there was a slim chance that Harriet had told her something useful. He'd have to wait an appropriate time interval for her to mourn before they approached her.

Rosa rinsed her mouth out with water and washed her face. "You made me get up. What's on the agenda for today?"

He spit a mouthful of toothpaste into the sink and noticed her tray of toiletries now included a box of condoms. He thanked God that he hadn't known the condoms were there earlier; making love wasn't what she needed. "Yesterday, I made repairs to everything that was broken in the house. How would you like a patio out back? And the sandpit needs repairing."

She stared at him. "You want to build a deck?"

"Would you like a deck?"

"I've put you out too much already. I'm sure Alton is having a fit."

"Alton came by yesterday with my clothes and his condolences. I know he's a real jerk, but he has his moments. In a way, he reminds me of David."

Her laugh tickled his heart. "Yeah, two assholes. Whew!" She calmed. "I miss him. I miss them both." Her eyes welled up with tears. Samson drew her into his body. "I can't lose Daddy," she mumbled.

"You're the strongest person I've ever met. No matter what happens, you'll survive."

Rosa watched from her kitchen window as Samson supervised the men unloading the supplies from the home improvement warehouse. His eyes locked on hers. He nodded his encouragement, then returned his attention to the flatbed truck and its contents.

"I love you," she mouthed.

The phone mounted on the wall beside the refrigerator rang. She checked the caller ID. "Hello, Daddy."

"Actually, it's Anna, darling. I need to charge my phone. How are you holding up today?"

"I'm feeling a lot better. Samson is being great."

"He seems like a good man. I'm sure you two will be happy together."

"Don't let Daddy overhear you." She returned to the window to watch Samson. "How's he doing?"

"Honestly," she sighed, "I'm worried about him. He hasn't been sleeping much lately and his eating... Well, he barely eats, especially since David's execution. You know how he tries to act all tough, but he's a big ol' softie."

"He hasn't mentioned anything about David to me," she said with a bitterness she didn't intend. "I'm sorry. I'm tired. I need to ask something. Something about you and Daddy."

"Go ahead."

"Did you ever suspect Daddy was..." She couldn't bring herself to say it. She pulled out one of the ladder back chairs from the kitchen table and sat. "Why didn't you know Daddy was working for David?"

"This was well over twenty years ago," came Anna's solemn voice. "Times where different back then, Rosa. I was almost forty. I had never been married, and I had this handsome, kindhearted, successful man interested in me." Cheer filled her voice. "The icing on the cake was he had this beautiful little girl. I'd always wanted a daughter."

"Thanks for stepping in. You're a great mother."

"It means a lot to me hearing you say that, Rosa. When Ernesto told me about his ties to David," she paused, "I wasn't surprised. I'd chosen to ignore the early signs."

"What do you think now?"

"He's changed."

"Why won't he go to the DEA? He's making himself look guilty, even to me." She fidgeted with the edge of the place mat. "I'm scared, Anna. What if he's one of those 'legitimate businessmen' that front for cartels? I feel so guilty for my feelings. Like I'm betraying him, but… I just don't know."

"You've lost so much and learned so many ugly truths these past few weeks; of course, you're confused. You know in your heart that your father is a good man. You know in your heart that he is trying to protect you. Hold on to what you know."

"It's hard to hold on when so much of what I knew two weeks ago is totally contradictory to what I know today. My whole reality has changed. I'm losing everything."

"This is your grief talking. You're not losing your father. He's innocent. Don't give in to the grief, Rosa."

"I'll try not to." She toyed with the edge of the cream placemat. "Are Angela and her husband there yet?"

"They took a taxi from the airport to their hotel."

"I thought you guys were supposed to pick them up. I figured they'd stay with you."

"Angela's husband called earlier and said they'd arrived last night."

"Maybe I should have invited them to stay here. I've been so self-absorbed."

"No, darling, you haven't."

"Can I speak with Daddy?"

"He finally fell asleep a few minutes before I called. I just wanted to call to make sure you were okay."

"Well, tell him I love him."

"I will."

Samson walked into the kitchen through the sliding door. Rosa held her hand out to him. "I love you, too, Anna." She hung up, then set the phone on the kitchen table.

"The men are finished unloading." He took her outstretched hand. "It's a beautiful Saturday. Let's enjoy it."

❧❧

"Why don't you just tell Ernesto you don't want to be CEO?" Samson asked.

Rosa's mouth flopped opened, closed, and then open again. She looked around, as if reorienting herself. "You're joking, right?"

"Nope." He rested his foot on the railing and gently rocked the porch swing as he looked at the moon, which was partially hidden by an overcast sky. "You love your company. Why give it up?"

"I don't have a choice. Daddy raised me to be CEO of Bolívar International. It's like he's the king, and I'm the only heir to the throne. I have a responsibility to fulfill." She leaned her head on his arm.

"But what about what you want? What about your dreams?"

"Bolívar Networks is my dream. Daddy won't retire for another decade or two. Until then, I'm free to live my dream."

"By then maybe you'll change your mind about being the CEO of Bolívar International." He wrapped his arm around her and continued rocking the swing.

"I doubt it, but I'll fulfill my obligation."

"You're a natural leader. Why don't you want to be CEO of one of the largest corporations in the world?"

"I don't care about being the largest in the world. I want my specialized company to be the best in the world. I have no need or desire to control such large entities. So, what does the future hold in store for you?"

CAUGHT UP

"If we don't turn anything substantial up in the next month, I'm resigning and returning to practicing law."

She grinned and batted her eyes. "For me? Why you shouldn't." He moved to the opposite end of the swing. "What are you doing?" she asked.

"Making room for your head." He laughed as he pulled her close. "If we don't find anything in the next month, the chances of us finding incriminating evidence in the near future are slim to none. I'd planned to leave the agency before I met you. My plans haven't changed." He kissed her lightly. "Well, maybe one of my plans has changed. I want at least four children. I used to want five, but since I'm marrying an old woman—well, you know how that is."

"And what old woman are you marrying?" she asked, brows raised.

He nuzzled his nose along her neck, whispering, "You wouldn't know her. She's a sugar mama." He licked her lips. "And she tastes like caramel."

She wrapped her arms around his neck, drew him into a kiss. She felt so good in his arms that he didn't want to release her.

Before he had the chance, she pulled back slightly. "You're gonna get me into trouble."

"Is that such a bad thing?" he said with bouncing eyebrows.

She playfully hit at him. "You are too much. I'm thirsty. Do you want me to bring something back for you?"

"Apple juice will be fine." With the knowledge that someday this would be their home, he sat back and watched her retreat into the house. He imagined their children in the front yard having water balloon fights and getting into trouble.

He'd need to change the basement into his and Rosa's bedroom and office space, so the children could use the three bedrooms on the main floor. His portfolio was worth over seven hundred grand. If he put seventy to a hundred grand into the house, their retirement wouldn't be harmed. Rosa may be worth over a hundred million, but he had no intention on allowing her to support his family. He was the man and would take care of his wife and children.

A small pinch on his arm interrupted his fantasy. He swatted, killing a mosquito. What was taking her so long? He went into the house. "Do you have any bug spray?"

He caught a glimpse of Rosa as she crossed the kitchen. She wore a simple cream sundress and was barefoot, singing an old Anita Baker jam as she carried a platter of sandwiches from the counter to the table. Just as he saw their children playing in the front yard, he could see her barefoot and pregnant, roaming around the kitchen. He chuckled at his thoughts, knowing she'd kill him for having them.

"The hallway bathroom under the sink," she replied, then continued singing.

He kicked off his shoes and joined her in the kitchen.

"Are the mosquitoes eating you?" She pointed at a spot on her forearm that had swelled slightly. "They got me, too."

He wrapped his arms around her waist and pulled her into his hardness. "You've got me." He swooped her into his arms and carried her into the bedroom.

"Put me down, you silly man," Rosa squealed.

Samson entered the dark bedroom and set her on the floor. "Your wish is my command." Arms wrapped loosely around her waist, he brushed his lips over hers. "What would you like?"

The wondrous sensations flowing through her body from his slightest touch were almost overwhelming. *To be your wife and mother of your children*, she thought, but breathlessly said, "For you to make love to me."

"I love a woman who knows what she wants."

She knew what she wanted all right. She wanted Samson. Just as Ernesto had come to terms with her moving to Chicago and starting her own business, he'd have to come to terms with whom she'd chosen to spend the rest of her life with. She slipped her hands under his polo shirt, drawn to his heat, his strength, his love. He was strong in so many ways. "I love you."

"Not half as much as I love you."

Feeling him wasn't enough; she wanted to *feel* him. As if reading her mind, he took off his shirt and tossed it to the side. Eyes closed and head resting on his chest, she listened to the steady beat of his heart. She'd been adrift so long. It felt good to be anchored again.

Heat rose within her as he planted kisses along her jawbone, down her neck to her shoulder. In an effort to cool herself and warm him, she nudged the straps of her sundress to either side. The soft material glided along the curve of her hips to the floor. The minute light making its way from the kitchen caught the glint of Samson's approving smile, sending her already racing heart into warp drive.

He glanced over his shoulder at the bed, then sat on the edge, positioning her between his legs. His mouth level with her breasts, he splayed his hands across her back and pulled her forward, suckling.

She moaned as she leaned into him. Her hands caressing his scalp for more pressure.

He looped his finger in her only remaining piece of clothing, her panties, and tugged.

How she wanted to give in, but not yet. She admired his body since day one and would take her time to explore the goodness that was Samson. He moved up on the bed and lay back as she straddled him. His feather-light stroking of her arms with his hands weakened her resolve. She squirmed a little, trying to shake the imaginary hold he had on her to no avail. She wanted him as much as he wanted her.

Holding onto her hips, he rocked her slowly over his hardness. Unsure if she could wait any longer, another moan escaped her. In one fluid motion, he rolled them both over, switching their places.

"You have me at an unfair disadvantage," she purred, unfastening his belt.

He ran his hands, then his lips, along her breasts, to her waist, until he finally found her panties. Her inner thighs quivered with pleasure as he tenderly suckled. Riding the waves of passion one second, the next her panties were gone, and he lay bare beside her.

Wanting a man this badly can't be healthy, she thought as her eyes finished adjusting to the minimal light. She laced her hands behind his neck and lowered his mouth to hers, fully tasting him. An indescribable rush flowed through her as visions of their life together played in her mind.

He took one of her breasts into his mouth as his fingers entered her. Shortly, her body heaved and arched as his hands and mouth sent her on a short run to ecstasy and back. Anxious to give him the same pleasure, she wrapped her hand around his hardness and gently stroked as she lowered herself.

"Rosa, I don't think that's such a good idea."

Loving him being vulnerable for a change, she continued her descent, then took him into her mouth and enjoyed herself.

A short time later, he suddenly pulled her up and rested between her legs. He glanced at the bathroom. "Are you ready to start our family?" he whispered huskily into her ear as he pressed his throbbing hardness against her heat.

Juan came to her mind, the little boy she'd taught to step at her birthday party. Giving him back to his mother was becoming harder every time she babysat him. She didn't want Bolívar International; she wanted her company, her own baby, her own husband, her own family. She wanted Samson.

She coiled her arms under Samson's and over his shoulders, then pulled. He filled her completely; mind, body, and soul. Their bodies instinctively moved together, sealing their bond forever. Legs linked around his thighs, she urged him to go harder, deeper. He happily obliged, lacing his fingers with hers as both shuddered from the turbulence of the passion rocking them to their final destination. Each cried out in pure ecstasy as his seed burrowed deep inside her.

CHAPTER EIGHTEEN

Samson looked up from the computer screen in Rosa's home office. "How are you feeling this morning?" Holding out his hand, he turned the chair toward her.

"I've been better."

He pulled her close and stood her between his legs with his hands on her hips. "My timing last night wasn't the best. I'm sorry. I'll understand if you change your mind."

She rested her hands on his shoulders and looked him square in the eyes. "The timing was perfect. I could use a taste of happiness about now." She nodded toward the computer screen. "What are you up to?"

"Writing my letter of resignation. I'll fax it to the chief tomorrow morning. In two weeks, I'll be a free man. In two weeks and a day, we'll be married." He paused. "If I can wait that long."

"I have no idea how I'll tell Daddy. He'll think I'm betraying him."

"You can do no wrong in his eyes. If anything, he'll think I'm manipulating you."

Face scrunched up, she said, "As if that's any better. I want for you two to get along." She backed away, blowing air out of her mouth. "I'm taking a walk before I change clothes. I'll have my cell on me."

The usual determination and confidence behind her steps was gone, and her shoulders were slightly slouched. He returned to writing his resignation with Rosa on his mind. A half hour later, the letter still only contained his return address and the date. He looked out the window. Rosa was in the backyard sitting on the ground near the sandbox.

"Give it time, baby," he mouthed.

He returned to the letter of resignation but couldn't focus. He checked the time in the lower right corner of the screen. One of the family limos would be there to pick them up shortly. He shut down the word processing program and went outside to ready Rosa.

She glanced over her shoulder at him. "I've never understood why people call these weeds. Daddy says my yard is in need of weed-and-feed." She handed him a giant dandelion. "They're beautiful."

"Yes, they are." He wiped away her tears as he sat with her on the blanket of grass, dandelions, and clover.

"I used to give Mom dandelion clover bouquets." She combed her hand through the grass and selected another plump dandelion. "They were the only cheap thing she ever liked."

"A clover's stem is so much shorter and thinner than a dandelion's. How did you make it work?"

She gathered a few dandelions into a big yellow bunch and handed them to him. She picked out several white clover flowers and placed them throughout the dandelions. "The clovers will die first because they can't reach the water." Her gaze dropped to her lap. "When I was a child, I used to wish Anna was my mom. When we moved, Daddy practically had to force me to answer Mom's calls. That's when her drinking got worse. It's my fault."

Samson tilted her chin up with his knuckle. "That's not true. I've interviewed her first husband. Her drinking problem started in her first marriage and gradually became worse. Don't start blaming and punishing yourself. I've been there, done that."

She rubbed her eyes. "I keep telling myself this was just a tragic accident, but it's hard. One minute I'm on cloud nine, the next I'm being drenched in a rainstorm."

He held her hand close to his heart. "We'll take this one second at a time."

❦

If one more person told Rosa they knew how she felt or Harriet was in a better place now, she'd scream. She saw her aunt, Angela, rush off to the back of the church where the Sunday school classes were located. Ernesto and Anna had just left the repast, so Angela was the only person in the room that might know how she felt.

"Rosa," Samson whispered into her ear, breaking her out of her trance. "If this is too much for you, we should leave."

She caressed his face, thankful he understood her so well. "I want to say goodbye to Aunt Angela. We haven't had a chance to say one word to each other."

Rosa searched the small classrooms for her aunt. "Hello, Aunt Angela," she said as she entered one of the rooms. "I'm sorry, we haven't—"

"How could you bring that murderer here?" Angela snapped as she marched toward her niece.

Head tilted and face scrunched up, Rosa held her hands up slightly. "I'm sorry, but I don't know what you're talking about."

"How could you disrespect my sister, your mother?" she raged. "I know Harriet had her faults, but this…" She lowered her short graying Afro. "How could you, Rosa? I thought you were different."

"Aunt Angela, I honestly have no idea what you're talking about."

"He killed her! He murdered her!" Shaking with fury, she clinched her tiny fists.

"No one killed Mom. It was a car accident." Rosa heard the door open, but didn't look to see who entered. The strength she felt silently supporting her told her it was Samson. "Calm down. You're upset."

The worry wrinkles adorning Angela's face seemed to deepen, making her look like a shattered, chocolate Valentine's heart. "Upset? Honey, I passed upset years ago. You turn a blind eye to Ernesto's treachery, then have the audacity to bring that murderer to my sister's funeral." She stepped closer to Rosa. "He murdered Harriet!" Closer. "He murdered her!" And closer. "Murdered her!" she drawled out, standing toe-to-toe with Rosa.

Rosa inhaled and exhaled deeply. "I love you, Aunt Angela, and know this is your pain speaking. Take it out on me if you need." She hunched her shoulders. "I can take it."

"Take it? You won't even admit it."

"There's nothing to admit. Mom died in a car accident."

An eerie giggle escaped Angela as she backed away. "How can anyone so smart be so stupid? Come off it, Rosa. I know the whole story." She raised accusing brows. "The story you pretend doesn't exist."

"What are you talking about?"

"Harriet's been calling me since you found out about David. As an insurance policy, she sent me a copy of the pictures she gave to you. She said that if anything happened to her, Ernesto was the cause."

"Mom hates Daddy and often made up stories to stir up trouble," she stated, truthfully. "He wouldn't hurt her or anyone," she said with more confidence than she felt.

"He killed her, so she can't hate him anymore."

"You're wrong. It was an accident."

"Step out of denial into reality, Rosa. Ernesto set his best friend up to be sent to death row because David wanted to tell you he was your biological father. Now, Ernesto had Harriet *murdered* because she wanted to show you that he is nothing more than a drug lord in sheep's clothing. She couldn't tell you because you never believed her. You always took Ernesto's side."

Rosa crossed her arms over her chest. "Daddy didn't make David murder anyone, just as he didn't make Mom drink and drive."

"I know Harriet liked to drink; but after Ernesto took you away from her, she replaced you with the bottle. Her becoming a drunk is his fault, too."

"Why couldn't Mom take responsibility for her actions? Did he make her drink during her first marriage also? Stop blaming Daddy for her mistakes. That was her problem in life. Now you're making it yours in her death. Mom could see me whenever she wanted. She left us, not the other way around. She told me Daddy didn't love me and was leaving us. Then, she left!" Rosa stepped back, slightly bumping into one of the tiny desk.

"How the hell could Harriet arrange to have her things moved in the middle of the night?" Angela made the sign of the cross. "Forgive me, Father, for cursing. This child has worked my last nerve."

"I was only six when they divorced. All I know is that when I went to bed, she was there. When I woke up, she was gone. When Daddy took me to visit her, *she* refused to see *me*." She poked herself in the chest as she spoke. "I heard her through the door. She didn't want me. Daddy didn't keep me away."

"Ernesto has you well-trained." She brushed by Rosa and Samson on her way out.

Missing the beauty of families enjoying the sunny Sunday afternoon, Rosa stared out the limousine window. She'd forgotten about the photo album. She remembered leaving it on the living room table, but why had Ernesto taken it? The possibilities, Angela's accusations, and Ernesto's behavior churned angrily in her stomach. There was only one real answer; Ernesto had arranged Harriet's murder to look like an accident, just as he'd set David on the path to death row.

"Rosa."

"He knows what buttons to push," she said aloud to herself.

"Who?" Samson asked as the limo turned onto Rosa's street.

"Daddy," she replied softly. "I'm scared, Samson." She glanced up and saw Alton sitting on her porch swing. "What is he doing here?" The car pulled into her driveway. "I'm in no mood for him today."

"I called him. After the scene with Angela, I thought we should hear what Alton's investigation into Harriet's death turned up, together."

"Do you think Daddy had something to do with Mom's death?"

He took her hand into his. "From what I've seen of him, no. She's the mother of his child." They watched as the chauffer rounded the car.

"But, David was my father and Daddy…" She looked away. "Daddy didn't even check on me after David's death. It's true, isn't it? What Angela said?"

"I don't know, baby. I just don't know."

The driver opened the door. Samson escorted Rosa along the walk and up the stairs as the chauffer slowly pulled out in the car. Alton stood, allowing Rosa to take his seat on the porch swing.

"I know I'm not your favorite person," Alton said with an apologetic grin. "But, I want for you to listen to me about something."

"It's been a long day—"

"Have you ever heard of a mean drunk?" he interrupted. "Well, my mother was the meanest drunk ever."

Ears perked up, Rosa relaxed her defensive stance and gazed into his sorrowful, blue eyes.

"I can't tell you how many times I wished she was dead. At the time, I thought I meant it. Late one night, this cop came by our house." He hunched his shoulders. "Actually, he came over to Samson's parents' because my mom had left me home alone, again. I was eight when she decided to get drunk and drive the wrong way down the highway. I blamed myself for years…" he trailed off. "I'd wished her dead, but I didn't mean it. I blamed myself. Of all the times for God to answer my prayers, he answered the one that took my mother away."

Rosa gently gripped his hand. "I'm sorry, Alton."

"I'm sorry for your loss." He cleared his throat and swiped the imaginary wrinkles off his Marlins jersey, then told Rosa what led to Harriet's death.

"So, Daddy didn't have anything to do with it," she stated, more than asked.

"No. I even have the phone records of the bartender calling the police when Harriet refused to wait for the taxi. It was a tragic accident. The same as my mother's."

Guilt washed over her relief as her shaky hands covered her mouth. "Oh, my God. How could I think such a horrible thing about Daddy?"

"I'm not trying to be insensitive, but just because Harriet's death was an accident, doesn't mean he isn't a part of the Martín cartel."

"Not now, Alton," Samson warned.

Alton has a point, thought Rosa. Ernesto had taken the photo album. She felt bile working its way up her esophagus. She ran to the railing, leaned over, and emptied the little contents of her stomach.

Samson whipped his white handkerchief out of his breast pocket and wiped her mouth. "Let's go into the house. Alton, hand me her purse. I need the keys."

Rosa shook her head. "You don't understand. Angela…" She inhaled deeply, praying some of the oxygen would make it to her brain so she could think clearly again. "The album… He took the album… This isn't happening."

Samson and Alton stared at each other for what seemed an eternity.

"How could he?" Rosa staggered across the porch. "I can't believe this is happening."

Samson quickly pulled Rosa's keys out of her purse and unlocked the door. "We don't know anything for sure." He opened the door and ushered her in. "I'll catch you later, Alton," he said as he closed the door.

Rosa didn't have the energy to make it to the living room. She leaned against the wall, willing the couch to her. "What if Daddy's a part of the Martín cartel?"

He dropped her purse and keys on the entry table, then held her close. "You'll make it through whatever the truth is. We don't know the truth yet." He led her into the living room where they sat on the sectional.

"He might actually be guilty, Samson. How could I have been so wrong?"

Samson sighed heavily, reached under the couch and pulled out the photo album. "I didn't think you wanted Ernesto to see this."

Eyes focused on the album, they wouldn't move. "He didn't take the album?"

"I meant to tell you I'd moved it, but I forgot."

"Daddy didn't have anything to do with Mom's death, and he doesn't even know the album exists." She brushed her hand over the album's leather cover. "I convicted him on the words of a grief-stricken woman."

"You've been through a lot. You jumped to a logical conclusion."

"But, I know Daddy." Flashes of Alton and Samson staring at each other, looking like they were caught red handed, bombarded Rosa. "How does Alton know about the album?" she asked slowly.

"I told him about it."

"And?"

"And he's working on identifying the men in the photos."

She snatched the album out of his hands. "You son of a bitch! You let him copy my album, didn't you?"

"The Martín syndicate is the largest in the world. It's my job—"

"To betray my trust!" she finished for him with a stomp of the foot as she stood. "You used me."

He reached for her. She moved away from his touch. "Get away from me," she hissed.

"I'd never betray you. I'm trying to catch a drug lord. Try to see this from my side."

"No! You see this from my side. My married mother became pregnant by her lover, David, and then marries a third man, Ernesto, who I thought was my father all of these years. Did I mention that David and Daddy were best friends? And, what do best friends do? Well, in this case, Daddy laundered money for David for several years, then he 'supposedly' set David on the path to death row, and now you suspect Daddy of being the head of the largest drug syndicate in the world. I'm just not having a good week."

"Rosa—"

"Is my name Rosa? Hell, everything else is out of whack: Alton's being nice to me, David's dead; my father's acting like he killed Jimmy Hoffa; my mother's dead; my aunt thinks I'm stupid; and the man I love has betrayed my trust. And you know what? I'm sick of you all. Now get the hell out!" She brushed by him.

Samson resisted the urge to follow Rosa into her bedroom. Instead, he went into the kitchen, washed his hands, and then rummaged through the refrigerator for something light to eat. Rosa had barely eaten a bite all day. The little that she had eaten, she'd thrown up.

He took a roasting chicken out of the freezer and placed it in the sink. Next, he prepared fruit salad and a toasted turkey, bacon, and tomato sandwich, then placed them on a serving tray. He was glad she was finally ready to consider Ernesto may be guilty, but wished she'd come around in a less dramatic fashion.

He took her running grocery list off the refrigerator, flipped it over on the back and took the ink pen out of the pencil holder on the counter.

I'm sorry I hurt you, but not sorry for pursuing the truth. The way I went about this was all wrong. I should have come to you first. Please forgive me.

He read his words, then lifted the paper to tear it. The wording was awkward, but this was an awkward situation. He lowered the paper.

I understand you need your space and to find your own way. Just know I'm here to support you in all that you do.

Love Always,

Samson

The events of the past two weeks ran on an infinite loop through Rosa's mind: secrets, deceit, drugs, betrayal, greed, murder. She looked up from washing the raw chicken in the sink to the early morning sun peeking through the trees. "No more," she whispered to herself. "I want the truth."

Ignoring the infinite loop, she massaged the chicken with crushed garlic, then sprinkled it with salt and lemon pepper. She wasn't sure what to do about Samson. Her rational side knew he had a job to do, and she'd be disappointed in him if he didn't do it. Then again, her irrational side wanted him to say, "To hell with the job. Alton can handle this on his own." But, her rational mind reminded her that Samson would ensure no corners were cut. He was honest and would find the truth. In intruded her irrational mind, saying it would blame Samson if Ernesto turned out to be guilty.

"Stop!"

She plopped the chicken into a roaster layered with wild rice and baby carrots, placed the top on the pot and set it into the refrigerator. Her whole life had been a tug of war between Harriet and Ernesto, and now—she sighed—now she couldn't tolerate being a pawn in any games. *No more games. No more hiding from the truth.*

The phone rang, startling her out of her thoughts. She grabbed the tea towel off the back of the chair and used it to hold the phone. "Hello." She trapped the phone between her ear and shoulder, then washed her hands in the sink.

"Hello, darling. It's Aunt Angela. Before you say anything, I want to apologize about yesterday. I was totally out of line."

"There's no need to apologize."

"Yes, there is. I felt like I'd failed Harriet, then took my pain out on you. I had to blame someone for Harriet's death, and Ernesto was an easy target."

"Forget about it." She ripped a paper towel off the roll and took a seat at the kitchen table. A long uncomfortable pause filled the line.

"Agents Quartermaine and Miles came by our hotel room last night," Angela said. Thinking he hadn't wasted any time, Rosa stiffened. "Agent Quartermaine told me everything surrounding Harriet's death and showed me the call records. He went on to say that I owed you an apology. I'd already come to that conclusion, but it was nice to see someone was looking out for you." She laughed nervously. "I'd say he has an interest in you that goes further than any investigation."

"I plead the fifth." Rosa crumpled the paper towel and tossed it onto the table. "The things you said about Daddy… Do you actually think he set David up or was that your grief?"

"All I know is what Harriet told me. Unfortunately, Harriet and the truth were mortal enemies. I don't know what to believe. I know that he used to launder money for David. And he did take you from Harriet. In all honesty, at the time I agreed with his taking you. I knew she had a drinking problem, then when you fell from that banister…" her cracking voice trailed off. "Harriet denied she'd been drinking, but… Well, you know how she was."

"Do you think Daddy's involved now?"

"I wish I had the answers for you, darling. I know he's always loved you. All three of them loved you." The awkward silence returned. "I'm not trying to rush you off the phone, but we have a plane to catch. I'll call in a few days. Goodbye."

"Bye." Rosa hung up, then went into the living room and curled up on the couch with the photo album. Page after page showed a bond between Ernesto and David that Rosa couldn't believe Ernesto would betray.

The doorbell rang. "Oh, Samson," she groaned as she placed the album on the coffee table and rushed to answer the door to tell him to leave her alone.

She swung the door open. "Daddy?"

"Of course." He hugged her. "How are you doing today?"

The security she used to feel when he embraced her was missing. She rested her chin on his chest. There were too many unknowns to feel secure. "I'm fine." She backed away. "But there's something I need to ask you."

"What's wrong?"

"I need to know the truth. The whole truth. Please, Daddy. I'm begging. Is there anything else you haven't told me about you and David?"

"There is nothing else. I know this is hard for you, but I'm innocent. Don't lose faith in me, baby. All we have is each other."

Her guilt over thinking he'd had a hand in Harriet's death weighed her down. Ernesto was her father, and he'd earned the benefit of the doubt. "You've lost weight. How about I cook you a little breakfast?"

"You sound like Anna."

"I've always liked her." She winked, then spun on her stocking feet and headed for the kitchen.

Ernesto grabbed the remote and turned the television to CNN.

"Yesterday was the anniversary of the first color broadcast television show…" said the newscaster. Ernesto tossed his keys. They hit the coffee table with a loud thud and slid into the photo album. A clip of a comedian making fun of CBS for having color shows when individuals didn't own color televisions at the time had Ernesto chuckling.

"What's so funny in there?" Rosa called out.

"How would you like to go to a comedy show later this week? I can check around."

"Sure."

His gaze returned to Rosa's new photo album. Thinking Anna had finally sent her the pictures from Rosa's birthday party, he pulled the album to his side of the table and opened to the first page—Ernesto and David being held by Maria. He frowned. After Rosa found out about David, Anna suggested giving Rosa a copy of his childhood pictures. He'd told Anna no, yet as he flipped through the pages, he could tell she'd disobeyed him. This wasn't like Anna, and she'd pay dearly.

The next set gave him pause. *How did Anna get these pictures of Harriet and Angela?* Scratching his head, he continued thumbing through the album. Angela could have given Rosa the pictures when she was in town. The smells of bacon, eggs, and brewing coffee were distracting, but not half as distracting as the photos of David with Rosa. There was no way Anna or Angela could have copies of these pictures.

He stiffened. *These are David's.* He quickly thumbed through the rest of the album and saw page after page of him with his drug contacts.

"Son of a bitch!" he bit out under his breath. Some of the pictures were as recent as a few months. "That fucking bastard!" he continued silently. "He's ruined everything." He closed the album and lowered his face into his palms.

"Rosa, I can't stay for breakfast." He snatched his keys and headed for the door. "We'll talk later." He rushed out past her.

Frozen in place, holding the serving tray with Ernesto's breakfast, Rosa's mind whirled. Ernesto was in such a hurry to escape that she doubted he noticed her standing there. Tears fell from her eyes. She'd heard it all: his fear, his rage. Feeling weak, she set the tray on the kitchen table before she dropped it. Ernesto's continually asking if David sent her anything screamed, "Pay attention to me!" There was only one logical reason she could come up with for his behavior. *He must think David sent me the album. What did David ruin?*

From the kitchen doorway, she looked from the album over her shoulder to the basement door. She didn't know who the men in the album were. Her old journals gave her Caldwell; maybe they held a few clues to the men's identities.

Ernesto pulled his Mercedes into a space at the grocery story parking lot. He wanted to regain control before he did something stupid. Thanking God Rosa was in the kitchen when he'd lost it, he rested his head on the steering wheel.

He knew Rosa would eventually search into the identity of the men in the photos. He chewed on his cheek. *I'll tell her David thought I had set him up to go to death row, and this must have been his way of getting me back. I just thought these were businessmen. I meet so many people. David must have had pictures taken with the crooked executives I cross paths with. There are so many businesspeople playing both sides of the fence out there. It's impossible to know who is who.* He felt his mind rambling. He'd clean it up before he presented his case to Rosa.

His mind switched to Samson, wondering if he saw the photos. The photos didn't prove anything, but he needed to give the DEA something, or even better yet, someone. He grinned as he thought of a way to protect Rosa and get the DEA off his back. He took out a throwaway phone and called in hits on Barry and Jeff Paige.

"Are you sure you want this done now, Ernesto?" his chief of security asked. "Cutting corners could lead to trouble."

"They're after Rosa. We have to move fast."

"I'll take care of everything."

❦

"It's noon. I'm heading over to Rosa's," Samson said as he cleared his desk.

"I'm no expert on women," Alton said. "But, I think you need to give her some space."

"She'll need me near when she starts looking into the men in the photos. She needs my support—" The intercom buzzer on the phone interrupted him. He picked up the receiver. "Quartermaine."

"Mr. Ernesto Bolívar is here to see you and Agent Miles."

Samson's brows rose. "Is his attorney with him?"

"No, sir."

"Give us five minutes, then send him back. Thanks." He hung up. "Ernesto's here, alone."

Both agents quickly removed or covered everything to do with their case in sight. "What do you think he's up to?" Alton asked.

"Your guess is as good as mine."

❦

Samson sorted through the file of information Ernesto handed them that showed several of Jeff Paige's connections to the drug trade, solid evidence the DEA didn't have. According to Ernesto, Jeff Paige was laundering money for David and was the Sierra No. 2 man. Jeff's alleged intentions were to join the two cartels.

"Why are you coming forward with this information?" Alton asked.

"David told me to give this information to the DEA if the Paiges ever came snooping around Rosa. As you know, Jeff Paige hired Rosa's firm," Ernesto answered smoothly, looking into Alton's eyes.

"But if Jeff is a part of the Martín syndicate, why would he care about Rosa?" Samson asked.

"Because David kept her secret." He had a far off look in his eyes as he focused on the window behind Samson. "They need to know what she knows. And if she knows too much, they'll try to silence her. If they find out about my early connections with David, they may think I want in." Ernesto stood. "I must leave, gentlemen. I have a business to run. If you have any questions, I'd prefer you ask me directly, instead of going through my lawyer. The fewer people who know about this, the better."

"We understand," Samson said.

They watched Ernesto leave the office and close the door.

"He just handed us Jeff Paige on a gold platter, lined with diamonds," Alton said.

"Do you believe Jeff laundered for David?"

"Hell naw! We know the Paiges run the Sierra cartel. Ernesto gave us Jeff, so we'd stop looking at his ass. Hell, I ain't mad at him though. Now they'll both fall, and I'll be running this joint some day."

"He didn't seem himself. He usually challenges me with his eyes. Not this time. This time, he wouldn't even look at me."

⚜

Rosa sat in the middle of her basement floor, surrounded by the photo album, a notebook and journals. An intensive search had revealed only three names, and one of those names was Caldwell's.

Banging broke her concentration. *What the heck?* She tossed her notepad and pencil to the side, then went to investigate the noise. She looked out the window above her kitchen sink and saw Samson. Her heart warmed. He was in the backyard, hammering away, building the patio. Sweat dripped from his brow and beaded on his skin. He took a washcloth out of his back pocket and wiped his face and bald head. She wondered how long he'd been out there in the hot afternoon sun.

She poured a glass of lemonade and took it out to him. "I'll leave the sliding door unlocked."

"Thanks."

She returned to the basement and cleaned up her mess, then went

223

into the kitchen and put the chicken in the oven and set the timer. Samson would be ready to eat a real meal in a few hours. She was glad he'd come, and overjoyed he didn't force himself on her. Somehow he understood that she needed him there for support, not for the solution. Ernesto's innocence was one question that she needed to find the answer to on her own.

She took her notepad and the photo album into her computer room and continued her search for the truth. A few hours later the oven timer dinged, startling Rosa. Unfortunately, her search had found her next to nothing.

She pushed away from the desk and let up the window. "Dinner will be done in about fifteen minutes."

"Here I come."

A few minutes later, Samson stepped into the kitchen with a canvas bag over his shoulder. "Something smells delicious." He kissed her on the cheek as she opened the oven. "I'll clean up and be right back."

She washed her hands, made a garden salad, and then set the table. Having Samson in the house felt so natural to her. *Maybe we'll make it.*

"Need help?" Samson, wearing a clean T-shirt and jeans and smelling fresh, took two glasses out of the cabinet and set them on the table beside the pitcher of lemonade. "I'm starving."

"I'll bet." They took their seats and said a blessing. "You got a lot done today."

"And how about you? Did you get a lot done today?" he asked between bites of wild rice.

"Not much." She thought about how Ernesto had acted at break-fast and felt nauseous. Something wasn't right, and she was determined to find out what. She pushed her plate away. Either Harriet had set Ernesto up—which was something she would do—or Ernesto was in deeper than he let on. "Do you know who those men are in the album with Daddy?"

"Yes." He cut a small piece of chicken leg, then picked it up with a fork and brushed her lips with it. "Eat."

"All you think about is eating."

"All I think about is how much I love you."

She felt her face flush as she took the bite he offered. "Can you give

me the information you have on the men in the photos? I want to…"
she trailed off. "Can I see it?"

He pulled his cell phone off his belt clip and dialed Alton's number.
"Hey, could you start making a file with the information on the men in
the photos with Ernesto that we can give to Rosa?… I know it's a lot…
I'll come by later tonight and help… Thanks." He disconnected, then
returned to enjoying his dinner.

"Thank you, Samson."

"I'll bring the files by in the morning. We can't give you everything
we have."

"I understand." She picked at her salad.

"We interviewed Angela last night, and Ernesto dropped by our
office this morning."

"Daddy came to your office?"

"Shocked the heck out of me, too. He's decided to cooperate, but I
don't know. There are so many lies to sort through."

"I know the feeling." They continued eating their dinner.

"I faxed my letter of resignation this morning. The chief called. He
wasn't surprised."

"Are you sure you want to quit?"

"David once told me I don't have the correct personality for a DEA
agent. I think he's right. After we clean the kitchen, do you want to go
for a walk?"

"Isn't Alton waiting on you?"

"Yeah." He took their empty plates and set them in the sink. "He
can handle things without me for another hour or so."

❧✖❧

Rosa lay across her bed, closely examining the photos. She had
slight recollection of some of the men. The phone rang, startling her.
She checked the caller ID. "Hello, Daddy."

"I just called to apologize for leaving so abruptly this morning."

"What's going on? Why did you rush out?" Silence. "Daddy, what
happened?"

"I saw the album on your coffee table and panicked."

"You, panic?" she asked slowly. "Tell me the whole truth, Daddy. I can't take these bits and pieces. It's making me lose faith in you."

"I know, honey, it's just… I worked for David until you were twelve. When we moved to Miami, I cut my drug ties. But some of those pictures are from a few months ago. I speak to thousands of people. Knowing David, those men in the photos have something to do with the drug world, but I honestly don't know. He set me up."

She leaned against the headboard. "Why on earth would he set you up?"

"Because he thought I had something to do with his being sent to death row. Because when you graduated from college, I refused to allow him to introduce you to the drug world. Because he was jealous of our relationship. There were millions of reasons."

She debated if she should tell him that Harriet gave her the photos. Unsure, she said, "This is the last time I'm going to ask. Please tell me the truth. Are you or were you involved in the illegal drug trade or any other illegal activities after I was twelve?"

"No, Rosa."

"So nothing else will pop up?"

"Only if I'm being framed. David's money reaches beyond the grave."

CHAPTER NINETEEN

Rosa and Samson cleaned and put away the breakfast dishes, then went into her computer room where he gave an overview of the files.

"Thanks for the information, but," she paused, "I want—need—to do this on my own."

"I thought as much. I'll most likely be in the office all day. You can reach me on my cell." He kissed her gently, then left.

Rosa broke out her notebook and highlighters, then began reading the information on the men. Two hours later, she had finished compiling a summary of what each man's legal and illegal roles were.

She set the summaries to the side, booted her computer, and logged into the Bolívar International network system as the super administrator. There were literally thousands of directories and millions of files on the network, and she planned to screen each one until she found the truth. She prayed, again, that the truth was Ernesto wasn't a part of any illegal activity.

She pulled up a search program that she'd made years ago and entered the names of each man separately. The name of the man, the title of the file his name was mentioned in, the name of the directory the file was located, and the last modification date of the file would be piped into a new text file; each result was one line.

Ten minutes later, the program finished the searches. She opened the extensive text file, engaged the sort portion of her search program to order the individual data lines by directory, then hit return. Within seconds, she had a twelve-page list, which she sent to the printer.

While the printer did its dirty work, she scrolled through the list, examining the date stamp.

Many of the files were recent; others were years old. The feelings of nausea returned. She went into the kitchen and grabbed the box of crackers off the refrigerator. She smiled, thinking Samson would kill her if he knew her lunch consisted of saltines.

She padded back to retrieve the printout. The last directory caught her eye—ZZAdjustments. Anxiety levels at an all-time high, she found it hard to concentrate. She couldn't remember an Adjustments department, and the ZZ prefix meant the whole directory had been deleted.

She maneuvered around the Bolívar network until she was in the ZZAdjustments directory. A few years back, someone had maliciously deleted a whole directory, so she'd created an update that renamed directories with the ZZ prefix and placed them in a temporary location for twenty-four hours before the files were actually deleted.

Crumbs fell down Rosa's T-shirt as she nervously gnawed on crackers. Ernesto owned the directory, thus he created it. He had also deleted it. She looked at the time of initial deletion, then the clock—one hour until the files would be deleted permanently.

"No, Daddy." She never thought it necessary to tell him about the updates she'd made to the system. He had no idea the items that he had erased weren't deleted.

❧✕❧

"I'd like two fried shrimp dinners," Samson said to the clerk. "What do you want, Alton?"

"A six-piece wing dinner, heavy on the mild sauce and some orange pop."

"Would you like soup or salad with your shrimp orders, sir?"

"Caesar salad for both, please."

"I don't eat rabbit food, so don't even ask." Alton's cell phone rang. He stepped a few feet away to answer. "Yeah, what?... No shit! How?"

Listening to Alton, Samson had missed what the cashier said. He handed her thirty dollars, assuming that would be enough to cover the bill. "What's happening?" he asked Alton.

Alton held up a finger and went outside.

"Your change, sir."

Samson accepted his change, then headed out the door. "What's happening?"

"Hold a second." Alton gave his full attention to Samson. "Give me a few minutes, and I'll tell you everything."

"Is there something wrong with Rosa?"

"No. If you would let me finish this call, I'd tell you. Damn!"

A few minutes later, Alton entered the restaurant and sat at the table with Samson. "Where are my wings?"

Samson pushed Alton's order across the table to him. On their way back to the office, he intended on dropping Rosa's lunch off to her. "What's going on?"

Alton opened the Styrofoam container and grabbed out a wing. "Guess who got himself shot up, Valentine's Day massacre-style, this morning?" He bit into a wing.

"Oh God, not Ernesto."

"Nope. These things are good."

Samson released a giant sigh of relief. "Who?"

"Barry Paige. I'll bet Ernesto organized the hit." He took another bite of the wing.

"First, he throws Jeff to us, and then has his father murdered. What is he thinking?"

"Sounds like he's panicking to me. You gonna eat or what?"

"Let's go."

"Where? I'm still eating. Barry Paige is dead. He ain't goin' nowhere."

"I need to warn Rosa about Jeff."

Rosa checked her email, and sure enough, there was an automated message telling her about the directory deletion. She closed the email program and entered the deleted directory. She didn't know which file to read first. Truth be told, she didn't want to read any of them. She clicked on the first file in the directory. The phone rang, giving her a short reprieve.

"Hello."

"Hello, baby, it's Samson."

The panic behind his voice set off her silent alarms. "What's wrong?"

"It's Jeff Paige. His father was gunned down."

"That's tragic. What's the world coming to?"

"There's more. Barry Paige was the head of the Sierra cartel. Jeff is the number two guy."

"No way," she gasped.

"We've got to get you out of town."

"Me? Why? Jeff came by snooping like you thought someone would. He couldn't have found anything, because I don't know anything."

"What if he thinks Ernesto put the hit out on his father? The only way to hurt Ernesto is to come after you. Jeff lost the tail we had on him. He must know about his father. I'm only five minutes away. Grab a few mementos, and we're out of here."

"Okay, but I need to copy something first."

"No, Rosa! We don't have time." He paused. "I'm sorry for snapping. Please, just do this for me."

"I'll be ready when you arrive. I need to hang up, or I won't be ready. Love you."

"I love you, too."

She disconnected, closed the file and reached in her bottom drawer for a blank CD. There was no way she'd leave without saving the directory Ernesto had deleted. She could pack while the system was copying.

The doorbell chimed several times. Samson had said he was five minutes away, so she didn't think it was him. Her curiosity almost overtook her common sense. The person stopped ringing the bell and instead banged on the door.

"Rosa, it's Jeff. I need to talk to you about something."

She speed dialed Samson's cell. "He's here. He's here!"

"Hide. We're almost there."

Jeff pounded the door. It was so loud that she was certain he was throwing his body against it. The pounding stopped. She looked around. There were no good places to hide. *How long before he remembers it's a lot easier to break a window than a solid oak door?*

Window. She stuffed the cell phone into her back jeans pocket and opened the window. Halfway out of the window, Jeff rounded the corner and yanked her the rest of the way out, dropping her to the ground.

She caught herself the best she could, but hurt her arm.

"Why didn't you answer the damn door?" He showed her his gun. "Time to leave."

Alton sped around the corner in time to see Jeff back out of Rosa's driveway. Her phone was still on, but the voices were too muffled for them to hear. "We can't rush up there," Alton said. "We'll follow at a distance and wait for our chance."

Samson rocked back and forth. "I'm not losing her. I can't."

Rosa had seen Alton's blue sedan in the passenger side mirror when they left her place, but she didn't let on.

"Ernesto murdered my father. That son of a bitch murdered my father!" He pointed the gun at her head. "His ass has to pay." He lowered the gun while continuing to steer through the congested streets of Oak Park with his free hand. "Take the phone out of my breast pocket and call that bastard."

She followed his orders. "Daddy," she said softly.

"What's wrong? Whose phone are you calling from? It says 'Private.'"

"Jeff Paige has a gun pointed at—"

Jeff snatched the phone. "You know that forest preserve off Thatcher..." He gave the details. "I like Rosa. I'll give you one hour. We swap. You for her." He threw the phone at the windshield. Rosa ducked as pieces ricocheted toward her and every which way.

Ernesto couldn't sort through the business cards fast enough. "Jill! Jill!" He hit the intercom. "Jill Walker, get Samson's number, now!"

Mrs. Walker ran into his office. "What's wrong?"

"He has Rosa!" He scrambled on his desk. "I can't find Samson's number."

"Who has Rosa?"

"That bastard Jeff Paige. He's supposed to be dead."

"Oh no, Ernesto. What were you thinking?"

"We don't have time for this. Get me the fucking number!" She ran out of the office. He looked at his watch. "Shit, shit, shit."

Mrs. Walker rushed into the room, dialing Samson's number. She handed Ernesto the phone.

"The bastard isn't answering. Call Alton." He handed her the phone.

She dialed Alton's number, then handed Ernesto the phone. He never though that he'd be relieved to hear Alton's voice. "Jeff Paige kidnapped Rosa," Ernesto said as he rushed out of the office. "You have to save her. He only gave me an hour to make an hour-and-a-half trip. Please. Please save her. He's headed to the forest preserve off Thatcher."

"Wait a second. Take a breath."

Ernesto swung open the doors of the stairwell and started running down the eight flights rather than waiting on the elevator. "I don't have time for games, Alton. This is my child."

"We're already trailing them."

Ernesto stumbled over Alton's words as he passed the fifth floor. "But how? Never mind. Just keep her safe. I'm on my way."

Rosa glanced over her shoulder as they walked further into the woods. Jeff had threatened to shoot into the crowd of people if she didn't do as he said.

She couldn't see how Samson and Alton would be able to save her, and there was no way she'd allow Jeff to kill both her and Ernesto. She stepped over several fallen branches as she took in her surroundings.

He pushed her forward. "Move it."

She stumbled to the ground. "Ouch." She grabbed her ankle. "I twisted it." She grimaced.

He stepped closer. "Well, hobble your ass on."

She leaned back on her elbows and kicked him in the groin as hard as she could. He fell to the ground. She took off, running deeper into the woods, worried because he hadn't dropped his gun.

A shot rang out. She didn't look back. She'd always stayed in excellent shape and hoped she could zigzag through the trees enough for the bullets to miss her. A second bullet whizzed past her ear. She cut a sharp right and continued, praying that Jeff ran out of bullets before she ran out of breath.

A shot rang out. Samson and Alton stopped. Samson recuperated first and ran toward the sound with his gun drawn.

"Slow down. We don't know what we're running into!" Alton hopped over a log and continued through the brush. "I'm the hot head. You're supposed to think things through."

"I have to save her." A second shot rang out. Samson caught a glimpse of Rosa's bright red T-shirt darting to the right. He couldn't see Jeff. "DEA! Drop your weapon!" he called out.

He saw flashes of Jeff between the trees, chasing Rosa and firing again.

Rosa cut right again. *That's it, baby,* thought Samson. Lead him across my path. He aimed to where she'd just passed and waited. A few seconds later, Jeff appeared. Samson shot. Direct hit in the upper thigh. Jeff fell to the ground.

"Rosa, get down and hide," Samson yelled.

Alton passed Samson on his way to Jeff. "Go find her, man. I got this."

Samson ran for the area where Rosa had headed. He heard something rummaging around in the brush a few yards from his position. He crouched down. "Rosa," he whispered. Shots rang out. "Rosa!"

"Shit!" Alton cursed. "Fucking bastard." More shots rang out.

Samson crawled along the ground.

"Samson, over here," Rosa said under her breath.

He quickly maneuvered through a patch of weeds, grabbed onto

Rosa, and held her tight. More shots echoed in the woods.

"I got his ass!" Alton called. "You can come out now."

❧⚶☙

"…and then he said he'd shoot into the crowd unless I did as he said," Rosa said to the gathering of FBI, DEA, and local police. "So, I went into the woods with him."

"How did you get away?" a burly female police officer asked.

"I pretended like I'd hurt my ankle, then I kicked him in the groin and ran." The small room filled with ewws, oohs, and sympathy moans.

"I don't give a damn!"

Rosa's ears perked up. "Daddy!" She released Samson's hand.

"Where's my child?"

"Daddy!" Rosa raced for the door, but she was stopped by the agents. "Let me go… Daddy!"

Alton left the room, then returned with Ernesto close behind.

Rosa ran to Ernesto and wrapped her arms around him. He combed his hands through her short curls and checked for scrapes and scratches. Seeing none, he pulled her close and rocked her gently. "I've never been so scared in my life."

"I believe you all have enough for your reports," Samson said. "Let's give them privacy."

Alton held the door open, while Samson rushed everyone out.

"I want you to stay, Samson," Rosa requested. He stood in a corner of the small office.

After everyone cleared, she said, "He thought you ordered the hit on his father, so he went after me." She shook her head. "That is the craziest thing I've ever heard. He wanted to kill me because he thought you *might have* put a hit out on his father."

"I'm sorry about all of this. This is why I left the lifestyle."

She backed away. "Did you leave it, Daddy? Are you putting out hits on men? Did you set up your best friend?"

"Of course not, Rosa. Where is this coming from?"

"I saw the hidden directory in Bolívar International's network that you tried to delete yesterday."

His eyes cut to Samson, then he returned his attention to Rosa. "We can't talk about this here. Come home with me. I'll explain everything."

"I've been asking you to explain everything for weeks. You kept saying you had, then I'd find more. I love you, Daddy." She hugged him. "I'll always love you. I need to hear the truth come from your lips."

"I'm sorry I've disappointed you. The truth is that I love you more than anything." His grip around her tightened. "We need to talk. I mean have a serious talk, just you and me."

Alton cracked the door open. "Sorry to interrupt, but the Sierra team is here and needs to speak with Rosa."

"Why can't I talk to them tomorrow or you give them an update?"

"The impatient assholes want to know about your meetings with the Paiges and what you found when you were testing their network. I know you're tired, but it's best to get this over with."

"Go ahead," Ernesto said. "Samson, bring her by my place when they're finished questioning her."

"I'm sure they'll have questions for you also," Alton said to Ernesto.

"I'm only answering one person's questions tonight." He kissed Rosa on the forehead. "I love you."

"I love you more."

<hr/>

"What do you mean he's gone?" Rosa asked from the back seat of Alton's car.

"While you were speaking with the Sierra team, I had Ernesto tailed. He went to the airport and hopped on his jet."

She took out her cell phone and dialed Ernesto's number.

"I'm sorry, Rosa. I love you more."

The line went dead. "He hung up on me."

"How he expects to get away in a plane is beyond me," Alton said.

"Are you sure he's on the plane?" Samson asked.

Alton laughed. "Excellent-assed question, but it doesn't matter anyway. It's not like we can arrest him for anything."

"Rosa," Samson said, but was greeted by silence. "Rosa."

"He's guilty," she murmured. "How many more people has he had murdered?"

"I know this is hard for you, baby, but I need your help. I need a copy of the directory Ernesto tried to delete."

She wiped the tears from her eyes. "There is no directory. He actually did delete it." She explained how Jeff kidnapping her had prevented her from copying the directory.

CHAPTER TWENTY

One week later

"Samson, would you please turn the food? I don't know what's wrong with me. The smell of frying fish usually makes me hungry, but today it's making me nauseous."

On his way to the kitchen, Samson stopped by the computer room. "That's my baby in there, Mrs. Quartermaine." He bent down and kissed Rosa's belly. "It's time for a home pregnancy test."

"I think it's time for you to turn the fish before it burns," she teased, praying he was correct.

"Your wish is my command."

She opened the next software sample. *I'm so far behind. I'll never catch up.* She unfolded the two page letter that accompanied the CD-ROMs.

Hello, Rosa.
My name is David Martín.

The letter fell from her hands. "Samson! Samson! It's David." She scrambled to pick the pages off the floor.

Samson ran into the room. "What's wrong?"

Her hands shook so badly, the letters looked like alphabet soup. "It's David. He wrote to me." She tried to focus through her tears, but couldn't.

Samson took the letter. "Where did you get this?"

"I thought it was a software sample." She handed him the package.

"The postmark is the week of his execution." He took out the CDs marked: "Sierra Syndicate," "Martín Syndicate," and "Images for Rosa."

"What does the letter say?" she asked. "I'm so nervous that I can't even see straight."

"Hello, Rosa. My name is David Martín. What I'm about to tell you will sound impossible, but I can't die without leaving you protected." He went on tell her about how he and Ernesto ran the Martín syndicate, he was her natural father, how Ernesto came to raise her, that he has always loved her, and that Ernesto knew about the Sierra CD, but didn't know about the Martín one. If Ernesto ever got out of line or someone by the name of Paige came snooping around, she was to find DEA agent Samson Quartermaine and give him the CDs. All of Samson's contact information was included in the letter along with the names, addresses, and phone numbers of his siblings and mother.

Samson put the Martín CD into the computer. David kept excellent records of distribution routes, accounts, pay-offs, hideouts, and every crooked businessperson, law enforcement officer, and government official he dealt with. "Wow," was all he could say.

By the time you receive this, it will be a full-length manuscript. Ernesto glanced from the computer screen out the window onto the rolling hills of his ranch. *I find myself sitting here writing to you several times a day, but can't bring myself to press the send. My draft box is just about full.*

You've always been so smart. I can't even open your emails because I know you've already figured out how to trace the area it's opened from. However, that's not the reason I haven't been in communication. I'm ashamed. His index finger paused over the backspace key.

Someday, you'll read all of my letters to you. My list of regrets is so extensive. I guess I do need to write a complete manuscript.

About David. He ran his hands through his graying hair and blew out an exasperated breath. *I honestly thought he wanted to bring you into our business. I loved him, but I love you more. I protected you the only way I could. By the time I realized my mistake, short of breaking him out of jail, there was nothing I could do.*

David thought I stepped in to care for Rosa Shields out of friendship. That was only part of the reason. The other part was my guilt. Please make sure she's taken care of. She's a good woman, just hurting. Jill knows her location. He shook his head. *I can't believe I betrayed my friend, my brother. I'll never forgive myself.*

I miss him. He sighed. *I miss you both.*

He saved the letter to his draft folder, then went through the house and checked the guns he'd hidden throughout the house. He would have hired security, but he didn't want to call attention to himself. No one would think to look for him in Wolf Point, Montana. If he lay low, DEA would never find him. He had over two year's supply of food and other necessities in storage. Anna was upstairs asleep.

He went out to the barn to get a box of photos he'd left in his truck. He hadn't spoken to Rosa since he'd skipped town. Thoughts of his baby girl brought a smile to his face. When he first agreed to raise her, he'd never imagined he could actually love her.

The sound of a car's engine sliced the country silence. He peeked out of the barn and saw a blue sedan approaching. It looked like there were four, maybe five passengers. He backed further into the barn, so they wouldn't see him. He wasn't in the mood for the Wolf Point welcoming committee or whomever it was.

"I'm not staying in the car," Samson said. "Are you sure the perimeter's secured?"

"If anything happens to you, Rosa will kill me, bring me back to life, then kill me again," Alton said. "This is your last day. Stay your ass in the car."

All five agents, including Samson, stepped out of the car. Alton rolled his eyes, then motioned an agent to wait at the rear of the house and one on each side. Samson walked up the stairs of the large Victorian style home and knocked on the door. Alton walked toward the barn.

"Ernesto, this is DEA agent Samson Quar—" The sound of a large engine revving to a start halted Samson's words.

Alton ran for the barn with the other agents in pursuit. A black SUV sped out of the barn. The agents ran for the car, some shooting at the truck's tires and missing.

Samson radioed to the blockade as he entered the car. "Ernesto's headed down the private road in a black SUV. Be ready for him. Shoot his tires out. Disable his vehicle."

Alton slammed the door of the sedan and gave chase.

Ernesto veered his truck off the main road onto what may have been a dirt path at one time. Gaining ground, Alton followed. The agents bounced in their seats as the car made its way over the branch-filled, stony path. "We need a four-wheeler," Alton said.

"That's exactly why he turned this way," Samson said, holding onto the dashboard for additional balance.

"Oh, shit. If he goes up that mountain…"

"Look!" Samson pointed to their left. A government four-wheeler truck sped out of the tree line and quickly gained ground on the SUV. The passenger shot at the SUV's tires.

Ernesto stuck his arm out the window to shoot back, hit a bump, and dropped the gun. He made a sharp turn to the right, heading directly for his neighbor's barbed wire fence. He burst through the fence and continued, weaving through cattle.

"He's driving like a madman," said one of the agents in the back seat.

"I can't go over that barbed wire." Alton drove south along the fence to the entry. "Hold tight!" Pressing the gas pedal to the floor, the wrought-iron gate flew off its hinges as he sped through it. "Where'd they go?"

"Over there, by that pond," Samson said.

They made their way to the pond, but had to stop at the base of a steep, rocky climb. "Damn mountains."

"Hills, Alton. Really big hills." Samson got out of the car and raised his hand to shade his eyes so he could see Ernesto's truck ascend.

"Semantics mean shit to me." Alton slammed his car door closed.

Ernesto's front left tire went over a large rock, tilting the SUV onto two wheels briefly. Samson's heart stopped. "Slow the hell down." No sooner did Samson get the word "down" out of his mouth than Ernesto's SUV tipped on two wheels again. This time, the SUV flipped.

Samson ran to Ernesto's aid as the SUV tumbled down the hill.

Rosa tried to push through the police officers that blocked Ernesto's hospital room. "What do you mean I can't see him?"

"We're sorry, ma'am, but we aren't allowed to let anyone…"

"Samson! Alton!"

Both agents came running down the hall, badges flashing. "She's alright," Alton said.

Samson escorted Rosa into the room.

The tubes, monitors, I.V., bandages, a broken man… Rosa ordered her tears not to fall. They couldn't even make an appearance. "Daddy," she whispered.

Ernesto cracked his eyes open. "Rosa…" He drew in a belabored breath. "Forgive me."

His obvious physical pain couldn't compete with the emotional pain she saw in his eyes. "You're my hero. You're my daddy."

His eyes slowly closed. "I love you."

"I love you more."

A few seconds and staggered breaths later, he said, "That's impossible."

She laid her head on the bed and her hand on his chest. "Stick around and prove me wrong."

One Year Later

Ernesto lifted his hand to block the sun. He'd bet there had never been a clearer, warmer, drearier day in history. He barely had a half second of freedom before the first reporter spotted him and charged with a microphone waving in the air.

"Mr. Bolívar, Mr. Bolívar!" A mob of reporters and spectators followed the young man up the cement courthouse steps, quickly surrounding Ernesto, his legal team and bodyguards.

Ernesto drew in a deep breath and snapped his game face firmly into place. Anna had ensured that he had the best legal team, judge and jury money could buy, so fear of conviction was never an issue. Yet, the one thing he wanted—needed—couldn't be bought.

"Mr. Bolívar, now that you've been acquitted of all charges, do you plan to reclaim your position as CEO of Bolívar International?" a reporter shouted over the crowd.

Microphones popped out from everywhere. At one point in his life, Ernesto craved the spotlight. He sighed internally. Now, all he wanted was to hide. The only light he longed for was Rosa.

His heart filled with pride as his voice boomed, "My daughter Rosa Quartermaine is doing an excellent job of leading the company. In the year that she's been at the helm, she brought the company through this troubling period, and she's taken thirteen percent of the market share from our competitors." He beamed. "She's managed to do the impossible. The company is in good hands." His bodyguards began clearing the way for him to get to his limo, which was waiting at the bottom of the steps.

"Mr. Bolívar," called another reporter. "Is it true that your daughter hasn't spoken to you since July of last year when you were upgraded to stable condition at the hospital?" The murmurs of the crowd increased.

The dagger plunged into Ernesto's heart by the reporter's question wasn't visible to the human eye, but the pain was no less severe. Once he was clear of danger, the realities of his betrayal had hit her hard. He offered a polite smile to the onlookers. "My twin grandsons are named David and Ernesto." He paused to allow the vultures to mull over his words. "Good day to you all."

The bodyguards led the way as he quickly descended the stairs. Marcus, the chauffer, rounded the limo and opened the door for him. Ernesto ignored the questions bombarding him. He was done with his life in the public eye. He nodded at Marcus, then slid into the back seat. Marcus closed the door, and the bodyguards double-timed it to their SUVs, which were parked, one behind and one in front of them.

A reporter knocked on the rear passenger window. "Is it true Martín willed his estate to Samson Quartermaine?"

Marcus pulled away from the curb and the crowd. Ernesto wished it were that easy for him to pull away from his old life.

"Ernesto," Anna calmly said as she placed her hand over his.

He'd seen her in the back seat, but he hadn't *seen* her when he entered the vehicle. His heart was other places. His head fell back onto the seat. "I've lost Rosa," he whispered. His eyes burned almost as much as his heart ached. This punishment was greater than anything man could dictate.

"She needs more time."

"She'll never believe in me again. If I'm not her hero, I'm nothing."

As the limo rounded the corner to merge onto the expressway, Ernesto barely had the strength to keep from falling into the door, knowing he had no one to blame but himself. He'd found himself caught up in the intricate web he'd woven. He watched out the window as Marcus weaved through the traffic.

"I told her you're working with the DEA. Teaching them the ins and outs of the drug trade."

"I told you not to tell her. She'll think I'm helping them to manipulate her into speaking with me."

She raised a brow. "I know what you told me. I also know that you're right; Rosa will never see you the same way, and things will never be the same between you two. But, honey, you were neck deep in the drug trade, hiding half of your life from her, manipulating and lying at every turn. You aren't that person anymore. Give her time to forgive him and learn this new man. She has to do this in her time, not yours."

Ernesto closed his eyes and prayed for Rosa's forgiveness.

ABOUT THE AUTHOR

Caught Up is Deatri's debut novel. Currently a Chicago area resident, she works as an editor. Three children, two dogs, and one husband keep her days pretty full. An avid reader since childhood, Deatri's idea of a great afternoon is a trip to the bookstore, followed by hours curled up on the sofa with her newly purchased novel. You can contact Deatri King-Bey at 2405 Essington RD. Unit B, PMB 212, Joliet, IL 60435, or email her at deatri@deewrites.com. Visit her website at http://www.deewrites.com.

If you'd like to learn a little something about our Afro-Colombian brothers and sisters, here is a place to start http://www.colombiasupport.net/choco/index.html.

Excerpt from

UNDER THE CHERRY MOON

BY

CHRISTAL JORDAN-MIMS

Release Date: January 2006

PROLOGUE

Paris rushed out of the indigo colored building. Eyes quickly adjusting to the dark of night, she checked her peripheral vision to ensure no one had followed her. Steps away from the deserted parking lot, she paused to squint up at the scripted sign. It blazed "Under the Cherry Moon" in red neon lights. She'd spent the last three years of her life here, but tonight had been her last shift. She fingered the cold metal in her soft leather purse, then pushed her teased hair from of her face. Tonight, she would get answers to the haunting questions that plagued her all of her life.

Black t-strap heels three-inches-high made click-clack noises on the hard pavement as she made her way to her black Porsche Boxter with the vanity plate *CARAMEL*. She'd gotten the plate after her boss had taken one look at her and exclaimed, "Add butterscotch to chocolate and you get caramel." Paris smirked at the memory of his unexpected and unnecessary comment, then focused on more imminent matters.

Pressing the black button on her key ring, her Porsche bleeped and the headlights flashed in response. Paris input the personal code, then paused as the door unlocked itself. She had a long drive ahead of her, so she hastily secured her safety belt and spared a quick glance to check the location of her mirrors. She'd stopped at the gas station earlier where she'd filled the tank, gotten a routine oil change, had the engine flushed and her tires rotated. Pleased that her car had received a clean bill of health; Paris knew there wouldn't be any interruptions in her journey. Paris slid the key in the ignition and smiled as the powerful engine trembled underneath her fingertips, resting on the steering wheel.

Every time Paris sat behind the wheel of this car, she appreciated it all over again. The power was intoxicating as it flowed from the engine. She felt empowered, driving at top speed always provided an immediate heady rush. Backing out of the parking lot, she checked her makeup in the rear view mirror, eased the car into the street, and then gunned the engine, taking off for the nearest exit. Paris was off to see her father.

CHAPTER ONE
KEEPING IT REAL

The phone rang loudly, interrupting Paris from her sleep. Irritated, she reached over and knocked the phone off the hook. It was two-thirty in the afternoon, and she was in the middle of enjoying a good sleep.

"Hello?" a female voice called out from the misplaced receiver.

Paris groaned as she extended a slender brown arm from her plush comforter to search for the phone.

"Hello?"

"Hi, Momma," Paris grumbled.

"How are you, baby? You must be sleeping. I can hear it in your voice."

Her mother's warm voice pulled Paris out of her sleep and provided the initiative to sit up in bed. Amidst the darkness, she rubbed her eyes and tried to focus on the surroundings of her bedroom. Her chocolate shades, pulled severely in attempt to block any cunning rays of sunlight. Outfits from last night's performance were strung over the back of her Queen Anne lounger in the far corner of her room. The closet was ajar, revealing a mirage of size six lingerie, costumes, and casual clothes. A vast collection of La Perla silk panties and 34C-sized brassieres decorated her wooden dresser and armoire.

I really need to clean this place up, she reluctantly admitted to herself.

"Yeah, Momma, I got in really late last night." She stifled a yawn.

"Baby, I wish you would reconsider that late night job. A young lady doesn't need to be coming in that late at night. I worry about somebody following you home or something."

Even though she experienced a brief stab of guilt due to her mother's incessant worrying, Paris smiled. She shuddered to think what her mother would do if she knew what she was actually doing at her midnight job. She led Deanne, her mother, to believe that she worked the graveyard shift at a twenty-four hour, customer-service call center. Though she hated lying to her mother, she knew it would kill Deanne to know her true profession. There was little chance that Deanne would discover Paris' secret because her mother lived in a tiny backward county in Mississippi and wouldn't dare travel all the way to racy, upbeat New Orleans.

The imaginary job wasn't the first misconception Paris planted in her mother's head, but merely the biggest in a rich history that spanned as far back as Paris could remember.

Deanne Jackson had been a single mother with an iron fist, a narrow mind and a propensity to hide behind her stern Baptist teachings. Paris and her brothers learned early on to rely on their imagination when dealing with their mother's intolerant rules. Now, Paris constantly reminded herself that as a twenty-six year old woman, she should be able to look her mother in the eyes and tell her she was a grown woman whose choices were hers and hers alone, regardless of whether Deanne approved or not. Unfortunately, one disapproving look from Deanne could still make Paris feel like an eight-year-old with an unfinished homework assignment and no pre-packaged alibi.

Her twin brothers Ivan and Sharp lived in Atlanta. Georgia was far enough from Deanne to keep her from being confronted by their less than conservative lives, but close enough for them to make it home for major holidays. The boys were three years younger than Paris. She had always been fiercely protective of her brothers and had travailed over the decision to enlighten them on her career choice, especially Ivan. Although Ivan was only a minute-and-a-half younger than Sharp, it seemed like years. Growing up, she and Sharp had recognized Ivan's naïveté and had tried to shield him from kids who would take advantage of him.

She had told Sharp of her true profession, assuming that he would do her dirty work and relay the bad news to Ivan. His accusatory response had temporarily bruised her ego, but it was what she should have expected from Sharp.

"You know that's fucked up, but hey you're a grown woman. I hope you realize that it won't last for long though, and then what are you going to do?" Sharp had asked.

It was almost a year ago since she had told Sharp her secret, and Paris hadn't paid his question much thought at the time. She also hadn't told him how much she made in a week, that being one of the biggest factors that convinced her to slowly disrobe in front of a room full of obnoxious men.

Paris considered her relationship with her brothers as close; but even then, she kept them at arm's length emotionally. Sharp was very much the same way, and the two of them shielded Ivan's emotions. When she was around her family, Paris kept quiet most of the time to keep from slipping up and revealing too much about her lifestyle. She never allowed herself to think about how her brothers would feel if they saw her perform. It was much easier for her to keep those parts of her life separate, both physically and emotionally.

Not wanting to deal with the hassle of being distant this year, Paris wormed her way out of Easter and had a plan for getting out of Thanksgiving in a few months, but there was no way Deanne would let her off the hook for Christmas. She was going to have to drive her old Camry, which would mean leaving her beloved Porsche in the covered parking at her building,

Paris smiled to herself, imagining her brother's jaws dropping if they could see her convertible limited-edition Porsche. Sharp would be extremely impressed, as he was much more materialistic than Ivan. She almost laughed aloud at the thought of Sharp's milk chocolate features turning green with envy. Fortunately, for him, she would never be able to drive her car anywhere near her family. There was no way she could justify having such an expensive car on her salary to her mother, and even if she could hide the fact from Deanne, the car would cause tongues to wag in Cleveland, Mississippi. So, although Sharp knew she was a dancer, she wouldn't be able to share her prized possession with him either. Paris and Sharp were kindred spirits, and she knew he'd never admit how much it bothered him that she was stripping for a living. If anyone understood doing everything in one's power to avoid ending up powerless and without, it was Sharp.

"Baby, are you there?" Deanne's question snapped Paris out of her daydreaming.

"Yeah, Momma. I guess I'm really tired."

"Alright, baby. I'd better let you get back to sleep. Call me later in the week all right?"

Paris returned her mother's goodbye, replaced the phone and pulled her down comforter over her eyes. She hoped sleep would not evade her as it usually did once her groove had been interrupted. It was Friday, and that meant she'd have to endure hell at the club tonight. The weekend would produce hordes of men who were ready and willing to spend their hard-earned cash on any and everything but their wives and children.

Paris still found it hard to believe that her customers spent so much money at the club. Many dancers told stories of exotic trips and grossly expensive jewelry lavished upon them by besotted customers. The majority of these men were married, and it was obvious by their constant offers that their wives were totally in the dark.

Last year a silver-tongued Italian executive from New York whisked Chocolate away on an all-expense paid tryst to Belize. Chocolate told Paris that the man called his wife three times every day and even answered a cell phone call from his daughter while they were engaged in what Chocolate described as physical recreation.

The lies never stopped with these men, from secret credit cards, covertly written-off expenses, surreptitious phone numbers to elaborate love nests and exorbitant cash advances. Their intricately spun web of lies magically avoided intersecting, leaving their wives and families none the wiser.

A very-married customer who owned an exotic car dealership talked Paris into test-driving a brand-new Porsche Boxter. He generously offered to help with the down payment on the car, then informed Paris that she would be the culmination of every man's secret fantasy driving the phallic-symbol of a car. After posing in several pictures for his dealership surrounded by various new Porsche models, Paris decided she liked the way she looked and felt sitting behind the wheel of the car. She fell completely in love with a sleek black convertible, and so the next week her auto dealer friend helped her put a hefty down payment on a '99 Porsche Boxter.

Paris bought her Porsche a month after the Mardi Gras celebration. The infamous New Orleans holiday was easily her favorite time of year, as she made the bulk of her yearly salary that week. The hedonistic French Quarters were bombarded with freaks and perverts, who, surprisingly enough, had tough competition outdoing the average Joe's ready to shed coordinating suit coats and slacks for a week of unadulterated fun. Since much of the celebration included strip bars and private parties, Paris, along with her co-workers cleaned up righteously. This year she'd worked twelve private parties, and that was working the Sunday before Mardi Gras through the Wednesday after. She cleared over twelve thousand dollars, and got another twenty-five hundred at the club that weekend. With that money, and help from a couple of friends who enjoyed her company, she managed to pay her penthouse off completely.

While Chocolate reminisced about how nice it must be to have someone love you enough to want to give you their last name, Paris reminded her it was much better to be on this side of the bank account. There was no way she wanted to end up being played out like the wives of her clients.

2006 Publication Schedule

January

A Lover's Legacy
Veronica Parker
1-58571-167-5
$9.95

Love Lasts Forever
Dominiqua Douglas
1-58571-187-X
$9.95

Under the Cherry
Moon
Christal Jordan-Mims
1-58571-169-1
$12.95

February

Second Chances at Love
Cheris Hodges
1-58571-188-8
$9.95

Enchanted Desire
Wanda Thomas
1-58571-176-4
$9.95

Caught Up
Deatri King Bey
1-58571-178-0
$12.95

March

I'm Gonna Make You
Love Me
Gwyneth Bolton
1-58571-181-0
$9.95

Through the Fire
Seressia Glass
1-58571-173-X
$9.95

Notes When Summer
Ends
Beverly Lauderdale
1-58571-180-2
$12.95

April

Sin and Surrender
J.M. Jeffries
1-58571-189-6
$9.95

Unearthing Passions
Elaine Sims
1-58571-184-5
$9.95

Between Tears
Pamela Ridley
1-58571-179-9
$12.95

May

Misty Blue
Dyanne Davis
1-58571-186-1
$9.95

Ironic
Pamela Leigh Starr
1-58571-168-3
$9.95

Cricket's Serenade
Carolita Blythe
1-58571-183-7
$12.95

June

Cupid
Barbara Keaton
1-58571-174-8
$9.95

Havana Sunrise
Kymberly Hunt
1-58571-182-9
$9.95

2006 Publication Schedule (continued)

July

Love Me Carefully
A.C. Arthur
1-58571-177-2
$9.95

No Ordinary Love
Angela Weaver
1-58571-198-5
$9.95

Rehoboth Road
Anita Ballard-Jones
1-58571-196-9
$12.95

August

Scent of Rain
Annetta P. Lee
158571-199-3
$9.95

Love in High Gear
Charlotte Roy
158571-185-3
$9.95

Rise of the Phoenix
Kenneth Whetstone
1-58571-197-7
$12.95

September

The Business of Love
Cheris Hodges
1-58571-193-4
$9.95

Rock Star
Rosyln Hardy Holcomb
1-58571-200-0
$9.95

A Dead Man Speaks
Lisa Jones Johnson
1-58571-203-5
$12.95

October

Rivers of the Soul-Part 1
Leslie Esdaile
1-58571-223-X
$9.95

A Dangerous Woman
J.M. Jeffries
1-58571-195-0
$9.95

Sinful Intentions
Crystal Rhodes
1-58571-201-9
$12.95

November

Only You
Crystal Hubbard
1-58571-208-6
$9.95

Ebony Eyes
Kei Swanson
1-58571-194-2
$9.95

By and By
Collette Haywood
1-58571-209-4
$12.95

December

Let's Get It On
Dyanne Davis
1-58571-210-8
$9.95

Nights Over Egypt
Barbara Keaton
1-58571-192-6
$9.95

A Pefect Place to Pray
I.L. Goodwin
1-58571-202-7
$12.95

Other Genesis Press, Inc. Titles

A Dangerous Deception	J.M. Jeffries	$8.95
A Dangerous Love	J.M. Jeffries	$8.95
A Dangerous Obsession	J.M. Jeffries	$8.95
A Drummer's Beat to Mend	Kei Swanson	$9.95
A Happy Life	Charlotte Harris	$9.95
A Heart's Awakening	Veronica Parker	$9.95
A Lark on the Wing	Phyliss Hamilton	$9.95
A Love of Her Own	Cheris F. Hodges	$9.95
A Love to Cherish	Beverly Clark	$8.95
A Risk of Rain	Dar Tomlinson	$8.95
A Twist of Fate	Beverly Clark	$8.95
A Will to Love	Angie Daniels	$9.95
Acquisitions	Kimberley White	$8.95
Across	Carol Payne	$12.95
After the Vows	Leslie Esdaile	$10.95
(Summer Anthology)	T.T. Henderson	
	Jacqueline Thomas	
Again My Love	Kayla Perrin	$10.95
Against the Wind	Gwynne Forster	$8.95
All I Ask	Barbara Keaton	$8.95
Ambrosia	T.T. Henderson	$8.95
An Unfinished Love Affair	Barbara Keaton	$8.95
And Then Came You	Dorothy Elizabeth Love	$8.95
Angel's Paradise	Janice Angelique	$9.95
At Last	Lisa G. Riley	$8.95
Best of Friends	Natalie Dunbar	$8.95
Beyond the Rapture	Beverly Clark	$9.95
Blaze	Barbara Keaton	$9.95
Blood Lust	J. M. Jeffries	$9.95
Bodyguard	Andrea Jackson	$9.95
Boss of Me	Diana Nyad	$8.95
Bound by Love	Beverly Clark	$8.95
Breeze	Robin Hampton Allen	$10.95

Other Genesis Press, Inc. Titles (continued)

Broken	Dar Tomlinson	$24.95
By Design	Barbara Keaton	$8.95
Cajun Heat	Charlene Berry	$8.95
Careless Whispers	Rochelle Alers	$8.95
Cats & Other Tales	Marilyn Wagner	$8.95
Caught in a Trap	Andre Michelle	$8.95
Caught Up In the Rapture	Lisa G. Riley	$9.95
Cautious Heart	Cheris F Hodges	$8.95
Chances	Pamela Leigh Starr	$8.95
Cherish the Flame	Beverly Clark	$8.95
Class Reunion	Irma Jenkins/John Brown	$12.95
Code Name: Diva	J.M. Jeffries	$9.95
Conquering Dr. Wexler's Heart	Kimberley White	$9.95
Crossing Paths, Tempting Memories	Dorothy Elizabeth Love	$9.95
Cypress Whisperings	Phyllis Hamilton	$8.95
Dark Embrace	Crystal Wilson Harris	$8.95
Dark Storm Rising	Chinelu Moore	$10.95
Daughter of the Wind	Joan Xian	$8.95
Deadly Sacrifice	Jack Kean	$22.95
Designer Passion	Dar Tomlinson	$8.95
Dreamtective	Liz Swados	$5.95
Ebony Butterfly II	Delilah Dawson	$14.95
Echoes of Yesterday	Beverly Clark	$9.95
Eden's Garden	Elizabeth Rose	$8.95
Everlastin' Love	Gay G. Gunn	$8.95
Everlasting Moments	Dorothy Elizabeth Love	$8.95
Everything and More	Sinclair Lebeau	$8.95
Everything but Love	Natalie Dunbar	$8.95
Eve's Prescription	Edwina Martin Arnold	$8.95
Falling	Natalie Dunbar	$9.95
Fate	Pamela Leigh Starr	$8.95
Finding Isabella	A.J. Garrotto	$8.95

Other Genesis Press, Inc. Titles (continued)

Forbidden Quest	Dar Tomlinson	$10.95
Forever Love	Wanda Thomas	$8.95
From the Ashes	Kathleen Suzanne	$8.95
	Jeanne Sumerix	
Gentle Yearning	Rochelle Alers	$10.95
Glory of Love	Sinclair LeBeau	$10.95
Go Gentle into that Good Night	Malcom Boyd	$12.95
Goldengroove	Mary Beth Craft	$16.95
Groove, Bang, and Jive	Steve Cannon	$8.99
Hand in Glove	Andrea Jackson	$9.95
Hard to Love	Kimberley White	$9.95
Hart & Soul	Angie Daniels	$8.95
Heartbeat	Stephanie Bedwell-Grime	$8.95
Hearts Remember	M. Loui Quezada	$8.95
Hidden Memories	Robin Allen	$10.95
Higher Ground	Leah Latimer	$19.95
Hitler, the War, and the Pope	Ronald Rychiak	$26.95
How to Write a Romance	Kathryn Falk	$18.95
I Married a Reclining Chair	Lisa M. Fuhs	$8.95
Indigo After Dark Vol. I	Nia Dixon/Angelique	$10.95
Indigo After Dark Vol. II	Dolores Bundy/Cole Riley	$10.95
Indigo After Dark Vol. III	Montana Blue/Coco Morena	$10.95
Indigo After Dark Vol. IV	Cassandra Colt/	$14.95
	Diana Richeaux	
Indigo After Dark Vol. V	Delilah Dawson	$14.95
Icie	Pamela Leigh Starr	$8.95
I'll Be Your Shelter	Giselle Carmichael	$8.95
I'll Paint a Sun	A.J. Garrotto	$9.95
Illusions	Pamela Leigh Starr	$8.95
Indiscretions	Donna Hill	$8.95
Intentional Mistakes	Michele Sudler	$9.95
Interlude	Donna Hill	$8.95
Intimate Intentions	Angie Daniels	$8.95

Other Genesis Press, Inc. Titles (continued)

Jolie's Surrender	Edwina Martin-Arnold	$8.95
Kiss or Keep	Debra Phillips	$8.95
Lace	Giselle Carmichael	$9.95
Last Train to Memphis	Elsa Cook	$12.95
Lasting Valor	Ken Olsen	$24.95
Let Us Prey	Hunter Lundy	$25.95
Life Is Never As It Seems	J.J. Michael	$12.95
Lighter Shade of Brown	Vicki Andrews	$8.95
Love Always	Mildred E. Riley	$10.95
Love Doesn't Come Easy	Charlyne Dickerson	$8.95
Love Unveiled	Gloria Greene	$10.95
Love's Deception	Charlene Berry	$10.95
Love's Destiny	M. Loui Quezada	$8.95
Mae's Promise	Melody Walcott	$8.95
Magnolia Sunset	Giselle Carmichael	$8.95
Matters of Life and Death	Lesego Malepe, Ph.D.	$15.95
Meant to Be	Jeanne Sumerix	$8.95
Midnight Clear	Leslie Esdaile	$10.95
(Anthology)	Gwynne Forster	
	Carmen Green	
	Monica Jackson	
Midnight Magic	Gwynne Forster	$8.95
Midnight Peril	Vicki Andrews	$10.95
Misconceptions	Pamela Leigh Starr	$9.95
Montgomery's Children	Richard Perry	$14.95
My Buffalo Soldier	Barbara B. K. Reeves	$8.95
Naked Soul	Gwynne Forster	$8.95
Next to Last Chance	Louisa Dixon	$24.95
No Apologies	Seressia Glass	$8.95
No Commitment Required	Seressia Glass	$8.95
No Regrets	Mildred E. Riley	$8.95
Nowhere to Run	Gay G. Gunn	$10.95
O Bed! O Breakfast!	Rob Kuehnle	$14.95

Other Genesis Press, Inc. Titles (continued)

Object of His Desire	A. C. Arthur	$8.95
Office Policy	A. C. Arthur	$9.95
Once in a Blue Moon	Dorianne Cole	$9.95
One Day at a Time	Bella McFarland	$8.95
Outside Chance	Louisa Dixon	$24.95
Passion	T.T. Henderson	$10.95
Passion's Blood	Cherif Fortin	$22.95
Passion's Journey	Wanda Thomas	$8.95
Past Promises	Jahmel West	$8.95
Path of Fire	T.T. Henderson	$8.95
Path of Thorns	Annetta P. Lee	$9.95
Peace Be Still	Colette Haywood	$12.95
Picture Perfect	Reon Carter	$8.95
Playing for Keeps	Stephanie Salinas	$8.95
Pride & Joi	Gay G. Gunn	$15.95
Pride & Joi	Gay G. Gunn	$8.95
Promises to Keep	Alicia Wiggins	$8.95
Quiet Storm	Donna Hill	$10.95
Reckless Surrender	Rochelle Alers	$6.95
Red Polka Dot in a World of Plaid	Varian Johnson	$12.95
Reluctant Captive	Joyce Jackson	$8.95
Rendezvous with Fate	Jeanne Sumerix	$8.95
Revelations	Cheris F. Hodges	$8.95
Rivers of the Soul	Leslie Esdaile	$8.95
Rocky Mountain Romance	Kathleen Suzanne	$8.95
Rooms of the Heart	Donna Hill	$8.95
Rough on Rats and Tough on Cats	Chris Parker	$12.95
Secret Library Vol. 1	Nina Sheridan	$18.95
Secret Library Vol. 2	Cassandra Colt	$8.95
Shades of Brown	Denise Becker	$8.95
Shades of Desire	Monica White	$8.95

Other Genesis Press, Inc. Titles (continued)

Shadows in the Moonlight	Jeanne Sumerix	$8.95
Sin	Crystal Rhodes	$8.95
So Amazing	Sinclair LeBeau	$8.95
Somebody's Someone	Sinclair LeBeau	$8.95
Someone to Love	Alicia Wiggins	$8.95
Song in the Park	Martin Brant	$15.95
Soul Eyes	Wayne L. Wilson	$12.95
Soul to Soul	Donna Hill	$8.95
Southern Comfort	J.M. Jeffries	$8.95
Still the Storm	Sharon Robinson	$8.95
Still Waters Run Deep	Leslie Esdaile	$8.95
Stories to Excite You	Anna Forrest/Divine	$14.95
Subtle Secrets	Wanda Y. Thomas	$8.95
Suddenly You	Crystal Hubbard	$9.95
Sweet Repercussions	Kimberley White	$9.95
Sweet Tomorrows	Kimberly White	$8.95
Taken by You	Dorothy Elizabeth Love	$9.95
Tattooed Tears	T. T. Henderson	$8.95
The Color Line	Lizzette Grayson Carter	$9.95
The Color of Trouble	Dyanne Davis	$8.95
The Disappearance of Allison Jones	Kayla Perrin	$5.95
The Honey Dipper's Legacy	Pannell-Allen	$14.95
The Joker's Love Tune	Sidney Rickman	$15.95
The Little Pretender	Barbara Cartland	$10.95
The Love We Had	Natalie Dunbar	$8.95
The Man Who Could Fly	Bob & Milana Beamon	$18.95
The Missing Link	Charlyne Dickerson	$8.95
The Price of Love	Sinclair LeBeau	$8.95
The Smoking Life	Ilene Barth	$29.95
The Words of the Pitcher	Kei Swanson	$8.95
Three Wishes	Seressia Glass	$8.95
Ties That Bind	Kathleen Suzanne	$8.95
Tiger Woods	Libby Hughes	$5.95

Other Genesis Press, Inc. Titles (continued)

Time is of the Essence	Angie Daniels	$9.95
Timeless Devotion	Bella McFarland	$9.95
Tomorrow's Promise	Leslie Esdaile	$8.95
Truly Inseparable	Wanda Y. Thomas	$8.95
Unbreak My Heart	Dar Tomlinson	$8.95
Uncommon Prayer	Kenneth Swanson	$9.95
Unconditional	A.C. Arthur	$9.95
Unconditional Love	Alicia Wiggins	$8.95
Until Death Do Us Part	Susan Paul	$8.95
Vows of Passion	Bella McFarland	$9.95
Wedding Gown	Dyanne Davis	$8.95
What's Under Benjamin's Bed	Sandra Schaffer	$8.95
When Dreams Float	Dorothy Elizabeth Love	$8.95
Whispers in the Night	Dorothy Elizabeth Love	$8.95
Whispers in the Sand	LaFlorya Gauthier	$10.95
Wild Ravens	Altonya Washington	$9.95
Yesterday Is Gone	Beverly Clark	$10.95
Yesterday's Dreams, Tomorrow's Promises	Reon Laudat	$8.95
Your Precious Love	Sinclair LeBeau	$8.95

Order Form

Mail to: Genesis Press, Inc.
P.O. Box 101
Columbus, MS 39703

Name _____

Address _____

City/State _____ Zip _____

Telephone _____

Ship to (if different from above)

Name _____

Address _____

City/State _____ Zip _____

Telephone _____

Credit Card Information

Credit Card # _____ ☐ Visa   ☐ Mastercard

Expiration Date (mm/yy) _____ ☐ AmEx ☐ Discover

Qty.	Author	Title	Price	Total

Use this order form, or call

1-888-INDIGO-1

Total for books _____

Shipping and handling:
  $5 first two books,
  $1 each additional book _____

Total S & H _____

Total amount enclosed _____

Mississippi residents add 7% sales tax